P9-CEU-790

ECHOES OF UNDERSTOREY

DURHAM COUNTY LIBRARY

Feb 14 2018

DURHAM NC

DISCARDED BY
DURHAM COUNTY
LIBRARY

BOOKS BY THORAIYA DYER

Crossroads of Canopy
Echoes of Understorey

ECHOES OF UNDERSTOREY

THORAIYA DYER

TOR

A Tom Doherty Associates Book

NEW YORK

This is a work of fiction. All of the characters, organizations, and events portrayed in
this novel are either products of the author's imagination
or are used fictitiously.

ECHOES OF UNDERSTOREY

Copyright © 2018 by Thoraiya Dyer

All rights reserved.

A Tor Book
Published by Tom Doherty Associates
175 Fifth Avenue
New York, NY 10010

www.tor-forge.com

Tor® is a registered trademark of Macmillan Publishing Group, LLC.

The Library of Congress Cataloging-in-Publication Data is available upon request.

ISBN 978-0-7653-8595-6 (trade paperback)
ISBN 978-0-7653-8596-3 (ebook)

Our books may be purchased in bulk for promotional, educational, or business use.
Please contact your local bookseller or the Macmillan Corporate and Premium
Sales Department at 1-800-221-7945, extension 5442, or by email at
MacmillanSpecialMarkets@macmillan.com.

First Edition: February 2018

Printed in the United States of America

0 9 8 7 6 5 4 3 2 1

For Mum,
who prefers her heroes extra heroic

Acknowledgments

Thanks to Evan and Diana for all the championing they did in front of my eyes and also the extra championing they must have done while my back was turned. Thanks to Cat for sponsoring my book tour and being a shoulder to lean on. Everyone involved with these books' editing, design, production, publicity, sales—you rock! Much gratitude for your patience with this baby writer, and baby writers everywhere. And as always, thank you, family, for being the immoveable roots of this tree.

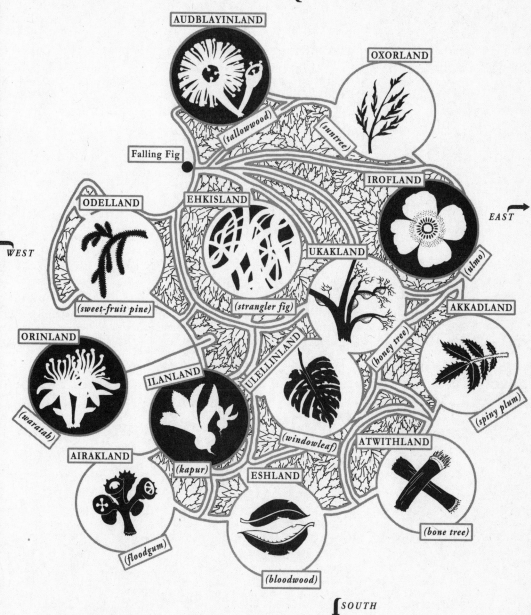

NORTH *(to the ocean)*

AUDBLAYINLAND

(tallowwood)

OXORLAND

(suntree)

Falling Fig

IROFLAND

ODELLAND

EHKISLAND

(ulmo)

EAST

WEST

UKAKLAND

(sweet-fruit pine)

(strangler fig)

AKKADLAND

ORINLAND

(honey tree)

ILANLAND

ULELLINLAND

(spiny plum)

(waratah)

(windowleaf)

AIRAKLAND

(kapur)

ATWITHLAND

ESHLAND

(floodgum)

(bone tree)

(bloodwood)

SOUTH

TEMPLE EMERGENTS OF CANOPY

ECHOES OF
UNDERSTOREY

PROLOGUE

IMERIS FEELS with little nine-year-old fingers high above her head for the smooth chimera skin. Youngest-Father has moved it to the top shelf, where he thinks she can't climb.

Frog song fills the fishing room, a room greenish lit by phosphorescent fungi. The growths make shapes like friendly pond ripples over the round wooden ceiling and walls. Imeris wrinkles her nose at the figgy stink of fruit bat guts. Middle-Father has hung a brace of the bats from a hook, his latest catch. A pitch-black, oval-shaped, floor-to-ceiling opening leads to the outside of the dwelling, to the nighttime winter forest. Smoke from smouldering leaves on the floor keeps the insects out.

She can't find the skin. Where is it? The top shelf is crowded with hooks and knives and traps with cogs and teeth, all the things made by Oldest-Father that he doesn't want Imeris to touch.

But she needs the wings.

She's old enough to fly. She is.

Their house has three mothers, three fathers, and three children. Everyone tells her how lucky she is to have all her mothers and fathers still alive, but it isn't that great! All they want is for Imeris to be exactly like them! A great hunter. A great healer. A great musician. A great mother. What's so great about being great?

Imeris will fly away from them. She will be great at being ordinary. Maybe she will keep salamanders, if she lives near the centre of the forest where it is darkest. Flowerfowl, if she lives near the edge. Oldest-Father, who is stupid and mean, says that Understorey is the best place to live. Youngest-Mother, who talks dreamily about sunshine and butterflies, is from Canopy. When Imeris is grown up, she will decide where to live. No time for that now.

Her hooked pinkie finally catches the hem of the precious hide, just as her feet slip on the shelf below. She lands on her back. The supple folds of the tanned demon skin fall with her, covering her face and hands, blocking out the room's green glow. Stunned slightly, she waits to recover without batting the skin or its light timber frame away, imagining for a moment that she's fighting the chimera herself. In her mind, the blow Imeris is recovering from is one delivered by the demon. Colour-changing camouflage. Claws that can carve gap-axe wood.

Then her nostrils catch the chimera's musk, still there beneath the smell of oily preservative. This demon had been her protector, not her enemy. She should not be thinking of battles. Confused, hissing like the chimera-mother half remembered in her dreams, Imeris kicks the skin skywards.

Emerald luminescence shows the baffled, round-cheeked face of Ylly, Imeris's sister, before the skin falls back into place. Imeris scrambles to her knees and then her feet, pulling the skin defensively around her shoulders. Because Imeris was adopted by her three fathers and three mothers, neither Imeris nor Ylly can be sure which one of them is older, but the more she calls Ylly her little sister, the more it feels true.

"Little sister," Imeris says innocently.

"I am telling Oldest-Father," Ylly answers at once, arms folded.

"If you do, I will tell Middle-Mother that you hate the new baby."

Middle-Mother is Ylly's birth mother. Ylly tries to please Middle-Mother the most.

"I do not!" Ylly clenches her fists at her sides. She's wearing a threadbare silk nightdress made from her old baby blanket. It's too short to cover her knees.

"You *hate* a not-even-born-yet *baby*." Imeris draws herself up like a goddess, lifting her chin, trying to disguise the fact that beneath the black folds of the hide, her restless fingers find the handles of the all-but-weightless wood frame that Youngest-Father has sewn into the skin.

"Do not," Ylly asserts.

"Give the baby that yucky old thing you are wearing, then."

"No!"

"Because *you* are a baby-hater."

"*You* are hopeless at keeping secrets, Issi." Ylly grips the nightgown as though Imeris might try to take it right now. "I do not hate the baby. I hate you! What are you doing? You are not old enough to fly. You will crash and die."

Imeris wriggles her shoulders so that the seams of the skin settle there. The finger spaces of the handles are too wide for her, the grips too far along the frame, but the elbow rings are warm in her clenched palms even if the too-long hem drags on the floor.

If only Ylly hadn't found her. She could've practiced with the frame in the fishing room for a while. Perhaps not even tried to fly right away. Now she's been seen.

If Imeris doesn't try to fly, Ylly will know she's a coward.

"If you hate me," she says haughtily, "you will not care if I die. If the new baby is a girl, you can call her Imerissiremi, and I hope you will not be a tattletale on her like you are on me."

Imeris takes three big strides to the edge of the room, barely avoiding getting her legs tangled in the skin as she kicks the smouldering leaves to one side. They burn her big toe, but she ignores the pain.

The blackness, the unknown, is terrifying.

Imeris knows that Youngest-Father keeps a sap-collecting platform on the trunk of the cidergum, across the hundred-pace chasm between the great trees, below the level of their home. Too far away for her to see in the dark, but she knows it is there.

I can fly to it. I will. Then I will fly back and climb up here again. That will give Ylly a fright. That will teach her not to tell me what I can and cannot do. It is only one short glide across.

The frogs pulse noisily in the night. If a silly old frog can get from one tree to another, Imeris can, too.

She spreads her chimera-skin wings.

"Issi, no!" Ylly cries.

Imeris's heart pounds. Heat rushes to her face. The floor beneath her feet feels abruptly sticky, like it wants to hold on to her.

She jumps.

For a count of five, she glides. It's the greatest feeling she's ever known. Warm, still air turns to a cool rush. Spore scents and the sweet rot of night-blooming orchids fill her nostrils. Nothingness forces her spread arms upwards. She pushes her arms back down. The speed of her flight astonishes and exhilarates her.

But there's no cidergum tree trunk in sight, and her strength cannot hold.

Her wings fold like paper. Her wrists touch behind her head. The chimera cloth collapses along her spine.

"Father!" she screams in a panic. None of them can help her. "Mother!"

And the mother that she screams for is the chimera.

Its smell comes back to her, strongly. Her three fathers took her from the gentle maw of the very demon they killed for this skin. The skin should protect her. It should somehow know her, even in death! The colours still change, don't they? Doesn't that mean the chimera's spirit lingers nearby?

Imeris feels herself slowing in the air.

She can't move her aching arms. They've tangled in the skin and frame behind her. Her feet begin to dangle downwards, and she feels desperately with them for the leaves and branches that must be striking her, that must be breaking her fall. She cannot have reached Floor. Floor is almost a thousand paces below, and she knows she has not fallen that far.

There *are* no leaves or branches.

There's nothing.

Has the chimera-spirit caught her after all?

It must be the magic of sorceresses. Or the spells of bone women. Perhaps the power of the very goddesses and gods.

Imeris hangs in nothingness, her panting filling the stillness and sudden silence.

Something has frightened the frogs.

She can't see anything. She's stuck between her home tallowwood tree and the cidergum, unable to swim through the nothingness that holds her, unable to move up or down. She considers stripping off the chimera skin to see if her wings fall, separated from the magic, but what if she's the one who falls? Besides, the skin is Youngest-Father's most prized possession.

Guilt. Terror. Imeris cries and cries, but nobody answers. Nobody comes. She cries herself to sleep.

A WOMAN'S voice wakes her.

"It is as he dreamed," the low, smoky tones surmise. "So young. It is too early. My heart weeps for him."

Imeris lifts her head. The voice is somewhere above her. Then she screams, because an open-jawed monster with a glowing gullet hovers over her, a tailless crocodile dangling from a rope of spider silk.

"God's bones!" the monster exclaims, jerking its head.

And Imeris sees it is an ordinary human head, after all. A hanging braid of black hair, woven with spiny fish fins, seemed a toothy snout before. The glowing gullet is a glass jar full of trapped blue lightning, such as Youngest-Mother once described to Imeris, a device of the lightning god, Airak. It dangles from the woman's hand.

Aside from a rope climbing harness, the woman isn't wearing any clothes. She rotates slowly on the rope end, and Imeris sees that her dark brown skin has a raised, bumpy pattern like a scaly crocodile's back from the nape of her neck all the way to her heels. Those scarred and tattooed heels, manipulating the rope, swing the woman up into sitting position, slightly above Imeris.

More terrible scars show where her breasts have been cut off.

"He sent me to find you," she says, holding out the hand without the lantern. "Come with me."

Imeris shrinks back into her chimera skin.

"I want to go home," she bleats.

Coward.

The woman puts her fist to her chin and raises one eyebrow.

"And where is that?"

Imeris starts to point, but she's gotten turned around.

"I do not know."

"Do you know whose protective magic has saved you from falling, even here, so far from his seat of power?"

The trapped lightning is the only clue Imeris has.

"Airak," she guesses.

"God's bones! It is not Airak that I serve!"

"Who, then?" Imeris's mouth is dry. Perhaps this crocodile-woman serves the old goddess of childbirth who once resided in the upper reaches of the tallowwood. A goddess of pain and blood, no matter what anyone says.

"The god Odel," the crocodile-woman says. "He who guards children from falling. Lucky for you, you are still a child. You fell once, but an offering was made so you would not fall twice. I will take you to Odel. Hold my hand."

That sort of god does not sound so bad.

The monster-woman grips Imeris's gingerly extended wrist and hauls her, still swaddled in chimera skin, to the level of her climbing harness, tucking

Imeris's arm around her neck and instructing her to hold on, monkeyback style, with both hands.

"But the god Odel lives in Canopy," Imeris says. "We cannot go to Canopy. There is a barrier." In all her whimsical wondering about where she would like to live when she is grown, she has never articulated this fact.

"It will be no barrier to me. Do as I say."

Imeris, who had hoped to see the next tree but never expected a whole other country, thrills with excitement and holds on with both hands. She grips Monster-Woman's waist with her knees. The chimera skin's wooden handles hang below them like the hooked thumbs of a broken-winged bat.

Monster-Woman climbs quickly, as though she carries no burden. Imeris has been taught that ropes are for children and helpless, spineless Canopians, but the woman shows no shame at the smoothness of her forearms and shins.

Hours go by, and Imeris looks up at what she thinks are the fabled stars. They grow brighter, and bluer, and she realises they are more jars of trapped lightning, shining on a network of snaking branch paths that connect the great trees in all directions. She hears human sounds over the frog chorus and the trickle of vertical rivers; drunken shouts, barrow bells announcing the movements of sellers and traders, children running and laughing, monkeys hooting, tapirs whistling, and the axes of fuel finders and chimney borers biting into trees.

"Is it morning?" she asks with wonder. The air is sweeter and colder.

"Not yet," the monster-woman says, "but the city of Canopy sleeps only in the monsoon. There is a platform. We wait here."

She swings them roughly out of empty air, a long way to the left, until they crash into the bark of a spiny plum tree. There is a platform there, narrow but solid, partially formed from a sealed-off stump of petiole. The stump was left behind when one of the young tree's fronds lost the light, shrivelled, detached, and fell.

"What are we waiting for?" Imeris asks.

"For my master," says the monster-woman. "He is not supposed to leave his niche once his visions begin, but he does not yet know that this was a true vision." She unties her harness from the rope that has held them suspended, simply releasing it. It falls back in the direction they swung from until Imeris can't see it anymore; she supposes the monster-woman will collect it later.

I cannot keep thinking of her as the monster-woman. I am not afraid of her anymore.

"What is your name?" Imeris asks, hugging the chimera skin around herself, abruptly needing its familiarity even though it betrayed her.

The woman, standing beside her on the tiny platform, looks down at Imeris with black eyes full of amused complacency.

"I am Aurilon, Bodyguard of Odel. You have not heard of me? I have never lost a duel. I am the greatest fighter the forest has ever seen."

"You are not," Imeris argues at once. "My middle-father, Bernreb, could beat you in a fight. He killed this chimera whose skin I am holding!"

Aurilon smiles and says nothing. She takes a waterproof, leaf-wrapped package from a hidden hollow in the tree, and there are leather climbing gloves with wrist straps inside the package. They are tipped with ferocious, curving obsidian-black claws.

And Imeris realises that Aurilon has killed a chimera, too.

PART I

*The Dovecote &
the Duel*

ONE

IMERIS DUCKED her head under the room's carved lintel.

At twenty-one, having reached her full height some monsoons before, Imeris was no taller than the average student at the renowned fighting school of Loftfol. Yet she ducked like everyone else. The entrance to the bow store was lowered on purpose. All who wished take up weapons were forced to first show respect to the long-dead founders of the school.

Braziers in six small hearths provided a low orange glow and helped drive monsoon moisture from the air. Familiar smells of flowerfowl feathers, used for fletching, beeswax for the strings, and oils for the long wooden limbs surrounded Imeris, but the sight of a messenger bird with a tiny tube tied to one leg, perched on an empty bow rack by the seventh, unlit hearth, brought her to a sudden halt.

She stared at it. Loftfol used lorikeets for its messages, birds bred in the hollows of the school's own boughs, but this was a blue-eyed bowerbreaker, near-blind, grey-feathered and brown-barred. These birds hunted flowerfowl in the utter blackness of Floor.

By smell.

It has found this room by smell, Imeris thought.

This room, where Imeris always arrived first, before the break of each day, lest she be forced to share the archery practice range with Kishsik and his cronies.

The bowerbreaker was only half tame, its hooked beak well capable of ripping out flowerfowl throats. When Imeris tried to take the message, it turned, wings raised, as if to escape back up the chimney. She seized it by the back of the neck and stuffed it into her armpit, trapping it long enough to take the tube.

Inside, a message.

Addressed to her in Oldest-Father's crude hand.

Youngest-Father must have told Oldest-Father about Kishsik, whom Imeris had injured during training. About the guilt that led her to avoid him, and how Kishsik's friends interpreted this as a weakness and fear of reprisal. Oldest-Father or his courier must be close by, or else the bower-breaker would have found itself a real live flowerfowl to feast on, instead of following the scent of old feathers into the bow store.

The message was a summons. A summons, when she should stay. She had demonstrated her proficiency in spine-fighting to Horroh the Haakim only yesterday, and today custom demanded her presence in the hall, to be recognised before the other teachers and students.

Their recognition means nothing. Horroh's pride is enough. His confidence in me repaid. The forgiveness he showed after the accident with Kishsik.

Imeris knelt by the closest brazier, seeking better light, fingers trembling. She read Oldest-Father's message again.

The witch has built a new dovecote, it said, *in the wilds of Wissin. An informant waits at the ti-house to meet your youngest-father and me. If you are coming, come quickly.*

The parchment was white against her liver-dark hand.

She had to go. She might already be too late. The bow she would have chosen for her practice called to her from across the room, but she could not burden herself with unwieldy weapons. The bony, retractable spines implanted in her shins and forearms were enough. Horroh had told her so, and she had proven the matter to her own satisfaction. Soon enough, the sorceress Kirrik would feel their bite. Her heart raced.

Time to fly.

She ducked out of the room, striding swiftly and silently down the polished corridor. Her best, closest exit was directly down, out of the hidden building that held the school's heart, through the aptly dubbed "dark temple." It would be disrespectful to the dead, but an effective way to avoid being seen by Loftfol's scouts.

The dark temple was a boarded-up complex of rooms, excavated within the southernmost branch of the triple-trunked river nut tree that hosted the school. Imeris had completed five years of study at Loftfol; during her fourth year, the dark temple had been closed for good after a fire killed six students and a teacher. But not before Lehhel the Odarkim had led Imeris, Kishsik, and three others through it on a practice raid. Despite the name, the dark temple had been brilliantly—perhaps overenthusiastically—illuminated, to mimic the sun-bright emergents of Canopy.

Imeris stopped at her bunkroom for her wings. They were rolled and stuffed inside a case to form the pillow on her bunk. Always waiting. Always ready to take her away, because Loftfol was a means to an end for her, nothing more. Despite her record-breaking climb to win the title of Heightsman, Imeris disdained her fellow students' desire for fame. She alone felt no yearning to bring down the gods and goddesses of the high kingdoms.

She touched the amulet hidden beneath her shirt, protection against foul, forbidden magic.

Her duty was simply to kill the sorceress, Kirrik, and then she would give up her armour, her knives, and her poison needles. Her days of performing the disciplines of cord strangulation and spine-fighting would be over. No more mad battles to win teachers of greater skill, of rarer talents, of seemingly impossible demands. Now was her chance, and she must not miss it.

Snatching up the pillow, she slipped back into the corridor, ignoring the delicious smells wafting from the kitchens, and found a chute for ash disposal at the corner junction of two halls.

Pillow between her knees, she squeezed into the chute, letting the wooden flap fall over the opening behind her. Counting the distance as she had been taught, she had her forearm spines out, ready, just as open air embraced her.

She stabbed them into the lip of the chute and swung hard, forwards through a cloud of ash, catching the bark of the river nut tree with both shins. Retracting her forearm spines, she dangled by her bent knees for a moment, rearranging the ashy pillow so it wouldn't fall, then taking advantage of wet bark weakened by the monsoon to pry the boards loose from one of the windows of the dark temple.

Letting the timbers fall, Imeris pushed her pillow in ahead of herself. If the window was a high one, the pillow could break her fall, but when she wriggled through, she found the floor only a pace and a half below the sill.

Inside the maze-like complex, fluorescent fungi stained the walls as they had stained the fishing room of her home. The fungi showed the greenish outline of dozens of life-sized wooden dummies carved to represent the soldiers of Canopy. Their faces were barely human, mouths open, wooden shins and forearms sheathed in heavy wooden robes, alien weapons raised. Sword slashes and arrow holes in the wood showed where students had scored points during their testing in the replica temple. Imeris found the effigies as creepy and repulsive now as she had on her first encounter. *Do not look at their faces,* Lehhel had barked. *Canopians have eyes, they have mouths, they have beating hearts, but they speak only lies. Look for the spines and seams of your brethren, and if you do not see them, let your knives and needles fly.*

Imeris had been momentarily grateful to him for not mentioning dark skin as an enemy trait, only to find him frowning furiously at her spines, as though they were somehow stolen.

In the second room she came to, the wooden dummies were blackened by fire.

I should not be here, Imeris thought, imagining the suffocating smoke. Impatience to find the hidden tunnel that led down to the emergency escape was tempered by shame at how quickly she had desecrated the resting place of her fellow students.

Then her fingers, feeling at head height along the wall, found the symbol of Loftfol, a pattern of thirteen points arranged in the shape of a spearhead. She pressed both thumbs into its centre, releasing the counterbalance within the wall, and the hidden door swung open.

Imeris darted down the tunnel. She came out onto a platform planed across the top of a house-sized burl, and in the relatively unsheltered space, the monsoon greeted her with a wet slap across the face. Loftfol was too far away from Canopy for much light to penetrate, especially in the rain, but it buoyed her to find the bulky, barely discernible shape exactly where she remembered it.

The school maintained a series of trebuchets for escape in case of catastrophe. Here, the lowest one waited. If any single enemy qualified as a catastrophe, Kirrik the body-stealing sorceress certainly did. Kirrik was an old, hated soul in a young, stolen body, and she had escaped Imeris once, because Imeris hadn't known who she was or what was happening.

Imeris knew now. Knew that the same sorceress who had brought down the Temple of Airak—in an attack spoken of in awed, exultant tones at Loftfol—had done her utmost to harm Imeris's Understorian family. Kirrik had died more than once at the hands of Imeris's fathers, but she'd always found another body to steal, another way to survive. That would not happen this time.

Imeris touched her amulet again. She was faster than her fathers. Stronger. Better trained. It could all be over—before the end of the monsoon—if she did not hesitate. If she was not too late.

Imeris pulled off the oilcloth protecting the machine. Exposing it to the damage of the downpour, she set about checking all of its ropes and counterweights, a difficult proposition in the dank dimness, carried out mainly by feel. She'd fix it later, would replace the ruined rope and wind the priceless granite counterweight back up into position before water and its own heaviness could see it lost back to the darkness of Floor.

An informant waits at the ti-house.

Youngest-Father didn't want Imeris to be the one to do it.

Nirrin was your friend, he'd said gently, *before her body was stolen by the sorceress. I should be the one to kill her a final time, and with one of Vesev's knives, too.*

But Youngest-Father wasn't the only one who kept the dead smith's handiwork at his fingertips. Youngest-Father hadn't been there in the forge. He hadn't seen Nirrin's sweaty face changing, her blue eyes widening, becoming vacant, before turning strangely triumphant. He wasn't the one who had offered an arm to Nirrin, the smith's daughter, as she spun on her heel and stumbled, as though she'd forgotten she wasn't wearing her leg brace.

The smith's son, Vesev, had just finished his sister's new brace. She'd gotten so tall since the last monsoon; they were of a height, both taller than Imeris. Vesev's eyes were olive-green where Nirrin's were blue, but they both had handsome smiles, pink cheeks, and a whorl of hair above the left temple. He handed the reshaped steel to her, carefully, because of the sharp hooks down the front of it that Nirrin used for climbing. With that brace, she was as nimble as anyone.

She'd immediately turned and knocked Vesev down with the brace. A single swift, unexpected blow. Imeris hadn't reacted as she should have. She hadn't understood what was wrong with her friend.

Now she understood. She would not hesitate again.

Oldest-Father understood, too. He might be deficient in kindness and generosity, but he knew all about revenge. Though Oldest-Father had trapped demons, he had never been to Loftfol. On some level, despite all the gruff criticism, he understood she had surpassed him and the time was right. No more murmuring about the elusive enemy around the hearth. No more frustration in Oldest-Father's eyes. Nor naked fear in the eyes of

Youngest-Mother, whose magical abilities made her vulnerable to possession by the sorceress, should their hidden home's location be revealed.

Imeris was not afraid of defeat. Her soul was safe while she wore the amulet. Nirrin and Vesev had been without the benefit of such protection. She was afraid that Oldest-Father would not wait for her.

Imeris fitted the final part, the crank of the windlass, into position. Ideally, ten or twelve people would leap up onto the trebuchet's throwing arm to bring it down quickly while the windlass was wound, but there was an alternate method, a series of pulleys attached to the mechanism, which would allow Imeris to lock the arm down, raising the payload in its woven basket.

She seized the tidily stored coils. It wasn't bark-rope, but incredibly strong and resilient strapleaf fibre, waxed for longevity. Imeris threaded the thick line through the sheaves in the dense, heavy turpentine blocks.

Then it was done. She pulled reams of rope through the system until her back ached and the trebuchet was ready to loose. Only the semicircular moving upper part of the platform still needed adjusting. Imeris used the same pulleys she'd used for loading the trebuchet to swivel it until it aimed east.

East. Wissin. That was where her fathers waited.

She checked the compass-points built into the fixed part of the platform a second time. It was dark in the school's shadow, though by now it was full day, and she had no brand or lantern for light; the marks were barely visible, and she touched them to reassure herself.

There was no more time to waste. She climbed into the sling designed for human use, pulled her wings out of the pillowcase, and connected the short lengths of bonewood that formed her climbing frame. Before long, she was shrugging into the seams and taking hold of the handgrips. The folded membranes were not chimera skin, but the next best thing, made from the leather of a dayhunter, the most common kind of demon seen in her part of Understorey.

After the sorceress is dead, my duty will be discharged, Imeris thought grimly, kicking at the release mechanism. It seemed stuck. *I will have revenge for Nirrin and Vesev.* They were friends she should never have had.

Having friends was dangerous. Is dangerous. If our home is ever found, villagers of Gannak will try to kill my fathers for refusing to raid Canopy. Loftfol will try to kill my fathers for opposing Kirrik, even though the school wants to kill Kirrik for stealing students' bodies. But Kirrik . . . Maybe Kirrik loses some of her memories each time she takes a new body, but she still remembers my fathers. She remembers they killed her before, and if she learns their location or if her memories of where they live resurface, she will try to kill them. Oh, and Canopians will come after them simply for existing.

She kicked it a second time, harder. *Yet my family wants me to be great at something? They think I have some glorious destiny? Killing Kirrik is it.*

Then I can leave Loftfol. My duels in Canopy will be done with. I will not need to train to fight anymore.

With the third kick, she felt the ratchet release and the ponderous load of stone begin its plummet through empty air.

Instead of plotting a course for war, I can live in peace. Canopy will stop searching for the sorceress. Their soldiers will stay above the barrier. My victory will seal the trust of both my teacher Horroh and my sister, Audblayin; I will become a bridge between Loftfol and Audblayinland, convincing them they need not quarrel. Kirrik's corpse will buy forgiveness from Gannak. Neither my Canopian family nor my Understorian family will need to hide anymore. I can make other friends wherever I wish.

Imeris flew, higher and faster than a simple drop from a tree trunk could ever provide. Her gliding frame snapped out into the locked position. Rain pelted off the sudden umbrella it formed. If not for the terrible swiftness of her flight, the water might have gathered there, weighted her down, and drowned her in the monsoon floodwaters of Floor.

All my separate faces will become one face. All my pulled-apart pieces will become one piece.

The Loftfol school built impressively robust and finely calibrated machines. Not a single errant trunk obstructed Imeris's path. She remained airborne for a count of two thousand, passing trunks that swarmed with creatures climbing up and away from the water, sweeping closer and closer to the lower limits of Understorey.

If there is no barrier down there, she had asked Youngest-Father as a child, *how do you know when you have reached Floor?*

When your feet touch dirt, Youngest-Father had said, grinning. *Floorians do not climb. They say they have a sacred connection to dirt and water. A Floorian might shoot you out of a tree, but she will not follow you into it. She would rather a floating house than a high branch for keeping dry.*

Imeris saw no floating Floorian villages below her, but she did see a handful of lantern-lit windows and coiled bridges, evidence of Understorian dwellings shut up tight till the end of the monsoon.

Then the grizzled, grey bark of the ancient magenta cherry tree she'd been aiming for widened across her field of view. In Understorey, the great trees were known by their body, texture, and scent before ever the shape or colour of their leaves was guessed at. This one bore a dimly seen pattern of scars from Loftfol students landing, the gouges too deep to be shed with the seasons. It smelled of sweet, sap-filled wounds turned dark, hard, and glassy.

Imeris cracked the frame of the glider with a sharp jerk of her tired arms, slowing her flight, changing it from a glide to guttural stutter, catching the tree with her forearm spines in the instant before she dropped.

She clung to the trunk, recovering her breath, blinking sweat from her brow out of her eyes.

Not that eyes were much use in the dark. She thought of the bowerbreaker, wishing fleetingly for its keen sense of smell.

Imeris climbed in an exploratory spiral. She couldn't have landed too far down from the emergency provisions cache that the school kept in this tree. The bridges of Wissin were stored away for the duration of the monsoon, but she could use the village's bridge-firing ballistae to fly to the next tree, and the next, until she reached the ti-house, Breeze, where her fathers no doubt already trespassed.

An informant waits.

Informants of years gone by had varied in utility. Sometimes they pointed the finger at spinewives with a touch of dementia, or village Headmen who seemed greedy for influence or resources. Other times, they noticed a pattern of fighting men going missing, or vanished graduates of Loftfol too canny to have fallen, which might indicate that the sorceress was building another sleeping army somewhere. During Imeris's childhood, there had been sightings of the bodies of Kirrik's one-time lover and of her son, both whose souls had been displaced by Kirrik in succession. The reports had stirred unease but not terror, since neither of those men were known to wield magical powers.

But Nirrin's possession transformed Oldest-Father's routine defences and Youngest-Father's casual information network into something more serious.

In the blackness, Imeris's hands found the sliding panel with its identifying pattern of thirteen points arranged in the shape of a spearhead. Inside were dry, slow-burning tapers, tinder, flint and steel, and a store of hard, translucent ghost-gourds. Lighting a taper and dropping it into the hollow of a gourd, with its narrow neck that admitted air but insufficient rain to douse the taper, she strung the makeshift lantern from her weapons belt, letting it dangle behind her with the collapsed wings of the glider, and continued her rapid ascent, this time in a small, soft circle of yellow light.

It wasn't enough light for her enemies to spot her from a distance, but it would help with a climb made more dangerous during the monsoon. Magenta cherry bark was hard, solid, and safe enough, but Breeze was built in a lemon ironwood tree. That fragrant favourite of ti-sellers was a hazard to its customers when saturated with water. In the rain, the wrinkled, grey-brown bark flaked away more easily, leaving even softer new orange bark beneath, occasionally sending unwary climbers to their deaths.

Imeris tried not to disturb any of the tree-dwellers holed up for the season. Smoke came out of chimneys, tickling the back of her throat. Occasionally, lights were visible in translucent windows. Many of the platforms were covered or dismantled.

She uncovered a bridge-ballista outside the carved, closed door of what must have been the Headman's house.

I will come back, she thought guiltily. *I will replace all the parts that are ruined.*

She refused to admit the possibility she wouldn't come back or that, if she did, she would be an empty shell with Kirrik's soul inside.

The bone amulet rested lightly around her neck.

Yes, her sister, once called Ylly, now Audblayin, had said gravely. *It will protect your body from being stolen by another, just as our fathers' amulets protect them. But I must ask you, Issi, to return all of the amulets to me when the sorceress Kirrik is dead. They're made from the bones of an Old God. They can be misused.*

Imeris had promised to bring the amulets to her sister when their task was complete. She had thought Kirrik's bones would be trophies enough for her. She had vowed to tattoo the enemy's face on her left shoulder, the way Middle-Father tattooed himself with demons he had killed.

She hadn't known that the face of the enemy would be Nirrin's.

TWO

IMERIS LAUNCHED herself from a third ballista towards the lemon iron-wood tree.

The jolt was uncomfortable and the elevation unsatisfactory, but the speed—the speed was good.

Imeris flew through the rain. The lemon ironwood tree rushed at her. She tipped the frame. Began to fall. Reached out with her spines but caught loose bark and slid down the tree trunk. Sloughed fibre and splinters enveloped her.

Gritting her teeth, Imeris retracted the spines in her forearms, but her upper body was being dragged back by the weight of her glider. She struck out with her arms again, but couldn't reach the tree at all.

Then her shin spines snagged in the thick, juicy body of a passionfruit vine, one that reached all the way from Floor into the sun-drenched arms of Canopy. Imeris hung by one knee gratefully, protecting her face with both arms until the broken bark and splinters fell away.

Not a very graceful landing. Youngest-Father would have been ashamed.

Tightening her stomach, Imeris pulled her body upright again. In the meagre glow of the almost-extinguished taper, she set her forearm spines more carefully into the solid sapwood of the tree. The strong, bitter-lemon smell that wafted down to her could have been the tree itself or a pot of ti-leaves brewing at Breeze.

Imeris climbed as quickly as she dared.

The path was more scarred than the magenta cherry trunk had been, evidence of the eagerness of decades of Breeze patrons. When she found one of the lower west-facing entrances, she admitted herself by an arched opening to the inside of the tree. The staircase was worn by many, many bare and booted feet. The establishment was lower down in Understorey and therefore that much warmer and more stifling than Imeris's home, but fire was always wanted for light, and Breeze was famous for staying cool all year around. Most ti-houses were shuttered during the monsoon, but not Breeze, because its magic needed access to the open air.

Imeris listened. Tried to be cautious. Heard a creak. A crackle. Whispered voices and the smell of cooking fish.

She lifted her wings off the floor with both hands and moved soundlessly up the stairs. They were cut directly into the tree, and when she turned a corner, where two entry staircases merged into one, she felt the famous breeze blowing full into her face, cooling her sweat. It brought the smell of smoke from a gobletfruit bark fire and the lingering hints of fruit syrups and dried lemon ironwood leaves.

She heard the voices clearly.

"Will you put that away? We cannot wait for Zhamahz any longer. It is midday, and his wife said dawn. He has either been killed by the enemy or his own inept climbing, and if the former, this place may be a trap set for us." The normally gentle voice of Imeris's youngest-father, forced now to a strained whisper.

"Fighting on an empty stomach," answered the idle voice of Imeris's oldest-father, "is worse than flying on one—that is to say, for burned ones and buffoons."

Imeris climbed the staircase and turned a second corner. The main sitting room of the ti-house was shaped like the interior of a bright, golden bell. The pace-long bone of the wind goddess, which imparted the continuous cool breeze, hung by the ceiling like the clapper of the bell. Multiple fireplaces, their chimneys bored sideways instead of upwards, were arranged around the wall, forming an outer circle. Low round tables formed an inner circle around the central stage below the magically hovering bone.

Imeris's fathers looked up at the same time from the single active hearth where Oldest-Father had laid lemon-ironwood-leaf-wrapped fish over the coals. They should have looked guilty, taking their ease in Breeze with neither the landlords' permission nor remuneration, but Oldest-Father smirked while Youngest-Father sighed at the sight of her.

Aside from the two men, the enormous chamber was empty. Out of season, none of the hallmarks of a renowned ti-house were there: no proprietors balancing wooden bowls of steaming beverages as they emerged from tunnels to the kitchens, and no customers playing checkers and sticks.

The aisles hosted neither women selling moonflower nor men selling bia. The stage was empty of poets and prophets of the Old Gods sermonizing or actively enlisting warriors for raids into Canopy, claiming they'd had visions of when and where the barrier would open for them.

Oldest-Father turned, silent and self-satisfied, back to his leaf-wrapped fish and prodded the blackening package with a poker deeper into the coals. His skinny shoulder blades touched each other in a hunch. He wore an olive-green woven-grass shirt and knee-length trousers. There were touches of grey in his short brown hair.

Youngest-Father wore only a waist wrap, gliding harness, quiver, and longbow, his belt heavy with coils of rope. His unlined face was boyish, and his blond hair was stuck down by rain. He rubbed his bare chin, beard abraded away by the regular use of sandpaper fig leaves, and sighed a second time.

"Issi," he said resignedly. "I should have known that was why he wanted to wait. You look well."

Imeris, no longer keeping quiet, let her wings drop and drag on the floor behind her, freeing her arms to embrace Youngest-Father. It was many months since she'd seen him. The Loftfol school did not permit frequent home visits. She was slightly taller than he was, and she felt their two bone amulets press against one another, hers beneath her shirt and his resting on his bare chest.

"So do you, Youngest-Father."

She went to Oldest-Father and hugged him from behind, wetting him, and he made a mock-disgusted noise and shook her off.

"You came quickly," he said. "The fish is not done."

"Who is Zhamahz?" she asked. "The informant?"

"He is a windowleaf fruit cutter," Youngest-Father explained. "He saw lanterns through a tangle of windowleaves."

"In Canopy? That is not unusual."

"Not in Canopy. We are below Ulellinland, the realm of the goddess of wind and leaves. Here, even Understorey is a labyrinth of tangled green growth. There are leaves on the windowleaf trees all the way down to Floor, but they are still windowleaves. They have holes in them. Lantern light shines through."

"Oldest-Father wrote that you had found Kirrik's new dovecote."

Youngest-Father rolled his eyes at Oldest-Father's turned back.

"The lantern lights were blue," he said, "and killed a bird that came too close. Who else in Understorey holds three of Airak's death-lanterns?"

Imeris was silent, recalling Youngest-Father's heroics, the Great Deed of his lifetime. She'd grown up hearing the story of how he'd rescued Unar, the Godfinder, from Kirrik's original dovecote beneath Airakland. Youngest-Father and the Godfinder together had used chimera skin to escape from the deadly ring of lanterns, bringing one of the lanterns along with them. Later they'd used it to escape a live chimera. The demon had not dared to enter the fatal blue glow.

Middle-Father had accomplished a Great Deed, too. He'd killed a chimera, and now he was Bodyguard to a goddess.

Oldest-Father pretended to scorn the notion of Great Deeds, yet he had killed Kirrik, or at least one form the sorceress had taken. She had worn the body of her son, Garrag. Oldest-Father had trapped her with a spring-loaded wooden cage and a ballista bolt through the heart.

Imeris might have felt pressured to kill Kirrik for her Great Deed even if the sorceress hadn't murdered her friends. Other families, she suspected, were not so keen on Great Deeds. If Imeris's birth mother had never dropped her, she might have gone her whole life without anyone demanding to know what her Great Deed would be.

Stop trying to keep her home, Youngest-Father had reprimanded Oldest-Father. *Our Issi is gifted. She can accomplish anything.*

Imerissiremi, Middle-Father had told her, *your Great Deed awaits. I took you from the maw of a chimera. It saved you so that you could save the world.*

Imeris had no intention of saving the world. Only, at first, of unmuddling her life, and now, achieving retribution. Revenge for Nirrin was why she'd overcome her reluctance to apply to Loftfol. It was why she'd gone to find Aurilon when her application to Loftfol had first failed.

I will kill Kirrik so far from any available bodies that her soul will shrivel into the ether before it can find a replacement.

"Which tree was it?" she asked Youngest-Father, tapping her foot. "Why are we waiting around for Oldest-Father's fish to cook?"

"The tale of the curious blue lanterns passed from household to household by no less than six messenger birds," Youngest-Father explained, scrubbing his sodden fringe back from his forehead with the fingers of one hand. "From Zhamahz to his seamstress wife. From the wife to her brother. From the brother to his wife, the distiller. From the distiller to her mother, the bolt turner. And the bolt turner remembered my songs. She sent me a message."

"How long did all this take?" Imeris unbuckled her wings from her body harness and spread them over several stools beside the fire. She lit a torch and set it into a bracket on the wall.

"Two weeks. The location of the windowleaf tree in question was lost along the way. But Zhamahz's wife expects a bird from him today. He cuts fruit during the monsoon because it is fattest and richest while the great trees' roots are underwater, and he has a trade arrangement with the Bird-Riders of Floor. They take one half of his harvest. In exchange, their bone women see him safely between the great trees where he makes his deliveries. Today, he is due to deliver here."

"And after the delivery, he will send a bird to his wife to let her know that he is well?"

"Yes."

"But he might not be well at all." Imeris kicked at a polished stool. The thought of Zhamahz, a helpless fruit cutter, being hunted by Kirrik enraged her. Kirrik should come to Loftfol if she wanted a true challenge; so many of the students had lost older siblings to her cause, voluntarily and involuntarily. "He might be dead. Or she might be in his body, coming to meet us. To see who we are and get rid of us."

"Yes." Youngest-Father shrugged. "I think we should go."

There was the thud and shudder of a bridge hitting a platform outside the ti-house.

Oldest-Father rose at once, the iron poker in his fist. He was a head taller than Youngest-Father, a decade older, but there remained swiftness and strength in his gangly limbs. Youngest-Father made a subtle, shrugging movement, disgorging the weapon that sat diagonally across his back, digging in his hip-pouch for a bowstring. Sliding his belt around his waist brought his quiver within reach. He stepped through the stave and strung the bow.

Imeris, instinctively after her hard previous year specializing in spine-fighting under Horroh the Haakim, held her arms out slightly from her body, resting her spines in their sheaths, bending her knees and gripping the wooden floor lightly with her toes.

Ugly, laboured breathing echoed in one of the entry tunnels.

"Quickly," a woman's deep voice shouted. "Into the ti-house!"

Imeris shared a glance with Youngest-Father. Their imminent visitor did not seem to be Zhamahz.

THREE

A FLOOD of villagers entered Breeze.

The women wore not the elaborate layered skirts and leaf-mosaic blouses of the House of Wissin, but the rope-secured, paperbark wrap skirts and breast bindings of those who made such clothes but couldn't afford them.

"This is opposite to our aims," Youngest-Father said quietly. "We need the sorceress isolated with no hope of fresh victims."

"Why have you loosed a bridge during the monsoon?" Imeris called to the closest villager. The boy, on the cusp of becoming a man, was rosy-cheeked and wide-eyed in the light from the torch on the wall.

"A demon climbed into our paperbark tree. A chimera."

A ripple went through the crowd, and the same woman's voice which had ordered the people into the ti-house shrieked, "Hurry! The wet bark is tearing! The bridge will not hold!"

Imeris shared another glance with Youngest-Father, who took the torch from the bracket without a word. They turned as one to Oldest-Father, who prodded his fish with an irritated scowl.

"Let it fall," he murmured to his left shoulder, "or else we all know what is to follow," but Imeris and Youngest-Father each seized him by an arm and bullied him towards the east-facing main entrance tunnel where the villagers kept arriving. At the far end of the tunnel stood a bulky, dimple-cheeked matron with a grey braid to her hip. The owner of the command-ing voice.

Imeris and Youngest-Father pointed Oldest-Father at the place where the great steel head of the bolt was beginning to ease back out of the tree, even as three distant, final stragglers pounded along the rope bridge.

"Who are you?" the matron demanded.

Every step that the stragglers took wobbled the bolt looser.

"I am Imerissiremi of Loftfol," Imeris said, seeking instant compliance by naming the school. "My father will save your people, but you must move deeper into the ti-house."

Without another word, the woman and the others around her obeyed. Imeris, Oldest-Father, and Youngest-Father now stood alone on the lip of the great entranceway, with its banisters made to look like the boughs of true lemon trees and the flower-laden branches of fabled camellias. The rope bridge was lit at this end by the taper at Imeris's hip and the flaming torch that Youngest-Father carried.

The other end of the bridge disappeared into the dark.

"My fish is burning," Oldest-Father said, but he took two chimera claw needles from his hip pouch. They were the span of his hand, curving and with eyes bored in the blunt ends of them, wide enough for him to thread the ends of his two thickest ropes through.

"Your eyesight is getting worse," Youngest-Father said calmly, holding the torch closer, as the bolt slipped another inch and the bark of the lemon ironwood tree began deeply splitting in multiple directions.

"Gods' bones, do not set my sleeves on fire!"

Then Oldest-Father hooked his knees around the banister, swinging upside down so his outstretched arms were level with the place where the bolt had struck. Imeris couldn't see him, but she waited for his instructions. She was prepared to hook her own legs around the banister and hold his ankles, to lower him down and give him more room to work.

"I can reach it," came his gasp, however, and she caught the needle ends of the ropes instead, pulling the chimera claws free and knotting the rope ends around the bases of the banisters. Oldest-Father hauled himself back up a moment later, securing the other ends of the ropes as well. He took his needles back from her, sitting with his back against the banister as he tucked them away.

"The end is fixed to solid wood," Youngest-Father called to the two men helping a small child along the final section of the rope bridge. He held the oil-impregnated torch out towards them. It sizzled in the rain but kept burning. "Go slowly and safely, if you would."

"Behind them," Imeris said. She sucked in a sharp breath. "They cannot go slowly."

For she had glimpsed the glittering eyes of the chimera in pursuit. The rest of its body, with the sleek, scaly, colour-changing skin, was invisible.

Before her fathers could stop her, she dashed out onto the bridge. Her added weight eased the bolt completely free of the tree in a shower of loose bark, but Oldest-Father had secured it well. His smaller, stronger ropes pierced the weave of the looser, thicker bridge ropes right behind the eye of the ballista bolt, and the bridge sagged and swagged but didn't fall.

Imeris put her arms out for balance. She didn't have her wings, but she had her training. On her toes, she danced along a single rope, past the men and the crying child, only dropping to the bark-lined bed of the bridge when she was between the villagers and the eerie glow of the chimera's eyes. Imeris knew from seeing stretched-out skins that chimeras were twice bear-sized, four-footed, long-tailed, and all but earless with a toothy, face-splitting maw. Yet the lamp-like gaze was the only part clearly visible, its body covered in colour-changing scales, a magical creature bearing the ultimate camouflage in the dark depths of the forest where it hunted humankind.

"Stop," she told the demon. Three paces separated them.

The chimera's glowing eyes rose to the level of hers, evidence that it had sat back on its haunches. Aside from the eyes, only a heaviness, a localized stability to the bridge, and a slight flicker over the pale bark and greenish-brown ropes betrayed the creature's powerful bulk.

Imeris stretched out her hand and took three steps forwards.

Hot breath warmed the back of it, but she didn't flinch. Her Great Deed would not be to kill a chimera. Bad enough the demon who had fostered her after her long fall from Canopy had been killed out of necessity by Middle-Father. He—all her fathers—had promised never to take the life of a chimera again.

"My mother was one of you," she whispered.

The forked tongue that touched her cheek was not invisible, like the rest of the creature, but pink streaked with black and blue. Imeris didn't flinch from it, either. She felt lost in half-true, half-dreamed memories of the metallic smell, milky taste, and blood-warm aura of the chimera. Though it was beyond impossible as a grown woman, part of her wanted to crawl past its teeth into its distensible throat pouch and go to sleep.

The golden eyes blinked and were gone. It had turned and was returning to the paperbark tree.

Imeris turned, too, reluctantly, returning to the ti-house. In the entranceway, beside her torch-bearing Youngest-Father, the two men whose lives she had saved stared at her in amazement.

"Are you a goddess of Canopy?" one of them gasped.

Imeris was often accused of being Canopian. Her dark brown skin, hair, and eyes were evidence of high origin, but her spines said otherwise. Perhaps that was one reason she now preferred her spines to any other weapon, why she preferred Horroh to her other teachers, for seeing only her spines when he looked at her.

"No," Imeris said. "My sister is a goddess of Canopy. I am just another warrior from the wilds." Not actually just another warrior. She was the youngest competitor ever to be crowned Heightsman at Loftfol. Only a necessity: They wouldn't take her otherwise. She'd needed them to take her. "That chimera will not go hungry. By saving you, I have doomed others."

The men put their palms together and bowed respectfully. The first one went deeper into the ti-house with the snuffling child.

The second man said, "Should we sever the bridge? There is nobody left in the paperbark tree."

"If you cut my brother's rope, who will wind up the bridge to protect it from the rain?" asked Youngest-Father, cocking his head. "And how will you go back home? Breeze has no bridges of its own. You will all have to stay here until the rain stops and bridges come from other parts of the village."

"The monsoon will end tomorrow or the next day," the man said, already pulling an axe from the loop at his belt. Imeris felt briefly distracted by his mentioning the end of monsoon. She had a recurring engagement in Canopy at the end of the monsoon, but she couldn't dwell on that now. "Better a ruined bridge than risk another demon attack."

"That chimera will not return," Imeris said.

"There are other demons," the man said. "Embracers. Needleteeth, which you of Loftfol call the spotted swarm. Dayhunters. Fiveways."

Imeris smiled, thinking of the demon-depicting tattoos across Middle-Father's shoulders. Lizard-like dayhunters had long, banded backs and great, curving claws. The spotted swarm were monkey-sized demons with short legs and long snouts, boiling over branches with fangs bared. Each of the five members of a fiveways troupe was monkey-shaped, but bigger. Their thick hides were all but impenetrable, and so rough brushing against them drew blood.

Then she heard the sound of wet bark pulling away from the tree trunk. She held up her hand for silence.

Youngest-Father and the man from the paperbark tree stared at her with foreboding.

Imeris dropped to the floor of the entranceway, onto her hands and toes, stretched out like a salamander, and peered over the edge.

Below her, at the furthest visible reach of the light from the torch, a man with a full basket of fruit on his back climbed up the lemon ironwood tree. He huffed a little with each sinking of the spines. The basket looked heavy. Ropes fell from the man's harness into the depths. His bare shoulders were broad, but his rust-coloured hair was grey-streaked.

His lower back stuck out from the tree the way men's lower backs did when they had potbellies from drinking too much bia.

"Who is that?" the man from the paperbark tree wondered aloud, poised with his axe over the banister and Oldest-Father's best ropes.

"Cut those," Youngest-Father instructed. Imeris felt the rush of wind as the severed ropes whipped past and the bridge fell. "It must be Zhamahz."

"That it is," confirmed the voice of the grey-braided matron. Imeris sat up, coming cross-legged at the edge of the entranceway to frown at the ample-bodied, paperbark-wrapped woman. She stood with her arms folded beside the banister and could not possibly see over the edge. "Can you smell what is in the basket?"

All three of them, Imeris, the axeman, and Youngest-Father, took a deep sniff of the rain-saturated air. Beneath the lemon tang was the hint of tart sweetness that belonged to the windowleaf fruit. Imeris had rarely eaten fruit in her fathers' home, but one of the teachers at Loftfol came from the Head family of Dul and had a sweet tooth.

"Just in time for lunch," Youngest-Father said.

"You cannot eat them straight after picking," the woman said. "Unless you wait for their scales to fall off, they will make your mouth bleed." She turned beady brown eyes on Imeris. "I am Zhamahz's wife, the seamstress Alenela. You have our gratitude for driving away the chimera."

"Accepted," Imeris answered. "We came to speak with your husband."

"Oh, yes," Alenela said, tossing her braid over her shoulder and glancing at Youngest-Father. "This one paid me a visit not so long ago. You might speak to my husband sooner if you threw him a rope. Also it might be safer for him, since the bridge has split the bark."

Imeris looked for Oldest-Father, but he seemed to have retreated into the ti-house. She took one of her own spare coils, secured it to the banister, and allowed it to drop past Zhamahz's head. The new arrival looked up at them with apparent startlement before hitching it to his harness and allowing Imeris and Youngest-Father to haul him up to the entryway.

He staggered past them to set the basket of green, patterned, oval-shaped fruit in a niche with a panel that slid back to accommodate provisions. His familiarity with the mechanism spoke of many previous deliveries.

Then he sat on the edge of the cupboard, rubbed at the seams on his forearms where his spines must have been bearing his weight for hours if not days, and drank from a leather bag brought to him by Alenela.

They embraced perfunctorily.

"You are late, my sweet," she said.

"The Floorians would not let me climb the tree yesterday," he said. "Their bone woman said a chimera was nearby. They waited for it to choose another tree."

"Did they?" Alenela murmured, waiting for realisation to make his jowly face sag and send his trembling right hand to the place over his heart.

"Is it . . . Is the demon in our tree, Alenela? But . . . the bridge. Did it hold? In the wet?"

"Everyone is here," Alenela said, placidly stoppering the leather bottle. "Everyone is safe. You have these strangers to thank for it. I suggest you help them with whatever matter it is that has brought them here to find you."

FOUR

IMERIS EXPLAINED curtly.

"There is a rogue sorceress. Sometimes called Kirrik. She carries the blue lanterns you have seen. We must know which tree they rested in. Lives depend on it. Can you tell us where it was? Can you explain how we may be sure of recognising it?"

"How do I know," Zhamahz asked, as politely as it was possible to ask such a thing, not meeting Imeris's eyes, "that the woman with the blue lanterns is not an innocent spinewife and you the rogue?"

"This woman faced a chimera to spare a tree full of strangers, my sweet," Alenela said, arms folded once again.

"If I were the rogue," Imeris said, "I would force you to accompany me. To be sure of finding the right tree. But I do not wish any unprotected persons to be near this sorceress when I strike her down, for she is a body stealer and sends innocent souls into the ether." She held up her amulet. "I do not have a spare one of these for you to wear. So I ask you again to describe in detail the direction and identifying traits of the tree in which you saw the lanterns."

Zhamahz gazed back at her with something like wistful contemplation for a long moment. Imeris had time to note the unusual placement of one implanted spine on the thumb of his huge, callused right hand, presumably for cutting stems. Also, a row of spines along his breastbone, useful for working with both hands free while stationary for long periods, but otherwise a danger, since spines weakened the integrity of the rib cage and made a vulnerable target in hand-to-hand fighting.

She tucked her amulet away.

Zhamahz shook his head, rubbing his bald spot with his left hand.

"The problem is," he said, "you would not be able to identify it, no matter what description I gave you. I have worked there only in the dark and the pouring rain. I know it by touch and by smell, but unless you had cut windowleaf fruit for forty years, I could not communicate these things to you."

"Then you must take us there," Youngest-Father said, "when the monsoon ends. And then get away as quickly as you can."

"There is another possibility," Alenela said, putting her hand protectively on Zhamahz's shoulder. They shared a glance, his expression reluctant, hers unreadable. "The Bird-Riders never forget a path once taken."

"That is not our bargain," Zhamahz argued. "Any Treefolk who set foot on the sacred soil must die—that is their law."

"They made an exception for you, my sweet. They may make another. You can but ask. It would be better than giving your body up to the use of a sorceress." Her hand tightened on his shoulder, and she shot a sharp glance at Youngest-Father.

Zhamahz nodded. He looked at Imeris and Youngest-Father in turn.

"I will go. I will ask them. That is the best I can do. It will take me the rest of this day and some of the night to drop back down to Floor and then climb here again. I am tired. You will wait?"

"We will," Imeris said.

The fruit cutter opened another hidden storage niche, this one on the other side of the entryway. There, a pulley on the end of a wooden arm swung out over the emptiness where the rope bridge had been. Zhamahz took the ropes hung from his body and threaded them through the mechanism. He emptied the basket he had carried on his back into the first niche, then reattached the empty basket to the ropes.

"Lend me your strong shoulders, Alenela."

Alenela smiled, showing her dimples, and tossed her grey braid over her shoulder. Stacking full water bags on his shoulders and her own, she joined him at the edge of the entryway, putting one arm around his neck and grasping the ropes with the other. Together they stepped onto the empty basket and sank slowly out of sight, as though they and the water bags were the counterweight to some other burden.

"You have traded with Floorians before, Youngest-Father," Imeris said, as they waited for that burden to appear. "Can we expect the Bird-Riders to agree?"

"Bird-Riders are not Fig-Eaters," Youngest-Father said. "The peoples of

Floor are more varied than those of the different villages of Understorey. Might as well ask a Servant of the death god what the birth goddess wants for breakfast."

Seven laden baskets of windowleaf fruit, each basket as tall as Oldest-Father, wound their way up the side of the tree. They stopped when the knots holding them to the ropes hit the pulley.

"Windowleaf fruit," Imeris said, taking one from the basket and breathing its delicious fragrance in again. "That is what the birth goddess would want for breakfast. I suppose we should secure the baskets and unload these?"

When they finished, they went to find Oldest-Father. In the chamber where the winds cooled the sweating, still-fearful crowd, he sat with the burnt leaf-wrappings, licking the last of the fish from his fingers.

"He told you which tree?" he asked. "Is it time to go?"

"Not exactly," Youngest-Father said. "Get comfortable."

After a while, inspired by Oldest-Father's example, some of the men went to set up a fishing net in the stream on the northern side of the tree. Children raided the kitchens for cups and drinking water. Families lit fires in the other hearths and sat around them drinking ti, playing sticks, and eating the syrups, gum-lollies, and other sickly sugary sap products that were added to ti for flavouring.

Imeris slept on the floor with her leathery wings for a blanket. She dreamed of Nirrin. Nirrin, flushed with pleasure at the news she was to be trained as a spinewife. Nirrin, teasing her brother about the relative prestige she would have compared to the village smith. Vesev answering that if she wanted any more metalwork done, she had better get on hands and knees and crawl. Handing her the heavy new brace with its seven curved, keen-edged spines.

Nirrin turning on him, brace in hand, eyes cold and glittering. And Imeris did nothing.

She watched and did nothing.

Youngest-Father woke her before morning. Still befuddled, half in the dream, she grabbed at her amulet. It kept her safe. Kirrik could not steal her body. She was not afraid. She was angry.

"Zhamahz has returned," Youngest-Father whispered in her ear.

Imeris forcibly loosened her fingers around the amulet. She took the time to use the toilet and to drink a cup of sweetened water. To stretch and loosen her muscles and joints, she practiced a quickening series of movements she'd learned at Loftfol, the first of their legendary forms. Then, gathering her wings and tightening her weapons belt and gliding harness over her sleeveless tunic and short wrapped skirt, she followed Youngest-Father to the east-facing entrance.

All was pitch-black. The noise of the sheeting rain almost made her miss Zhamahz's urgently whispered words.

"No light is permitted," he said. Imeris's hand met his rough, pudgy fist on the banister. She stood close to the edge. Youngest-Father's warm shape was between her and the long fall. She heard the pulley rattle; someone was angling the ropes. "That is their first and most urgent condition. They know about the sorceress you are hunting. To protect their bone women, they insist on total darkness. They say a bone woman's body can only be stolen if her face is seen and known."

"No light," Youngest-Father agreed. He took Imeris's hand, guiding it to the ropes.

"Step together onto the basket," Zhamahz said. "Your journey may be a little alarming. I did not know there were three of you."

Not enough fruit as a counterweight, Imeris supposed.

We are fliers, she thought. *We are not afraid to fall.*

She felt Youngest-Father's weight shifting, and she stepped after him, feeling with her foot for the edge of the basket, taking the rope in her hands.

"Gods' bones," Oldest-Father cursed as they swung out and hurtled down.

The coolness of the plunge was not unlike the wind in the ti-house. Imeris closed her eyes and tried to enjoy the relief of it, the way that it kept insects away from her, and not think about their landing. She was still tired. She wished she'd eaten some fish before falling asleep. The alertness she'd gotten from the sweetened water was fading.

Something heavy knocked her hard under the ribs, and only Oldest-Father's arm around her kept her from falling free of the basket. The shock made her mind flail for enemies—was it the sorceress? Had the Bird-Riders betrayed them?—before she remembered the tart fruit smell that had accompanied the blow. Not a human smell. Choking for breath, she endured Oldest-Father's grip until her midriff came unparalysed and she could speak.

"Was that . . . Was that . . ."

"It was the fruit," Youngest-Father confirmed in her ear. "On the way up. We are halfway down."

Imeris tried not to think what would have happened if she'd been carrying her bore-knife a little further towards the front; it might have been driven up into her chest by the fruit basket. She breathed slowly as her pulse settled. Tried not to think of the stories about Floorians being hideous and misshapen, about them mating with the beasts they shared their dirt with, and about their thirst for fresh blood.

You have traded with Floorians before.

Trade was not a thing she knew very much about. Oldest-Father prided himself on not needing anyone else. He'd trap a hundred beasts for their bones before he'd send Imeris to Gannak to trade for a single steel blade.

Middle-Father, when he had lived in Understorey, could not go to Gannak because of crimes he'd committed there before Imeris was born. *A hunter is no better than his weapons,* he'd told her a hundred times, though, and sent her to the forge for the things he needed, and later, the things she needed. Not just metals but salt, too. *Salt is the secret to a warrior's stamina, Issi.*

Imeris carried salt on her person at all times, in a pouch on her weapons belt.

Youngest-Father, in contrast, had brought back spoils from his travels among the villages of Understorey to their home in the tallowwood. He and Youngest-Mother had learned new music. Performed old. Instruments were bought and songs sold. The pair of them had used Youngest-Father's eye for beautiful fabrics and jewels to build a web of connections from Hundar to Lit. Those connections had paid off for him during the hunt for the sorceress. But even he had never sought to forge long-term alliances with Floorians.

Bird-Riders are not Fig-Eaters.

What was a Bird-Rider, anyway? What sort of monstrous birds were of a size to be ridden? And if the birds could climb or fly, why hadn't Imeris ever seen one? Middle-Father had hunted most of the great beasts and demons of the forest, and he had never mentioned any such thing as a bird big enough to ride upon. Imeris imagined enormous grey owls with hooked beaks and eyes like golden moons. Night-parrots the size of giant tapirs that drummed together in the dark.

Floorians do not climb. They say they have a sacred connection to dirt and water.

The greatest danger from owls was their talons. If Imeris was to fight one, she would try to trap the feathered legs together, to catch them with a rope and throwing stones. That would leave only the beak to worry about. Before she'd learned spine-fighting from Loftfol's Haakim, she'd learned from the Scentingim to weight ropes, hang from them, throw them, and strangle with them.

A Floorian might shoot you out of a tree, but she will not follow you into it.

Parrots had slightly less rotational ability in the neck. Imeris visualised the pertinent anatomy. The knife work she had learned from Middle-Father would be applicable in such a case. A strike from beneath the chest would need to be very deep to reach the heart in its spacious cavern of air-filled sacs; a spine-severing slice from behind the head would be more effective. The beak, though a danger, relied on strength in closing to open nut cases and tree trunks, not strength in opening. Perhaps a noose around the bill would be prudent, as with the owl.

Imeris felt surreptitiously for the spare ropes that still hung from her harness, half ready to loosen them, to use them, to string them with drilled stones for throwing.

The basket juddered to a halt. The earth smell was more powerful than Imeris had ever known it, drowning out the lemon ironwood smell. She felt buried in soil and leaves and half submerged in steaming water. The wood smoke clinging to their clothes and hair would make her own party easy enough to detect.

They could shoot her with arrows or mark her with a javelin, even blind in the black.

No, she thought. *I have not set foot on it. Not yet.*

"Is anyone there?" Youngest-Father called into the hot, heavy unknown. "We pay our respects to the Bird-Riders. I am called Marram. My brother is Esse. The young woman is my daughter, Imerissiremi."

There was only the whisper of running water around the roots of the tree and the howl of an unknown animal in the distant dark.

And then soft laughter. A splashing sound, as if someone had dropped down into knee-deep water. A nearby animal made a sharp *kek-kek-kek* sound and was soothed by human murmurs.

Imeris smelled eel and ginger on a stranger's breath but squared her shoulders and did not recoil.

"Who are you?" she demanded.

"Gumblossom," said a deep-voiced man whose mouth sounded about at the level of her eyes, a pace back from her. Though Oldest-Father tugged protectively at her, trying to turn the woven basket so that he was the one facing the stranger, she didn't help him and it didn't work.

Imeris, mortified by her foolish imaginings and determined to quash her dread, put her hand out to touch the man. She touched feathers instead, startling the creature before her into a *kek-kek-kek* that threatened to burst her eardrums. She couldn't let go of the rope with her other hand, so she wrapped her one loose arm around her head instead.

"Do not boke her eye," Gumblossom said when the animal was quiet.

"Do you mean poke her eye?"

Gumblossom laughed softly.

"This sound! Bah! We do not use it. Bah! Bah!"

Each time he tried it, he came closer to saying *pah!* without quite managing it.

Imeris stifled a giggle.

"Are all Floorian men named after flowers?" she asked. "Or just your leaders?"

"All children are named for the first fallen flower their mother feels after the birth," Gumblossom said. "But I am no leader. I talk with Treefolk because when my mother was bregnant with me, she ate some of the sbeaking-bone of an Old God. So I was born with some Treefolk words in me. Some Elephant-Driver words, Crocodile-Rider words, Rememberer words, Fig-Eater words, and words from the Bright Blain. Took me longer than other children to learn my own language, the language of the Steed-folk. But now, all these words, is useful to my beoble, correct?"

Imeris was taken aback. She'd heard other languages spoken about in Loftfol as historical irritants in the translation of fighting technique texts, not as things that still existed. Words were words.

"Correct," Youngest-Father said, sounding amused.

"You can be useful to my beoble, also. You hunt the sorceress, correct?"

"Correct," Oldest-Father said. "Will you take us to the tree, or will we stand here on this basket in the rain until dawn?"

"Our bone woman asks that I remind you. No light."

"No light," Oldest-Father agreed.

"The lightest of you will ride with me. But out your hand again, Im-mimissimi."

This time, Imeris did laugh. When she reached out her hand, a man's wide, muddy palm clasped hers and dragged her from the basket onto something broad, slick, and warm. She felt that she was seated in front of Gumblossom, that his chest and abdomen were naked and covered in mud. His eel and ginger breath tickled her ear.

"She feels like a wet feather bed by a fire," Imeris said.

"She looks like a giant flowerfowl," Gumblossom answered. "Her feathers are glorious, black and blue, and her toes are four body lengths long. It is a shame you are not bermitted to see her. She walks on the lily bads that float on the surface of the water. But we must move, so that your companions may mount."

His knees pressed the great bird's sides. It lurched forwards and back before coming to a halt again with its neck feathers brushing Imeris's nose.

"Her head bobs back and forth when she walks," Gumblossom warned. "Do not get a bloody nose. Lean back."

Imeris leaned against him. He felt like a normal man, albeit with bulky muscles and a bushy beard. Not hideous and misshapen at all. Imeris wondered if he had green eyes. There was a special place in her heart for men with green eyes. And he ate eels with ginger, not blood.

"You carry no weapons?" she asked.

"My steed is my weabon," Gumblossom replied as shuddering basket sounds and a close-by *kek-kek-kek* indicated that Imeris's fathers were being helped onto their own giant birds. "Her beak and her claws and her sbeed. Do not feel shamed by the way I will hold you. If you fall off, you cannot rid us of our shared enemy."

FIVE

The giant bird raced through the dark.

Imeris lay back at a sharp angle, eyes to the sky. Gumblossom's burly arms were wrapped around her, and the steed's feathered head brushed her breasts with every swift stride. It would have felt like a dream, if not for the thought that the battle with the sorceress lay ahead.

An hour or so had gone by. Imeris had never seen a water clock outside of Loftfol, but her time in the school had given her a good sense of how the days and their divisions passed, even in pitch-blackness. If she'd been in Understorey, she might have hoped to see the first light of day, but here there wasn't so much as the twinkle of false stars.

"Have you ever seen the sun?" she asked Gumblossom.

"When I was a child," Gumblossom replied. "One of the great trees fell. That was when these lilies grew. They bloom in the sun after a giant dies. These ones likely will not bloom again for a hundred years. Life is very batient, here."

"We do not see much of the sun. But if I never saw it at all, I think I might go mad."

"And I would go mad if my feet did not touch the earth. Here is the tree that your friend the fruit cutter bade us bring you to the base of."

Imeris felt the steed's pace falling, the feathers brushing her at lengthening intervals.

"How can you see? How can you know?"

"The steed knows," Gumblossom answered. "She does not like to come close to trees. They bend her toes." He had to help her to sit upright when they stopped, for Imeris's lower back had seized up in the awkward angle she'd adopted while riding.

There was no time for her stretching exercises, though. Gumblossom swung her out over the right side of the giant bird, and she had no choice but to trust him and let go of his hand. Her feet landed together on a tree root; her waving arms found the chunky, fibrous bark of a floodgum criss-crossed by the succulent stems of the parasitic windowleaf.

"Imeris," Youngest-Father said quietly beside her, and then Oldest-Father landed right on top of both of them. There was more laughter and splashing from the Floorians, and cursing from Oldest-Father, as they untangled themselves.

"The mud at the foot of the tree," Gumblossom called from a distance, "will brotect you from insect stings, but do not go deeb into the water. Bad things wait there. Good hunting to you, Treefolk."

"Thank you," Youngest-Father called back to them.

But the Bird-Riders were gone.

Good, Imeris thought. *Now Kirrik will not be able to use any of them.*

Obedient to Gumblossom's suggestion, they smeared each other's bodies with mud, wherever there was bare skin. Youngest-Father wore the fewest clothes, so carried the most mud, while Oldest-Father and Imeris only had necks, faces, arms, and lower legs to smear with the fine-grained, decay-smelling silt.

"This is a fortune to a potter," Imeris said.

"Status symbols for half-wits," Oldest-Father muttered. "Pottery."

"Is the water clean, I wonder?" Youngest-Father asked.

"We should have asked the bone woman to purify some for us," Imeris said. Long before she had gone to Loftfol, Middle-Father had taught her how to stay strong for a battle at the end of a long climb. *Drink all the water you can hold. Piss it all against the trunk right before the attack, marking territory like a demon and lightening yourself for combat.*

And what of the warriors below? Imeris had asked him, giggling.

You are marking them, too, was Middle-Father's answer. *Marking them as weaklings and cowards who did not reach the battleground before you.*

"This will have to do." Youngest-Father sighed, sharing a leather water bottle and balls of cidergum sap between them.

They began to climb.

"At least it will be easy to see the lanterns in this," Imeris whispered.

"We can only hope," Youngest-Father whispered back. He had taken the lead. Imeris climbed behind him, with Oldest-Father lowest down the trunk. Spines weren't necessary, with the windowleaf stems offering easy purchase, even without being able to see a thing. The occasional cool leaf blade slapped Imeris's cheek; she had been warned that the windowleaf trees here had leaves all the way down.

They didn't need to speak of battle plans. Those were long ago made and many times practiced. The first time the three brothers had killed Kirrik, it had been by arrow. The second time by trap and ballista bolt. Both times, the sorceress had inhabited a body incapable of magic. Imeris had listened avidly to those tales by the fire, proud of her fathers, but it hadn't been personal to her, then. Nirrin had still been herself.

They feared that Nirrin's body had been chosen because she was destined to be a spinewife. They feared that this time, Kirrik would be able to use the gods' powers against them, the way she had once before.

Middle-Father had formulated a plan whereby Youngest-Father, with his chimera-skin wings, would fly down right on top the sorceress while Oldest-Father distracted her with talk. Chimera skin blocked the use of magic. Middle-Father would reach under the edge of the hide and cut her throat while she was entangled in it. Perhaps the skin would hold her soul inside it, too.

If not, the three brothers would be wearing amulets and there would be nobody else on the tree; nobody close enough for Kirrik to take over before her soul faded into the ether.

It was a good plan.

Middle-Father was in Canopy right now, being Bodyguard to Imeris's sister, his amulet passed on to Imeris, but Imeris was more than willing to do the throat-cutting. She'd practiced the motion with her right-forearm spines, of cutting an imaginary throat from the other side of the edge of a demon hide. Horroh the Haakim had watched without asking why.

Nirrin was your friend, Youngest-Father had said, *before her body was stolen by the sorceress. I will be the one to kill her a final time, and with one of Vesev's knives, too.*

Youngest-Father had been afraid of the village smith, Sorros, and his two children, Vesev and Nirrin. He'd agonized that Imeris would let slip the location of their dwelling, or her fathers' real names. If anyone from the village learned the truth about her family, the people of Gannak would come for the three brothers, to force them to face their version of justice.

Imeris hadn't cared about her fathers' so-called crimes in the days before they'd fled the village. She only wanted a friend who wasn't her sister or brother. Someone to tell her secrets to, who could tell her what was going on in the wider world, and who was sympathetic to her desire to escape the expectations of her parents that she would carry out Great Deeds.

When they were both about twelve, Imeris had dared to visit Nirrin at her house in Gannak. Nirrin's mother had gone out to the ti-house to sell moonflowers, and Vesev had been at the forge with their father.

The two girls, alone in the house, had made ti themselves, stealing honey from the pantry and luxuriating in the smooth sweetness it gave the ti. They'd put a tarantula in Vesev's bed and tried on Nirrin's mother's wedding headdress, which she was keeping for Nirrin's wedding. It had metal and gems in among the feathers and bright-dyed fibres, and they'd fought over who would hold it up to the firelight and coo over the glitter and gleam of it.

Nirrin had wanted Imeris to try the dresses next, but Imeris hadn't dared take off her wings and gliding frame.

If I suddenly jump out the window, she'd said nervously, *it will be because I see Oldest-Father coming along the bridges to find me.*

Of course, Oldest-Father hadn't come. He rarely left the tallowwood tree trunk that was their home. It was Youngest-Father who rapped smartly on the door to interrupt Imeris's illicit visit, and it was a Defender of Gannak who tried to detain them both. They'd managed to fly away that time, though Imeris hadn't been able to fly away from the beating Oldest-Father gave her after, nor the confiscation of her wings.

Now she wished she'd disobeyed Oldest-Father more often and visited Nirrin more while there had still been time.

Remembering how strict he had been while she was growing up made her want to piss on him, right here and now, but this was no place for childishness. She was a Heightsman of Loftfol.

"I see the lanterns," Youngest-Father said, going utterly still against the trunk.

Imeris froze, too, gazing upwards at the ghostly glow. Very faint, filtering through many layers of broad, black-silhouetted, hole-filled windowleaves, but the blue blush was unmistakeable. She wrinkled her nose. Smelled male sweat that belonged to neither of her fathers.

"There must be a sentry," she murmured. "Buried in leaves. Let me go ahead and find him. His body must not be made available to the sorceress."

"Wait," Youngest-Father replied, "until I am away."

"Do you need help with your wings?" Imeris whispered. When he didn't answer, she knew he had unwrapped them himself. The sound of him sliding them over his shoulders always took her back to the moment of her first flight, the smoothness of the too-big handles, and how the god of falling children had saved her from her own stupidity.

Today there must be no mistakes. This was her chance to break free of her old segmented life and start anew, to truly find herself. Only Kirrik stood in the way. *Kirrik,* Imeris had heard that name whispered, a curse, a thousand times. From now on when anyone said it, they would look to her, admiringly, knowing she had rid the forest of a terrible scourge, but not knowing she'd had no choice, bred to the task and now led to the task. She must not fail.

"Find the nearest tree for me, brother," Youngest-Father called softly down to Oldest-Father, who brought two hollow blocks out of the bundle on his back and clapped them together.

They made a sound like a branch cracking, which was a normal enough sound in the forest and not bound to cause too much alarm, but the echoes of the sound told Oldest-Father, who had practiced with them, where the neighbouring tree trunks stood, and where there was only emptiness for thousands of paces and more.

He climbed up past Imeris and, in the lantern light, she saw him lift Youngest-Father's arm, chimera cloth hanging from it like a bat's skin folds, and point it slightly to the left.

"There," Oldest-Father murmured, retreating out of the way.

Youngest-Father launched himself with a crack of frame setting and a rush of air. Imeris couldn't follow without a ballista, in the rain, with her inferior wings, but she didn't need to. Youngest-Father would climb the neighbouring tree until he found a position suitable for gliding down to the level of the lanterns.

Oldest-Father's job would be to lure the enemy onto some nearby, obvious, clearly visible platform close to the death-lanterns, without being killed by them.

Before Oldest-Father moved into the open, though, Imeris would have to make sure the sorceress was isolated. At least one sentry seemed likely. Above the dovecote if Kirrik was most concerned about discovery by Canopians. Below if she was most concerned about Understorians.

Imeris was willing to bet the man she could smell was a guard stationed below.

She pulled slightly ahead of Oldest-Father, motioning for him to be still. Without waiting to see if he'd obeyed, she used her spines to slice away a section of windowleaf between its long, stringy veins. It made a swishing noise, but single swishing noises could be ignored. Breaking twigs, falling fruit, and disagreements between birds could all make a single swish. Imeris had heard and ignored plenty in the last few minutes. It was sustained swishing that attracted attention.

Ducking her head under several other of the leaves, she located a handful of mosquitoes on their undersides, captured them unharmed, made a leaf-tube from the cut section in her hand, and blew the insects into the air above her.

They dispersed silently, wings catching the sparse light. Imeris watched them closely.

At first they spread out in a random pattern. Then some of them seemed drawn to a particular gap between leaves above her head.

Somebody is there. Breathing.

Imeris listened. Heard nothing. Saw nothing further. Manoeuvred with all the stealth she naturally possessed and had honed at the Loftfol school, contorting her limbs to avoid brushing leaves and branches, at times her entire body weight borne by one handhold as she strained to lift herself up and over some half-furled sheet of green.

Then she peered through a slit in the leaves, spotted the underside of a boot and part of a knee, and felt all her mind and muscle focus to a killing point. She had to end whoever crouched there without alerting the sorceress to a struggle.

Imeris reached overhead, forearm spines out. They slid easily between the windowleaf trunk and the rootlets that held it to the host tree. Immediately, the trunk segment sagged under the weight of the hidden sentry, leaving the person no choice but to stand up and scout out a safer perch.

Imeris glimpsed the man's startled, black-skinned Canopian face. His back to the tree, his arms went wide to steady himself. Imeris's concentration was so absolute, she could almost feel herself in his place, thinking his thoughts. It was not magic. Only the total empathy possible in a one-on-one encounter.

His eyes darted to his right. He was preparing to pivot on that foot, turning his front to the tree, stepping onto a secure trunk with rootlets intact.

Imeris visualised where his neck would be when he pivoted. Felt the roughness of the weighted ropes in her hands. She would not have room to give the ropes the full turn she had been taught to add power to the throw, nor could she use her preferred length, in case the weights hit the tree and bounced off instead of wrapping around his throat. The wooden blocks were neither barbed nor poisoned.

He shifted his centre of gravity. Imeris sank her shin spines into the tree and reared back, right arm pushing free of the foliage. She swung the cord. Loosed it. The throw was perfectly timed.

Unable to shout his warning, the sentry wobbled at the brink of falling, hands instinctively coming to his throat instead of securing him to the tree. One shin managed to catch in a thick stem. Abruptly his head dangled level with hers, upside down, his back arched, eyes bulging and mouth opening and closing.

She drew a fish knife and tried to cut his throat. Her first kill. She had to grit her teeth to stop her own mouth from opening and closing, still in terrible sympathy. She could have been the one hanging there, an instant away from death. He blocked the knife. She sliced his palms. *Hurry,* her mind berated her. *Do not make a commotion!*

Before she could stab him through the heart, Oldest-Father was blocking her way, pulling a brain-coated bore-knife out of the man's skull.

"Quickly," Oldest-Father whispered. "She might have heard. Follow me."

Imeris swallowed with a dry mouth. The moment of sympathy was over; she was a woman on a branch who might have died; her flesh was vulnerable; there was no amulet to shield her from physical attacks. Yet her lifetime of training was as good as a magic amulet. Better, since it could not be taken away from her. The flicker of fear was overtaken by exultation, which was overtaken in turn by regret. For a moment she couldn't look away from the blood, diluted by rain, dripping down the sliced, hanging hands of the dead sentry. His soul was winging its way through the trees even now, swiftly towards rebirth.

Then, she put her fish knife away and climbed after Oldest-Father.

SIX

IMERIS CREPT with Oldest-Father along a broken lateral branch.

The branch had no doubt been a strong and vital bough when the flood-gum was young and growing. Shadowed by the canopy, though, and dragged on by the weight of windowleaf vines, it had long since cracked and fallen away. Most of her mud had washed away in the rain, and Imeris suppressed the urge to slap at insects.

The side of the sorceress's dovecote came into view.

"You will never get past the lanterns," Imeris breathed, "to reach the central vein."

The building took the shape of two enormous windowleaves, jutting out twenty paces or so from the side of the tree, connected by slender columns of equal lengths. Ceiling-leaf and floor-leaf were perfectly parallel, one about two body lengths above the other. The leaf-perforations that ate away a fifth of the edge of each dark green, leathery surface matched one other, too. Rainwater collecting on the ceiling-leaf fell through the upper holes in glittering, bluish streams and straight through the corresponding lower holes.

It was beautiful.

But the death-lanterns that shot lightning bolts into any body that blocked their light were hung strategically from the twisty, creamy-brown columns at the tip and both sides of the lower leaf. The lanterns' blue glow defended not only the gaps between leaves where Oldest-Father might enter, but also the upper and lower perforations. There, the shafts of light looked like ghostly blue spears.

Only the central leaf veins, where there were no perforations, were safe. The sorceress must sleep on the lower vein, sheltered from the monsoon by the upper one.

"The leaves are tough," Oldest-Father whispered, "but not like tallowwood.

If I cut around the base of that column closest to us, column and lantern will both fall."

"Killing you on the way down," Imeris said dolefully.

"We still have enough rope between us. Give me yours." His hand touched her arm. "I can swing out of the way." Oldest-Father always carried more rope than anyone. He was afraid to glide, even in the dry season. If he had to cross the spaces between great trees, his preferred method was to tie one of his ropes to the belt of a person who *did* have a glider, and once they'd made the crossing and secured it for him, to swing across after them.

Imeris looked down at his hand. They were close enough to the lantern light for her to see the spots and scars on the back of it. He was old, too old to be trying acrobatics, and she was a Heightsman of Loftfol.

"Let me do it, Oldest-Father."

He scowled.

"Did I summon you here to watch you die?"

"Did you summon me," she retorted, "to carry rope for you?"

"The plan is not altered, Imeris. You will take Bernreb's part. You will finish her off at the end. Not before."

I am my own woman, she thought angrily. *You do not command my obedience anymore.*

When Imeris had made that forbidden visit to Nirrin's home, aged twelve, she'd been known by everyone as Issi. *Issi, did you know that women can be Heightsmen, too, if they beat all the men in the race to Loftfol?* Nirrin had said. *Issi, did you know that Loftfol is a school for training war leaders to raid Canopy?*

Usually it was Nirrin who enlightened Issi, but that day, the day they had tried on the wedding headdress, Issi had found herself able to contribute. *Nirrin, did you know that if our people get captured in Canopy, they snap off their spines and make them slaves forever?*

Nirrin had been horrified, clutching her arms. Issi had clutched her arms, too. Only for a moment. Her blood was Canopian, but her spines made her Understorian, or so she thought. But the idea of slavery was fresh in her thoughts. So when Oldest-Father punished her with a beating and by taking away her wings, she had tried to hurt him back by calling him a slave.

Do you wish we lived in Canopy? Oldest-Father had asked her scathingly.

That I truly was a slave, and you were not Imerissiremi, but Imeris? Imeris was your Canopian name, before your blood mother dropped you over the edge to be eaten by demons.

He'd called her Imeris from that moment on, a constant reminder, and she had defiantly reclaimed it, though her other two fathers still called her Issi or Imerissiremi. And he'd taken away her knives, replacing them with chimney brushes, saying she would not hunt again until the chimneys were cleaner than her filthy mouth.

She hadn't known how to fight with her spines then.

"At the end," Imeris acceded. "Not before."

She gave him her rope. He whisked away.

Imeris climbed after him, slowly and arrhythmically, trying to disguise the drag of her glider wings as leaves rustling in the rain. If Oldest-Father was able to cut any of the leaf-dwelling away, it would be because the sorceress was sleeping. In her head, as her fingers and toes found holds in between the fleshy stems, Imeris practiced the throat-cutting move.

My Great Deed.

The end of the sorceress Kirrik, and the end of my family's ambition for me.

She would not leave the fatal blow to others, as she had with the sentry. Her heart thumped.

Then she flinched back, flattening herself between leaves, as the blue lantern fell. Abandoning silence, pushing her way up through the foliage to find a viewpoint, she glimpsed, through the hole he had cut, Oldest-Father climbing through the lower windowleaf of the dovecote.

Imeris peered into darkness in the direction where Youngest-Father had glided, hoping he was in position and ready to begin his glide towards the dovecote. She clambered higher up the trunk, forced to go around several of the huge, flat leaves. Behind a clump of them, several paces higher than and around the trunk from the dovecote, she waited, hugging the stems, feeling her spines quiver, scanning for a second sentry, seeing no movement and smelling nothing but windowleaf fruit and the faint stink of panther musk.

She rearranged several of the leaves so she could see.

Oldest-Father knelt on the upper leaf of the dovecote, putting his head through one of the holes to peer inside it.

Whatever he saw made him leap back. There were ten paces of safe space around him devoid of the direct, deadly light. Imeris unfolded her glider frame, snapping it into place, ready to launch in Youngest-Father's place if Oldest-Father could not buy enough time.

"Kirrik, who was once Rannar of Dul," Oldest-Father shouted, "and the tanner Aaderredaa before her! I seek an audience."

His thin body was straight and unafraid.

How can a man be afraid of heights but not of a body-snatching enchantress?

A young, dark-haired woman pulled herself up through the hole where Oldest-Father had peered. Her back was half turned to Imeris, but her figure was achingly familiar. A huge bosom contrasted with a thin boy-bum and wide bare feet. The woman wore a sleeveless black shirt, a short olive-green split skirt, and one leg brace with steel hooks.

Nirrin.

Nirrin's spines had never taken in that leg, which had been broken when a dayhunter tried to snatch her out of her cradle. Imeris felt nauseated. Memories of the moment in the forge threatened to overwhelm her.

No. It is not really her.

"How," the woman who was not Nirrin asked imperiously, lifting Nirrin's chin, "do you know those names?"

"I had a bird from one of your sons," Oldest-Father said. "He is a slave in Canopy and seems to think it your fault. You never taught him to switch bodies. He says switching bodies is the only way he can rid himself of the mark upon his tongue."

"He has asked me to pay his ransom before," Kirrik said, putting her fists to her hips. "Now he sends you. What can you offer that he could not?"

"I am a problem solver."

"You would serve me?"

"I am a machine maker."

"No machine is worth the loss of my lamp." Her tone turned dangerous. "I shall have to risk the climb to Floor to recover it."

"I have slain many demons."

"I have slain more. Also, many women and men."

"Yes," Oldest-Father agreed, "many. Including Sikakis, who was a prince. Garrag, who was another of your sons. Nirrin, who would have been a spinewife of Gannak, if you had not sent her soul into the ether."

Silence between them. Stillness.

Hurry, Youngest-Father, Imeris thought, her pulse racing, her spines vibrating with their need to spring from her forearm and shinbone crevices.

"Those names," Kirrik said at last, menacingly, "are not known to my son."

A bird made of chimera cloth swooped out of the darkness, covering Kirrik in a heartbeat with colour-changing wings.

SEVEN

Imeris prepared to launch herself.

The sorceress was trapped. Enfolded.

No. Imeris hesitated.

Something was wrong.

Something was happening.

The twisting, creamy-brown columns separating the two great leaves were coming alive. They were not wooden. Squeezing out from under the upper leaf through the perforations in it, they had the chimera skin in their mouths; they dragged Youngest-Father back. He was still strapped to the frame of the glider. Kirrik was revealed, her lips moving but not making any sound.

Snakes.

Nirrin was going to be a spinewife.

These were the vipers that served as donors for the fangs, magically embedded in bone, which became an Understorian warrior's climbing spines. Imeris's spines had come from reptiles like these.

Nirrin, fists stretched out to either side, had spines erupting from all sorts of places they shouldn't. A crown of them stood up from her skull. Lines of them tore through her black shirt, emerging from every rib. They pushed out all along her spine, ripping her shirt and her olive-green skirt.

The sorceress was out from under the chimera skin. She was escaping, all of Imeris's hopes and plans escaping with her. *She must not escape!*

In a panic, Imeris launched herself without first making sure she was clear. She cursed as her glider wing tip snagged on a leaf. Instead of plunging to her fathers' aid, she careened in a half circle and slammed, upside down, into the tree trunk. All the breath was knocked out of her.

"You should have let them sleep on, Core Kirrik," Youngest-Father shouted. "They cannot maintain this structure without the coldness and rigidity of hibernation."

"You!" Kirrik shrieked. "I healed you. I spared you. I should never have kept you in hibernation!"

Imeris wrenched her arms out of the straps of the frame and righted herself, still gasping. The blood had run to her head, suffusing her along with the sense of failure.

Kirrik turned to face her, eyes blazing. It was not over. The enemy was still there. Imeris leaped, wingless, down onto the upper leaf, dodging away from the lantern beams. She skipped over a writhing carpet of snakes towards Kirrik, her spines out, heedless of the danger.

Her weight collapsed the upper windowleaf around her. The dovecote sagged, threatening to spill all of them. It was nightmarish. Like being trapped in a vertical river, unable to go forwards or back. Imeris couldn't see her fathers or Kirrik. She pushed the leathery leaf surface away from her, spines catching in it, only hoping that the sorceress, with her many added spines, was trapped in it, too.

Oldest-Father's bore-knife blade emerged from the leaf, a hand-span from Imeris's face. It scored her shoulder in a downward curl; Oldest-Father's hand, when it seized her harness, turned slick with her blood. The harness rope pressed into the wound, making her cry out.

Her stomach lurched. Everything fell away. The huge pair of window-leaves, detached from the tree, drifted in slow motion, left behind in darkness by the two remaining, fast-falling lanterns. Imeris's wings and their frame fell, too. Vipers fell, looping around nothing. Clothes and blankets, books and scrolls toppled. They must have been inside the dovecote.

Imeris dangled by her harness from Oldest-Father's hand. His other arm was caught by the spines in the trunk of the tree. Their eyes met. His tight expression softened with relief. Imeris lunged at the tree, sinking her own spines into the juicy windowleaf stems. Oldest-Father let go of her harness, letting her take her own weight.

When she looked up, in the fading blue lantern light and the greyish daylight now reaching them from the distant sky, she saw Youngest-Father hanging from the floodgum bark by his spines. A few body lengths above him, the sorceress hung from a rope made of snakes.

Imeris smelled the same sap she had smelled before, but it had smelled like hope before, and now it smelled like catastrophe. Kirrik had the height advantage, and they had lost the element of surprise. As the sorceress climbed higher and the lowest snake became superfluous, it detached itself from the chain and fell onto Youngest-Father's upturned face. He slashed it with the spines of his other arm, just in time for another viper to drop onto him, and another. Kirrik's lips moved, again in silence, and Youngest-Father's movements slowed. His eyes closed, and his body went limp.

"What's happening?" Imeris cried, lunging upwards, wanting to climb to Youngest-Father's rescue, but Oldest-Father jerked her wrist painfully.

"No, Imeris," he hissed. "Keep this distance, or she'll put you to sleep, too. She must be silenced before she kills him. Use your throwing rope."

Childish instinct to obey him kicked in. Youngest-Father's slumbering form slackened, and his spines loosened from the tree. Imeris ducked her head, feeling around herself to find the weighted rope, and while she was distracted, Oldest-Father slipped upwards, past her.

"Wait," she cried, but he was already halfway to the sorceress, a bore-knife in each clenched fist.

Nirrin—Kirrik—stared down at him with contempt. The windowleaf stems around him shuddered to life, sending new, green shoots wriggling into the open air. The tree itself was betraying Oldest-Father, joining the fight on the side of the sorceress.

Vines lashed his body and limbs to the trunk. Imeris heard the crack of his neck breaking. She wanted to believe she had imagined it. When his body turned in the grip of the writhing shoots, she wanted to believe that he was struggling.

Escaping.

Instead, he was pulled in between the trunks of windowleaf and host tree. Imeris saw his dead, glazed eyes popping in the moment before every part of him was covered, sealed into the titanic trunk of the tree.

She screamed her denial, and Kirrik's predatory glare left the place where Oldest-Father had vanished, settling on her instead.

Imeris didn't pause to aim. Once she had the weights swinging at speed, they left her hand and connected almost instantly, across five body lengths, to the sorceress's mouth. The hardwood bloodied Nirrin's lips. Perhaps broke a few teeth. Imeris's spines sprang from her forearms. She climbed rapidly towards the injured sorceress, but when she stopped, halfway, to raise her head above the tangle of leaves and sight her prey a second time, she saw

Youngest-Father's slumbering form about to fall, between her and the escaping sorceress.

She set her shin spines and prepared to catch him. Nirrin's steel brace made a characteristic sticking sound in the tree. Its spines were neither as slender nor sharp as snake-teeth spines, and in the time since Vesev had made them, tree sap and rain had rusted them. Imeris raised her voice so that the fleeing Kirrik could hear her. "I will find you again! You are an abomination! Every part of the forest you corrupt will point the way to you!"

The tree shuddered. Youngest-Father fell. Imeris's joints jolted as she caught him.

She pressed his limp form against the same fleshy stems that had murdered Oldest-Father, having no choice but to trust that these ones would not open and envelop them both. She planted her forearm spines to create a cradle for him.

A windowleaf stem grew impossibly fast over their heads, blocking the feeble daylight. It stretched across the chasm between great trees, vanishing into darkness, carrying Kirrik with it.

Youngest-Father had spoken of seeing such horrors before, when Kirrik wielded the Godfinder's power. How could she have forgotten?

Imeris felt paralysed by Oldest-Father's loss. A storm of unbearable shame and fury filled her.

I was not quick enough. I was not strong enough.

There is no greatness in me. My mothers and fathers were wrong.

Oldest-Father is dead. My Great Deed. I can never meet their eyes again.

EIGHT

IMERIS SHIVERED in the doorway, holding Youngest-Father's body before her.

It was Oldest-Mother, Ylly the elder, whose wrinkled hands urged her inside, closer to the fire. Imeris shuffled into brightness and warmth. She put her father on the enormous slab of quandong wood that comprised, with ironbark frame and pegs, the central table.

"Where is Esse?" Oldest-Mother asked.

"Gone," Imeris answered, staring at Youngest-Father's relaxed face, his cheeks brushed by closed lashes. "Dead. Killed by Kirrik."

Five days since their defeat at the hands of the sorceress, Imeris was weak with exhaustion and grief, and dizzy with hunger. She hadn't stopped to forage or hunt, uncertain as to the effects of Youngest-Father's continued deep sleep. He'd fallen under Kirrik's spell before. The Godfinder had slept peacefully under the influence of a similar spell for many years. This one, though, had been cast with malice.

"Marram isn't dead," Oldest-Mother said, feeling Imeris's forehead, pinching the loose skin on the backs of her hands. "He isn't, or you'd have put him in a tree-bole with his wings and brought back only a token."

"He is not dead," Imeris agreed, still shivering. Heat from the blazing fire shrank her woven clothes as they dried. It made her eyes gritty. There was a painful, pinpoint throbbing between them. Her bones ached from nights spent dozing vertically, roped and wedged by her spines in the sides of trees.

It was night now. She recalled it when her roving eyes found the embroidered hangings that covered the passages to other rooms deeper inside the tree, the cavernous fireplace lined with stone stolen from Floor and the multiple rows of spits of drying fish, but no Middle-Mother or Youngest-Mother.

They were sleeping.

"I'll wake Oos," Oldest-Mother said, lifting her hands reluctantly from Youngest-Father's throat where a pulse should have beat strongly. She bent under one of the embroidered hangings, hesitated. "His wings." She jerked her chin at the chimera cloth and handles which hung from Imeris's climbing harness. "They shouldn't stay so close to the fire. If you won't go and lie down, go and oil them. He'll need them."

Oldest-Mother left the room. Imeris pulled the wings away from her harness. She was still standing there, holding them, mind too fogged to remember what she was going to do with them, when Youngest-Mother arrived.

Youngest-Mother, whose name was Oos, was much taller than Oldest-Mother, and the better part of two decades younger. Where Oldest-Mother had straight white hair and skin the colour of mother's milk, Youngest-Mother was dark as polished blackbean seeds with beautiful full lips, her hair like a thundercloud with the first few threads of white for lightning.

She held her thirteen-pipe flute gently in long, slender fingers. There were no spines in her forearms or shinbones. She had come from Canopy, not long after Imeris herself had fallen as a baby.

"What happened?" Youngest-Mother asked in her melodious voice.

Imeris flinched, recalling her clumsy launch. The way the leaves had caught her and the glider had failed. A movement she'd performed a thousand times but bungled when it really counted. Kirrik would be dead now if not for her blunder. Oldest-Father would still be alive. Youngest-Father's condition was all her fault.

There must be no mistakes, she'd told herself, and then done the exact opposite.

"Oldest-Father is dead. Kirrik put Youngest-Father to sleep. He has not moved—"

Youngest-Mother released her breath sharply all at once. She embraced Imeris, whose arms did not respond until after Youngest-Mother had released her.

"Thank the goddess you're not hurt."

"It was my fault."

"No. This is Kirrik's work and hers alone."

"Can you save Youngest-Father?"

Youngest-Mother turned to the limp shape sprawled across the table.

"One who walks in the grace of Audblayin can and must revive him. Unar found a way to wake him once before. So will I."

Youngest-Mother had spent her youth as an adept in the Temple of Audblayin. Unar, the Godfinder, had been her friend. At one time, Youngest-Mother had been a target of the sorceress herself, though she wished now to believe that Kirrik had forgotten her.

She set the thirteen pipes to her lips. They vibrated with her exhalation, but no sound came out of the flute.

Imeris shivered.

"What have you discovered?" she whispered when Youngest-Mother lowered the flute.

"I'm not sure," Youngest-Mother replied, her thick brows knitting. She was still staring in consternation at Youngest-Father when Oldest-Mother returned to the room.

"The monsoon is finished," Oldest-Mother said meaningfully to Imeris, but Imeris couldn't think about going to Canopy until Youngest-Father was safe. She gave a slight nod to acknowledge the information, returning her attention to Youngest-Mother's face.

Imeris didn't like to interrupt Youngest-Mother's train of thought, but Oldest-Mother said, "There are bite marks on his legs and arms, Oos. Over the old scars."

"Kirrik had control over snakes," Imeris said dully. "Her latest dovecote was constructed of them."

"Spinewives practice hatching the snakes from clutches of eggs," Youngest-Mother said absently, "to save the villagers having to catch them."

"She had spines," Imeris went on, her eyes never leaving Youngest-Father's face, "implanted in all parts of her to prevent anything coming close. Her magic put him to sleep. Vines under her control broke Oldest-Father's neck and dragged him inside the tree trunk. I hit her in the mouth with a throwing weight. She escaped on a windowleaf stem that carried her to another tree before falling away."

Oldest-Mother brought a bowl of water and a cloth. She began cleaning Youngest-Father's dirty face; she put a second, wetter cloth to his cracked lips.

"You're lucky," Youngest-Mother said, "that her focus was on escape. That she didn't send windowleaf stems through your heart."

"How have these strongest of her powers returned, Youngest-Mother? Are they not Audblayin's powers?"

"Yes." Youngest-Mother's lips puckered. "Nirrin would have been a spine-wife of Gannak. In Gannak, which lies closest to the seat of Audblayin's power, the natural affinity of anyone born gifted is for life and birth magics. Kirrik couldn't displace your souls, because of the amulets you wore, but she could use Nirrin's skills."

"And how," Imeris asked, "do we defend ourselves from those, Youngest-Mother?"

"You'll have to ask that question of your sister. Quiet, now." Her brow relaxed. "I think I see a way to wake him."

She blew into the pipes, silently, again. The flames in the huge hearth flickered. Youngest-Father did not immediately stir. Oldest-Mother drew the damp cloth away from the patient's mouth. She sat with her hands on her knees, watching.

Then Youngest-Father drew a deep breath. His lashes fluttered. His spines relaxed partway out of the seams in his arms. He breathed out again.

"You've done it, Oos," Oldest-Mother said, relieved.

"He was only brushed by the edge of the spell, I think," Youngest-Mother said, lowering the flute for the second time. "Or it's simply that Nirrin's power is an order of magnitude weaker than Unar's was. Help him to drink and then take him to his bed, Ylly."

Oldest-Mother obeyed.

Only when he was gone from the hearth room and Oldest-Mother had returned did Imeris feel as though she'd relinquished his weight. She collapsed into one of the chairs. Her shoulders trembled, and she took Oldest-Mother's damp cloth, putting it to her own lips.

"The monsoon is over," Oldest-Mother told her a second time. "The old year is over. The new one has begun. Will you go to Canopy?"

"Yes," Imeris said wearily. She wanted sleep more than she wanted anything, except to defeat Kirrik, and clearly she needed more training, more practice, if she was ever to hope to do that. Oldest-Father would not want her to hide in a hole and weep. He would want her to carry on along the path he had chosen for her.

"Then I won't need to send any messages to your sister or your middle-father. You can tell them about Esse."

"Send a message to Leaper. I may not see him."

"Do not die, falling from the wet bark of your own tree, because you are too tired to think. Your sparring partner will still be there next year."

"Will she?"

"If she isn't," Youngest-Mother said wryly, "and your famous duels are finished, you'll have won by default."

Our duels are not famous, Imeris thought. *Nobody will hear of them until the day I win one, and even then, if it takes too long, they will say it was because she was old and her strength failed.*

The monsoon is over. Why now? Why tonight? You are a cruel goddess, Ehkis, Bringer of Rain.

Imeris would have to climb through the night to reach the Temple of Audblayin by morning. Her sister would be waiting for her. Imeris had an ongoing appointment with Aurilon, the most feared fighter in Canopy.

"His body is already sealed into a great tree," Imeris said. "Will you perform some ceremony anyway? Put his rustiest fishing traps into some wax-filled hollow?"

Youngest-Mother and Oldest-Mother shared a glance.

"We'll speak with Marram in the morning," Youngest-Mother said.

Oldest-Mother put a grilled fish on a leaf-plate in front of her.

"Eat," she said gently.

But it was Oldest-Father's voice Imeris heard in her head at the sight of the fish.

You do not need fruit. You do not need Canopian food. Good Understorian river fish is best.

Imeris remembered glancing up at him, meeting his serious and unbending eye, seeing her face, many shades darker than his, reflected in it.

You do not know what is best for me, she'd thought angrily. *If nobody needs Canopian food, and Understorian river fish is best, why do the women of Canopy have healthy babies every year while Understorian mothers fall pregnant once a decade? How many unborn ones did Middle-Mother lose?*

Imeris had fantasised, constantly, about the things she could say to Oldest-Father to cut him to the bone. Yet she'd been taught that respect for elders was paramount. She had never used those tempting, mentally practiced word-weapons, and now she never would. Was she glad of it? Relieved? Or resentful? Perhaps if she'd been raised in Canopy, things would be different.

Imeris gazed at the pale flesh of the fish next to her liver-brown skin. Youngest-Mother reached out and enfolded Imeris's fingers in hers.

"Every time you came back to us from Loftfol," Youngest-Mother said, "without a promise-band around your arm, Oldest-Father would fret. He was terrified that one day you'd go to Canopy and never return, like your brother and sister before you. In the end, you were with him. In the end, you fought by his side."

In the end, I failed him.

Now, more than ever, I must find a way to destroy our enemy, whether that way is Loftfol or the teachings of Aurilon.

They cried together for a good hour or more. Softly, so Middle-Mother and Youngest-Father would not wake. All the times Oldest-Father had been cantankerous and cruel were forgotten, as were the times when Imeris had been obedient and dutiful. All she could remember of him was integrity. All she could remember of herself was defiance.

Imeris dried her eyes. She touched her left arm where a betrothal-band was traditionally tied. So Oldest-Father had wished for her to find a mate at Loftfol, perhaps as much as he had willed her to supersede them all.

She thought of the young warriors at the school, every one of them disciplined and athletic. Attractive. Youthful. They were dream mates and could be valuable allies in battle. Yet each was fanatically Understorian to the core. It was not that they had initially mistrusted her Canopian origins. They might scorn her for being a woman, but until the accident with Kishsik, they had never scorned her for that. Babies fallen from Canopy were gifts of the gods. Fortune smiled on them, if they survived, and Imeris had survived in a more unusual way than most.

No, it was not until Kishsik's injury that they doubted her loyalties. In two more years, Imeris would reach the black cloth rank; she would have studied the warrior arts at Loftfol for seven monsoons in total. If chosen as Leader, she would be set the task, the Great Deed, of recruiting an army to take with her into the sunlit city of the cruel oppressors.

But Imeris had a birth mother she'd never met, somewhere in the city of the cruel oppressors. Her brother and sister were Canopians.

"Oh, Youngest-Mother." She sighed. "I could not wed a warrior of Loftfol."

"Because there aren't any other women there?" Youngest-Mother asked with an arched eyebrow. It was Oldest-Mother who shared her bed.

"Not that." Imeris picked at the edges of her leaf-plate, eyes downcast. "Though I once wished that I could love Nirrin the way you love Oldest-Mother. When I think of bedmates, it seems I solely think of men. But who could I trust with my family's secrets? And what stranger could truly see me, not just my fighting skills or as the way open into Canopy, do you suppose?"

"I don't know." Youngest-Mother hesitated. She straightened the twisted shoulder strap of Imeris's climbing harness. "To an Understorian you're a weapon. To a Canopian, a slave. I couldn't begin to tell you where to seek for a companion."

"Perhaps in Floor," Imeris said with a hoarse laugh, "where they cannot see me at all."

NINE

IMERIS CLIMBED through the hole in the barrier that her sister had made for her.

The cacophony of Canopy was welcome. She heard the piping of a pair of plovers nesting on a platform nearby, the creaking of barrow wheels over tree-roads and the whooping of children let loose for the first day of the season to chase complacent birds and rainbows. Most would return safely home. One or two might fall.

Middle-Father waited for Imeris, hanging ape-like from one forearm, scratching his beard in a bored way with his free hand.

"Are you injured?" were his first words when she drew level with him. He was a big man in a leather vest and woven trousers cut off at the knee. Tattoos of beasts and human enemies he had killed covered his pale Understorian skin. Though he served the goddess Audblayin, he could not enter within the warded walls of her Garden on account of having wilfully taken human life.

It seemed the goddess, formidable as she was, hadn't been able to keep him in the formal Canopian clothes denoting his office as Bodyguard, either.

The sliver of spines visible between his forearm and the tallowwood tree was a little more yellowed. His cheeks were a fraction hollower and his waistline a little thicker. Otherwise, he hadn't changed since last year. She drew breath.

"Middle-Father," she said, forcing the words out despite the lump in her throat, "you are my oldest-father now."

"Issi," he rumbled, "poor Issi, my Issi. I am your middle-father for always. Do not mourn him. He is already reborn. The goddess came out through the Gate to say as much to me last night. Esse is dead, she said, and born again, I cannot tell you where, only that his soul has passed safely through me."

They hugged, one-armed. He smelled like sunburn and sap, furs and ripe fruit.

"You have not slept," he observed. "Did you go directly from Loftfol to battle and then back home alone?"

"Not alone. Youngest-Father was with me. He will make a full recovery, Youngest-Mother said. He will be fine."

Middle-Father shook his head.

"He will not be fine. I think it almost time for me to leave Canopy. Your sister must find herself another Bodyguard."

"I think," Imeris said, attempting a reassuring smile, "I might need to borrow your bed for an hour or two before I go to battle."

"More than an hour or two," Middle-Father advised. "Your old foe will not want to take advantage. She will wait."

"I suspected the break in the barrier would not wait."

"Indeed. Over our heads, the Gatekeeper has instructions to mend the breach. Within the hour, if you did not come. I waited here to ensure no demon came through."

Imeris couldn't suppress a semihysterical laugh.

"What a shame that one did not come!"

"Yes, I know. With Esse gone, perhaps one will get past his traps occasionally and give me something to do."

Tears might have risen to Imeris's eyes again if there had been any spare moisture left in her. She climbed past Middle-Father into the brightness and colour of the high branches. Troupes of monkeys and flocks of birds swooped and rustled everywhere in the wet foliage. *Be aware of your surroundings at all times,* her Loftfol teacher, Horroh, urged constantly, but that was hardly possible in the high branches of the great trees, where the wind and weather kept everything in motion all the time.

Imeris felt more at home in the dim and secret stillness of Understorey.

She found the Gatekeeper sitting cross-legged outside the Garden's mighty, half-open, carved wooden Gate. To the left of the Gate stood a round-bellied dwelling grown from the living wood of the tree. It was a dwelling made distinctive by an arched entryway with a trickle of water dividing it. A chimney opening belched smoke that smelled of old coconut palm fronds. To the right, the high wall of the Garden concealed the fecund abundance within.

"Good morning, Aoun," Imeris said, though the sun wasn't high enough yet for either of them to cast a shadow and she thought this might be the worst morning of her entire life.

The open sky above the Garden was fearsomely vast and mysteriously changeable. Cream and purple-coloured clots of cloud formed a convoy close to the horizon. It was the retreating caravan of the monsoon, dividing sky the colour of molten bronze from a greater, lemon-pale expanse where the last stars of the previous night resisted being extinguished.

"Sister of my mistress," Aoun acknowledged with a quirk of the corner of his mouth. He was a long-limbed, tapir-brown, quiet Canopian with a warrior's muscular build, though Imeris had never seen him take a weapon to hand. No spines, Imeris knew, were concealed in the creases of his forearms and shins. His eyes were very deep set, and silver hairs sprinkled his short, black beard. He was a few years older than Youngest-Mother, who had been his friend.

The shiny lantern of his office sat beside him. His feet and knees were tucked under the hem of his white robe.

"I am going to sleep in my middle-father's house," Imeris said. If the goddess already knew about Esse's death, there was no need for them to meet immediately.

"There is a lavishly appointed bed there," Aoun said. "Wasted, since Bernreb doesn't use it."

He meant Middle-Father. Bodyguards didn't need to sleep. Wakefulness was a gift given to them by the god or goddess they served. An additional aptitude bestowed on Audblayin's Bodyguard was the ability to fly, but only adepts could take advantage of it, and Imeris's middle-father had not been born with magical gifts.

His gifts were patience and hunting prowess. His bed was for entertaining his wife, but she had vowed never to visit him in Canopy in the hopes that his term as Bodyguard would finish sooner rather than later.

Before Imeris could go inside the dwelling, a lofty, brown-skinned woman in a floor-length dress and long, straight black hair slipped out of the Gate. She flung herself at Imeris, holding her tightly, so that the diamonds on the dress pressed painful pinpoints into Imeris's neck and arms.

"Issi!" the new arrival cried softly.

"Hello, Ylly," Imeris answered, widening her stance, steadying herself against her sister's enthusiasm. "I mean Audblayin. I mean Holy One."

It was never clear which element of her sister's personality was strongest at any particular moment. A year ago, Imeris had greeted Ylly-Audblayin with the same playful ear tugging she'd performed when they'd shared a bedroom, teasing about her tiny ears and saying she would keep pulling until they were stretched to normal size. Only to have the imperious goddess remind her that the penalty for laying hands on a deity was death.

So Imeris allowed her sister to make the first move, always. Even now, when they had both lost a father. Because Ylly had three fathers, all beloved, but Audblayin had hundreds, if not thousands, and not all were remembered fondly.

"Come with me into the Garden," Audblayin said. Her hair smelled of woodfern and quince, a scent Ylly had always favoured. Imeris herself would rather rub eucalyptus-oil-rich tallowwood leaves on her skin to hide her human scent from prey.

"Holy One," Aoun said from his seat, "I think your sister must have travelled all night to come to the barrier in time."

"That's why we'll feast together!" The goddess took Imeris's hands, tugging at them in unison, taking backward steps towards the Garden, ignoring her Gatekeeper. "Before you go to fight with—"

"Wait," Imeris said uneasily, resisting, leaning away from the Gate. "We must speak of Oldest-Father first. You must discharge Middle-Father from his duties. Let him go to pay his respects. If they do not hold a ceremony at home, he will need to travel to the part of Understorey below Ulellinland where Oldest-Father died to say his farewells." But Audblayin didn't stop drawing her forwards, shrugging off her concerns.

"I am the birth goddess, Issi. Middle-Father is my Bodyguard. We do not say farewells. That is nonsense. Oldest-Father is not gone, he is renewed, and by my power. Middle-Father will—"

"You have to let him go home, Ylly!"

"This is his home!" She stabbed a finger at the dwelling by the Gate with its trickle of water and merrily smoking chimney.

"No, his home is with Middle-Mother in Understorey."

Audblayin's eyes narrowed.

"*She* told you to say all this. *She* sent you to harass me in her stead. This is the same tree where he has lived—"

"But the barrier separates him from his family—"

"I am his family. Leaper is his family, and Leaper lives above the barrier."

Audblayin tugged her onwards as they argued. They passed through the Garden Gate. Imeris felt a shiver at the meeting of Aoun's powerful wards with the magic that lived in her protective amulet.

"I am glad you had that amulet," Audblayin said softly, apologetically. "Did you use the things you learned at Loftfol to fight Kirrik? Most of the ones I love use my power to fight. I feel it. But not you."

"Everything I did was useless," Imeris said. The Garden was greener and brighter than any other place she had ever been. Her eyes ached. Her throat ached. Every part of her ached, but she walked on along the tidy, winding dirt paths and singing bridges. When the fern fronds and the flowering creepers whispered and shifted, trying to get closer to Audblayin, whom they loved, Imeris was reminded of the windowleaf tree coming alive to break Oldest-Father's neck. "Kirrik escaped. She used your power to break his neck."

"I felt that. Faintly." Audblayin took Imeris's hands again. "You were far from here."

"Then you can tell me how she got away. After Oldest-Father hit her in the mouth, how did she grow that branch and escape?"

"She couldn't sing or speak, but she could howl around a mouth full of blood. She used that awful sound for her spells. I heard it."

"Eliminate unknowns," Imeris muttered. "That is what Horroh says at Loftfol. Now that Kirrik is in Nirrin's body, how can I eliminate unknowns? The power of goddesses and gods is one huge unknown. Could you not sever Kirrik from yourself, sister, from the source of the magic?"

"No." Audblayin squeezed Imeris's hands sympathetically. "I'm sorry."

"Could you give me an amulet, like this one, but one that will cancel her ability to use your power?"

"No."

Imeris wasn't sensitive to magic, but the sudden sternness of Audblayin's voice let her know that the memories and personality of the girl she'd grown up with were being suppressed by the uncompromising immortal within. The question had touched a nerve.

"Then I must find some other way to kill her!" *I will. If I spend my life trying, I will.*

In her mind's eye, she saw herself in the Temple of Odel, humbled yet again by defeat. Every year, she challenged Odel's Bodyguard to a first-blood contest of hand-to-hand combat. Aurilon was famous for never having lost a duel.

Aurilon knew secrets not taught at Loftfol and would only teach them to Imeris if Imeris managed to surprise her.

How will I know if I have surprised you? Imeris had demanded before their first clash.

You can trust me, Aurilon had answered, giving a rare, reptilian smile. *I will let you know. Oh, and there is a time limit. You only have the time until you are beaten in which to show me something new.*

Each year, for four years, Imeris had studied hard from books, her fathers, her other teachers. Just as Understorians were vulnerable to the novelty of Canopian fighting styles, she felt convinced Canopians such as Aurilon must be vulnerable to the novelty of Understorian techniques.

Loftfol was the key to defeating Aurilon.

Aurilon was the key to defeating Kirrik.

Kirrik could come after Youngest-Father while I am in Canopy. To finish the job. There is nobody with him to protect him. Imeris shook off the despairing thought.

The first time she'd met Aurilon in a duel, Imeris had fought in overlapping-metal-scale armour, attacking with her curved dagger the way that Middle-Father had taught her. The next time, she'd tried the traps taught by Oldest-Father, but Aurilon hadn't been lured into them. During the third battle, the Bodyguard had turned back on Imeris the poison needles given to her by the Odarkim; the resulting three days of paralysis had been humiliating. On her return to Loftfol, Imeris had next gone to the Scentingim to learn wrestling methods and rope strangulation.

I was not surprised, Aurilon had informed Imeris as Imeris had woken from a knockout blow to the head, her assassin's cord lying all but weightless across her lax palm.

Each year she'd delayed defeat a little longer, but to no avail. This year, under Horroh's tutelage, she must prevail, despite her fatigue. Her attempt on Kirrik had failed, and now the sorceress knew her face. The situation was even more desperate.

Imeris traditionally spent the morning before her yearly duel breaking fast with her sister in Audblayinland, brimming with hope and focusing her determination, just as it was fast becoming tradition that she spent the evening of the second day after her defeat with her brother, Leaper, in Airakland, brooding among the charred, lightning-struck trees. *What do you expect, Issi?* Under the cold stars, he'd conjured a flicker of lightning over his hand to read her expression by, shrugging when he saw the misery of defeat. *You shouldn't be surprised. All she does is kill people all day. What have you been doing all day? Gutting fish for Oldest-Father, right? You should challenge her to a fish-gutting competition.*

"Issi?" Audblayin's voice was soft again.

"Yes?"

"You could give up trying to kill Kirrik. She can't get across the barrier. We're safe from her in Canopy. You could become my Bodyguard. Replace Middle-Father. You've been trained by Loftfol. I know you'd be more than capable, and though it seems we'd be breaking the Law of the Balance, which ensures the forest's vitality, we would not, for neither you nor Middle-Father are capable of drawing on my magic. Aoun's maleness would suffice. The strength he has accumulated as Gatekeeper and the greater portion of power allotted to him already replaces the traditional strength and power allotment of my Bodyguard. Middle-Father could go home, like you said. Like you wanted."

"No," Imeris said, with all the steel the goddess had mustered only moments ago. Even if what Audblayin said was true and there was some kind of exception to the rule that the Bodyguard of a female incarnation of Audblayin must be male, she could not abandon Understorey to the sorceress. "We will breakfast together. I will sleep for a day and a night in Middle-Father's house. Then Aurilon and I will clash for what I hope will be the final time."

She forced herself to see the changes in the Garden since the last time she had visited. Whistling ducks *peep-peep*ed in the tallowwood pools, having found their way somehow from the Bright Plain. A goat grazed the grass garden, two suckling kids at foot; Imeris supposed it was the gift of a wealthy patron, an ongoing source of milk and fibre and, later in life, guts for string. The world wore on, and Imeris felt she was trapped, spinning in place, not going anywhere, ever chasing, never catching.

And now Oldest-Father was dead.

This time next year, she vowed she would be laughing instead of crying.

By the end of the next monsoon, Oldest-Father, I swear to you.

Kirrik will be no more.

TEN

ODEL'S EMERGENT stood high above the other great trees.

Imeris took a moment to gaze down at the green patchwork. It looked so different from above. She was used to gazing up at it from deep down among sombre, towering trunks.

The gaps between leaves were dark instead of cloud- or sky-bright, their shifting and flailing movement hypnotising to watch. Wind and the foraging of creatures four- and two-footed made the many shades of citron, lime, emerald, beryl, and gleaming greenish-black ripple like the fur or feathers of some breathing thing.

She couldn't see any boundary to the forest in the east, west, or south. To the north, a half circle of pale yellow plain divided Odelland from the edge of Audblayinland. The Floorians who lived there, Imeris supposed, must see each other in daylight all the time. She remembered the feel of the Bird-Rider at her back.

She remembered her clumsy attempt at gliding down to kill Kirrik.

Now, as then, her spines trembled in their long bone sheaths.

Today I will win.

Aurilon will share her secrets.

And when I have learned them, Kirrik will not escape from me again.

After her long, nightmare-filled sleep in Middle-Father's dwelling, she felt Oldest-Father's death, not as proof that Kirrik's defeat was impossible, but as part of his final command to her and her final responsibility to him.

Odel's Temple above her was a great edifice of golden sweet-fruit pine heartwood. Formed by magic or metal tools into the shape of a scaly carp balanced on its parted lips, it rested where the growing shoot of the tree should have been, at the apex of a white spiral plank-stair around the outside of the tree connecting a handful of wide branch paths. Below the stair was a gaping, east-facing tree hollow, Odel's Test, where parents had once flung their children over the edge to be sure of the god's protection.

The tree's arms, cast wide around it, formed a picturesque frame but offered minimal shelter from the wind. The Temple's wavy fishtail stuck up far beyond the drooping fingers of fine moss-green needles and tiny, scaly, branch-tip fruit. Imeris walked along one of those arms, flattened on top into a smooth pathway with a low, woven rail of pegs and vines. She had borrowed a pair of her father's loose Canopian trousers to cover the creases in her shins where her spines lay.

Her forearm spines, she didn't wish to cover. Inside the fish-shaped Temple, she took off the pretty embroidered robe that Audblayin had given her and draped it over the edge of a vast, floating dish where offers were given to the god. Her sleeveless tunic freed her arms but covered her good climbing harness so that enemy hands couldn't grasp it.

She tried not to feel naked without knives, traps, cords, or poison.

Your own Understorian body, Horroh had said, *is all that you need. Trust it.*

Several slaves were there, setting tributes from their masters on the dish and whispering the names of young children, but the god himself and his Bodyguard were nowhere in sight. The internal staircase that led down to Odel's Test had been covered by a perfectly fitted sweet-fruit-pine plug, but Imeris knew where it was.

She waited until she was alone in the Temple with the hovering offerings and the blue-tinged lanterns.

Then she knelt on the floor, set her spines into the fitted puzzle piece, and pulled it open like a trapdoor.

The stairwell wasn't lantern-lit, but yellow sunlight entered it from somewhere, most likely the outer opening into the hollow below. Imeris slipped quietly into Odel's Test, pulling the trap shut over her head, listening intently.

Aurilon owned a colour-shifting chimera skin, too, and she used it, not for gliding, but to move invisibly through the darkness. It was the skin of the demon that had killed Odel's previous incarnation, ending a middle-aged man's life but not the eternal soul of the god.

A curse had fallen upon Aurilon at the chimera's slaying.

All killings of chimeras ended in curses.

But it hadn't affected Aurilon so far, not where Imeris could see, anyway. Odel had told her that curses were patient.

Turning a corner, she found Odel's Test newly repurposed as a kind of library or scholarly study. The gaping eastern hollow did admit the morning light and permit a view of supplicants approaching the Temple. On the other side of the much-widened space, a west-facing annexe like a beehive had been built onto the side of the tree, with tall, elliptical glass windows.

Odel sat behind a desk in the annexe. His black hair was in short twists, and his head dipped low over parchment. According to Aurilon, Odel's previous, older incarnation had been prone to sleeping by day and wandering restlessly at night by taper light. The smoke and smouldering heat of the taper had provided a focus, a way to help him distinguish between visions and reality.

This younger version had a keen instinct for recording histories. He valued ink galls and a comfortable chair over walking boots and silks. Imeris admired his physique, the strong hands, ink stained, so often covered by gloves, bare to her scrutiny for once. In this place, contrasting with the way he appeared in public, he cared only to wear a robe unlaced, uncrossed and slipping away from his bare brown shoulders. Imeris could make out the hem of a short wrap skirt covering his thighs. That was all.

There was no sign or sound of the Bodyguard.

It was warm in the room. The glass windows, Airak-made, didn't open and the air was still. If Odel were to cover the open hollow with a curtain, the study would become an oven.

"You are one day late," he said pleasantly, without looking up from his work. It appeared to be a copy of an older, torn manuscript: *On the Flourishing of Temperate Trees in the Event of Concurrent Weaknesses of Sun and Rain Goddesses.* Beneath it, she glimpsed an unrolled scroll titled *Predicting the Rare Occurrence of Snow in Winter: A Study of Airak's Emergent.*

Not answering immediately, Imeris moved silently into the circle of direct sunlight, taking care that her face remained shaded, searching the dim corners for Aurilon's camouflaged presence.

"There were complications, my lord," she said after she'd completed half the circuit.

"Remember, Imeris. If you touch my bare skin, your life is forfeit."

"I know the laws of Odelland, my lord." She slid across the smooth wood, searching.

Searching.

"I'm sick of the pair of you breaking my things."

"She finds it entertaining to watch me struggle to avoid you, my lord."

"It's not entertaining," Odel said, frowning but still not looking up, "to execute someone for no reason except that they've brushed up against an immortal."

"Could you not change this unjust law, then, my lord?" Imeris cracked open a cabinet, peered inside, and found it full of shelves and papers.

"I can't change all the laws at once." He set the quill in the well and raised his hazel eyes at last. The honeyed light turned them the colour of tallowwood; the colour of old amber. "They already take any opportunity to murder me. Can you imagine if I stirred them up too much? Aurilon tells me you're quite free with the person of Audblayin, but then again, your sister lives in her Garden behind her Gates and wards and is generally safer than most."

Imeris circled again, still keeping her back to the blinding sun.

"Perhaps you could tell me where your Bodyguard is, my lord. I could try to draw the battle out of your holy Temple—"

She felt the slight give beneath her feet in the instant before the second trapdoor opened. As she started to fall, Imeris's instinct was to put her spines out and stick to the lip of the opening.

Aurilon had used her instincts against her before. Imeris made two parallel bars of her forearms in front of her face, protecting her head. She dropped, unresisting, into darkness.

Impact with the smooth, flat floor came a few seconds later. The trapdoor closed, cutting off the last light. *Sealed inside, as Kirrik sealed Oldest-Father into the windowleaf tree. No. Focus.* Imeris rolled backwards. Was the trapdoor mechanical or operated by hand? If Aurilon had waited near the ceiling and heard Imeris's near-silent steps, the assumption would be that Imeris would roll forwards in the direction she'd been facing.

She'd made a trapdoor herself, once, in preparation for their second duel. Now she'd fallen into one. *Careless! Remember what has gone before!*

This was their fifth fight. For every move and countermove that Aurilon made and Imeris remembered, the reverse was also true.

They hadn't fought in the dark before, though. Who had the advantage? Aurilon might have assumed it would favour her slithering, constant-contact fighting style, but then again, Imeris was Understorian and she'd visited with the Bird-Riders.

The clarity that reduced the enemy to moving parts instead of persons took over Imeris's mind. She moved into the steps of the form called Floor, slashing the air with her spines. She felt for the shape of the chamber with her feet, finding its circumference. It would be deliberately deceiving. She must make out any obstacles quickly, before her opponent could drive her into them. Ropes. Nets. Stumbling blocks. Allowing the Bodyguard to choose the battleground was a serious mistake.

No, she admonished the weaker self who wished to remind her of recent losses. *There is no sorceress, no family defenceless in the dark. There is no past or future. Only here and now, and I am Imeris, a Heightsman of Loftfol.*

She heard a sound like splinters lifting behind her.

Imeris spun and slashed again, pinning Aurilon's fingers against the wooden wall with her spines.

Not fingers. A shock ran through her. She'd hit something harder than a human hand. Chimera claws.

She had time to realise Aurilon's hand had escaped the climbing glove, time to calculate where the Bodyguard's knees had hung and to guess where her opponent's feet would fall. Shoulder to the wall, Imeris kicked out behind her with a leg that was sweeping, not cutting, interrupting what could have been a gracious recovery by the Bodyguard.

Aurilon gave a *whoof* of emptied lungs as she landed, facedown, on the floor.

This year, I will be the victor. Imeris dropped to one knee, following the sound of the exhalation with a driving fist, all her force behind it. *Keep the fight short,* Horroh had advised. *Keep your secrets to yourself.*

The blow connected only with empty floor, splitting the skin over Imeris's first two knuckles.

Aurilon's exhalation had been a decoy, and Imeris had fallen for it. Her second mistake. Aurilon's huge hands which, every meeting, had sought a grip on Imeris's clothes, now closed on spineless elbow joint and the back of her collar.

Imeris flew through the air, away from the wall. But Aurilon had thrown her before. An attempt at locking Imeris's extended arm was how the Bodyguard habitually followed through. Aurilon's weight lay across Imeris's hips, her hands at Imeris's wrists, again seeking holds where there were no spines. Imeris curled her arm, spines withdrawn, against her body, to prevent the painful, immobilising hold.

She kicked hard against the floor to turn over. Now the Bodyguard lay beneath her, naked and slippery, no softness where her breasts should have been, yet without the flayed-to-muscle feel of a fighting man of Loftfol.

Imeris swung her right forearm, spines extended, at the Bodyguard's face, and again Aurilon managed to unbalance her so the spines stuck in the wooden floor.

As Imeris moved to withdraw them, Aurilon's left shoulder wedged the spines against the grain. The seven snake fangs curved downwards. They were intended to hold Imeris's full weight against the vertical trunk of a tree. Without raising her elbow, she couldn't retract them. She struck towards the Bodyguard's temple with her left elbow, but with her weight removed from Aurilon's other shoulder, she felt both the Bodyguard's arms snaking around hers like lianas.

Like sorceress-possessed vines. Imeris imagined her eyes popping as Oldest-Father's had. She smelled Temple incense and Aurilon's sweat; she imagined the smell of windowleaf sap. In a single motion, Aurilon flipped them both again. Aurilon's thighs now held Imeris's neck and shoulders to the floor. Between them, Imeris's arm extended from Aurilon's crotch to her throat.

The last time this had happened in one of their duels, Imeris had tried to twist her thumb downwards, to roll backwards, bend her elbow safely, and slip away.

This time, angrily, she tried to turn the blade of her hand downwards, prepared to sink her spines straight into Aurilon's rib cage. To Floor with first blood. To Floor with duels to submission. *I cannot lose again. I do not have another year to spare!*

Before she could do it, she felt her elbow joint pop. It was agony, but, impotence spurring her to a blind rage, she tried to ignore it, to keep turning the limb, to push out her spines.

The bone in her forearm where her spines were embedded snapped.

She screamed with pain and fury.

Aurilon released her. Rolled away. Imeris lay there, still screaming. A few paces back from her, Aurilon struck a spark, blowing a taper to life.

She stepped forwards, looking down at Imeris. Her face was wet with perspiration but relaxed and expressionless. Now the shape of the room was clear. It was gently curving and bare except for a rough ledge at head height around the room. No tricks. No traps, apart from the one that had brought her down from the Test. Just two women, a pair of chimera-claw gloves, and an ineffectual curse that was yet to afflict Odel's victorious Bodyguard.

"You should have stopped when it was only dislocated," Aurilon said smoothly.

"Did I surprise you?" Imeris managed to demand through gritted teeth.

"No. You idiot. Did they teach you that at Loftfol? Sacrifice your arm, for what?" She shook her head. "Something a man would do. I am disappointed. But not surprised."

ELEVEN

ODEL'S SLEEPLESS Bodyguard, like Audblayin's, owned a rarely used bed.

"Lie still," Aurilon ordered, setting Imeris and her loosely splinted arm into a mattress that rustled with windgrass thatch stuffing. The secret hollow lay behind a false wall of the Temple, inside one fin of the fish. Two tiny bores were barely enough to keep the air fresh, and there was neither smoke nor fire. A single blue lantern hung from a brass chain in the centre of the domed ceiling, and a small, red-spotted gecko lingered there hopefully, waiting for tiny flies.

Later, when night fell and a frog refrain relieved the choir of cicadas, Aurilon brought water and Imeris asked, "Are you sure she received your message?"

"Quite certain," Aurilon said. "But Airakland is far away. It may take some time for her to come."

"I thought I could outmatch you, in the dark," Imeris said, distracted by pain, barely hearing Aurilon's answer. "I am from Understorey. You are the Canopian, the one who relies on the light, or so I thought. But I suppose the ones who gave you your markings see no more sunshine than the Bird-Riders do. I finally figured out where they are from."

"Yes," Aurilon said, taking the water gourd away.

"You fell, the same as I did."

"Not quite the same. I was older. Maybe seven? The wealthy children dared each other to jump over a gap between branches." Aurilon offered a bedpan. Imeris eyed it. Her legs were quite well. Apparently Aurilon, or her master, did not want a fully spined Understorian seen loitering about Odel's Temple looking for a suitable place to toilet. The Bodyguard went on. "I was smaller than the other children. They had Odel's protection and knew it. I did not. They goaded me anyway. That is how I fell."

Imeris could easily imagine it.

"You want to teach me." She took the pan. Used it. "Why else give me so many chances? You feel a kinship between us."

"Not enough of a kinship to teach you before you are ready." Aurilon's mouth firmed. Her black eyes flashed in the blue lantern light. "A fool speaks to one without ears."

Then she turned her scarred, bumpy, scale-like back to Imeris and opened the panel in the false wall, departing to empty the pan. Afterwards, Imeris guessed, she would lurk in some high place, defending Odel from dangers while he dreamed his horrible, prescient dreams.

Two DAYS later, the Godfinder came.

Unar didn't need to stoop, as Aurilon did, to enter the hidden room. She was shorter, softer, plumper, and slightly lighter-skinned than the Bodyguard. Her hair was loosely woven into two shoulder-length braids tied with tallowwood twine. Permanent frown lines scored the spot between her bushy brows.

The adepts of the Garden from which she'd been expelled didn't permit her to wear the white robe of a Servant, nor the red robe, crimson shirt, and spinach-coloured trousers of a Gardener. Unar wore, instead, the rough brown woven shirt of an out-of-nicher; the ankle-length, split wrap skirt of a Bodyguard, in nobody's colours; and her Godfinder's cloak, a long, hooded brown robe patched with dried and preserved leaves of a hundred faded hues.

All the niches of Canopy knew and respected that cloak. Since Unar had taken it up, the faithful bereft of their goddess or god no longer had to wander, naked and half-starved, from niche to niche, in hope of finding their deity.

Imeris remembered her as the sleeping princess in their home, a mystery that her three mothers and three fathers refused to properly explain to her.

Did you sneak into the roof, Issi? little Ylly, six years old, had whispered to Imeris one night, shivering with anxiety and awe. *Did Oldest-Father stay sleeping? What is in there?*

A girl, Imeris answered, creeping under the blanket with Ylly, unable to shake the mental image of the round, sooty face with its wide nose and generous lips, nestled in a pillow of springy black hair, which Imeris had searched for its resemblance to her own. *A girl is sleeping up there. I had to wait for ages before I felt her heart beat. She sleeps like a tree bear through the monsoon.*

Do you think she is a princess? Excitement replaced fear in Ylly's voice. *A cursed princess? Is she our sister, or your birth mother, Issi?*

Imeris had been irritated her sister had guessed her motive so easily. Her birth mother. No. The sleeping girl did not seem old enough. She had no stretch-stripes on her skin, and her breasts were too small.

Maybe she is our sister. Maybe when she wakes, she will tell us.

When Unar had woken, however, all she'd done was reveal Ylly as the goddess Audblayin and split their family forever between Canopy and Understorey. What she'd done was take Imeris's little sister away, and her little brother, and her middle-father, and foreshadow the fact that Ylly-Audblayin would be the one that sagas spoke of, that Ylly-Audblayin was the one whose famous name would live forever.

A child their three mothers and three fathers could truly be proud of. Yet the goddess had done nothing to stop Kirrik. Considered her an Understorian problem, like dayhunters and chimeras.

"Fighting again, Imerissiremi?" the Godfinder asked wryly, and Imeris knew from the heat and reduction of pain in her broken arm that her injury was being magically appraised.

"I did not break it on my own," she answered peevishly.

"You might have lost the use of your spines in this arm if I hadn't been able to come."

"Can you heal me or not?"

Unar's smile transformed her unremarkable features.

"The old Odel," she said, sitting on the bed beside Imeris, "wouldn't have allowed me to use Audblayin's power in his niche. And the old Audblayin would have thrown me out of a tree years ago for my disobedience. But since we're together at this particular crossroads in time, yes, I can heal you."

You might have lost the use of your spines. Imeris's lip trembled. It wasn't the pain. She had a high tolerance for pain. It was fear of never completing the task. Now that she had failed at earning Aurilon as a tutor, who in Loftfol should she learn from next? The Litim, Dammammad, who taught the short sword? What about Saliailas, the Huntingim, who was unmatched in the use of the javelin? Clearly, choosing Horroh had not helped. She could not tell him so. He knew nothing of her matches in Canopy. None of them did.

When will it be over? When will I be free?

"I am lucky you were able to come, Godfinder," she said. "And grateful my sister is a goddess."

Unar closed her eyes. Her smile faded.

"She knows I'm with you. She's willing me to help you. But you should be more careful."

"I will be," Imeris lied.

The Godfinder's lids flickered open again.

"Daughter of a chimera," she mused, "in the place where I once came to see a chimera skin."

"There was a chimera in Wissin. It knew my smell. It turned back from my tree. The villagers were amazed."

"They should have been horrified." Unar scowled. "Chimeras turn back from the stench of sorceress's souls."

"It knew my smell," Imeris repeated. "I wonder if they have a language. I wonder if they speak to one another."

Healing magic was unspectacular. Nothing like when Leaper called lightning to his piles of black sand. Imeris's arm became numb to the feeling of broken pieces of bone moving. The eerie shifting beneath her skin showed them fitting together and knitting.

But when feeling flooded back, the seam remained bloody and raw. Her spines protruded like the red-smeared teeth of a rough-made saw.

"You know how it goes," the Godfinder said grimly. "I can't heal a spine-seam completely, or you'll lose your climbing hooks. Wrap them up in the dressing and come with me. Aurilon has had enough of coddling you. You can stay with me in Airakland until you're ready to climb back down. And you can see your brother while you're there. You're very lucky to have a brother. To have your family looking out for you."

"Yes," Imeris murmured. *They used to tell me how lucky I was to have all my mothers and fathers still alive.* "I know."

A great hunter. A great healer. A great musician. A great mother. A great Bodyguard. A great goddess. A great Godfinder.

There's nothing great about being great. I just want it all to be over.

TWELVE

AIRAK'S EMERGENT fanned up and out of the canopy like a charred, skeletal bat wing.

Of the thirteen Temples in the teeming treetop city, Airak's was the only one that was dead. Even the death god, Atwith, was connected to the soil of Floor through the living body of a great bone tree. The fingers of this blackened hand were floodgum branches which had once been white and covered in long, leathery leaves, now hollowed spears where lightning bolts entered through the open culminations at the command of unseen adepts wielding magic within.

"Leaper will be sleeping now," Imeris said, stopping on the twisting gobletfruit road. "Does he know about Oldest-Father? Has somebody told him?"

Sunlight flooded the stretch of Airakland ahead of them. Many homes and workshops were in other, lesser floodgums just as blackened and scarred as the emergent. Glassmaking was not confined to the Temple. The king of Airakland's palace was similarly visible, its pale, magic-sculpted wood roundly cloud-shaped with windows shaped like jagged bolts to let the blue lantern light shine through. It, too, was hosted by a floodgum, but that tree was alive, draped in wet, gleaming foliage of dark grey-green. Tree and palace were turned rowdy by yellow-tailed black cockatoos ripping up the bark for beetle larvae and screaming at each other over territorial incursions.

Imeris noted the way the birds dropped underneath the branches, holding on by a single foot or clawed toe, then opened their wings to catch the air and sail away. It was so effortless.

She remembered pushing off the tangle of windowleaf stems, in so much of a hurry to join her fathers she'd felt like she was already standing with them against Kirrik. Then the swish and jerk of the tangled wing tip. The pendulum swing. The crunch and judder as she hit the trunk.

Disgrace. Death.

"I told him about Esse," the Godfinder said, a deepening of her frown, quickly smoothed away, the only sign of her own feelings. "I passed on to Leaper what your sister said, which was that she was pleased to announce his glorious rebirth, in any case. You Understorians don't take it very hard when warriors die, do you? Everybody seems to expect it. You'll see Leaper after dark. Come on. I'm not as fit as I used to be. I can't run around Canopy all day like you young things." It was a joke. Imeris and the Godfinder were physically about the same age, early in their third decades of life.

Imeris followed Unar again along the gobletfruit path. They took two turnings along floodgum paths, then skipped along the prickly, seldom-used branch path of a false palm heavy with huge, head-sized nuts.

That branch ended at the hollowed node of a scented satinwood tree. An arch in the horizontally striped bark admitted them to a sheltered cross-roads where paths radiated out in two dozen directions. Traders, eager faces lit by the omnipresent blue lanterns, had sprung up around the edges, and one old woman, perched on a pyramid of grain-filled sacks, called out to Unar.

"Your ugly little children need a feed, then, Godfinder?"

Unar laughed and shook her head as they passed. The old woman frowned at Imeris's bandage-wrapped arm and Understorian tunic and said no more. The satinwood branch they walked out on from the cross-roads, ten paces wide and flattened on top by the power of the wood god, Esh, led in a straight, level line to the innocuous-looking gate of Unar's flowerfowl farm.

Imeris couldn't hear any of the two hundred birds clucking, pecking, or fussing. That was because they flew down to Floor during the day, a drop of some six hundred human body lengths, to gorge on mineral-rich mud and mate with the heavy, Floor-bound, mature male birds.

When evening came, the hens returned to the farm to eat grain and roost for the night in their woven wicker pens. Unar had made the pens to pro-tect them from owls, pythons, and spotted cats. The birds soon learned to be grateful when the Godfinder locked the gate.

Imeris halted before the entrance with Unar at her side. She hadn't been to the farm before, only heard stories of the flowerfowl and their adventures from Leaper. The gate spanned the whole width of the road. Everything that lay beyond it belonged to the Godfinder.

It appeared to be only a simple arch with dead vines hanging from it.

"Lend me your injured arm," Unar said. Imeris held it out to her, grimacing.

One of the dead-looking vines blushed bright green, sent out a new climbing tendril and wound lovingly around Imeris's wrist. Magic at play, again. Imeris did not draw her arm away from Unar, even when she felt the growing shoot curl between her still-tender spines.

"What is it doing?" she asked, as if the vine had a mind of its own.

"Tasting your blood," Unar said. "So it knows, in future, that you're to be allowed through. It's my thief-catching vine. Mostly for young boys after eggs, too lazy to climb for their own."

Imeris forcibly relaxed her forearm tendons as the playful green shoot withdrew. It spiralled back around the arch, turned grey and became still. The two women walked under the arch. Beyond it, the flat branch road widened into a burl sixty paces in diameter.

If the burl was perfectly spherical when it first formed, it was now flattened on top like the road, and that was where the fences and pens waited for the flowerfowl. Pitcher plants full of drinking water grew in a ring around the circumference and steps led down from the near edge to the dwelling inside the burl.

"Be my guest," the Godfinder said, waving Imeris ahead of her. "Choose any place to rest."

The inside of the burl was not very much like Imeris's trunk-hollowed home. The brownish-pink satinwood smelled like caramel, the scent intoxicating as Imeris moved further down the stairs and away from the daylight. *This is what I could do. This is how I could live.* The walls felt dry and rough to her tracing fingertips; they weren't self-polishing like tallowwood. Woven hammocks hung from the ceilings of three little half rooms that came off a main room.

In the main room, a small charcoal-burning oven with a thin, diagonal, metal chimney pipe opposed a table covered in clay pots of tiny trees and moss. A suspended blue lantern replaced the blazing Understorian hearth for giving light. Cushions stuffed with feathers lay on woven blue carpets against the curved walls. Blue-painted wooden chests sat beside them. Three steep stairs at the far end descended to another sunken little half room with pipes that came through the roof to refill three tapped water-barrels. A basket of leaves for wiping sat tidily by a toilet hole and a curtain.

Imeris looked up to find Unar's expression expectant.

"The blue light," Imeris said, smiling, "and no fire. It seems cooler."

Unar nodded.

"I'll send a bird to your brother to let him know you're here."

"I saw no cages," Imeris said. "No writing implements."

Unar stripped off her sandals and put them under the table with the tiny potted trees. She went down the stairs to fill a modest copper kettle with water and set it on the stove. Then, instead of lighting the laid fire with bedded coals or by striking sparks, she took the blue lantern down from the ceiling and opened one of its glass panes by sliding it up out of the frame.

A miniature bolt of lightning struck from the blue glowing heart of the lantern into the stove. Shortly after, flames licked up around the charcoal. Unar slid the glass pane down and rehung the lantern. Imeris was amazed.

Tiny trees. A tiny, trapped storm. She half expected a tiny man to pop out from behind the cushions and prepare the ti.

"When I was teaching my flowerfowl to return safely to me," Unar said, taking two cups out of one of the blue chests, "I used a trickle of your sister's power to make them trust me. Other birds came to that call. Songbirds, but also those who can mimic human voices. They carry my messages to Leaper and bring his messages back to me."

"You live in a wondrous world, Godfinder."

"One you were born to. It wouldn't seem strange to you if you'd stayed in it instead of falling. Anyway, with birds to carry my messages and a market at my door, you can understand how I've lost some of my stamina. Will you drink? Sleep? I'll have an afternoon nap, myself."

Imeris shook her head ruefully.

"I will take ti with you, Godfinder. Before I can sleep, though, I must practice the seven disciplines and the six flowing forms. This is a good wide space for them."

Unar smiled.

"Suit yourself. I'll be sawing wood in that hammock."

Imeris assumed her host was joking. The woman had slept for seventeen years in Imeris's home without making a sound. But after the ti had been drunk and a talking parrot sent to Airak's emergent, the clothes washed and hung to dry and the cups put back in the wooden chest, Imeris found her immersion in the first discipline, the Discipline of the All-Body Breath, tested by the gargling horror of the Godfinder's snores.

THIRTEEN

As the sun went down, scratching, preening, and soft conversation announced the arrival of the flowerfowl and two Skywatchers of the lightning god.

Imeris dragged her guilty thoughts away from Oldest-Father's final words—*She must be silenced before she kills him. Use your throwing rope, Imeris*—and arranged a slightly more carefree expression for her brother. Leaper was sixteen, quick-thinking, and supremely confident, almost as broad-shouldered and muscular as Middle-Father if not as pale-skinned.

Only, his hair had been shorn close to his scalp. That had the look of a punishment about it. He grinned mightily when he saw her.

"What are you so pleased about?" Imeris asked, embracing him. "Is it so amusing that I am beaten by Aurilon again?"

"Of course not," Leaper answered. "I'll tell you what I find amusing after you've told me what happened and how you're going to beat her next time."

Leaper had a way with words. He'd lost his Understorian accent within a year of coming to Canopy, adopting a highborn's formal speech when necessary by sheer force of will. Now he strutted like a king's son in his Skywatcher's black velvet skirt and bearskin sandals. Heavy brass bracers inscribed with silver bolts covered the spines hidden in his forearms and shins, the intricate clasps and locks secured by the lightning god himself, who kept the key. Those in the Temple who accepted Leaper's service had not crippled his climbing ability, but nor would they allow him to roam unattended.

Aforis, his eternal chaperone, kissed Imeris on both cheeks. The older Canopian was a Skywatcher, too, demoted from a Servant's silver around the time that Imeris was born. It was a story she hadn't been able to get anyone to tell her, though she suspected the Godfinder had something to do with it. Unar looked momentarily stricken when she saw Aforis, but she composed herself, offered him the best cushion, and served him ti before anyone else.

"I do not know how to beat her," Imeris told Leaper, resisting the urge to rub her bandaged arm. "When I return to Loftfol, I will choose a different teacher."

"She's pretty old, isn't she, old Aurilon? Maybe she'll die soon of old age."

For all his broad shoulders, muscles, and fancy clothes, he was helpless when she turned on him. She seized his little finger with her good hand and twisted his arm behind his back. Learning to fight had never interested him. Working hard at anything, day by day, until all aspects were mastered, had never interested him either, unless it was kissing the backsides of royalty.

"Ow! Let go, Understorian savage!"

"I do not want Aurilon to die!" Imeris growled. "I want her to teach me!"

"She's never going to teach you, dimwit, that's the whole point, don't you understand? How does it go, again? You can't beat her till she teaches you, and she won't teach you till you beat her. Any idiot could grasp immediately that's an unwinnable scenario."

I do not have to beat her.

"Imeris," Aforis chided, "your ti will get cold."

She let Leaper go. At least the smirk had disappeared from his handsome face. They sat down on cushions, sipped ti, and glared at each other.

"I'll tell you what Leapael was laughing at," Aforis said. "We passed the king's palace on the way here. Soldiers of Orinland have come to Airakland at the goddess's request. They're trying to enlist our king's soldiers in the search for a criminal."

"Must be a dangerous criminal," Unar said, blowing nonchalantly on her ti to cool it. "Imagine sending soldiers across two niches after some petty lawbreaker. Very provocative."

"Not a petty lawbreaker," Aforis said. "This man, called Anahah, was the Bodyguard of the bird goddess. Now he's fled Orinland."

"The king of Orinland threatened to call a Hunt if the traitor isn't found," Leaper said excitedly.

"A Hunt can only be called for a demon," Unar said, rolling her eyes. When she saw Imeris frowning in puzzlement, she waved her half-empty ti cup and elaborated. "In the early days of Canopy, when the barrier was first built, there was an agreement between all thirteen royal families that if it was breached and a demon came through, each niche would send its best hunter on the Hunt."

"No demon has come through the Airakland barrier for a hundred years," Leaper boasted. "Our god keeps his part of the barrier—"

"All the goddesses and gods do their best," Unar said shortly. "People are always killing them."

"When a chimera came through in Odelland," Imeris said, "Aurilon killed it by herself."

"Aurilon this," Leaper muttered. "Aurilon that."

"How come your head is shaved?" Imeris asked keenly.

"I was trying out a hairstyle to see if it suited me. The Shining One didn't like it."

"Who is the Shining One?"

"The Servant of Airak who makes the death lamps," Aforis said.

"What kind of hairstyle were you trying?" Unar asked.

"Half black," Leaper replied, "and half white. It's only a matter of time."

Unar snorted her tea. "I, too, expected to become a Servant," she said darkly.

"Is that who has half white hair and half black?" Imeris asked. "Servants of the lightning god?"

"Yes," Aforis said.

"I've still got a souvenir," Leaper said. "Even though the Shining One held me down and shaved my head." He hooked his thumb into the top of both wrap skirt and loincloth beneath, pulled sharply downwards, and showed Imeris the top two finger widths of his pubic hair. It was half black, half white.

"Stop! Disgusting!" she cried, leaping to her feet, spilling the dregs of her ti.

"Not about to shave me there, is she?" Leaper's laugh was warm and loud, echoing in the space.

"I think I need to vomit."

"I think I need the amenities." Aforis sighed. "Too much ti. Down the stairs, Unar?"

"Down the stairs," Unar confirmed.

When Aforis was gone and the curtain lowered behind him, Leaper leaned forwards towards Imeris.

"I found out," he whispered, "what Aforis got demoted for."

Imeris wanted to stay standing, indignant, but she couldn't help herself. She sat back down, cross-legged on her cushion, and leaned conspiratorially towards Leaper.

"Trying to sleep with the god?" she guessed.

"No. What? I mean, yes. He broke his vow of chastity," Leaper said, "but not with the god. With some woman, right?"

"Now who is the dimwit?" Imeris said with satisfaction.

Leaper's eyes bulged. He reached from his knees across to hers and squeezed them, hard. Their faces were only a hand-span apart.

"He's never made a single move towards me."

"Maybe because you both have made chastity vows and submitted to the magic, idiot, and maybe because he is fifty and you are a child. You really think you are so beautiful that nobody can resist you?"

"That's right, I am! Whereas the whole of red-blooded Loftfol can easily resist you, no magic required!"

Imeris was deciding whether to resist breaking his face when the curtain swished aside and Aforis began washing his hands beneath the tap in one of the barrels.

"Must I seat you in opposite corners, children?" Unar asked, and Leaper abruptly slid his bottom back on his cushion, away from Imeris. Aforis rejoined them.

"One who walks in the grace of Airak was sorry to hear about the man you called Oldest-Father, Imeris," Aforis said. Imeris and Leaper immediately sobered, looking in silence at one another with shining eyes and long faces.

"I thought Esse would be the last to go," Unar said, sighing. "He never left that tree."

"He left it to fight Kirrik," Imeris said.

Unar and Aforis looked at each other again. Unar opened her mouth as if to say something, but Aforis gave a slight shake of the head and Unar lapsed into silence.

"When will you return to Understorey, Imeris?" Aforis asked.

"Tomorrow," Imeris said. "Or the next day."

"She broke her arm in the fight with Aurilon," Unar told him, and Leaper's head came up interestedly. "One more night, and her spines will be able to take her weight again."

"Who is the best hunter in Airakland?" Imeris asked Aforis, changing the subject. "How is it decided, if a Hunt is called?"

"There's a relic of the Old Gods," Aforis said, eyes drifting to Unar. "A tool of Ilanland, a thin bone needle set in a compass. The needle points to the best hunter present at that time in that niche. The compass travels to each Canopian kingdom until thirteen Hunters are found."

"Quite specific," Unar murmured. "Not unlike a rib bone that I have heard of, from Akkadland, which allows a person to find their blood relations."

Imeris glanced from Unar's face to Aforis's. Her knowledge of magic, as always, was woefully inadequate. She thought of the bone that made the cool breeze in the ti-house in Wissin. She touched the bone amulet at her throat that protected her from Kirrik's body-stealing sorcery. Those were simple functions in comparison to the ones the Canopians spoke of.

They went up to the flowerfowl pens to lock the birds safely in for the night. The hens had brown bodies, hatchet-shaped tails, and bald red-and-yellow heads. They honked softly as they finished eating and sorted themselves out among the provided perches. Imeris watched them with envy and longing.

Unar brought out the lantern she'd used for starting the fire in the belly of the stove. She set it above a particularly large pitcher plant full of water and opened up all the panes. Aforis gave the Godfinder a disapproving look but said nothing.

"Is that dangerous?" Imeris asked.

"It's a failed attempt at a death-lantern," Unar replied, "by a person who is not allowed to make them. He's lucky he wasn't sent away."

"Our sister is famous in Canopy for her power and grace," Imeris mused, "while Middle-Father is famous in Understorey for being a murderer who escaped retribution. Will Leaper be renowned for serving Airak or for burning down his house?"

"I think the Godfinder," Leaper said, leering, "knows something about bringing down Airak's house."

"It kills the insects," Aforis explained mildly to Imeris. "They're drawn to the light, stunned by the lantern, and fall into the water. What the birds don't eat in the morning is left for the plant to feed on. That's why this pitcher is so much bigger than the others. It's time for us to go, Leapael."

The higher branches of the scented satinwood obscured the silhouette of Airak's emergent, but the direction it lay in was plain enough. Imeris allowed her gaze to be drawn to the flicker of lightning striking, cold and with quick, quiet ripping sounds, from a clear sky.

"I suppose it is," Leaper said, coming to stand beside Imeris, looking in the same direction. "Want me to come educate you some more tomorrow evening, Issi?"

"No." Beneath the bandage, Imeris tremored her spines in their sheaths. The pain was fading. "I shall be gone. Want me to carry your love to our mothers and remaining fathers? Or have you been sending them message birds?"

Of course he hadn't.

His smile was rueful as he kissed her good-bye.

FOURTEEN

It was midday when Imeris made ready to depart the Godfinder's farm.

Unar packed her a full basket of flowerfowl eggs.

Imeris had few possessions to gather. With the rivers still running, she shouldn't need to carry water. She still planned to repair the bridge ballistae she'd abused on her way to Wissin before returning to Loftfol, but she'd need supplies for that task.

Unar pressed some silver coins into her hand.

"I know you can sleep stuck to the side of a tree," she said, "but there's no point doing it if you don't have to. You could trot along the low paths this afternoon, sleep tonight in the far corner of Airakland and then cross Ilanland and Orinland the next day."

"Yes," Imeris said, flexing her freshly unbound forearm. "The branch roads require less effort. I will not drop below the barrier until I reach Audblayinland. Airakland tonight is my plan. The next night I will spend in Ehkisland. There is a lodge near the southern border where I have stayed before. Where I will not be . . . bothered."

She avoided the Godfinder's gaze, but Unar blocked her exit.

"Bothered? And what do you mean by that?"

Imeris gave in to the Godfinder and dropped down onto a cushion. Then she glared up at her host, made furious by the recollection.

"They tried to make me a slave. Never mind. It was monsoons ago."

"Who tried to make you a slave?"

"Five louts in Orinland." Imeris clenched her fists. "Dirty. No clothes. Carrying rusty scythes and cracked hammers. The slaves who passed them on the road stuck out their tongues. I was amazed. What new caste was this? Who were these people that even slaves would scorn them?"

Unar sat on the cushion beside her. "It wasn't scorn," she said.

"No." Imeris laughed at her assumption. "The slaves were not showing defiance but displaying their ownership marks for the louts to see. They had the protection of their rich, influential owners. When I made no such display, they tried to stop me."

"Did you kill them?"

Imeris remembered her stroll with Audblayin through the Garden. The Garden, which did not admit killers.

"I injured one of them. I took his scythe and cut his hamstring. The others soon dragged him away."

The Godfinder smiled darkly.

"You taught them a lesson. Not all unowned women are defenceless. Not all those with spine-seams are slaves."

"They could have raised an alarm." Imeris shrugged. "Brought the king's soldiers down on me. An Understorian warrior, free and unfettered in Orinland? I was too complacent. I still am. I wear my own clothes and do not hide my seams as you and my brother do. Look at me." She indicated the gliding harness over sleeveless Understorian tunic that she wore. "What have I learned?"

"To travel during the daytime," Unar said, kissing her cheek. "And not to take the low roads through the province of beasts."

MISTLETOE LODGE at the southern edge of Ehkisland tunnelled through the sapwood of a tallowwood tree whose smell and feel reminded Imeris of home.

Smaller than the emergent that hosted the Garden of Audblayin, it none-theless provided two dozen small, tidy rooms in a trunk-encircling ring. Individually seeded mistletoe plants hung down over each wide, arched outer window. There were no lamps in the rooms, but light from the upper paths streamed in through the unshuttered openings. When snacking on the sweet, yellow-fleshed mistletoe berries, guests were cautioned to extract the poisonous, barbed seeds that caught on their tongues.

It was just after sunset. Imeris paid for her room with one of the silver coins that the Godfinder had given her. She had no luggage to unpack be-sides the basket of eggs and, without clean clothes to put on, no real reason to bathe. The mirror showed her short-cut, fuzzy hair compressed at the back from sleeping in one of the Godfinder's ridiculous hammocks, her sweaty brow smudged with bark and her neck speckled with bug bites. Not exactly a pretty picture.

The whole of Loftfol can easily resist me!

Imeris could not have cared less what she looked like. In a fight, short hair could not be grabbed. Functional clothing would not restrict her movement. Perfumes and unguents could warn enemies of her approach, and so she would not use them.

When she leaned over the window's edge to consider high and low escape routes in case of emergency, she spotted somebody else leaning out a window above and to the right of hers. A blond slave with broken spines and brown eyes.

He stared at her with something like hostility.

Then he was gone.

Imeris pulled her head in the window. She was certain she'd never seen the man before. Peeked out again and found him peeking down at her, too.

The next time she peeked, he wasn't there. But a moment later, she heard a swish of wings and saw a bird leaving the lodge with a message tied to its foot.

It flew down.

She left her room and went to the upper balcony of the lodge. It was deserted. She supposed the other lodgers were dining. This tallowwood was no emergent, and she had to look up to see the two closest neighbour trees, Southeats and Northeats, both crowded food markets with public eateries open all day and night. Bartering voices were raised in mock outrage, enticing smells wafted down, dead-end roads were set aside for toileting, and Imeris spotted a row of bare arses. Gibbons and tree kangaroos lurked in the lower branches to catch and clean up bits of bread and fruit dropped by clumsy children.

Her empty stomach rumbled.

Perversely, she felt like eating fish. Not Canopian lake fish, crusted in nuts, stuffed with herbs, and smothered in decadent fruit syrups, but tough, smoked, bark-tasting, and bark-textured Understorian fish.

Oldest-Father's fish.

Imeris checked that nobody was watching—the staring slave and the released bird had heightened her sense of caution—and tested her forearm spines in one of the rising branches of the crown. Bending her knees, she raised her feet from the balcony floor. The spines held her weight with only minimal hurt. Unar had done it. Healed Imeris as though the disastrous error of judgement with Aurilon had never happened.

The upper reaches of the tree beckoned. Imeris climbed higher.

She perched in a fork with a partially obscured view of Southeats and reviewed her duel with Aurilon. Fighting with spines was a centuries-old Understorian tradition. Maybe learning the old forms from Horroh was exactly what had made her predictable. She was going about it all wrong. Understorian methods might ultimately defeat Aurilon after decades of study had turned Imeris into a teacher herself, but defeat or displays of skill weren't the true aim. Surprise was what she needed. The short sword was a Canopian weapon. Aurilon would surely be surprised if she pulled out one of those. Maybe she really should seek the oversight of the Litim.

Next, she contemplated her failure with Kirrik. Gliding was something she excelled at. It was impatience at fault there. That could be cured. It must be. Oldest-Father had not died for nothing. She would use what she had learned. She would grow stronger.

Finally, hair raised and skin prickling on the back of her neck, she considered the blond slave and the bird.

He saw me, and he sent a message.

The branch she was in, no thicker around than her thigh, shook as though something heavy had landed in it.

Imeris came up into a crouch, left shin spines sunk in the branch, the sole of her right foot firm against the bark. Her right hand rested by the knife at her left hip, ready to slash or to spring away.

The message could have been a coincidence.

She heard shouts from Southeats. When she glanced across the gap between great trees, she saw soldiers on the branch roads and in the market. They were Ehkisland soldiers, wearing kingfisher-blue wrap skirts, their black bracers and breastplates strapped over sky-blue tunics. The men's long hair was twisted into ropes that ran river-like down to their lower backs.

They carried short spears with long blades and black feathers hanging from the hafts, threatening market customers with them. Seizing shirt-fronts. Shaking women. Knocking food away. Smashing a stall.

Searching for someone, or, at least, for information.

It was no coincidence. That bird went to the king's palace. But how could it? The palace is up. The bird went down.

She would have to escape via Northeats.

"Wait," a man's voice called softly as she turned and gathered herself to spring.

Imeris froze. She searched the branches for the voice's origin and saw nobody. Nothing. The branch shivered. Someone who weighed the same as she did approached along it.

They were invisible.

Someone else who has killed a chimera, she thought, heart racing. *Has everyone killed one except for me?* It was too late to leap. She prepared for a fight to the death with an enemy she could not see.

He rippled into visibility right in front of her. A young man, sitting with one leg on either side of the branch, leaning on both arms for the purpose of inching forwards. He was small, thin, and light, with greenish-gold skin and hair. His eyes had no whites to them. He wore only a short brown wrap skirt over a loincloth.

Where his hands and feet should have been were the black, padded paws of a panther and he smelled slightly of male panther musk.

Imeris blinked. When she looked again, he had human hands and feet the same greenish-gold as the rest of him.

Magic. Always magic.

Her right hand lingered on her knife handle. But he had spoken to her and revealed himself, and she wasn't sure that stabbing him through the heart was the politest response.

"Are you a scout?" he asked in his soft voice, betraying no alarm. "The forerunner of a raid from Understorey? You're disappointed to see the soldiers, aren't you? How could they know you were coming? Have you been betrayed? But if you have been betrayed, if they're really waiting to kill you, why was your instinct to flee upwards and not downwards? That just makes no sense at all."

"You have so many questions," Imeris said, keeping her eyes on him to make sure he didn't change into something more dangerous while she noticed, despairingly, in the corner of her eye, that soldiers were coming along the branch path from Southeats to the lodge.

"I ask questions when I'm nervous," the man said.

"Do I make you nervous?"

"The soldiers do. They mean to use those weapons on me. The goddess Orin, Queen of Birds, gave them those black feathers for their spears. The feathers point the way to me, unless I'm invited into a human-made room. If I become a human guest in a human space, the Mistress of the Wild can't find me."

He was an adept of some kind, there was no doubt of it. Imeris hated deities and all their Servants in that moment.

"Who are you?" But she suspected she already knew.

The green-skinned man licked his full lips, looked left and right, and shifted his grip on the branch ever so slightly.

"I'm Anahah. I was Orin's Bodyguard, though she now names me traitor."

"Soldiers searched for you in Airakland, too." It popped out of her mouth before she remembered not to give anything away about who she was or where she had been. *Keep the fight short. Keep your secrets to yourself.*

Anahah smiled sadly.

"Orin sent messages to all the kings saying that whoever had a hand in my slaying would receive tribute in her stead for a full year."

"What did you do to make her so angry?"

"That's a long tale. The soldiers will be here soon. Won't you make way for me, warrior? I wish you no harm. The soldiers will go when I'm gone. If you've come to slaughter gods, though, you might want to choose a different day."

His eyes flashed, perhaps in anger, perhaps with a sense of urgency. Imeris stared into them. The irises had turned a darker shade of green. A thin black rim separated them from the paler green where the whites should have been. Was he preparing to use Orin's power on her?

"The king of Orinland threatened to call a Hunt," she said. "As though you were a demon. Are you a demon? Does that green skin of yours change colour because you are a chimera's child?"

I am a chimera's child, she thought.

"No," Anahah replied, unblinking. "I am what I am. No Hunt can be called on my account, though one might argue that this Canopy-wide search is worse than a Hunt. Orin can't revoke the gift to transform that she bestowed on me when I was her most trusted adept. I'll use that gift to elude her forever."

"Come into the lodge," Imeris said. "To my human-made room. Be my human guest, for tonight, in a human space paid for with Canopian silver."

He arched one eyebrow. "They'll search the lodge."

Imeris could not let the opportunity escape her. This man had been

Bodyguard to a goddess. All the kings of Canopy were after him, and yet he remained free. He could teach her new fighting techniques. She would surprise Aurilon and destroy Kirrik.

All she had to do was put him in her debt.

"You are an adept," she said. Her temporary ownership of the room could protect him, but only if she was not dragged away by the soldiers for being Understorian. "Mark my tongue. Make me a rich merchant's slave. Make yourself invisible against the room's ceiling. Then remove the mark when they go."

He looked shocked, his irises reverting to their lighter green hue.

"Aren't you afraid they'll kill me and you'll be a slave forever? Children are taught in Canopian classrooms that Understorians are slinking cowards."

"I am not as brave as you think," Imeris said. He couldn't know that her sister was Audblayin, or that Imeris could think of at least two other Canopian adepts who would remove slave marks from her tongue if she asked.

"Quickly, then, warrior," he agreed, and they both climbed down and slipped back inside her window. "While I'm here, not only can the feathers not point to me, but she can't sense what I do with her power. I'll give you the slave master's kiss."

Anahah lifted her chin with one hand. Imeris forced herself not to pull back as their mouths met. She felt a searing on her tongue like the press of a hot poker.

She clenched her teeth and did not scream.

FIFTEEN

THE SOLDIERS went.

Anahah dropped down from the ceiling of the room.

Imeris rose from her genuflection by the side of the bed, closing the door after the king's men. She watched her guest ripple from empty air into a greenish-gold-skinned man in a brown skirt once more. Standing on the same level surface as she, he was a head shorter. She stared, fascinated, as his clawed cat-feet faded into slim, bare fingers and toes. Her clothes needed straightening after her subservient crouch on the floor in the soldiers' presence, but his skirt was either part of him or he was able to transform it, too.

Her tongue throbbed painfully.

"They could've snapped off your climbing spines," Anahah said quietly. "They could've raped you. They could've killed you for fun."

"You do not have a high opinion of soldiers," Imeris said. "Nor of me, if you think I would have let them do any of those things."

"I don't know you." Anahah gave his small, sad smile again. "But I can see you're fit and trained to fight. That harness you're wearing is for gliding. The rope is of excellent quality, and you carry a great deal to spare. I've heard of a warrior school that lies below Ehkisland where men and women are trained to kill deities. It's called Loftfol."

"Loftfol," Imeris repeated, sighing. She should have been there days ago. Her absence would be remarked on. It seemed she would have to tell the former Bodyguard something about herself, to stop his guessing. She sat down on the bed. "Listen, Anahah. My name is Imeris. I was born in Canopy, though I fell and lost my arcane aura decades ago, and I have no interest in killing deities. I came to test my skills in a duel. I lost the duel. Now I am going home."

Her stomach grumbled again, but she did not dare go to find the proprietor and ask for food. When she'd paid for the stay, she'd presented herself as an out-of-nicher. She hadn't identified as a slave. What would they say if they saw a bleeding mark on her tongue that hadn't been there before?

"Your home is Understorey?" Anahah asked, coming to sit beside her. "How do you find living in darkness?"

"I am hungry, and it hurts to talk," Imeris said, leaning indignantly away from him so their bare arms didn't touch. "You are the one who promised a long tale."

"Did I promise? Here." He leaned after her and kissed her a second time. Pain and the sensation of the ridges of the glyph dissolved away as effortlessly as his panther paws had dissolved. Imeris had been too distracted by the soldiers to be aware of his closeness before. He had no detectable human odour, but the panther smell and a hint of crushed banana leaves hung around him. The lips he briefly pressed to hers were soft and cool like the velvet bracts of a banana flower. "Is that better? Please tell me about Understorey." He shifted back, allowing her the hand-span of space between them that she'd sought.

She sighed again. Pressed her tongue to the roof of her mouth. She hadn't liked having the marking there and felt soiled somehow, though she'd been a slave for less than an hour.

"How do I find Understorey? Let me think," she said, closing her eyes. "In Understorey, when you lie on your back on a branch or a platform and look directly upwards, it is no different to seeing true stars in the night sky. The foliage is so far away. It heaves and shifts like clouds, letting through only tiny flares of blue or orange or white light. When these lights touch your skin, they are like weightless rain. Light is a treasure the leaves of Canopy try to hoard, but some of it always escapes, even if there is no extra warmth to it."

"Is it cold where you live?" Anahah sounded surprised.

"No. Hotter than here. The smells are so thick you feel you are pushing through them, like pushing through a river. Water is louder." Imeris thought of the river that ran down the side of the tallowwood, Audblayin's emergent, her home, and also of the one that frothed through the heart of Loftfol, the split-trunked river nut tree. "Here, rain strikes the leaves in a thousand separate blows. There, it roars. One single angry creature. There are few human sounds."

"How old were you when you fell?"

"I do not remember it." She opened her eyes. Met his strange ones.

"Have you a blood family here?" he asked.

But Imeris had had enough of answering his questions. It was his turn to answer.

"Have you no family or friends, Anahah, to invite you into their homes and keep you safe?"

He lowered his gaze to the floor.

"Orin killed every living member of my family. All my friends. Anyone she remotely suspected might provide me with shelter."

Imeris felt a lump in her throat.

"Could you not have defended them?"

He laughed a quiet, stuttering laugh, like a child dragging a stick along a paling rail.

"I didn't know. I was busy defending Orin. She left me unsuspecting until the end so there'd be nowhere for me to go."

"But how did you wrong her?"

Anahah did not reply and would not meet her eyes.

A footstep sounded in the corridor outside the door. He looked at her, and his irises had gone the darker green. His body twisted, turning invisible as he leaped for the ceiling. Somebody knocked on the door.

Imeris strode calmly to answer it. The landlady stood there in a robe embroidered with keys and falling rain. She had a sculpted, conical tower of hair, silk shoes with curled toes peeping out from the hem, and a blue-blazing lantern in her hand.

"Good evening," she said. "One who walks in the grace of Ehkis is simply checking that all of our esteemed guests are unharmed."

"My room was searched," Imeris said. "Did they find what they were looking for?"

"I'm afraid not. I apologise. You must understand." The landlady lowered the lantern as though correcting the impression that she, too, was searching for something. "The fugitive from Orinland. They say he turned on the very goddess he was supposed to protect. He planned not just to kill her but to trap her soul in between bodies, never to be incarnated again."

"Is that what they say?" Imeris tapped her lips with one finger. Had she kissed a man with no scruples at all? If she had, surely he would have left her marked as a slave and made himself comfortable in her lodging. Then again, perhaps to withdraw her protection, all she had to do was stop considering him to be her guest, and he would not wish to risk that. "All is well here. Though I do not quite feel safe going to the food markets with such a man on the loose. Could you bring me some supper?" Imeris handed over another of the Godfinder's coins. She had no idea what the things were worth, but it seemed to please the landlady, who promised to return shortly with provisions.

Imeris closed the door and sat back down on the bed.

"She hoards her coin," Anahah said from the empty air, "in a chest that she lowers on a chain down her private lavatory. They would've taken it, if they'd found it."

"That is fascinating," Imeris said. "She is coming back soon. You had better stay there for now."

"I'll tell you if I get tired," his disembodied voice replied.

Imeris snorted. She supposed Bodyguards did become tired, even if they didn't need to sleep. Aurilon had never showed any sign of fatigue, however. And her middle-father would never admit his arms were aching, even if he'd spent a week hauling some heavy carcass back home.

"Did you really plan to trap Orin's soul? I did not know souls could be trapped in between bodies."

No reply.

Imeris was not especially interested in the workings of souls, any more than she was interested in the working of magic outside what she needed to know to defeat her enemy. Fighting interested her. Killing Kirrik interested her, and then being able to get on with the rest of her life.

"You must have killed many times in defence of Orin," she said. "You must be an accomplished warrior. You could teach me—"

"No," Anahah interrupted, his soft voice sounding slightly sulky. "I couldn't. Is that why you helped me? I change into animals when I need to fight. They have instincts you and I couldn't hope to have."

"Oh." Imeris glanced up at the ceiling, but even knowing exactly where he was, she still couldn't see him at all. "What kind of animals?"

"Mostly jaguars. To kill by swift ambush and a bite right through the assassin's skull."

"That is a skill we practice. Dropping onto enemies. A bore-knife can go through a human eye socket or the base of the skull." Imeris nodded. "A jaguar is an obvious choice."

"Ah," Anahah said, "but the jaguar is easily beaten by a fiveways troupe. Four fiveways demons seize a limb each, while the fifth one holds the tail. Their arm and shoulder muscles are dense. Inexorable. They can pull a jaguar into pieces in moments."

"Can you change into five separate animals, then?"

"No. But even one fiveways male, using his long arms as clubs, can smash a would-be killer from a high branch road."

"So the jaguar assumption was incorrect." Imeris pulled her long legs up onto the bed, sitting cross-legged in the attitude of learning she assumed on the wood floors of Loftfol. "The fiveways is the best fighting form."

"The fiveways can easily be killed by the embracer," Anahah said, naming the demon that took the form of a constrictor with the girth of a great tree. They were too heavy to hunt often in Understorey. Imeris had never seen one. "Yet young embracers are routinely snatched up and eaten by swamp harriers on the Bright Plain."

"What is a swamp harrier?"

"A bird," Anahah explained, "like a kite or a hawk. Long-legged, for grasping snakes in long grass or through dense canopy. Then again, I have heard that jaguars will sometimes make a meal of swamp harriers by twitching their tails in sunlight. When the bird drops down on what it supposes is a snake, it ends up between the jaguar's jaws."

"Do you mean to say that all is cyclical?" Imeris asked, frowning. "Or that fighting is futile, for all die in the end?"

"I mean to say that all have their weaknesses."

She smiled.

"Understorians? What are our weaknesses?"

Anahah gave his distinctive, fluttering, interrupted laugh.

"Tonight we are friends, but we might be enemies someday. Telling what I know of your weaknesses could armour you against me."

Imeris's decision to learn the Canopian short sword silently firmed. She would literally armour herself once more. She would dig out the lovely bronze-scale breast- and back-plates, and even the neck piece and helmet that she hated. Sword slashes and thrusts with their longer reach would leave her lower abdomen and thighs vulnerable. Perhaps Vesev's father in Gannak, Sorros the Silent Smith, could make her a split skirt piece as well. Sorros should have been retired but had been in demand since his son's demise.

The landlady returned with a platter of salamanders and bulrush roots boiled in oil, garnished with edible water-plant blossoms and the berries of swamp-loving bushes. Ehkisland boasted more lakes and ponds than any other niche. There was also an unstoppered gourd of jackfruit wine, which gave off a powerful pong. Imeris thanked her host and promised to put the platter outside the door when she was done.

"You can come down now," she said, munching on a blossom. "You do eat animals, not just become them?"

"Yes." The floor shuddered as he struck it, hands and feet first, like a cat. Anahah straightened as he became visible. He took a bulrush root from the platter and eyed it. His closeness made her hand jerk reflexively to her mouth. She lowered it and offered Anahah the jackfruit wine, which made him laugh mirthlessly. "I know a story about a jackfruit tree."

"Tell me." Imeris picked up a bulrush root of her own, still hot enough to burn.

"There was a border dispute between Orinland and Ehkisland. Orinland is a smaller territory, and its queen coveted a mighty and most productive jackfruit tree whose trunk straddled the two niches."

Imeris thought of the borders of Audblayinland, fairly certain that they were fixed.

"How can there be disputes when those limits are set by goddesses' power?"

"The queen of Orinland didn't care for that. She stationed her soldiers around the tree, evicted the Ehkislanders, and had a winter residence, not to mention a private jackfruit winery, built in the upper branches." Anahah smiled. "Ehkisland soldiers came, of course, but quickly withdrew when they discovered the five-year-old son and heir to the throne of Ehkisland being held hostage in the winery. Orin knows how the kidnapping took place, but once it was done, the family was helpless to defend their rights."

"Did Ehkis not intervene?"

"Ehkis was weak. Only a child, recently reborn." He broke his bulrush root in half and blew on it to cool it. "Ilan was strong. The goddess of justice and kings might have intervened, had the Ehkisland royals paid her any tribute in recent times." He shrugged, and bit into the white flesh of the root. "They hadn't. The queen of Orinland threw extravagant parties in her winter residence. The revels increased in licentiousness and magnificence year after year, until she took a drunken fall from her own balcony. That was two monsoons ago."

"But what about the child? The hostage? The prince?"

Anahah took the time to chew and swallow.

"Oul went back to his family at last, five monsoons older, lonelier, and sadder." He gestured with the other half of the root, in the direction of Ehkisland. "In exchange, Ehkisland ceded the jackfruit tree. Which turned out to be pointless. It was boarded up as a permanent memorial to the Wild Winter Queen."

"His name was Oul," Imeris mused.

"Poor little shadow wandered the servants' passages of that place until they dumped him at the Temple for getting under their feet once too often." Anahah shook his head. "He was small. Silent. Nobody spoke to him, except for me. Nobody played with him, except for me. He liked to make paperbark wind catchers and keep pet frogs."

"You speak about him as if he died."

"Orin numbered him among my friends and had him poisoned. A twelve-year-old boy." He looked as woeful as a twelve-year-old boy in that moment. Imeris squeezed his shoulder.

"I am sorry."

"So am I." He reached for more food, breaking the contact between them. Imeris set the brittle skin of her bulrush root back on the platter.

"Are you certain," she asked, "you cannot teach me anything about fighting?"

Anahah contemplated her darkly over his fried salamander.

"I forget how to fight when I'm in human form."

"So become a beast and show me. You said Orin could not take back her gifts. You said that while you were here, she could not feel it when you used those gifts. For fighting. That is why she gave them to you."

"Not just for fighting. To accompany her, too." Anahah took a tidy swig of the jackfruit wine. "She spends at least an hour shaped like a human each day. That's when she receives supplicants and orders her Servants about. Most of the time she's a kite, though, or a spotted cat, or a boa. Her Bodyguard has to be able to keep up with her."

"A boa," Imeris murmured. "Not so different from an embracer. I would win all my duels if I could do what you do." She imagined tying Aurilon in knots with a strong, flexible snake's body. Or diving on Kirrik in the form of a giant falcon.

"There's a price to be paid." Anahah made a pile of salamander bones on the platter's rim. "That's why I won't show you. Every time I take the life pattern of another creature, the closest creature to own that pattern dies. If I changed into a snake, here and now, somewhere in Ehkisland or below it, a scaly old matron would fall out of her tree, never to lay a clutch of eggs again."

Imeris tilted her head to one side.

"What if you changed into a chimera?" It seemed like the power to exterminate demons from a distance might be a good thing. But killing chimeras also came with a cost. Anahah's expression turned wry.

"A real chimera would die. And the curse would fall on me, unless I used that form to save another's life. Who wants a cursed Bodyguard?" He offered her the gourd, but Imeris wouldn't drink wine in Canopy or anywhere outside the safety of her home. She shook her head, and he took another swig.

"If you took my form?" she asked.

"I can't do that." He seemed relieved that he could not. "This is how I look, now, when I'm human. I can't disguise myself as another person."

"What about when you turn invisible, or grow panther claws?"

"That's different. That's me imagining a change to myself. I don't gain the instincts of a panther, or a chimera, when I do that. I've imagined all sorts of things, to find out what's most useful. Growing extra arms, or thumbs. A tail. Even"—Anahah's free hand alighted on Imeris's forearm where it was braced beneath the platter—"spines."

Imeris narrowed her eyes at him.

"Spines are awarded to Understorians who demonstrate they are worthy," she said with disapproval. But then she couldn't resist asking, "Did you find them useful?"

Anahah smiled and set the wine gourd down on the far edge of the bed, propping it against the wall so it wouldn't spill. Holding up his hands, he curled his fingers, making them into panther paws. The claws came silently out of their sheaths, every bit as deadly as hers.

"Truthfully? Not as suited to me as these. To use Understorian spines, to climb with the elbow and shin, good strength and stamina in the shoulder blades and upper back will complement flexibility in the hips and power in the thigh. Long limbs are no disadvantage." His smile deepened as he watched her face change, her eyes narrowing in concentration. He had tried to tell her this already, but she hadn't been paying attention; she hadn't made the link between her yearning to learn better techniques and his skirting the issue of weaknesses.

He had lied when he said he'd forgotten how to fight in human form.

"And your paws?"

Anahah switched his focus back to them. The black toe pads elongated into fingers, the claws turning pale green and pressing flat into fingernails.

"To climb with the hands and feet," he said, "heavy muscles in the arms as well as shoulders and sides are needed. Men find some advantage over women, and smaller men over tall." He met her curious gaze. "There is no secret to winning duels. No magic required. Only know yourself."

She pulled back from his strange perspective, his focus on fighting animals. People were not animals. He had admitted that humans didn't have the instincts. Trying to fight like a bird or a demon was all wrong.

"That is not true." *There are secrets. Aurilon knows them. She will tell me.*

Anahah shrugged and took up the gourd again.

"Keep seeking a teacher who'll tell you what you want to hear."

"I have one." *That is, I have found one that I wish would teach me.* "She is a Bodyguard. And she has never been beaten. And she has only her own human form to fight with."

"I've been cheating, all this time, haven't I? I told you so." He laughed, louder and less restrained, and Imeris realised the gourd was empty, that although he was not a large man, all the jackfruit wine was gone. His cheeks were flushed a deeper green. "I'm sorry it wasn't Aurilon of Odelland that you were able to place in your debt. Perhaps I can repay you some other way."

Imeris was slow to catch his meaning.

"I have no need of coin."

He dropped to the bed beside her and slung an arm over her shoulders, which she permitted.

"Perhaps you should not have drunk all of that." Her fingers rose to her lips.

"You keep doing that."

"What?"

"Touching your mouth." His strange eyes were intent, an almost luminous green.

"Have you kissed a lot of slaves?" Imeris asked behind her hand, not lowering it. "Is that how it has to be done?"

"No, and, no. Would you like to try it again? Without the stinging intervention of the goddess?"

Imeris lowered her hand.

"No," she said firmly. "You can share the bed, if you wish, but keep your hands—claws—paws—to yourself." She remembered one of the Loftfol boys pretending to stumble in the dark so that he could grab her breasts. He'd laughed at her outrage until she'd pinned him to the wall by his spines and left him there. Her mothers had warned her to be wary.

"Just as well," Anahah said softly. "Winning duels can be difficult with a full womb. Running from your enemies, too."

"How would you know?" Imeris turned away. She thought of Middle-Mother, pregnant in the Garden, awaiting her masters' ruling on her baby's fate, and Oldest-Mother, raped by a king and ruined by a princess. Both of them marked with a Canopian owner's glyph since birth.

"I'm sorry. I wouldn't know, of course." Anahah shook his head ruefully. "Perhaps I shouldn't have drunk all the wine, but you see, I can't risk outstaying your ownership of this room. I'll sleep beneath the open window. The need to piss will wake me. I'll be gone before the sun rises. Safe travels, Imeris, and thank you."

SIXTEEN

"You didn't win," Youngest-Mother guessed sympathetically.

"I will next time," Imeris said without real enthusiasm. Anahah hadn't taught her much of anything, and the tutors at Loftfol would be angry enough over her going missing for so long that they'd send her back to white-cloth chores for weeks.

"You've started this month's bleed, too?" Youngest-Mother indicated with a lift of her chin and a pointed glance the stain in the crotch of Middle-Father's too-big trousers.

Imeris stared past her at the place by the blazing fire where Oldest-Father should have knelt, iron skewers bundled in his hands, spitting river fish. The hearth room was too empty. Oldest-Mother and Middle-Mother had gone in disguise as Nessans by a lower-down, temporary bridge to the new year market at Gannak.

"Is Youngest-Father here?" Imeris asked.

"Youngest-Father," Youngest-Mother said, "is in Wissin, trying to discover where Kirrik might have gone after you three pulled down her new dovecote. I'm so sorry, Issi. Is there anything we can do to help before you go back to Loftfol?"

"Just a place to rest. I will stay tonight and go tomorrow." Imeris began unbuckling her harness. Home was the only place where she ever took it off. "My bleed lasts for only two days. When it is finished, I will be safer from demons."

Circling around the huge slab table back to Youngest-Mother, she shrugged out of the shoulder straps that secured the egg basket and handed it over.

"These are for you. From Unar."

"Wonderful!" Youngest-Mother's commiserating expression brightened. "Thank you for carrying them so carefully. Not a one is broken."

Imeris followed her into the comforting green gloom of the fishing room. There, the wall of water beating past the opening kept foodstuffs much cooler than by the side of the constantly roaring hearth. Imeris took off her trousers and washed her legs, helping herself to moonflower and a loincloth to stuff it in. Youngest-Mother set the eggs on a high shelf where the child Imeris had once felt about for Youngest-Father's wings.

Her own wings had been lost in the battle with Kirrik. She'd have to go back to Loftfol by the bridges, which meant travelling only in the middle of the day when the ballistae were in operation.

"Wait," Imeris begged when Youngest-Mother made as if to return to the hearth room.

Youngest-Mother waited. She curled her fingertips in her long hair. Today it hung down in the Understorian style.

"You were a Servant of Audblayin in the Garden." Imeris felt her way, hesitantly, towards what she wanted to say.

"I was," Youngest-Mother replied. It was no admission. She had said so a hundred times before.

"Did you mark the tongues of slaves?"

In the fishing room, there were only the luminous fungi to light Youngest-Mother's face, but Imeris saw her plump mouth flatten and her broad, black brows draw down.

"I was shown how. I wasn't a Servant for very long before Unar dragged me down here. I used the spell they showed me on Aoun, in practice, and he practiced on me. But I never marked anyone for the first time. I did change Sawas's mark, and your sister Ylly's, from the mark of the Garden to the mark of the House of Epatut. It was Unar who removed them."

"There is no mark of the Garden anymore," Imeris said.

"No, there isn't." Youngest-Mother's shoulders were hunched. Tense. "Your sister put a stop to it in that sanctuary, at least. I've heard that Odel doesn't keep slaves, either. Nor the wood god, Esh, but his ways are strange and frightening, and nobody really understands them."

Imeris raised her fingertips to her lips.

"Did you kiss them?"

"Did I kiss whom?" Youngest-Mother's eyebrows shot up. "Odel and Esh?"

"No!" Imeris dropped her hand from her mouth to her side. "The Understorians you were turning into slaves. To make the mark on their tongues."

Youngest-Mother sighed.

"No," she said. "Though kissing was said to decrease the pain."

"By magic means? Or because of the distraction?"

"I don't know, Issi."

They stood together, sad and contemplative, for a minute or two, before ribald gibes and indignant squawks announced the return of Middle-Mother and Oldest-Mother from the marketplace.

Imeris found them in the hearth room. Over the wide quandong table they spread bags of salt, baskets of fruit, bottles of coconut oil, and gourds of medicine-precursors and mordants. Oldest-Father had always provided enough animal skins and dried fish to allow them to trade for whatever they needed. They might have to be more frugal without him.

"Issi!" Middle-Mother cried, flinging her arms around Imeris. Her birth name was Sawas. She was plumper than Imeris's other mothers and smelled of expensive stone powders that prevented perspiration. "We feared you'd been killed by that monstrous fiend Aurilon!"

"Sawas feared you'd been killed," Oldest-Mother said, smiling wryly, kissing Imeris on the cheek, "as she does, dramatically, every year. Aurilon is no monster, Sawas, but a role model for our dedicated warrior daughter. But, Issi, you can't have surprised Aurilon, either. You can't have beaten her, or you'd have stayed on in Odelland as her disciple."

Imeris grimaced, still squeezed in Middle-Mother's enthusiastic embrace.

"I did not surprise her. I failed again."

"You've plenty of time."

Middle-Mother put her hands to Imeris's cheeks, inspecting her foster daughter's face critically, Imeris knew, for the appearance of wrinkles.

"You don't have plenty of time," she corrected Oldest-Mother, scandalised. "You have twenty-one monsoons behind you. You want to kill, because your friends were killed, because your father was killed, but killing is not the way to defeat death. Death is defeated by new life."

Imeris couldn't help but smile.

"New life? Now you sound like the great goddess Audblayin."

"She's the one who sounds like me. I came first," Middle-Mother said, jiggling Imeris's squished cheeks between her palms. "She can't take her own advice, though, and give me grandchildren, so it's up to you, Issi."

"What about Leaper?"

Middle-Mother released Imeris, throwing up her hands.

"I never see him. I never hear from him. It's like I never gave birth to him at all. Worse than my husband, and did you see Bernreb while you were in Canopy? Did you tell the great goddess Audblayin that I need my man back? Five years is too long! It's about time she chose herself another Bodyguard."

Audblayin asked me to do it, Imeris thought. *I could stay in Canopy, safe from Kirrik. I could forget every claim that Nirrin and Vesev and Oldest-Father have on me.*

"Can I sleep in Youngest-Father's bed?" she asked. Her old bed had been removed when she went to Loftfol. Youngest-Father's wooden slab was now her favourite napping place. The room where the three children had slept had been turned into a workshop divided in two. Half the workshop was for Youngest-Mother to fashion the musical instruments she sold in her occasional dry-season tutoring forays. The other half was for Oldest-Mother to concoct healing unguents and home remedies. Those had been taught to her by a deceased friend of her mother's, one whom Imeris could barely remember, an old fighter and herbalist called Hasbabsah.

"I'll give you clean sheets," Youngest-Mother said, stoppering the coconut oil she'd been smelling and twining her fingers in her hair again.

Imeris enjoyed a few hours of dreamless sleep.

When she woke in the early evening, she acquiesced to Middle-Mother's desire to swim before supper.

Imeris tied sturdy knots in the rope ladder that would allow Middle-Mother to climb down to the pool. It was a diversion of the river that ran down their tree. Oldest-Father had fashioned it, decades ago, to trap day-hunters. Imeris knew there were old bones in the bottom of the pool, but it was deep and dark in the hollow of the tree, and she'd never been able to see them.

Middle-Mother couldn't convince Imeris to dive down and try to touch them, but then Imeris had never been as good a swimmer as Middle-Mother. They left their clothes and Middle-Mother's harness on a railing Oldest-Father had fashioned for the purpose.

"I'd a child by the time I was your age," Sawas said, sighing, standing on a carved shelf, tracing the stretch marks on her naked belly and thighs before reaching across to pat Imeris's smooth skin.

Imeris batted Middle-Mother's hands away and slipped into the water. She splashed out into the middle of the pool. It was twenty body lengths across. Water poured in from the river through a bored chute and over-flowed from the lip. There was a good arm's length of air between the surface and the domed wood ceiling. She couldn't see it, but Imeris knew the engraving was still there, of her name, and Ylly's, and Leaper's, done with a bore-knife one day after a writing lesson with Oldest-Mother. Leaper had been the youngest, but his writing had been the tidiest.

Imeris had punished him for it with repeated dunkings. He'd been forced to become a better swimmer than she was, just so he could escape her.

"Tell me again about Ylly's father," she said.

Middle-Mother dived neatly, entering the water without a splash and emerging on the other side of Imeris, spouting water playfully.

"He was a thatcher from Oxorland," she said. "They've got ridiculous names. His was Ofondness. Ofondness thought he'd heard Audblayin's call, but he was wrong. Just farted too hard, or something." Middle-Mother laughed. "I liked his long arms and legs and his little brown bottom. His teeth were all crooked, but Ylly's teeth grew straight, like mine. Mostly, I wanted a baby, and there he was. You know that most men who serve a deity have a spell on them so they don't want sex. I suppose your brother has a spell like that on him. He'll be a dead end like the rest of the Servants."

"That hardly seems fair. What good is an oath to remain chaste when it costs no effort to keep it? Without temptation—"

Middle-Mother splashed her.

"Oh, so you know something about temptation, do you? Tell me about those Loftfol boys. Or is there somebody else? Are you sure that you keep going to Odelland to fight that monster Bodyguard? Are you sure you don't love the feel of her skin against yours? Or is it the handsome young incarnation of Odel?"

Imeris hardly heard her, so vividly was she picturing the lanky Canopian thatcher with crooked teeth. Of course he would want to make love to beautiful, mischievous Middle-Mother. But with no intention of going away with the man to Oxorland, hadn't Middle-Mother cared that her child would be a slave?

"Middle-Mother, how could you be with that thatcher while he was free and you were a thing owned by the Servants of Audblayin?"

"Was he free?" Middle-Mother shrugged. "He woke up in the morning, and he went to work. He hauled bundles of cut windgrass up the sides of great trees from Floorians even poorer than he was. He ate tasteless food. Slept on splinters. I ate meat and beans and nut porridge and slept in a bed in the great Garden."

"Of course he was free," Imeris said angrily, but Middle-Mother splashed her again.

"Nobody is free," she said irritably. "Not the goddesses, not the gods. Is my husband free to return to me? What about my baby, whose body is home to the most coveted soul in Canopy? She ended up trapped in the Garden just the same as I was trapped. Worse. Until death."

When they climbed back up to the dwelling, Imeris using her spines and Middle-Mother the rope ladder, they found Youngest-Father at home. He'd also brought in a net of fish, gutted them, and spitted them over the fire.

"Now everyone is here," he said warmly. The family sat around the quandong table to eat fresh-caught fish together.

"How can you say that?" Middle-Mother wailed. "What about my husband? What about my children?"

Youngest-Father ignored her, which spoke eloquently of how often the lament came up at the supper table. Oldest-Mother reached across her for the salt.

"I ruined the ropes and mechanisms of some of the ballistae I used between Loftfol and Wissin," Imeris told Youngest-Father. "I wonder if you would help me to fix them. It would be faster with both of us. And with some of"—she almost turned to ask him, as if he might be sitting there, silent and scowling—"Oldest-Father's rope."

Youngest-Father said, "I have fixed them, Issi. It was my excuse for staying in Wissin."

"Did you hear any rumours about Kirrik?" Youngest-Mother asked quietly. Only one finger and the thumb of her right hand were greasy; she ate fastidiously.

"No," Youngest-Father admitted.

One by one, they left the table, heading for their beds, until Youngest-Father and Imeris were the only ones left in the hearth room. Youngest-Father watched in silence as Imeris put more wood on the fire.

"Short sword," she said to him after a while.

"What about it?" he asked, bemused.

"You have not asked me which discipline I will take up next. Short sword, I think." She mimed a few experimental slashes and thrusts.

He nodded. "You will do well at it. You do well in all the fighting arts."

Imeris gazed at his boyish, carefree face. She thought about how he had never had a spell on him to inure him to temptation.

"What will happen if—" She wanted to ask, *What will happen if the short sword is a waste of time, too? What will happen if I never kill her? If she kills me?* She couldn't finish the question, couldn't speak it aloud. Instead, she asked the lesser question, the one that never troubled her sleep, but which clearly troubled Middle-Mother. "What will happen if I never fall in love?"

Youngest-Father looked surprised.

"Do you ask because you think I have never fallen in love?"

It was Imeris's turn to be taken aback.

"Have you?"

"Yes."

"With Youngest-Mother?" she guessed. "Before you knew that she loved Oldest-Mother?"

"No!"

They both stared, astonished, at one another. Then they looked away. The firelight leaped higher over the fresh fuel. Smoke ran over the drying racks of fish like an upside-down river.

"Listen," Youngest-Father said. "Our mother, Moonoom, was a travelling wet-nurse. She was even smaller than me, and as a girl she loved to fly, but there was one thing she loved more than flying, and that was babies."

"I suppose she could not fly pregnant or with young children?"

"You suppose right. Esse, when he was born, was everything to her. She nursed two other babies between him and Bernreb and three more before having me. We were all born in different towns. Her husbands kept dying, but she was happy. Just like Sawas was happy when Oos, Ylly, and I went travelling. She didn't envy us our adventures. Sawas loves babies. She loves children."

Imeris looked at the remains of the fish bones in the fire and thought again about how much easier it seemed to be for Canopian women to fall pregnant. Maybe it had nothing to do with the food. Maybe it was simply that Audblayin walked among them.

But maybe Sawas would have had more children if she had stayed a slave. Imeris shook her head to be rid of dark thoughts.

"Yes."

"This is what our mother told us, many times," Youngest-Father said. "Boys, if you wish to father children, be sure to choose a wife whose dream is the raising of children. You will be hunters, and that is a dangerous trade. It is unlikely you will see your children grow. Especially you, Marram."

Imeris tilted her head, not understanding.

"Why especially you?"

"Because I love flying, the same as she did." Youngest-Father squeezed the back of Imeris's neck. "The same as you do, wild child. I have beaten chance to live this long. Twice I have been saved just in time from the sorceress."

"I have been saved twice, too," Imeris said, ashamed, touching her amulet. "Once when Kirrik took Nirrin instead of me. The second time, with you, when I tried to fly to you but crashed into the tree instead. Oh, Youngest-Father."

"Bernreb has escaped his likely death at the claws of a tree bear or the coils of an embracer by being snatched up to Canopy by your sister." He raised his eyes to the ceiling. "Yet he chose well with Sawas."

"He chose her?" Imeris teased. "The way I heard it, it was Middle-Mother choosing from the three of you."

Youngest-Father shook his head ruefully.

"I did fall in love, once. Her name was Immi. She was funny and lighthearted—and careless, Issi. She hated the sound of babies crying. Though she sang like the goddess of beasts and birds and wept when I went, I had to leave her. Better to leave her before giving her a child she did not want than leave her afterwards."

"Yes," Imeris said after a while. "You were a good boy for listening to your mother. How did Moonoom die?"

"She took her wings from the peg one morning and never returned."

Imeris shivered.

"I do not want that to happen to you."

Youngest-Father laughed softly.

"I am completely safe. For the near future."

"What do you mean?"

"You messed up my bed," he said, "and did not change the sheets, but

I am too tired to change them now. Crawl in, if you like, or sleep in the chair after you have finished your forms. Tomorrow when you go, I may still be sleeping. But I will not have you walking on the bridges to Loftfol like a lead-footed Canopian. You will take my wings."

Imeris gazed at him for a long moment. Since she'd stolen the chimera cloth twelve years ago, he hadn't needed to tell her again not to lay a finger on it. Bringing the wings back to their home after the futile attack on Kirrik had been a necessity.

"But you need them."

"I will come for them. After I have crafted a new set of wings from day-hunter hide for you."

He went to bed, and Imeris struggled to tip the great table, by herself, onto one side. She stacked the chairs and benches against it, to make room for her daily exercises.

Oldest-Mother emerged from one of the hanging tapestry flaps before Imeris had finished the Discipline of the All-Body Breath.

"Did the sound of dragging furniture wake you, Oldest-Mother? I am sorry," Imeris said.

"Not that," Oldest-Mother replied, her smile reassuring. She moved stiffly over to the fire and put a kettle over it. "I've got this pesky pain in my lower back. Crushed snake vine stems with a little warm water and fish fat helps."

"I am not listening," Imeris said, smiling. "No matter how you try and make me a healer, I am a warrior, Oldest-Mother."

Until Kirrik is dead, at least.

She moved easily through the Discipline of Balance, followed by the Discipline of Strength. With a pause for a sip of water and to help rub the fish-stinking ointment into Oldest-Mother's lower back, she carried on with the Disciplines taught to her by Middle-Father and her Loftfol teachers respectively.

The Discipline of the Knife.

I was never so clumsy with a knife when I was at Loftfol, Oldest-Father had muttered one day when she was practicing under Middle-Father's eye. He had been full of needling remarks like that—*I kept the tidiest bunk at Loftfol; I was the best dressed at Loftfol; my fish fed a thousand warriors at Loftfol*—until Youngest-Father revealed to Imeris that Oldest-Father had never been to Loftfol.

The Discipline of Administering Poison. Taught to her by the Odarkim, whose faint praise after a year of study had been that he had never seen a woman do better. This could have been because he had never taught a woman before, but Imeris knew she excelled at the subtle discipline. The problem was that Aurilon's skills were simply superior.

The Discipline of Cord Strangulation. Taught by the Scentingim. Rope use had always been one of her weaker areas. She did not have the strength in her hands nor the knot-tying knack Oldest-Father owned, but she had tried her best to improve.

Finally, Imeris danced the Discipline of Spines.

"That last one," Oldest-Mother remarked as a sweaty, tired Imeris came to sit beside her, "is terrifying."

"Why are you waiting here for me to finish?"

"Oos and Sawas were whispering about you. They said you had unusual questions."

"Ha!" Imeris banked the fire. She moved all the furniture back to where it belonged, as quietly as she could. There was no need to disturb Youngest-Father; the chair in the hearth room would be fine to sleep in. She sat back down beside Oldest-Mother. "Maybe I do."

"You always have questions when you come back from Canopy or school. Last time, you had questions for your fathers, because you'd cut off an Understorian's hand by accident. The time before, you'd hamstrung a man from Orinland. This time it seems it's your mothers you need. Have you met a young person of interest to you, Issi?"

Imeris thought of a green man with green eyes who could make himself invisible. She shrugged.

"If I have, that is not the question I have for you or anyone, Oldest-Mother. It is slavery that concerns me, and the question of where I belong. If Canopians are cruel and wrong, leading a raid against them is not acting against my ancestry, but instead setting things to rights. Yet my sister is a goddess and to bring the Garden down is to betray her. Who is my family? Who are my people? How did you know, growing up in Canopy, that you were a person, the same as any Servant of the deity? How did you know you were an Understorian woman and not a collection of tradeable Canopian goods?"

"My mother told me who I was," Oldest-Mother murmured. "That's how I knew."

"But I have three mothers, and they tell me different things."

"That is your curse and your good fortune, my Imerissiremi. I loved the one mother that I had, but she couldn't always tell me what I needed to hear. She couldn't speak to all my different selves, and I couldn't speak to hers. She had a warrior self I couldn't understand, and I had a nurturing self she couldn't understand."

"Nurturing!" Imeris exclaimed. "That is not how Middle-Mother describes you. Killer of kittens, she calls you. You lived in a palace and were punished for throwing one of the king's pet kittens down."

Oldest-Mother nodded.

"I did live in a palace. We weren't treated well. My mother did awful, desperate things to hoard food for me. When she found me feeding the bread she'd saved to baby birds with broken wings, she took them away from me and wrung their necks. She tossed them over the palace walls. Whatever wasn't worth feeding went over those walls. Including my mother, eventually. I wanted the king's family to hurt the way that I hurt. Otherwise I would have treasured that kitten. If I'd been allowed to keep Sawas close to me for longer than a few seasons, I would have treasured her, too."

"I don't think I want to have children, Oldest-Mother." Not even when she did discover where she belonged. Youngest-Father was right. She was not like Middle-Mother. Her first love was not children, but flight, and peace, and quiet. "If I have a child-nurturing self, she is a dwarf beside the titan that is my lone-warrior self."

"You don't need to have them, my Imerissiremi. The world is full of children. Our many selves are renewed, without end, in the hearts of strangers we never meet and whose names we never know."

SEVENTEEN

IMERIS, BORNE up by the chimera-skin wings, sped like an arrow towards the Doorstep.

The Doorstep was a simple wooden platform. Loftfol's masters had it built on the side of a river nut tree, a smaller one than the triple-trunked tree whose heart hosted the school itself. The smaller tree's trunk was only a few paces across. The platform, with its flickering beacon of fish-fat-burning flame, was not much wider. Any visitors openly aimed at the Doorstep were allowed to approach Loftfol. The Doorstep could be reached by bridge or glider.

Trespassers trying to surreptitiously approach from any other direction were caught by the school's scouts and hanged. Their corpses were left to rot in wooden cages, which dangled from chains below the Doorstep platform.

Imeris aimed her glider at the beacon, her mind already in the star-shaped Hall where the river ran through the school and the teachers stood in the corners, waiting for pupils to select their subjects. She might have missed the recognition ceremony, but she would not have missed the new year's choosing. Her bronze armour weighed her down, but it was no longer monsoon and the lightness of the demon-hide glider bore her up. The short sword she'd traded for and had sharpened at a forge in Lit made her weapons belt lopsided, but the detour had been worth it.

The short sword teacher, Dammammad, was the Litim. It felt right to carry a blade fashioned by the smith of his home village.

Imeris judged the angle and speed of her approach. Shifted her weight. Arched her back. Ran a few steps along the platform as she shifted her shoulders to collapse the frame of the glider behind her.

She came to a halt, panting. Her booted toes hung off the edge of the platform.

"Not a bad landing," said a deep, rich voice behind her. Imeris turned, wings dragging, to find the spine-fighting teacher, Horroh, leaning against the beacon post. His brawny arms were folded across an amethyst-studded purple silk vest; the stones, in clusters of thirteen, repeated the spearhead emblem of the school.

Imeris's first instinct was to smile at the sight of him, before it occurred to her that he should not be at the Doorstep. She showed her respect with right fist pressed into left palm, but she couldn't help looking around nervously for the usual low-ranking sentry. Was she in trouble? Was Horroh here to warn her, as he had warned her once before to avoid the boys who followed Kishsik through the halls, the ones who had adopted him since his injury and muttered about Canopians bearing spines? Perhaps signs of her passing had been found in the dark temple, and she was to be scolded for disrespecting the dead.

A rope ran from the beacon post into the darkness between trees. It led to Loftfol. The sentry should have sent a message in a cylinder across to the school, and the school should have rung its bells to let the sentry know that Imeris was permitted to pass.

There was no sign of the cylinder. Or the sentry. Or the grips and metal clips that would send her skimming down along the rope herself.

Be aware of your surroundings.

Horroh did nothing to relieve her unease. His colourless eyebrows and pasty, creaseless face made his intentions difficult to read at the best of times. His shaved head, which had once reminded her of a flowerfowl egg, now bore a finger-thickness of bristling blond hair, as though he'd meant it to remind her how long she'd been away.

Eliminate unknowns.

"Horroh the Haakim, wise teacher of my past year," she said, making the gesture a second time, "you must have known I was on my way. You must have given my name to the scouts. Am I to be reprimanded?"

"Something like that," Horroh said, moving slowly into a ready stance, which unnerved her even more. "It is two weeks since monsoon ended, Imerissiremi. Were you caring for your mother?"

I could tell him everything. About Kirrik. About my sister being a goddess, and about Aurilon. He would understand.

No, he wouldn't. Telling him everything would only confirm what Lehhel said in the dark temple, that Canopians have eyes, they have mouths, they have beating hearts, but they speak only lies.

"Her illness," Imeris said, stepping forwards and away from the small platform's edge, "is always the worst at the end of the monsoon." Youngest-Father's wings rustled, folding back along their pattern of seams and grooves.

"Your mother is Canopian? From Ehkisland?" Horroh asked lightly, and Imeris, biting her lip, saw again in her mind's eye the blond, brown-eyed slave who had released the messenger bird from the lodge.

It had flown *downwards.*

To Loftfol.

She held out her empty hands. Tried to keep her voice steady.

"My birth mother is Canopian, as you see from the colour of my skin. My foster mother is not."

"When a bird came from Canopy to report your presence there," Horroh said, raising his forefinger, "I found your application in the archives. Despite all the sick mother excuses you have used over the years, her name is not the one written there. Your sponsor is Marram, a Heightsman and one-time student at Loftfol. His birthplace listed as Gannak. Until now, although you are a woman, you performed satisfactorily. We had no cause to send to Gannak for news of him."

Imeris's hands trembled.

"He is my youngest-father," she said. "He killed a chimera. He made this glider from its hide." She hadn't meant for it to sound like a threat, but it came out that way.

"Marram was not born in Gannak. He is the youngest of three brothers exiled from Gannak for murdering an innocent man."

"They did not want to raid Canopy." Imeris wanted to pull her hands back, but feared Horroh would interpret it as reaching for a weapon.

"Of course not. Your fathers are traitors." He shook his head sadly. "So are you."

"What do you mean?" Her heart started pounding.

"In the year that you were led on a practice raid through the dark temple, you lit the fire that destroyed it, did you not? That is why you did not hesitate to invade that sanctified space. The dark temple was too good. Too accurate a replica of the Canopian Temples that you are loyal to. You could not permit it to remain in use! Once it was ashes, you maimed the only other student who had shown an aptitude all but equal to your own, the boy Kishsik, who came second to you in the climbing race to become Heightsman. I am getting old. I have been blind."

"No!" Imeris gaped at him.

"You and your fathers are spies for Canopy." He said it with the same grave calm in which he had confided, *Your own Understorian body is all that you need. Trust it.*

"No!" She *had* trusted it. She had trusted *him.* Tears threatened. She had lost one father and now stood in peril of losing another. "How can you think that? Horroh, you know me."

"Unfortunately for you," he went on inexorably, "we have our own spies." *He cannot be as certain as he seems. He has had more time to prepare himself for this confrontation, that is all.* More time to stare at her footprints in the dark temple, to let the hate and fear of the other teachers breach his barricades, to wonder why she had wanted to evade the sentries upon departure. And she had not confided in him. *Another terrible mistake. How many have I made, since the monsoon ended?* "Now you will come to Loftfol, Imerissiremi, but not as a Heightsman. You will surrender your things and suffer the healing out of your spines."

Alarm electrified her. He was not indecisive, as she'd hoped. Loftfol's decision was made. Her status as a warrior was forfeit. She would have to submit, or fight. Again. *The healing out of your spines.* It was what Unar had spared Imeris in Canopy. She could not let him do it.

"Let me explain, Horroh." Imeris glanced left and right, looking for other gliders or ropes descending. Horroh would not have expected to subdue her himself. *Others must be coming.* Or must they?

"You!" Horroh thundered, egg-white face reddening, spittle in the corners of his mouth. "You will come in an iron cage worth more than your wretched traitor's soul to tell us how you were able to breach the barrier and when it will be open again!"

Where were the others? Did he really think he could capture her alone? His confidence belied skills he had not shown her, or anyone.

Keep your secrets to yourself.

It struck her, then. He was a spinehusband. Not just a spine-fighter. He had served, in Haak, as the seeder of viper teeth in teenaged girls and boys. He was confident because he had magic as his ally.

"I cannot breach the barrier," Imeris said truthfully, begging him with her gaze to believe her.

"Is it the amulet?" Horroh demanded. "Does it do more than protect you from sorcery? Does it open the way to Canopy?" And her amulet grew warm on its woven cord, as did the long bones in her forearms and shins.

The healing out of your spines. Physical contact was not necessary; she was within range of his magic. Yet he was too close for her to simply open the wings and drop away. The harness tip would clip him as it had clipped the leaves of the windowleaf. She would be completely vulnerable to his magic, as Oldest-Father had been vulnerable to Kirrik's.

No more mistakes.

Imeris lured him closer with a bared throat. She pretended panic; she pretended to look up for sentries along the slender trunk of the Doorstep.

There were no sentries. Climbing bodies on the daughter tree would have sent telltale vibrations through it. It was less stable than its counterpart. While Horroh thought her attention was diverted, predictably, he lunged. His spines did not extend. He wanted to knock her out, not draw blood.

Imeris pivoted again, sharply, turning her torso safely away from the arc of his arm. Exploding with pain and rage at his betrayal. The teacher who had told her to trust herself had turned on her. Without even hearing her explanation. He thought she was a spy, that she had burned her former teacher Lehhel the Odarkim to death in the dark temple, that she had cut off Kishsik's hand, all cold calculation, and then feigned her remorse. What breed of ruthless predator did he truly believe Canopians to be?

Your own Understorian body is all that you need. Trust it.

Imeris slammed the chimera cloth down over him while his upper body was overextended. Youngest-Father's gift, to snuff out magic like water on a wick. Her action doused the burning in her bones immediately.

Keep the fight short.

Hardly knowing what she was doing, she twisted into the movement she had practiced so many times under Horroh's idly curious gaze. Her left arm wrapped around his cloth-hooded head and jerked it back. Her right arm swept under the edge of the chimera skin. Spines extended.

Spines cutting. Catching on cartilage. On bone.

The resistance, the determination needed to follow through, the sweetly painful vibration of it ran through her whole body. It was nothing like she had expected. Nothing like her victorious reveries.

She cried as her teacher's blood fountained over the Doorstep. As he gurgled. As he grew still. If she was a ruthless Canopian predator, he had forced her to become one. He had trained her to kill.

He was now her first kill.

"Why?" she shouted, rolling him over the edge like a Canopian throwing down a slave. Not like an Understorian should treat the body of an enemy, sealing it into a great tree, but she didn't want to see what she had done, to remember him as ruined meat. "Why did you want me to be a spy? Why did you want so badly for me to be Canopian?"

She knew next to nothing about him. Their most intimate act had been his killing, and now she would never know.

The bell began tolling at Loftfol, but it was not the welcome bell.

It was the signal that the school was under attack.

As Imeris tried to wipe Horroh's blood off onto the knobbly grey trunk of the tree, she felt the vibration of approaching warriors under her stained hands. There was no time to think. There was nowhere to climb.

She snapped the glider's frame into extension. She had no choice but to fly.

PART II

*The Slave &
the Hunt*

EIGHTEEN

IMERIS POUNDED on the invisible barrier below Odel's emergent.

"Aurilon!" she shouted until she was hoarse. "Aurilon!"

It was all day and most of a night since she'd fled Loftfol. The blood on her spines had mingled with the sap of a hundred great trees but not worn away completely. She tried to tell herself Horroh had deserved to die, over and over again, but she couldn't really make herself believe it.

This is how it starts. One day a child dreaming of Great Deeds, the next day a killer with Understorian blood as well as Canopian on her conscience, with both the Garden of Audblayin and the great school of Loftfol closed to her forever. *Who am I? Where do I belong?*

"This is beneath your dignity," Aurilon's smoky voice advised from slightly above her, and Imeris lifted bleary eyes to see Odel's Bodyguard hanging upside down from rope and harness as she had the very first time Imeris had seen her. "You did not squeal this way as a child."

"Warriors from beneath Ehkisland are close behind me," Imeris panted.

"Then I can hardly advise my master to make a way through the barrier for you."

"Do something! Help me! I am so tired, Aurilon!" *And I will never rest in my Loftfol bunkroom again. Never rise before the sun to take a bow to hand and bend it in the Unrolled Room of Echoes, never glimpse my dark reflection in the pond under the bridge at the halfway mark or pull shafts from the straw god target on the far side.*

A place of safety from Kirrik, where I knew she could not come.

Imeris tried to think what she might do if Odel refused to let her through. There had to be some other way. No ideas came. She gazed at the Bodyguard in mute appeal.

Aurilon sighed. She plucked something, a coin or a counter, pale as shell or bone, from the dense weave of her bark-ornamented hair.

"I could mark you with the sigil of the slaves of the king of Odelland. The barrier would recognise you as belonging to the world above and not the world below. It would let you through, as if you'd fallen only hours ago instead of decades."

"And then?" Imeris asked, waiting for Aurilon to reassure her that the mark would be removed. Anahah had reassured her. The mark he'd given her was gone before the fear had had time to really sink its teeth in. She couldn't understand why Aurilon didn't hurry up and say it. That it was all a trick to escape pursuit.

"And then you would feel gently, but over time, ever more powerfully compelled to go to the palace of Odelland," Aurilon said, "where your sister's great-grandmother served and died. They might take you in and give you work to do, or they might throw you down to choke before breaking. I am no mighty magic wielder. My master cannot free slaves that are not his own. The bone coin that makes the mark was given ages ago, as a hint that I might send human gifts to the king."

"A hint," Imeris repeated woodenly. "That you might send human gifts."

"Children have been given as tribute to save other children before." Aurilon held the bone coin up between thumb and forefinger. "This has the power to admit you to Canopy, not I. It will also admit you within the wards of the king's palace. Once within those wards, you could not leave except by his orders. Are you really being hunted?"

"Yes, Aurilon. The pursuit is mere minutes behind me. Please! Ask Odel to open the way! You cannot mean for me to be a gift to the Odelland king."

Aurilon bared her teeth.

"I cannot allow you to lead a raid on Canopy, whether by design or by accident, student of Loftfol."

"No longer a student. I killed my teacher. That is why they come for me!"

Odel's Bodyguard held out the bone coin.

"Take it," she said, "or stay below the barrier where you belong. You were right. I do feel a bond with you, Imeris, but I serve the Protector of Children."

Imeris took the coin with unsteady fingers. She turned it over in her hand. So innocent-seeming. Like the effigy of Orin in the archery practice range at Loftfol. It seemed a clumsy straw thing, shaped by new students the same way the old students had shaped it, but what it really reflected was generational rage. This coin pretended to be a tiny thing of value, a wondrous instrument of magic; instead it represented all the cold, cruel indifference of Canopy to the lives of the less fortunate. Her fingers clenched around it, and she suppressed the urge to throw it away.

"I could share it with the ones who pursue me," Imeris said suddenly, savagely. "I could mark them all. Gently, you said, but over time, more powerful. We would have time to raze your Temple! Would that surprise you, Aurilon?"

"Yes," Aurilon said without blinking. "I would be surprised. But you would not do it, and if you did, I would kill you. The dead make poor pupils. Besides, I know truth when I hear it, and when you said the words *I could*, I heard *I could never* beneath them."

Aurilon tipped herself upright in her harness and shimmied up the rope, arcane aura permitting her through the invisible barrier that was solid as stone to Imeris, leaving the ex-student alone with a racing heart and jumbled thoughts.

My master cannot free slaves that are not his own.

She tried to remember what Anahah had said, how he had explained the process of his marking, but tiredness warred with urgency and everything was a fog. Had Anahah specified which sigil was to be used, or how he had gained authority to use it? Was it stolen and copied, the way that Anahah's different animal forms were stolen and copied? Had a slave died in the marking and unmarking she'd endured?

Once within those wards, you could not leave except by his orders.

Who would come to save her, if she branded herself this way? The Godfinder? Middle-Father? Leaper? None of them would be her owners. None of them would have the power to free her. All her confidence from the earlier episode was eroded.

"They will buy me somehow," Imeris whispered, and pressed the bone coin to her tongue. She might argue with her family constantly, but she knew she could rely on them. Canopian or Understorian, they were one.

It was agony, as it had been before.

How will my family know I am there?

She spat the coin into her palm and slipped it, slick with saliva, into her salt pouch. This time, when she raised her hand to the barrier, it passed through.

To a Canopian, it is only empty air.

Imeris glanced down. She couldn't yet see the scouts she knew were in her wake. Her breath tasted suddenly foul. She panted with hope and with fear; she drove her spines into Odel's emergent to continue climbing and wondered if someone would come to save her before her spines were snapped off and cast away.

My wings. Youngest-Father's beautiful wings, from the skin of the chimera who saved my life.

She would never be allowed to keep them. They were hundreds of times more valuable than a slave. Only a king could buy them back for her. It would be better to hide them somewhere.

Odel could use them to buy me back and then free me.

She looked up and saw Odel's Temple, tail of the leaping fish and the highest branches of the emergent licked by the lemon light of sunrise. Would Aurilon hide the wings for her in the secret room? Or perhaps stored with the skin of that other chimera, the one that had killed Odel's previous incarnation?

As if the marking on her tongue was sensitive to her plans to divert and delay its demands, the urge to find the palace rose irresistibly up in Imeris like the urge to vomit.

She ran out along one branch until it crossed another, then ran back towards the entry to the Temple.

Aurilon wasn't inside. Or if she was, she was by the side of the sleeping god below. Imeris started to go to the trapdoor, but the urge tugged at her again, more insistently.

There was no time.

No!

She couldn't just shed the glider onto the floor. Anyone could take it. The bronze scale armour was valuable, too, but replaceable. In desperation, she placed Youngest-Father's wings on the pile of tributes. He would understand. Even kill another chimera, take the curse onto himself, if that was what was required. He'd never sired his own offspring, but his dedication as a father was never in doubt.

Good-bye, Chimera-Mother. Forgive me, Youngest-Father. Better to give the skin to the god than allow the Odelland king to keep it.

"This tribute," she said with tears in her eyes, "is for a child whose name I do not know. She is like me. She has a warrior self." Imeris groped for more ways to describe the child she wished to protect, the one that Oldest-

Mother had told her was out there, in the forest somewhere. "She yearns for a quiet life. She has a Canopian self. She has an Understorian self. Even— even a chimera self."

Blurting her last words, Imeris obeyed the urge and turned, retching, both hands over her mouth. She walked with as much dignity as she could manage from the open door of the Temple. Obeying did not lessen the urge, but seemed to make it stronger. Trying to avoid a misstep that might force her to reveal her unbroken spines, she descended the winding staircase and stepped out along the branch road that led to the king's palace.

It lay to the southwest, lower down in Canopy. Imeris kept her eyes downcast, still fighting the urge to vomit. She watched her feet, the feet of passing strangers, and the road. Her boots were given a blue cast by Airak's lanterns.

Each time she saw a blue quandong branch road, Imeris glanced up to check the signposts; she knew the palace was in one, and she knew blue quandong in Understorey by its hard, grey, moss-blotched bark. Blue quandong in Canopy meant something else; it meant javelin-bladed emerald foliage with scarlet leaves interspersed with green and brilliant blue fruit swollen to ripeness by the rain. The sun rose higher and the nausea grew more powerful, and still none of the signposts were marked with the king's toucan crest.

And then they were.

Imeris sobbed with relief as she made the turning, cheeks wet and tongue burning. The road, widening all the time, had deep parallel ruts from the passage of barrows, and at the end of it the palace filled the quandong crown like an overweight ibis balanced in a sapling. Humankind made two types of dwelling in the arms of the forest; one was hollowed from and yet considerate of the great trees; the other was tacked on to the outside to boast mastery over branches. This palace was the second sort. To Imeris's eyes, it was a larger and even more immodest version of a Headman's house in Understorey.

The road ran between paired, thatched wooden guardhouses connected by iron gates. It broadened again on the other side of the gates, forming a north-facing forecourt-cum-practice yard, which currently milled with soldiers.

A stream ran over the road between practice yard and palace, with a low-ered drawbridge across it. Then the branch road disappeared into the palace, a tall building of stacked red-and-white timbers. Its symmetrical towers and main hold were crowned with pointed roofs thatched with grey windgrass. The place where the branch road connected to the tree was hidden in the heart of the palace.

Sweet-smelling smoke belched from every window, keeping the royal dwelling insect-free. The thatch was fresh and sweet-smelling, too. How could it stay so clean, the seat of a lineage so stained with blood?

Imeris looked for the west-facing window that had belonged to a long-dead princess. It was the nephew of that murderous princess who now ruled Odelland.

That nephew was also Middle-Mother's nephew. Sawas was Oldest-Mother's unwanted child by the old king.

Middle-Mother, was the thought Imeris clung to as another wave of nausea doubled her over. *Middle-Mother is descended from the royal family of Odelland. If she is, then my sister and brother are, too. They can free me. They own me!*

Soldiers in Odelland's pale orange tunics and short, bloodred skirts caught her as she stumbled towards the guardhouse. She stuck her tongue out for them to see, and they cracked the iron gate open for her to pass, pushing her roughly through.

She didn't care what the commotion in the practice yard was. More and more soldiers seemed to be emerging from the thatched barracks building to the west. There, the stream that ran by the palace entry fell off the edge of the yard. Soldiers rinsed their mouths, scrubbed their hair, and pulled on armour by the edge of the stream.

They had different armour—lighter, layered, and lacquered—to the armour of some other soldiers, who made loud demands in the yard. Those soldiers wore solid ebony plate edged with silver and studded with black glass.

Soldiers from Airakland.

Imeris dragged her hands away from her mouth and pressed them over her ears. It didn't matter what they were saying. The turmoil was none of her doing. She had to climb inside the wards around the palace before the sickness of being newly marked made her insensible.

One of the black-clad soldiers, an officer by the raven's feathers in his hair, pointed straight at her.

Imeris lowered her eyes and stumbled on.

Of course I look odd. Out of place. There is another entrance. A slave's entrance. Walking over the drawbridge like an honoured guest is not for scum like me, but what can I do?

Both kinds of fighting men crowded around something that was in the officer's hand. They looked at it. Then they crowded around Imeris.

"This is the one!" somebody boomed. A hand caught her wrist. Bodies pressed against her.

"'Ware the unbroken spines," somebody else shouted, and her other wrist was seized. Her arms were pulled wide apart. She needed air. She couldn't breathe. Her tongue was swelling.

Choking her.

"There is no mistake," the officer growled, waving the thing in his hand in front of Imeris's face just as the sun speared through the branches and blinded her.

I can let the darkness take me, I suppose. She closed her eyes. Consciousness slipped from her grasp. *Surely someone will carry me inside before I die.*

NINETEEN

IMERIS OPENED her eyes to blue sky through the quandong crown overhead.

She was still in the forecourt.

The drive to move, to find the palace, was gone, and she was able to conceive the thought *I have been seen by hundreds of people.*

Loftfol will hear from their enslaved ex-students that I am here. One Forest has spies in Canopy also. Kirrik will know that I am here. Neither can pass through the barrier, but both can call on their agents to act. I have to hide. I have to get out of sight.

A neat-bearded man in a tall cylindrical hat crouched by her side. He wore loose silk robes patterned with a repeating toucan-pair motif, in colours that were nearly but not quite Odel's, as was custom in Odelland. He took his broad, dark brown hand away from her chin. She felt her tongue. The slave's mark was gone. He had used magic on her.

"Who are you?" she asked faintly.

"One who walks in the grace of Odel attends the court as king's vizier. I am Ubehailis of the House of Ikkased, once a Servant of Odel. Nobody here knows you, slave, but the Hunt has been declared by the king of Airakland. The device points to the heart that beats beneath your weak woman's breast, and by our law, you're to be freed from the palace and given over to serve." He shook his head, whether in dismay or puzzlement, Imeris couldn't be sure.

She sat up, the scales of her armour clinking. Beside the vizier stood a wrinkled, white-haired man. He wore metal-studded leather over rainbow-hued tunic and short skirt, and he could have been Middle-Mother's brother; he had the same wide mouth, bright gap-filled teeth and crease-cornered, amused-seeming brown eyes. His were sunken with age, though.

Soldiers of both coloured cloths whispered behind their hands. The scowling officer with the raven feathers shook the device as if he could force it to give a different answer.

"Aurilon," Imeris said woozily. "Aurilon is the greatest hunter in Odelland."

"Apparently not," the Airakland officer said, still scowling.

I am free again, Imeris thought. *The mark is gone, and yet again my slavery has not lasted an hour.* She felt humbled. Wretchedly relieved. It was hard to concentrate on what the soldiers around her were saying.

"Kill her," the vizier suggested, "and the device will point out another, sure enough."

That got her attention.

"You should be content," the king said sternly to his adviser, "that Aurilon is not called to the Hunt. Odel's safety is imperative."

"I'm not sure how it works, Warmed One," the officer admitted to the vizier. "It might choose another, or it might simply leave us one person short of a hunting party."

"You will be one short in any case," the vizier said, straightening to his full height, pulling Imeris up after him. Their eyes were level. "Orinland will surely not supply a man to destroy the horror that its mistress has created."

"Perhaps not," the officer said with a crooked half smile. "We go next, and lastly, to Orinland." He bowed deeply before the king, an unnecessary courtesy to a monarch not his own. "We thank you for discharging this obligation in such a timely manner, your majesty of Odelland. May the thirteen protect you."

The Odelland king inclined his head. He withdrew in a stately fashion across the drawbridge into the palace, his vizier and several soldiers by his side.

"What are you called, slave?" the Airakland officer asked. He put the device away in a leather satchel, removed and unrolled a parchment, and waited, poised with a stick of charcoal, to record her name for posterity.

Only then did Imeris feel nausea returning, deeper than the relief that she'd escaped whatever fate waited for her within the walls of the palace of the king of Odelland.

I am to kill a chimera, after all. I am to join the Hunt and track a demon through Canopy.

She made a decision quickly.

If am to kill my fourth mother, I will do it swiftly and with dignity. I will take these other Hunters for the teachers that Loftfol will no longer supply me, and in the meantime, surrounded by the greatest fighters in all of Canopy, I will be safe from both Loftfol and Kirrik. There will be time to think. Time to plan my reconciliation with the school. They must listen to me. I am not the enemy. The sorceress is. She threw her shoulders back. Stood tall.

And I will teach these Canopians a thing or two, no doubt.

"I am—" Abruptly, words failed her.

Was she Imerissiremi, of the wilds near Gannak, or was she Imeris of Audblayinland? Was she Issi, daughter of Marram, Heightsman of Loftfol, or a nameless fallen child returned to win honours in the city of her birth?

"Yes?" the officer said impatiently.

"I am Imeris," she said simply. She'd chosen. The Canopian form of her name. It didn't sound the same forwards and back, was not auspicious for travelling in both directions. The officer scribbled it down on the parchment.

"Really?" a man's voice boomed. "You are named after a children's story about a giant silkworm?" He guffawed. The sound of Gannak was in his speech. A white-skinned, bare-chested brute pushed through the black-clad, black-skinned soldiers. Imeris looked up into an unfamiliar blue-eyed face even as she instinctively shifted her weight and edged back, making room for combat.

The brute had snapped-off spines: definitely a slave. He had a kite-shaped head with a short, heavy jaw, high forehead, and bow-shaped mouth. Thin, tented brows quirked as he turned side-on to her, matching her aggressive stance. Both hands went up and over his shoulder, hovering near the hilt of the longest sword Imeris had ever seen. Leather strips between his massive shoulder blades held back his long, straight, black hair.

"Who are you?" Imeris asked, feeling her spines in their sheaths. If he drew that beast of a weapon, she'd be out of his way before the blow could land, adding his blood to Horroh's in her spine's serrations before he could swing again.

"These are your fellow Hunters," the Airakland officer said in a bored voice, tucking the parchment away. Imeris's quick glances revealed even more non-black-uniformed types oozing to the fore. "I'm Captain Oniwak of Airakland, leader of the Hunt." He slapped the back of a thin, hungry-looking fighter in red and grey with a shaved head and prominent canine teeth. "I've named this man my second, to take the lead in the event of my death, but I doubt the Hunt will last long. He is Eeriez of Eshland. You'll want to seek the company of your own kind, though. Your fellow slave is Daggad, a fighting captive Understorian chosen by the device from the niche of Audblayinland. He remains the property of one of their merchants. The House of Epatut has no wards, and so it wasn't necessary to free him."

The brute lowered his hands and put out his tongue. Imeris eyed the loom symbol burnt into the wet pink flesh. He waggled it suggestively before he put it back in his head.

"He," Imeris said, relaxing her stance, "is not my own kind."

Daggad's enormous fists went to his hips. There, hung over the short skirt and leather loincloth, he carried a round shield with a cloth-wrapped bundle stuffed into the back of it. His studded sandals looked expensive. Ugly red scars crisscrossed his fishmeat skin. He was perhaps twenty years older than she was, a survivor of many battles.

"Maybe we do not look alike, little sister," he said, "but you talk like a child of the dark. 'Ow else did such a sweet citizen's face get a slave's song stuck down 'er throat?"

"Later," Captain Oniwak barked. "Fall in, Daggad. Proper introductions come later, at the monument tree. There, the full company will receive detailed instructions on the boundaries of our mission. For now, if we march all day, we can be at the border of Orinland by nightfall."

"I am in no 'urry to confront the Queen of Birds," Daggad drawled, but he moved into the double line that the black-clad Airakland soldiers began forming. Imeris joined the line by the side of the Eshland Hunter, Eeriez. They linked arms at the elbow; the intent was to balance one another while running along thin branches, weapons drawn on either side in case of aerial attack.

She did it casually, as though she'd been trained in a Canopian barracks and not overheard Loftfol teachers speaking of how to counter Canopian tactics. The pair in front of her were not soldiers and didn't manage so easily. One wore the foot-tangling sky-blue and storm-black robes of a Servant of the rain goddess. The other was a mere child, dirty-soled, dressed in a pauper's drawstring trousers and woven bark shirt.

"We aren't going to confront the goddess, but to claim the thirteenth member owed to us by ancient accord," Oniwak corrected Daggad, adjusting the crossbow slung over his shoulder.

But the little boy whispered to the richly robed Servant, "Lakekeeper, when Orin hears that we mean to murder her pet beast, won't she be angry? Maybe unleash it upon us?"

"Maybe," the Lakekeeper whispered back kindly. Beneath his jewelled and heavily embroidered costume, he had broad shoulders and a thick neck, but no weapons visible on his person. "If she does summon it to us, the Hunt will be over very quickly. Oniwak is very good with that crossbow. You'll have wealth and fame without ever having lifted a hand."

And Imeris thought, *Orin's pet beast? I thought we were hunting a demon.*

Besides, there was no way, short of growing eagle's wings and flying, that they could reach the palace of Orinland before dark.

THEY SET off, trotting along high roads cleared by the captain's omnipresent scowl.

Every two hours, the twelve Hunters and their escort of Airakland soldiers stopped at the edge of public markets to rest, share marching rations, and drink; a gourd-flask was passed around by a stumpy, bearded old man with a strange parchment stole covered in inked symbols hanging around his neck.

"Are you a Servant to a deity?" Imeris asked the first time, taking a sip from the gourd when he insisted. It tasted of nothing. She held up the gourd, puzzled, weighing it with her hand, feeling the heft and the slosh of liquid inside.

She tried to take another sip. More nothing. She'd made the motions of swallowing but couldn't tell if she'd gotten any of the drink. The stumpy little man smiled impishly at her confusion.

How she hated magic.

"That'll suffice," he said. "It's the potion of the winds. One who walks in the grace of Ulellin is no Servant, but it's from Ulellin's Temple that one acquired this rather valuable magically enhanced concoction. Speed can be advantageous in a hunt, wouldn't you agree?"

Imeris stared after him as he took the gourd to the next member of the party. She licked her lips, trying to taste the so-called potion.

When she rose from her crouch to continue the march, her limbs jangled oddly. Her whole body felt lighter. Heat burned in her joints. The world seemed brighter, her vision less colourful yet keener.

She linked arms with Eeriez and they did not run, but raced. Wind whipped past her as though she guided a glider. The giant slave, Daggad, moved to the front of the column. He kept up a warning bellow that barely reached the ears of citizens ahead of the river-quick party.

"Make way for the Hunt!"

When their pace slowed, breath threatening to burst Imeris's armour-constricted chest and pinpricks of light exploding around her, they stopped for a rest and another sip of the intangible potion before hurtling onwards to Orinland. In fact, it seemed to work better each time.

"We're getting closer to Ulellinland," the old man with the parchment stole told Imeris when she remarked on it. "Some deities' magic won't work at all outside their niche, but all of them are strongest in the seat of their own power. Our friend there, the Lakekeeper, could drown you in a deluge by his mistress's lake. Here, he can't even fill a cup with water." The Lakekeeper didn't look up from his seat on a kink in the branch two paces away, where he tended a blistered toe, but a rustle of his silks told Imeris he was listening. "We have a black-robed Servant of Atwith in our Hunting party also, though his death-touch here is but a tickle." Imeris looked for the Servant and found him, folded patiently in on himself at a platform's edge. "Yet the wind does not stop at the borders of Ulellinland, and if Esh could not shape wood outside his own domain, how would we live?"

Eeriez, the Eshland Hunter, broke into a toothy grin. He, too, lingered only a few paces away, but his teeth and the whites of his eyes were all that Imeris could see of him; he'd subtly arranged himself by a piece of bark which matched the colours and textures of his tunic and armour, assuming a petrified stillness that had made her forget he was there.

I can see why he was chosen, she thought.

Abandoning doubts that her own selection had been a mistake, she wondered which qualities she owned that made her suited, in this case, to victory. *What kind of "pet beast" has Orin set against us, and why?*

"It would help if I knew what we were hunting," she said to Captain Oniwak. "What to look for."

"When we have our thirteenth, woman," Oniwak said, turning away.

"When he came to our bakery," the ragged boy confided in Imeris, "he shouted at my mother. No good reason. In the middle of the night, he shouted at a stranger that she was stopping me from being a soldier. As if I ever wanted to be a soldier! Would've broken his filthy fingers where they grabbed me. But mother's mouth was all sucked in the way which means she's too proud of me to speak. So Irof smile on me, I'll make her even prouder."

They set off again.

Orinland felt at once wilder and quieter than Odelland. Imeris saw no written signs or splashed deity's colours, but pedestrians' clothing changed from light, bold, and ornamented silks and seed-wool to dun-coloured linen and leather. Instead of grass screens and smoke guarding entrances to homes, Imeris observed glass or horn windows and metal grates. Washed clothes fluttering at the sills of open windows vanished in favour of closed-in, guarded, gourd-shaped market-hollows, workshops, and schools.

Those on the roads spoke softly to one another behind raised hands.

Imeris remembered hamstringing a man on the low roads of Orinland. He and his four companions were around here somewhere. And Horroh's blood was on her spines.

Are you proud of me, Oldest-Father? She shivered as she ran, though Canopy was warm and she was covered in a sheen of sweat. *Will your memory rest when I have killed Orin's beast with these others? Will I not have done better than any son? Will my work finally be done?*

She knew it would not be. Not until Kirrik was gone from the forest for good.

TWENTY

THE PALACE of the king of Orinland filled the crown of a firewheel tree.

It was easily five times the size of the palace of the king of Odelland. No part of it was crafted by human hands. Not a timber was sawn; not a nail marred the hard, pale bark of the firewheel tree. It appeared as if the tree had simply chosen to split and grow in the form of five grey, identical, parallel towers. Fallen autumn leaves of previous years provided mulch for flat roofs fragrant with blue-flowered flax. Over all five towers spread a second roof of glossy, dark green firewheel leaves and flowers like flaming red wheel spokes in palm-sized circles, yellow-hearted and with the tip of each spoke graced by a tiny golden sphere.

The façade of each tower crawled with realistic, high-relief representations of battling birds and beasts. Somewhere out of sight, screw-pumps must have turned by magic or the sweat of slaves; fountains frothed from the mouths of the wooden birds and animals, falling into a perfectly circular lake that ringed the tree in a level forty body lengths below.

A huge processional road ran from the front of the palace towards Orin's emergent, five hundred paces distant in a dimly glimpsed waratah tree. The road was twenty paces wide, the biggest that Imeris had seen.

The old man with the parchment stole saw her looking.

"The king pays his respects at the Temple of Orin often," he said. "The goddess, when she comes to bless the royal family or to watch the Games, travels along this road in a jaguar-drawn chariot."

The little boy in the bark shirt sniffed.

"In Irofland, our high-ups have better things to do than praise each other in public and give out purses to naked, fake men in fancy poses."

"This palace," Imeris said, ignoring the boy, "must have been built by Esh." She glanced at Eeriez, who said nothing. "In Audblayinland, they mock the wood god for having neither Servants nor proper Temple, for wandering mute and friendless. I have seen Audblayin's Garden Gate, which depicts with some skill historical instances of its defence. I never could have imagined anything like this, and this must be nothing compared to the palace in the labyrinth of the king of Eshland."

"Bet there's people starving here," the boy muttered. "Take care of us, our high-ups do, not just themselves."

"We passed through the labyrinth of the king of Eshland," murmured a middle-sized, crop-haired Hunter, "on our way to fetch Eeriez. They have no soldiers, it's said, but Eeriez was in there selling skins. I would rather hunt a hundred beasts than die in that place." The neck of the fiddle he carried ended in a roaring bear's head, and the back of the instrument was carved with swarms of bees. Imeris supposed he hailed from Ukakland. If he had any weapons to hand, they were well hidden in his silks, or perhaps in the leather case across his back.

A young woman in a brown shirt and trousers and a crimson cloak, carrying a lyre, approached Captain Oniwak and asked him if he'd like her to sing him the songs of the beasts portrayed on the palace walls. He waved her impatiently away.

"It's a common misconception," the old man with the parchment stole told Imeris, "that Audblayin and Atwith are the mother and father of this Titan's Forest. Birth and death are the moments when life is weakest. Orin and Esh represent animal life in its prime and tree life at its greatest strength. Orin and Esh are the true mother and father of Canopy. That's why we find Ilanland between Orinland and Eshland. Justice must always temper strength. The Hunt can't be called against the innocent. It can only be called after a demon draws human blood."

The boy sniffed again. "Just ignore old Ingaget's teacher talk, slave. He'll fill your head with dung when what you need is hunting smarts."

The old man, Ingaget, clapped his hand on the hilt of a short sword hanging from a belt at his waist.

"Don't I have hunting smarts, whelp?"

A small, sharp, steel dagger appeared in the boy's grip by impressive sleight of hand.

"Fall in!" Captain Oniwak barked, and both child and elder put their weapons away. Imeris linked arms again with the Eshland Hunter, guarding the left side of the column as they progressed down the processional road, ready to slash wide at a moment's notice with the spines of her left forearm.

For the cavernous mouth of the central tower offered no hospitality. It presented only the open jaws of wooden serpents, wasting jets of water in wide, decorative arcs. This extravagance, outside of monsoon season, boasted of power and excess. Imeris stepped over a line of regularly spaced holes bored knee-deep into the wooden floor.

Deeper inside the cave-like entrance, a pair of inner doors covered in carved demons, everything from fiveways to chimeras in the act of terrorising wide-eyed humans, remained resolutely shut. Again, nobody appeared to receive them, or even to turn them away.

"This is an insult, Captain," Eeriez called to Oniwak at the head of the halted column. His voice echoed.

"I have a mandate," Oniwak replied, leaving his crossbow in place but removing the artefact of Ilanland from his satchel. He bent his head to study it. "The compass points deeper inside this tower."

"Many women and men have met their deaths here," the Servant of Atwith said softly from his place at the front beside Oniwak. Imeris hardly heard him. In the dim light, she'd noticed wooden gratings at ground level all around them.

Maybe the gratings were for ventilation. If so, why were they large enough to admit a person? Surely that was a flaw in the tower's defences.

Then she saw a pair of animal eyes glittering in one of them.

"Retreat," she cried, extruding her spines, "or be trapped here with wild animals."

Instead of ordering the withdrawal, Oniwak clapped his hands over his ears.

"Slave," he hissed. "Silence your shrill woman's voice."

Imeris could have gone by herself, saved herself. She didn't owe them anything. Their silly Hunt was for fools. Yet she had been chosen. A thing of the gods had sought her out. She must meet whatever fate it promised her.

I am one of them.

In the gratings, the points of wooden stakes withdrew silently into the walls, as if the palace yawned with two dozen deadly mouths. In the high archway behind the Hunters, sharpened logs thundered from the fountain-edged opening down into the hollows that Imeris had stepped over, caging them in the confined space.

"As you wish," she said to Oniwak, furious. "I will be silent."

A slat-ribbed tree bear, as tall at the shoulder as Imeris was, emerged first. Its black-and-yellow face was scarred, long lips drooping, black nose twitching. Imeris had never known a tree bear to attack a man except in self-defence. Their teeth were for grinding tough shoots and cracking beehives, their claws for opening wood and bark in search of grubs.

This one swung a paw at the Servant of Atwith, knocking him down. The column of Hunters and soldiers closed into a circle with bear and Servant at its heart. Imeris saw, in the corner of her eye, Oniwak putting a crossbow bolt between the bear's ribs.

Then she was in the outer ring, staring into the face of an approaching, half-starved jaguar. Beside her, the fiddler made no move to abandon the musical instrument and draw weapons. Instead, he set bow to strings, eliciting a low hum reminiscent of a hive of bees, and out of the curling holes in the soundboard came the very insects depicted on the back, making for the black viper emerging at the jaguar's heels.

Magic, again, but this time on her side.

"Towards the fountainheads," Oniwak ordered, and the circle, fending off bears, cats, and raptors as it moved, crept back towards the archway where the regularly spaced logs blocked the way. Stripes of light showed more and more animals coming through the open tunnels. Crocodiles. Yellow-furred apes. Smaller, grey tree bears. Flightless birds with bladed heads and taloned toes. Beasts like the goats she'd seen in the Garden but with horns as long as swords.

Imeris could focus only on the creature closest to her.

Mostly jaguars, Anahah had said. *To kill by swift ambush and a bite right through the assassin's skull.*

Imeris ducked as the animal sprang at her. Front legs enfolded her. Front claws tried to shred her shoulders, hind claws her abdomen, carving her bronze scales instead. Imeris allowed its weight to collapse them both. Rolling backwards beneath it, forearms raised, she couldn't cut upwards, because her spines were blunt on their distant edges, but when she pulled her spines back down towards her chest, they opened both of the jaguar's carotid arteries and made parallel splits down either side of its rib cage. It felt like killing Horroh all over again.

Imeris lay under it, stifling a sob, washed with blood, waiting for it to die. She heard the sounds of an axe biting into wood. When the jaguar gurgled its last and shuddered to stillness, she heaved it off her and saw that the disciplined circle had broken apart. Amidst the chaos, the Hunter from Ilanland, wearing purple-stained, iron-studded leather armour, had chopped handholds in one of the logs with a double-bladed axe not designed to be used on wood. As Imeris scrambled to her feet to face the next frenzied animal, a kind of hard-hoofed tapir with tusks, the black-skinned Hunter returned his axe to its loop and seized the log, lifting.

The pair of them, Hunter from Ilanland and Daggad the white-skinned slave, were matched in hulking size and strength. After a long moment of struggling and swearing, they heaved the log by its fresh-cut handholds, out of the hole that had received it, high enough for a human to escape through.

"Send Ibbin through to scout the surrounds," Captain Oniwak bellowed. The boy in the bark shirt pulled his dagger from the white breast of a harpy eagle and looked up towards the light. The bird's talons had scored his hands and face, barely missing an eye. Before he could obey and tumble towards the hole, the old man, Ingaget, garbled some objection and pushed his way ahead of the child.

"Soldiers," Daggad panted in explanation. "Orinland soldiers waitin' out there."

Oniwak ordered the Airakland soldiers to go after the old man. Oniwak put a bolt through the neck of the tusked creature as it charged Imeris. She dodged it as it rushed anyway, hoping it would go down, but she was forced to draw her short sword at the last, slashing at its face to keep it back while it bled out. She glanced at the hole to see how many of her allies were out into the open and how many there were still to go.

"You'll go last, coward," Oniwak shouted at her. Imeris cut the head off a constrictor that struck at him while he reloaded his crossbow. The impact jarred both her shoulders in their sockets. He gave her no thanks, but turned to fire at another tree bear.

The bolt missed. Imeris's sword was too short for her to want to close with the heavy, thick-furred, long-armed animal. She danced around it, trying to confuse it, trying to give Oniwak time to reload, but he was gone through the opening.

Imeris was the only one remaining in the dim space.

"Out, woman," Daggad cried, his arms straining and the sweat standing out on every inch of him. "Go!"

"How will you follow?" Imeris demanded, sheathing her sword and lunging for the sunlit gap. Blinking in the brightness outside, she was forced to duck by the swinging blade of a curved spear wielded by one of her companions. Hunters fought the crimson and brown-clad soldiers of Orinland on the grand Temple road.

Behind her, the log thudded back into place. Daggad and the Hunter from Ilanland were trapped inside.

Imeris used her spines to scale the archway, sinking them deep into the water-spouting serpent heads. At the apex, the log that the two men had lifted emerged from beneath the most ferocious-fanged gargoyle of all.

Hanging from her left forearm and shin, Imeris drew her short sword again, hacking at the serpent head. Chips flew, and the lifelike sculpture shuddered, until it was weakened enough that the pressure of the flowing water came to her aid, blasting the head away and sending a much wider, forceful jet over the soldiers fighting on the road below.

Imeris kept on cutting, towards the socket where the log was held. Her sword was blunt, ruined for flesh. Her right arm ached. Below, six or seven of Orin's soldiers seized the Servant of Atwith and tossed him off the edge of the road, down to die in darkness.

Captain Oniwak had been afraid their Hunt would have to do with only twelve. Thanks to their hostile reception in Orinland, they were down to eleven before they'd begun. Nine, if the two trapped in the cavern were torn apart by animals before Imeris could set them free. A crossbow bolt splintered the wood a pace away from her, but she couldn't spare any energy to seek the shooter.

"I'll help," Eeriez said, quick grin flashing his pointed canine teeth. He'd climbed up carefully on the other side of the arch, carrying the axe. The Ilanlander must have passed it to him through the gap between logs. "Hold this for a moment."

Imeris put her sword away. She took the axe, drawing it through the erupting water that separated Eeriez from her, almost losing her grip on it. It was heavy. Too heavy for her to swing. Eeriez roped himself swiftly to one of the other serpent heads.

When he took the axe back from her, he had both hands free and room to swing it. Each blow drove deep towards the log-trap's housing, and when he split the socket, the log toppled with a groan, pushed by the water towards the battling Hunters and soldiers.

Eeriez didn't pause to untie the ropes. He cut himself free using the reversed axe-blade. The weapon clattered down onto the road only slightly ahead of Daggad and the axe's owner. They emerged, bloodied but not limping, into the melee, with half a dozen animals at their heels.

"Form up," Captain Oniwak screamed from somewhere in the midst of the fighting. Imeris slipped down from her perch to join a double column, her right elbow linked with Eeriez's left. She couldn't effectively use her sword to attack with her nondominant hand, and it was too blunt to be much use, anyway, but by holding it reversed, so that it lay along her sheathed spines, she was able to block steel blows that came driving towards her. The animals were fighting each other, or fleeing. "Proceed to alternate road!"

Imeris understood his aims. The traditional method of retreat while in the double-column was to leave the front pair fending off the enemy while the rest shuffled back and then, when that pair became exhausted, for them to dash back and absorb themselves in the back of the column while the next pair took their turn. That would only work on a branch road that was one or two men wide, however.

Defending themselves desperately, like a spider surrounded by ants, the Hunters and their escort of Airakland soldiers inched towards a smaller path leading off the processional highway.

TWENTY-ONE

ORIN'S BEASTS and her king's men harried the Hunters all through the night, to the border of Orinland and Ilanland.

Imeris's whole body deflated and swayed with each drawn-out exhalation. She'd changed sides with Eeriez countless times to try to rest her left arm and Eeriez's right hand, which wielded poisoned knives. He'd almost cut her five times, and she'd twice torn his tunic sleeve with a careless swipe of her spines.

This cannot go on.

Owls came, talons first, towards her eyes. Imeris sheared off a slew of flight feathers, and the birds spun away.

I should climb down into Understorey.

Snakes tried to coil around her legs. Her shin spines went through them as they tightened their grip, and bloody cubes of dead meat fell.

Orin cannot touch me there. I will go home. I will tell them I have fled the Hunt.

Eeriez pulled her down, saving her from a sword swing. She sank her spines into the trunk of a purpleheart tree, saving both of them from a fall.

I will tell them I have fled Loftfol. That students may be searching for them to kill Middle-Father and Youngest-Father. That Loftfol will never accept that Oldest-Father died trying to rid Understorey of the sorceress. She kept some of their students asleep in her lair for years, until their families gave up hope of finding them. They should hunt her themselves.

She managed to get up again, to continue down the branch path, but one of Airak's lanterns seemed to leap up and catch her feet. Her hands and knees landed hard against the path again. Eeriez crouched beside her, his face a mask of blood turned tarry by blue lantern light. Daggad's shield moved over them, appearing from nowhere, protecting her or perhaps

Eeriez from the driving arc of a thrown javelin. It bounced away, bound for Understorey.

Imeris smelled overpowering incense.

A woman's commanding voice rang out between the trees.

"Stop!"

Imeris struggled to rise and could not. She didn't recognise the voice. It spoke again, louder.

"Back to Orinland, soldiers of the Untamed King. Your Mistress of the Wilds does not rule here."

Sounds of clashing weapons slowed and ceased. Owls departed on silent wings. Snakes slithered away. Imeris stayed kneeling on the purpleheart branch road, gasping for breath. Daggad's shield hovered above her.

"Holy One," came a man's gruff shout in reply. "These intruders attacked the palace in Orinland. This is justice, Holy One."

"Don't dare to tell me what is and isn't justice." Fury filled the voice this time. "Justice is my domain. Return to your own niche at once before I stop all your hearts as justice for one man's insolence. Go!"

Imeris sank further into a graceless sprawl on the edge of the branch road, raising her eyes to the sight of a short, slender woman of maybe thirty monsoons, wearing a purple silk tunic and long skirt painted to look like the armour of a king. Her hair made a black halo around her head.

"Ilan," Daggad said stupidly, lowering his shield. Crimson and brown-clad Orinland warriors retreated in the direction from which they'd come.

"Can she do that?" Imeris asked Eeriez softly. "Stop the hearts of thirty men?"

"She can do anything," Eeriez whispered, shrugging, "so long as she believes justice is served. Bring the dead back to life, I've heard, if they haven't been reborn already."

"Of those who are called to the Hunt," Ilan intoned, and Imeris struggled to remain alert, "which of you represents Ilanland?"

"I do, Holy One," said the blood-smeared soldier with the double-headed axe, picking his way along the path towards her through his wounded and drained fellows. An even bigger man, who must have been Ilan's Bodyguard, blocked his approach, and the Hunter sank to his knees, bowing his head instead. "My name is Erth."

"Erth," Ilan said, "I charge you to keep your company out of Orinland. Clearly, you aren't welcome in that niche."

"That's no surprise, Holy One," Erth said. "It's Orin who unleashed the creature we hunt. Made it from bodies of her own Servants, they say, shaped to look like a panther with the head of a boar. She made it to sniff out and rip apart her one-time Bodyguard, a man called Anahah."

Imeris couldn't control the tremor of powerful, unspecified emotion that coursed through her. The body of a panther. The head of a boar.

Anahah. Green-skinned chimera-child. Where will you hide? Who will shelter you?

"Tell me more, Hunter Erth." The goddess Ilan sounded surprised and displeased.

"As you wish, Holy One. The Queen of Birds and Beasts is so consumed by rage that she doesn't care who else is killed by getting in the creature's way. Reports say it killed an old woman, a crafter of wooden clocks, in Eshland. She lived not far from Esh's emergent. The god, nettled by the beast's intrusion, caused a bloodwood tree to cage the giant creature. The creature came apart into many smaller pieces and was able to escape."

"Esh could not capture it, you say." Ilan's eyes narrowed.

It comes apart, Imeris thought dazedly. *It cannot be caged.*

"Holy One, it was the king of Airakland who called the Hunt. The creature came to Airak's niche not two days after killing the clockmaker. It may have killed an innkeeper in Ehkisland along the way. In Airakland it killed a farmer and fivescore flowerfowl."

"How do you mortals hope to proceed?" Ilan sounded incredulous. "Wouldn't it be better for this matter to be resolved by diplomacy, among deities? It sounds as if only Orin can choose to end the beast's rampage. Perhaps you should help it by searching out this Anahah, the sooner that the creature may be unmade."

Imeris put her fingers to her mouth. Captain Oniwak came forwards, crossbow dragging awkwardly behind him, to kneel beside Erth.

"Holy One," he said, "you've seen how open Orin is to diplomacy at this time. Her disregard for casualties has raised Airak's ire. Once the Hunt is called, it can't be called off, as you know. We mortals hope to proceed by showing faith in the Hunt's compass, ourselves, and your power and grace." He dug in his leather satchel, holding up the device that had led him to Imeris. "The lightning god set us in motion, and we must follow the path to its end. The Hunt is complete only when we die or the creature is destroyed."

Ilan moved into her Bodyguard's lantern shadow, close enough to take the compass. She turned it over in her fingers.

"So," she said. "You'll take the list of names to the monument tree."

"That is my intention, Holy One," Oniwak said.

"I charge you, as I charged your companion Erth, to track and kill the beast only outside the borders of Orinland. If you agree, if you keep to the course of justice, which demands that a deity's demesne is respected, I'll be able to keep Orin's human and nonhuman allies from tracking and killing you."

"We would be grateful for such protection, Holy One."

"You'd best find shelter." The goddess of justice turned away, her Bodyguard by her side. The cloud of incense which had enveloped them faded, leaving the smell of insect-repelling smoke from some houses on the next tree.

"You heard her," Oniwak said, returning to the main cluster of Hunters and soldiers by the trunk of the purpleheart. "We'll find an inn. I'll see what I can find nearby, and if there's nothing, we'll have to evict some of these out-of-nichers from their hovels."

Daggad, Imeris, and the boy, Ibbin, watched him lope off along a branch road. Feeling no inclination whatsoever to evict anyone from any hovels, Imeris found a handful of leaves for cleaning her sword.

"Evict out-of-nichers?" the boy repeated incredulously. "In Irofland—"

"Spare us any more talk of Irofland," Daggad groaned, and Ibbin glared at him and slunk away.

"I am interested," Imeris called after him, "in Irofland."

"You should have heard Captain Oniwak when we went to Eshland," the fiddle player said. He stood behind them, and when Imeris turned, she found him turning a screw in the bow to loosen the tension on the dried, stretched tree bear tendons. "Insulting the god. Insulting the king. I thought he was going to start a war, just the two of us against the Thousand Wooden Soul-Eaters of Esh."

"There are no Thousand Wooden Soul-Eaters," Eeriez corrected him. "The king of Eshland relies on his labyrinth for protection. Speak only what you have seen, Servant of Ukak."

"Very well," the fiddler agreed, bemused, unlacing the leather case he'd had stowed across his back, which turned out to be empty. But his music and bees had served him well enough as a weapon, despite his being out of niche. "One who walks in the grace of Ukak saw not only the king of Eshland's labyrinth but also the hatred on Captain Oniwak's face as the device led us safely through it to the palace. What a shock to a man who walks in the grace of Ukak, one who cooperates in a kind and neighbourly fashion with his neighbours of Irofland, to hear Captain Oniwak brazenly brand his own neighbour's monarch a coward and a thief in his own halls."

"Irofland and Ukakland are indeed the best of neighbours, their deities the best of friends," advised Ingaget, the old man who had given them the potion of the winds, leaning wearily on the fiddler's shoulder, "but over the past hundred years, the niches of wood god and lightning god have fought intense, bloody battles."

"The Battle of the Labyrinth," murmured the adept from Ukakland, rubbing blood from the back of his bee-and-bear-carved fiddle with a square of felt. "I heard Captain Oniwak say his father fought there."

"And died there?" Imeris guessed, thinking with despair of how many inherited enmities swirled around her; it was a wonder the air wasn't thick enough to choke them all.

"No. Apparently he lost his sire when Understorians brought down the Temple of Airak." The fiddler's glance flicked briefly from Imeris to Daggad. "Many a wise, experienced commander was lost in that traitorous blow, sorely missed by junior recruits along the branch roads of Airakland. Captain Oniwak was the best of what they had left. He commands his own men well because his prejudices do not come into play." The fiddler stowed his now-full instrument case, with no need to finish his thought. Imeris could finish it for him: *Oniwak does not cooperate well with any but soldiers from his own niche.*

"You musta done somethin' amazin'," Daggad told Eeriez as Oniwak became distantly visible again, returning to the group, "to impress our Eshland-loathing captain. He picked you for his second."

"I stayed still," Eeriez said silkily.

"You stayed still." The fiddler chortled. "He couldn't see you. That little bone needle pointing right at you, and he couldn't see you. And then you saluted him and told him he had the look of an ancient, worthy foe, and all of a sudden, he desperately needed you at his right hand."

Daggad nudged Ingaget with his knee. "What about you, old man?

Any grudges I should know about? Any of your relatives killed off by Understorians?"

"None that I know of. Stop that. You'll bounce me off the branch, you exuberant man-child."

"What do you mean, none that you know of?"

"I was a Servant of Odel." The old man lifted his chin. He was still shorter than Daggad by a head. "Odel's Servants don't live in his Temple, mind. He sends them all over Canopy, to brighten the lives of children he knows will die, or to comfort the grieving left behind. I met a leaf cutter in Ulellinland whose child had fallen and comforted her rather more than either of us were expecting. It was all in the timing, see? Odel's Servants lose their magic powers when they grow too old. I felt myself released from Temple service, and happily remained with my leaf cutter in Ulellinland."

"You cannot 'ave been so old, if you were doin' all that comfortin'." Daggad made a crude gesture for crowd approval before turning away from Oniwak's approach. Ingaget was oblivious, gazing into the past with a brief, blissful smile.

"Her name was Ettuf. She became my wife. I became a teacher. She loved to harvest in the rain. She tempted the monsoon, and one day the winds took her. Understorey took her. Perhaps Floor did, too. Who can say whether my leaf cutter lived or died? Who can say whether her son, who fell before her, lived or died?"

"You could ask the wind goddess," the fiddler said wryly. He flicked his gaze at the flask on Ingaget's belt. "Her fortune-telling would've cost less than that priceless potion you share around with strangers."

"I don't really want to know." Ingaget rubbed his right eye with one blood-spattered fist. "They live merry and colourful lives in my head, in my sorry imagination. I'm certain they're dead, and yet. If I have enemies in the dark depths, I'd rather not know them."

"I have found a suitable inn," Oniwak announced, coming to a halt in front of them.

But Eeriez snored already in a heap by the side of the road, his back propped against the trunk of the tree. Daggad, sitting beside him, turned his shield so that he could stuff his bundle back inside. Then he held it, soft side upwards, and patted it like a pillow.

"This spot looks good," he said, picking flaking blood off his face and rummaging through the items on his belt for a water gourd, which turned out to be empty. "I vote we sleep 'ere."

"Take mine," the Lakekeeper said, offering his gourd to Daggad. He was already curled up with the boy, Ibbin, at Eeriez's other flank.

"We'll be murdered while we sleep," Oniwak growled. "Robbed at the very least." Imeris imagined she could still see the reflection of the comfortable and expensive inn in his eyes.

Daggad slaked his thirst and returned the water gourd to the Lakekeeper. He yawned.

"Dawn is almost 'ere. Oxor watches over us. Ilan as well." He beckoned to Imeris. "Turn your backta mine, woman, if you want it protected. Your virtue is all you 'ave got worth stealin'. That sword is the shoddiest work I 'ave seen. From Understorey, is it?"

Imeris told herself that the small rebellion against Oniwak's authority was enough to satisfy her; she did not need to rise to Daggad's taunts. She sank down beside the hulking slave, faster than intended as her muscles gave out.

"She's still got her spines," Oniwak snapped. "At the very least they should be broken before we let down our guard with her in our midst."

"Do not be more of a fool than the fool that led us inta Orin's trap, Oniwak," Daggad said. "Those spines helped get me outta the palace. We might need them again. Better than the sword, as I said."

Imeris wanted to cut Daggad for insulting her sword. She wanted to cut Oniwak for his contempt and mistrust. She wanted to send a message to Youngest-Father, to warn him that she'd angered Loftfol.

She had no way to reach him. Her armour was bent out of shape, and she removed the front and back pieces carefully. She wanted to sink into sweet oblivion, but just as her head came to rest on her bent arm, her eyes bulged and her mouth dropped open; the import of what Erth had said to Ilan struck her.

Orin's beast had killed a farmer in Airakland.

The Godfinder.

TWENTY-TWO

THE MONUMENT tree was a fig tree.

Its white arms contained a wide, clear lake. Its inner walls were magically inscribed with the names of Heroes, Minstrels, Games Winners, and Hunters. In the late afternoon, the surface of the lake was half deep shadow, half shimmering reflection of the stark black letters and silhouetted profiles of the noteworthy stamped into the pale bark.

Imeris's group of Hunters and soldiers slept by the purpleheart for four or five hours, then roused themselves to reach the monument tree before dark.

Two lanterns flanked the narrow approach to the lake. They were each as tall as Imeris, made of bronze and panes of glass, blue-lit by the grace of the lightning god. Children filed along the approach, jugs balanced on their heads, bringing water back to their homes for evening meals and washing. Fisherfolk paddled palm-frond rafts out into the centre of the lake and dipped baited wooden hooks on the end of strapleaf lines beneath afternoon-sun-warmed lilies.

Captain Oniwak took the parchment with all their names to the closest lantern. He hadn't crossed out Ootoo, the name of the Servant of Atwith who had died.

It was an Understorian name. Imeris wished she'd had a chance to speak to Ootoo before they'd reached the palace of the king of Orinland, but Oniwak had been in such a hurry.

"The Hunt is called," Oniwak said. He opened a pane on the side of the lantern and thrust the parchment into the crackling blue light, withdrawing his hand swiftly with a hiss of indrawn breath, slamming the pane shut. The list crisped in an instant and crumbled to ash. At the same time, an empty place on the white walls around the lake blazed blue, and twelve names appeared in black.

Beside the names appeared a drawing of a creature. The size was not indicated, but the features were clear. A short-snouted, maned head with
tusks longer than the head was wide. *A boar,* Erth had named it, and it
matched the animal Imeris had seen for the first time at the palace in Orinland. Small eyes. Short, tufted tail. These contrasted with huge, padded
cat paws and long, powerful, smooth-furred legs.

Imeris looked at the engravings of other demons who had triggered
Hunts. Here, a fiveways troupe. There, an embracer. A pair of floating eyes
to indicate a chimera.

Nothing as unnatural as the creature these Hunters faced.

Cries of awe and surprise went up around the lake. Children abandoned
their jugs and rushed over to touch Oniwak's armour and grip his hand.
He tried to shake them off, but they laughed, undeterred, clinging to him
harder.

Imeris stared at her name. The letters were an arm's length tall. Whether
she lived or died, they would stay there for as long as the forest survived.
She didn't know what to feel. The distinction wasn't earned. Not yet.

*Is this how my sister feels? That she must fight all the harder to be worthy of
the honours she already receives? Could I use this acclaim as currency to bring
Canopy and Understorey together against the sorceress?*

A chill passed through her at the recollection that in the levels below,
in the Understorian town of Hundar, the monument tree carried other
names carved by axes in human hands and rubbed with char. The names
of Leaders who returned gloriously from raids on Canopy. Those who died
or were captured as slaves.

*Youngest-Father will never be able to pass through the barrier to look with
pride upon my name.*

Yet, had she stayed to be a Leader at Loftfol, Leaper and Audblayin would
never have been able to look with pride upon those honours, written down
in the dark.

*Did they not think of that, all my mothers and fathers with their grand
wishes and dreams? Did they think it would be obvious to me that I am Understorian when every one of my mothers besides the chimera is Canopian-born?
When my brother and sister live in Canopy? When* this *is the colour of my skin?*

Imeris shook her head and wondered if Floorians, too, used the same
monument tree for their own mysterious memorial purposes.

"The creature's trail goes cold!" Oniwak shouted, trying to be loud and look serious while surrounded by cheering children. "I've decided to split our forces. Eeriez, you'll take Owun, Erth, Omt, and Iraffahath to Eshland to investigate the death of the clockmaker."

"Yes, Captain," Eeriez said, grinning.

"The rest of you will come with me to Airakland. Daggad, Ibbin, Ay, Ingaget, and you, woman. We'll see what clues we can find in the wreckage of the flowerfowl farm."

"My name is Imeris," Imeris said. She pointed. "It is written on the walls."

Some of the children with the water jugs, startled by the sound of her woman's voice issuing from beneath the blood smears and bronze scale armour, abandoned Oniwak's side for hers, singing her name over and over.

"Imeris! Imeris! Imeris!"

Imeris beamed until one of them chanted, "Imeris the giant worm, fat and furry for certain! Made a cocoon the size of the world, and died to give us curtains!"

Daggad laughed uproariously as her smile faded.

"Let us go to the weapons market, Imeris," he said. "Before we go anywhere, you need a better sword."

Imeris glanced again at the animal depicted on the wall.

"I do not want a sword," she said. Oldest-Father would say that a trap was best to defeat any kind of creature, humankind included, but without Anahah, Imeris had nothing to bait a trap with. Perhaps armour, spines, and knives were best against tree bears and jaguars at close quarters for an Understorian clinging to the sides of trees, as Middle-Father had taught her, but battles here were fought as often as not on flat roads and even ground, where range was a more important factor. Youngest-Father's weapon of choice would serve her better in this Hunt. "I want a longbow."

"You couldn't draw a man's bow," Oniwak said.

"Then we shall get one made for a woman," Daggad said. "Others of us could no doubt use whatever sharpenin' services are on offer." He snatched up the closest cheering child. "Girl! Which wayta buy weapons?"

The Ilanland weapons market, when they found it, ran through the heart of a pink peppercorn tree. One entrance to the tunnel, which was kinked to avoid the structural heart of the tree, was the public entrance. The other end came out on a path running directly to the palace armoury.

The six Hunters destined for Airakland—Oniwak, Ingaget with his parchment stole, Ibbin the bark-shirted boy, Ay the Lakekeeper of Ehkisland,

Daggad the slave, and Imeris with her forbidden spines—gathered on a platform outside the market. The ferny fronds, clusters of hundreds of pink berries, and powerful aroma of the peppercorn tree surrounded them.

"Be quick," Oniwak instructed, eyeing a leashed, bell-covered tree bear dancing for its keeper's benefit on the back of a barrow.

"First," Daggad said, engulfing Imeris's hand in his, which she reluctantly allowed, "you need coin. Sell that shoddy sword if you do not intendta use it."

Tight-lipped, she nodded. She still had some of Unar's coins, but there was no reason to keep the sword. She would never go back to Loftfol. Never train under the Litim. *Not even if I am able to make peace with them. That would be too much to expect.* They entered the tunnel together, squeezing between people. On the left and right sides, round openings to roomy workshops alternated with narrow display fronts. The locked doors of stockpile strong rooms stood behind them. Colourful flags hung over the shop entrances, stitched with house symbols of makers and traders.

The air wafting through the tunnel was hot and dry. Many of the workshops contained forges, crewed by smiths of all flavours of metal. They wore hoods, despite the heat, to keep sparks from catching in their hair, and their wooden walls were lined with fire-resistant flax fibres coated in clay.

Goods being drawn from quenching barrels ranged from trap jaws and axe heads to shears, combs, and coins bearing Ilan's profile. Weapons racks hung from every wall, and polished items gleamed from tables blanketed in oilcloth.

"Where—" Imeris had time to say before Daggad pulled her through a curtain of insect-repelling smoke into a pond. At least she heard the splash and stepped out of the trough into something soft and gritty before the water could seep through her boot-stitching.

"A banner that I recognise," Daggad said. "They will pay you the metal's proper worth." He noticed her staring at the yellow grit. "The sand protects the floor against fire."

"Also good for sharpening steel," the smith said cheerily, and Imeris laid out her short sword for appraisal. The smith mentioned neither the chipped and bloody blade, nor the maker's stamp from the Understorian village of Lit. Instead, a set of scales appeared from under the table and the weighing commenced. Imeris allowed Daggad to do the haggling, and walked away from the smithy with two gold coins in her hand and an empty sheath.

They washed the sand from their shoes into the trough on their way out; the water was there to make sure none of the valuable sand was lost. Then it was on through the tunnel until Imeris spotted a yellow flag with crossed, pace-long arrows embroidered in black.

The bowyer's bowl-shaped booth smelled of yellowrain sap, beeswax, and feathers, giving Imeris a swift flashback of the room at Loftfol where she'd found Oldest-Father's bird. Myrtle and yellowrain staves, some taller than Imeris, leaned against the peppertree wood wall. Completed bows, some flat, others recurved and laminated with thick risers of myrtle or floodgum, rested on purpleheart pegs above her head.

"You need—" Daggad began, reaching for something light and accurate, suited for shooting birds on the wing, but Imeris, ignoring him, went straight for a heavy stick of yellowrain, the rich red heartwood contrasting sharply with the white sapwood. *Yellowrain is the very hardest of softwoods,* Youngest-Father had told her in his gentle voice. *The sapwood is the best wood under tension, while the heartwood is peerless under compression. A natural spring.*

"This one," Imeris said, reading the inscribed draw weight of the bow, represented by nine tiny notches. It was one third of her bodyweight. "With a sinew string."

"You should 'ave a silk string"—Daggad smirked—"with a name like yours."

Imeris turned with the bow in her hand to the short, wide man behind the shop counter.

"A sinew string, please," she said, "and two spares."

She tried not to look at Daggad, but they had to wait some time for the three strings to be measured and made. He hummed a tune reminiscent of the rhyme the children had recited at the monument tree.

"Stop that," she said eventually.

"Stop what?" Daggad asked innocently.

"That song about the fat silkworm. I can hardly believe you are the best hunter in Audblayinland."

"But of course I am not." Daggad guffawed. "First thing that 'appens when a Hunt gets called is the deities' Bodyguards and the kings' secret guardians and assassins send birdsta each other with messages to get down."

"Get down where?" Imeris said incredulously. *I knew it. Middle-Father is the best hunter in Audblayinland. Aurilon is the best in Odelland.*

"Get down below the barrier, inta Understorey." Daggad pushed his finger hard against the tabletop as though he could force it through the wood. "So the device cannot sense them. So they cannot be chosen. Goddesses and gods do not give up their personal safety so easily!"

"But Oniwak. He's a king's captain. And Irrafahath is Oxor's Bodyguard."

Daggad shrugged.

"The king of Airakland was the one who called the Hunt, so Oniwak would 'ave 'ad no time to sneak away. Besides, 'e seems too stuffy and honour-bound for 'is own good—perhaps 'e would have stayed anyway." Daggad laughed. "As for the Bodyguard of the goddess of love, maybe the others do not like 'im enough to send 'im a bird. Or maybe it is a jest, you know, the one about the jaguar that goes 'unting flowerfowl in Oxorland and they end up bedded instead. You know what they say about Oxorland!"

"No," Imeris said. "I do not know."

Daggad leered, and appeared about to tell her when the bowyer returned with the strings. Imeris paid for everything, including a full quiver with thick, sticky fig sap in the bottom to keep the arrows from falling out when she climbed, and a waterproof leather cover and back strap for the bow. An attached leather cap came with the quiver; fig sap would hold horizontal arrows in place but could not grip them if the quiver was turned upside down. Imeris preferred her quiver be open, in case she needed to shoot quickly, but took the cap to keep the earnest bowyer happy.

They found Oniwak pacing in agitation on the platform outside the market.

"Ready to go?" he demanded.

"I must test the new bow," Imeris said.

"Must you? In the dark?"

"A fool takes an untested weapon into battle, and you Canopians have no idea what true dark is."

Daggad spectated with interest, buying a bag of roasted nuts from one of the little girls who scurried from shop to shop setting gathered hoards on unoccupied coals wherever they could find them. Ibbin, the boy from Irofland, filched a handful out of the bag. Ingaget glued new strips of silk around the grip of his short sword, parchment stole fluttering in the breeze. Ay, the Lakekeeper, adjusted his blue and black robes.

"You don't take orders well, do you, woman?" Oniwak said.

Imeris, ignoring him, shot a few arrows at the great tree opposite them, a rata growing over a sweet-fruit pine, some hundred paces away. One of Airak's lanterns illuminated a pace-wide section of branch suitable for setting her sights. She lost her first arrow, but the others struck in a tolerably tight group. There was hardly any shock to her wrist with the release; she was satisfied with the bowyer's craftsmanship, superior to Youngest-Father's if she was being truthful.

Daggad accompanied her over a rata branch road that bridged the gap to retrieve the arrows.

"Should a true Hunter not make all 'er own bows and strings?" he drawled. "Seem more like a figure of legend that way, less like a silkworm."

"Did you make that?" Imeris answered, slapping the sheathed broadsword on his back, refraining from seizing his long tail of black hair and jerking it sharply downwards.

Daggad laughed. He laughed again when she couldn't pull her arrows loose from the tree.

"You know plenty about wood," he said, snapping a sprig of notch-tipped rata leaves away from his face and crunching another mouthful of nuts. "You picked that bow quick enough. What you do not know is that although the bark of rata in Understorey is all soft and full of air holes, in Canopy they borrow the wood god's powerta make it 'ard and durable wherever the rata is used for roads."

"Help me, please," Imeris said, as politely as she could manage.

Careful not to stand behind the nocks, Daggad wrapped his huge hands around the shafts and drew them out for her, one by one.

TWENTY-THREE

It was still dark when the Hunters approached the Godfinder's farm.

There had to be hundreds of farmers in Airakland. Imeris had no information, no reason to suspect that the creature's victim was Unar.

Yet she stepped up to the false palm path with a sense of dread. Oniwak led the group to the crossroads in the scented satinwood tree. There, the barrows and hollows of the traders were covered in weighted blankets and tight-woven leaf mats to keep furry nocturnal pests and blown-in rain away from the grain.

Flame-coloured climbing salamanders hunted slugs and moths in the lantern light. Crickets used the acoustics of the hollow to amplify their calls. A pair of hungry-looking out-of-nichers dozed on a pile of empty sacks. Otherwise, the crossroads were abandoned.

"Wake one of them," Oniwak said. "Find the way to the farm."

"The farm is this way," Imeris said, stepping onto the straight satinwood branch which led to Unar's gate. She half expected him to call her a liar and attempt to bring her back, but the Hunters fell in behind her.

The path wasn't lit. The last time she'd come this way, she'd been preoccupied with her failure and humiliation, longing for what she considered the easy life of flowerfowl farming. When she came to the archway with the dead-looking vines, she flung out her arms to bar Oniwak's passage.

"It is a magical gate," she said. "The rest of you cannot go through."

"I don't see a doorbell," Ibbin piped up.

"There may be clues left behind by the creature," Oniwak said.

"The Godfinder lived here." Imeris's voice came out huskily. She remembered the sleeping woman in her fathers' home. The tea they had taken together so recently. "Her magic controlled the vines. Only she could have taught this gate to recognise you for a friend. You must not approach the arch. This is as far as you can go."

"But not you?" Daggad asked shrewdly.

In response, Imeris put her upturned wrist into the archway. She held her breath, waiting for the vines to come to life. Waiting for them to taste her, to withdraw and let her through.

The vines trembled, but they didn't move. No new tendrils grew out of them.

"Someone's coming," Oniwak said in a low voice, peering keenly through the night. "Be ready."

A cloak-wrapped shape stopped several paces back from the other side of the arch. Unar's voice issued from it, and Imeris's heart leaped.

"Unfortunately," the Godfinder said drily, "my thief-proof gate has been ruined by a goddess's pet impossible for me to kill. The Hunt, is it? There don't seem to be enough of you. Imeris, I'm surprised to see you again so soon. Aren't you supposed to be at Loftfol?" Daggad grunted and stared at Imeris at this revelation. "This isn't the usual hour for receiving guests." Unar put her fists on her hips. Imeris blinked back tears of happiness at the familiar sight. "Come on. You might as well all come inside and have some ti."

Oniwak sipped his ti without lowering his gaze from Unar's face.

"So you heard screaming. Then what happened?"

They sat across from each other on feather-stuffed cushions. Daggad sprawled on the blue carpet behind them, propped up on one elbow to drink his ti. Ibbin swung in one of the Godfinder's hammocks, whistling quietly to himself, while the Lakekeeper sat as far back from Unar as he could manage with a barely disguised expression of distaste. Ingaget turned the blue lantern over curiously in his hands.

Imeris squirmed in her cushion-seat, wanting to get Unar alone. The caramel smell of the satinwood was stifling. Her relief and happiness on finding the Godfinder alive had faded. A sense of urgency had overtaken all else.

Unar could get a message to Understorey. To Youngest-Father. To tell him what had happened at Loftfol. That Imeris had killed her teacher Horroh and was now outcast. Hunted.

That the students might be hunting Youngest-Father, too.

Oldest-Father had many clever traps, but he was no longer alive to maintain them, and Youngest-Father couldn't fight off all of Loftfol if they found out where he was. She thought of the spy who had seen her at Mistletoe Lodge in Ehkisland. How many spies did Loftfol have in Canopy? What if they were watching her now?

Her name was written tall on the wall of the memorial tree, and twelve Hunters being chased out of Orinland by the king's soldiers and waves of wild animals could hardly stay secret. Informers could be lurking outside the farmhouse at that very moment. If they were, they might not dare to strike at the Hunt, but they might tear Understorey apart looking for her fathers, to punish them instead.

Imeris squirmed again.

"I went up the steps," Unar said. "I saw something enormous with its head stuck in my vines, trying to wrench them out by the roots, but the vines kept growing, wrapping it in deeper and deeper layers—"

"Enormous?" Oniwak interrupted. "How big, exactly?"

Unar raised an eyebrow at him.

"Longer than it was wide or tall. Maybe ten or twelve paces long. Three paces high at the shoulder. The head, as I said, was wrapped in vines, but the front legs and haunches were black-furred. Powerful, but with red scars running all over. At least, I thought they were scars at the time."

"Could you see who was screaming?"

Unar's nostrils flared and her eyes lost their focus.

"I saw legs and shoes sticking through the arch, between the creature's front paws. Veiny old legs with green-dyed sandals. They belonged to the woman who sold flowerfowl fodder at the crossroads. She was delivering a few bags for me, and the birds had gone to greet her, eager to get at the grain."

"Do you know the grain farmer's name?"

"To my great shame, no," Unar admitted. Imeris tried catching her eye. Tried to stare at her from behind Oniwak's head, to signal that she had something important to say.

"How did you drive the creature away?" Oniwak sounded irritated, and Imeris couldn't decide if it was because he wished Unar had left the creature tangled in the vines by the head, or if it was because he was starting to suspect that magic would be more effective in the Hunt than the crossbow that he carried.

"I didn't. It pulled back from the arch, and its head came away from its neck. The red scars that I saw weren't scars. They were places where it could break apart. Once the body moved back to make room, the head broke into these writhing chunks. A handful of them, half red-raw, half furred, or half tusked. They rolled back along the bloodied path and stuck back onto its body again. It stood there breathing heavily for a few moments, as though that had been an effort for it. I think—I thought—there might have been more than two eyes."

Daggad snorted with apparent amusement, but Oniwak didn't blink.

"How many?" Oniwak wanted to know.

"There might have been two eyes in each piece that made up the head. It turned around and went into the crossroads. I went to the woman's body, but it was gutted. Gored. A whole lot of my birds had been crushed as well. There were lots of feathers and blood. Her grain barrow had been knocked down, I think. My archway was poisoned, nearly dead. I tried to find the woman's family at the crossroads."

"They'd already gone to the palace," Oniwak said, "to report the attack."

"I went to Airak's emergent to do the very same. I have a—a relative, there."

Unar glanced at the Lakekeeper, who scowled and looked away.

"You're an interesting woman, Godfinder," Oniwak said. "You're acquainted with an Odelland slave girl as well as the Lakekeeper of Ehkisland. You were a Gardener, serving Audblayin, and now you claim to have a relative among the Servants of Airak. That is very interesting. Can you think of any reason why Orin's creature would seek you out? Are you acquainted with the traitor Anahah?"

"No."

"Could the traitor have been hiding here? Could the creature have been following his scent? Before the attack, did any of your grain or fowl go missing?"

"No."

Imeris went very still. Her heart beat faster.

Could the creature have been following his scent?

"Could you have been," Oniwak pressed ruthlessly, "anywhere that the traitor could have been, where his scent could have gotten on you, or his stolen magic mixed up with you or yours?"

"Not unless he's disguised himself as Odel. Since the monsoon ended,

Odel's Temple is the only place I've been that is further from here than the next tree."

Imeris struggled to stay motionless. Her queasiness deepened. Oniwak gestured towards Ingaget.

"Pass me the lantern, Ingaget. I'll send a message to the others in Eshland. Godfinder, have you parchment, quill, and ink to spare?"

"Yes," Unar said, stiffly unfolding her legs from the cushion, pushing one hand off the floor to rise.

Imeris seized the opportunity to go after Unar into the next half room.

"What's wrong?" the Godfinder asked her, and Imeris grabbed her by both upper arms, turning her away from the main room, spilling in desperate whispers the disaster of her return to Loftfol, the death of Horroh, the loss of the chimera-skin wings, the slave-branding and its overturning when she was chosen for the Hunt.

"I beg you," she said at last, searching Unar's face, "warn my fathers."

"Of course," Unar said. "You don't need to squeeze the blood out of my arms. And don't worry about them. They've been dodging Gannak far longer than you've been dodging Loftfol."

Imeris let go.

They returned to the main room. Oniwak wrote a message out on the parchment before opening one of the panes of the lantern and stuffing it inside.

"Eeriez of Eshland!" he cried as the message was consumed, the blue glow intensifying. A moment later, the blue glow flared brighter again. Oniwak thrust his hand into heat and light that should have seared him to the bone, pulling out a piece of reed paper scrawled on in charcoal.

"What does it say, Captain, if your fellow Hunters are permitted to know?" Ingaget inquired, while Daggad craned his neck over Oniwak's shoulder, trying to read it directly.

"It says," Daggad boomed, "that the wooden clockmaker killed by the creature in Eshland 'ad been commissionedta craft somethin' for the traitor. A soul cage, made of bone. Eeriez cannot say if the cage was completed before the clockmaker's death."

"What is a soul cage?" Ibbin called from his swinging hammock.

"What does it sound like?" Daggad said, guffawing.

"There's no such thing as a soul cage," muttered the Lakekeeper.

"Superstitious nonsense." But when Imeris glanced at the Godfinder, Unar looked contemplative and said nothing.

"We'll meet them on the southern border of Ehkisland," Oniwak said. "At a place called Mistletoe Lodge. The innkeeper was killed there. We must discover the connection between them."

"Must there be a connection?" Daggad drawled. "It could be killin' indiscriminately."

"No," Ingaget mused. "Its mission is neither to sow fear nor cause chaos. And anyway, to accomplish either of those things, it wouldn't need to expend energy ranging so quickly or so far. The captain is right. There must be some common connection to Anahah, the creature's quarry."

Unar's gaze snapped sharply into focus. Imeris felt it strike her like an arrow.

The Godfinder's farm. Mistletoe Lodge. Imeris was the connection. She had sheltered Anahah there.

If I become a human guest in a human space, Anahah had said, *the Mistress of the Wild cannot find me.*

He had also said, *Orin killed every living member of my family. All my friends. Anyone she remotely suspected might provide me with shelter.*

Orin's creature had killed the poor innkeeper and then followed Imeris's scent from Mistletoe Lodge back to the Godfinder's home. To make sure Anahah was not being sheltered there. It must own more than an ordinary beast's intelligence. It must still be partly human.

She pressed her tongue against her palate, keeping herself from sharing all she knew with Oniwak, but also remembering the feeling of the slave's mark there. Anahah had mixed his magic up with her. That much was certain.

And Imeris now had bait for a trap, if she cared to use it.

Herself.

TWENTY-FOUR

IMERIS HESITATED at the edge of Southeats, looking down at Mistletoe Lodge.

It was late in the day. The open, mistletoe-draped windows should have echoed with guests, and the insect-repelling braziers should have been lit. Neither of those things were true.

Oniwak spoke with the owner of a crab-stick cookery. They stood behind the barrow a dozen paces away, at the edge of Imeris's hearing. The owner's story sounded similar to all the others'. A hundred bystanders or more had seen something like a great black bat drop down onto the slightly lower canopy of the smaller tallowwood tree, covering it like a sheet over a bush.

The shadow had shrunk into a denser, four-footed shape and begun sticking its maned, tusked head into the windows of the lodge. At the same time, men and women had run screaming out of all available exits and along the branch roads to Northeats and Southeats.

Nobody knew why the creature decided to crush the innkeeper when it found her hiding under a bed in one of the rooms. Nobody could say why it left all the others unharmed, including the terrified patrons of Southeats, by which route the monster departed, or why it went up instead of down into the darkness where it belonged.

Imeris thought she had answers to all three questions, but the answer she spoke aloud was in response to the final one.

"It cannot go into Understorey."

"What are you mutterin' about?" Daggad asked, spraying saliva and bits of soft tree-hollow crabshell from around the stick it was skewered on.

"The creature. It cannot pass below the barrier because it is made of magic and the magic of the Temples will not work in Understorey."

"If you are right, that might be a good wayta kill it." Daggad wiped his mouth with his leather bracer. "Make it fall." He let go of his crab stick.

They both watched it fall.

"I do not know enough about magic to be sure," Imeris admitted. "Do you?"

"The only magic that concerns me is this," Daggad said, sticking out his tongue to show the emblem of the House of Epatut to which he belonged. "Let us bother the Lakekeeper about the barrier."

Imeris hesitated. The House emblem had seemed suddenly familiar, but she couldn't worry about that now.

Ay slumped gloomily against a stack of empty barrels. His robes no longer looked fine. They were stained and rumpled. He missed his lake, Imeris supposed, and his goddess. At least they were now within his niche, where his powers were strong. When he had fought Orin's beasts and the king's soldiers, he'd occasionally flung his tears like acid at the enemy, but mostly he'd ducked and weaved and used a green branch broken from a tree to block edged weapons and bodily beat the attackers away.

Here, he could walk sideways and upside down, call a thunderstorm inside a man's lungs to drown him, or boil the eyes out of an enemy's head if he chose. According to Ingaget, anyway.

Daggad repeated Imeris's speculation about the beast, but the Lakekeeper only shrugged.

"The gods and goddesses have power everywhere. If they're sometimes weak when they fall to Floor, it's because the people of Floor make no tributes to Canopian goddesses and gods. Surrounded by those who are devoted to them, our deities can venture wherever they choose to carry out the deeds it is in their nature to carry out."

"You could try harder to be of help," Imeris said. "Even if you wish you had not been chosen as a Hunter."

"One who walks in the grace of Ehkis finds it difficult," Ay answered stiffly, "not to be resentful when deities manufacture such conflicts to satisfy their pride. The goddess of rain has been twice murdered in two decades, yet where is the Hunt declared to find the sorceress Kirrik?"

Imeris stared at him in shock.

"Who, now?" Daggad asked.

"I have met with the Godfinder far too often." The Lakekeeper picked up a handful of fallen leaves and scattered them vindictively. "My Lady

Ehkis, an immortal, is as vulnerable as a child. She is a child! And I'm stuck here, chasing down the product of another Temple's frivolous internal quarrel, instead of teaching that child, and her Servants, how to navigate their powers."

The Lakekeeper knows about Kirrik. Of course! Imeris had known about only one occasion when the rain goddess's body had been stolen by the sorceress, but much went on in Canopy that she didn't know about.

"Could you wash the beast away with a magic river," she asked, "if it came on us here in Ehkisland? Could you use water to get it off the side of a tree and down beyond the barrier? Would you try?"

Ay met her gaze and shrugged again.

"I'd try," he said. "But I see no reason for it to come back here."

"We do not know what reason it hadta come 'ere the first time," Daggad said.

Oniwak called for them to follow him. Daggad offered a hand and lifted the Lakekeeper to his weary feet. In single file, the Hunters crossed the gap, down the tallowwood path to the Mistletoe Lodge. As they approached it from the south, the dying sun gilded the left side of it.

Imeris noticed deep claw marks on the outside of the lodge. They were deepest by the window opening of the room in which she had stayed.

"There," she said, touching Oniwak's shoulder, pointing.

"The room where the innkeeper died," was his gruff reply.

He made a perfunctory examination of the abandoned lodge, beginning with the room where Imeris had sheltered Anahah. Blood made brown blotches on the tallowwood.

"Why haven't her relatives cleaned it up, taken it over?" Ibbin wondered aloud. "Expensive bit of property, this."

"They're afraid the creature will return," Ingaget said. "They can't be sure why she was taken. Was it something about her? Something about the lodge? Or something about that room?"

Imeris stayed silent.

The lodge with its bloodstains and emptiness reminded her of the dark temple at Loftfol. How her poisoned throwing knives had gone deep into the wooden effigies of Canopian Servants and how Kishsik, then two-handed, had helped her to dig them out with his bore-knife. His poison-dipped needles peppered another of the effigies. Imeris had hesitated to compliment him on their accuracy, to be the first one of them to speak since her victory in the climbing race to become Heightsman.

How her back had ached from the weight of the bow the day she'd won that race against Kishsik. How her heavy breathing had echoed in the humid, noonday stillness of the week before the monsoon, when the bark was driest and safest to pierce with blade or spine or bore-knife. Many of the men, arms like coconuts squeezed into bear stomachs, had raced with forearm spines alone, but Imeris had known her upper body strength was not equal to theirs. For the first half of the race, she'd lain back on lateral branches, more common in river nuts than other trees, and used Youngest-Father's bowfishing arrows with a heavier, stiffer, foot-drawn bow to send ropes arcing over even higher branches. Holding the guide rope lightly in her hands for balance, she could then crawl up the bark on shin spines alone, using the muscles in her thighs instead of her shoulders, bow at her back, the scent of river nut sap sharp in her nostrils.

It had been time-consuming, but energy efficient, leaving her with reserves for the last stage of the climb, where she'd abandoned bow and arrows, attacked the tree with fresh forearm spines, and overtaken Kishsik in the final dozen body lengths of the race.

His intense, hazel eyes had fixed onto her face, his expression unreadable. In their practice raid in the dark temple, Imeris had held back from speaking to him because she assumed that he hated her; all his friends had made that clear. So it was a shock when he said mildly, *I wanted to be the best. I wanted to kill the goddess in her true Temple. Now I see that it does not matter who kills her, so long as she is thrown down. You will throw her down, Imerissiremi.*

Imeris had ventured a guarded smile, thinking sadly, *She is my sister, and I love her. I will never throw her down.*

The sun sank out of sight, and there was no sign of the other Hunters, the six men under Eeriez who had gone to Eshland. Daggad speculated that those six should have in fact reached the lodge first; south Ehkisland was equidistant from Airakland and Eshland, but Oniwak's group had been forced to detour around Orinland.

"Bring me one of Airak's lanterns," Oniwak ordered Ibbin. "Any one will do."

He used the mysterious communication method of his patron god to pass another message to Eeriez and quickly received one in return.

"'Bird brought news of an attack in Audblayinland,'" Daggad read out again over Oniwak's shoulder, and Imeris's heart leaped. *Audblayinland! Middle-Father!* "'Audblayin's Bodyguard met the beast outside the Garden Gate. Wards repelled it. The Bodyguard escaped by droppin' down inta Understorey. We go to interview the Bodyguard.'"

"We might as well get comfortable, then," Oniwak said, crumpling the message in disgust. "Seems we'll be waiting here a few days or more."

Daggad's eyes were bright.

"It is as you guessed," he told Imeris. "The creature cannot go below the barrier."

"Or it wasn't really after Audblayin's Bodyguard," Oniwak snapped.

"Who's brave enough to sleep in the room where the innkeeper was killed?" Ibbin jeered.

"Nobody needs to sleep there," Ingaget said reprovingly. "We've the whole place to ourselves."

"I will sleep there," Imeris said. *Leave my family alone, beast. If you're following me, come and find me.* She wanted to laugh. Hunted below the barrier by Kirrik and the students of Loftfol. Hunted above the barrier by Orin's monster.

And they called her a Hunter.

"I will sleep with you," Daggad drawled. "You do not wanta be alone if the creature comes back."

Imeris stifled her immediate instinct, a scathing response. She really did want to be alone when the creature came back.

But she might not be able to set her trap without Daggad.

"We'll set a watch for the creature," Oniwak said. "Southeats might be the best vantage point. Any sign of the creature, put a handful of popping nuts into one of Airak's lanterns and say my name. I'll keep the lantern by my head. The noise will be sure to wake me. Boy, you can take first watch."

Ibbin shifted his feet guiltily. He pointed at Daggad.

"He told me we were allowed to eat them."

Oniwak glared.

"That wasn't table salt they were coated in. It was signalling salt, to make coloured flames."

Ibbin gazed at the Captain for a long moment in wide-eyed uncertainty. Then he doubled over and vomited on the floor.

"Now I really don't want to sleep here," Ay murmured, holding his robes away from the colourful bile, exiting the room in disgust. Ingaget and Oniwak followed him. Ibbin peeled a bit of bark from his shirt and used it to wipe his mouth. Daggad, struggling to contain his amusement, went for a bucket and mop.

"How can a child be the greatest hunter in Irofland?" Imeris asked, at the same time as Ibbin asked, "How can a woman be the greatest hunter in Odelland?"

They laughed together.

"I'm a baker's son, like I told you," Ibbin said. "Got very good at catching feathertailed gliders in my hands for my mother to put in the pies. Lots of little gliders in Irofland. They drink the nectar. Real sweet, glider flesh, with plenty of fat."

Imeris was impressed. The fist-long gliders were extremely quick. It was a struggle to simply keep an eye on one, much less to catch it. Flowers were few enough in Understorey, but she couldn't imagine catching a glider without a trap.

Daggad came back with the mop and started cleaning the floor. His back was turned to Imeris, but a wheeze of laughter escaped him at the sight of the multihued spew.

"I fell when I was a baby," Imeris said to Ibbin. "My birth mother was bumped by a beewife in the silk market. A she-demon cared for me until three fierce hunters, brothers, found and raised me."

Daggad stared at her, mop abandoned.

"Audblayin's bones," he swore.

"I would rather," Imeris said, "you did not use that expression. She is my sister, you see."

Ibbin and Daggad looked at each other. They looked back at Imeris.

"So that's how you can fight," Ibbin said. "You're half goddess yourself."

"No. A woman does not have to be a goddess to be a fighter. There is another woman fighter in Odelland who has beaten me many times." Imeris went to the window and began measuring it as Oldest-Father had taught her, using the length between the base of her middle finger and elbow as one-third of one pace or one-sixth of one body length. "But Daggad tells me the Bodyguards all go into hiding when a Hunt is called. At least, that explains how he was chosen."

Daggad guffawed.

"Seems the Bodyguard of Audblayin runs away to Understorey often."

"He is my middle-father," Imeris said with disdain, "and no coward. He has killed a chimera." She didn't turn around to check, but she guessed from their silence that Daggad and Ibbin were sharing glances again.

When the vomit was mopped up, Ibbin departed to take his place in Southeats. Imeris, alone with Daggad, her measuring complete, gave him the money she had remaining.

"Before you get undressed," she told him, "there are a few things you must find for me and bring back here, or at the very least put in orders for them to be made. I could not carry them myself. Two curved axe-blades, each two and one-third paces wide. Set into heavy hardwood blocks, a finger width short of two palm thicknesses deep, so they will fit into the grooves I will gouge tonight with the adze you will buy and bring me. A good sharpening stone also. And rope. I will need ten coils of palm-thickness strapleaf. Grease for the grooves. A block and tackle and two half-pace belaying pins with eye-bores. The money is not enough, I know. The landlady kept her coins in a chest dangling from a chain down her private lavatory. Steal them. If the beast is travelling from Audblayinland, we may have enough time."

"Enough time for what?" Daggad stood frozen in the act of unbuckling his sword harness and laying the monstrous weapon down on the bed. It was fairly loose, anyway, to aid in the necessary two-handed draw; only a sword shorter than the arm could be drawn single-handed from the back.

"Setting a trap for the monster," she said.

"What do you mean? We are not trappers. We are trackers. Hunters."

"Yes, of course!" Imeris said, throwing her hands up in the air. "No plan is needed. When we find the beast, we will each rush at it with our various preferred methods. Oniwak will shoot it with his crossbow. You will swing your great sword. Ay will call the rain, and Ibbin will pounce on it with his bare hands. Irrafahath and Ingaget will stick it with their short swords, Eeriez will poison it, and I shall put a pace-long arrow through one of its twelve eyes. So what if it does not die? We can surely expect the goddess of justice to appear again to save our skins!"

Daggad sat down on the bed.

"We 'ave each worked alone," he said. "We 'ave each laid our enemies low. Each of us believes our own method is best. Each of us believes we will be the one to kill the creature single-handed and bask in the glory. But not you."

"Not me."

He blinked.

"I was there when the Godfinder spoke," he said. "I was afraid when she told 'ow it broke apart and re-formed. You wanta build a trap with a blade two and one-third paces wide? You wanta cut off its head, knowin' that it 'as parted head and shoulders before and survived?"

Imeris put her fists together and pulled them apart.

"I want to *keep* its head and shoulders parted. The wooden blocks will see to it. I want Ay waiting outside to bring the rain and send the body down below the barrier. I will speak to him about volunteering for the watch at Southeats."

"Captain Oniwak might not—"

"To Floor with Captain Oniwak!" Imeris trembled with anger. "He is as stupid as he is blind. I am asking you to help me, not him."

"Sounds like tellin', not askin'." Daggad grinned. "I am usedta that. I am a slave. But I remember 'ow it was before." He stood up. Moved closer. Reminding her of his physical strength. He was so tall. His shoulders were so wide. He blocked out the lantern light from the mistletoe window. Imeris stood her ground. "I was born in Gannak. It lies below Audblayin-land, but you know that already. When I was a barely a man, a Leader of Loftfol found a breach in the barrier and led two dozen villagers of Gannak through. Most of us died. The rest became captives of the king of Aud-blayinland."

"I am sorry." Imeris lifted her chin, trying to stand taller.

"I remember the Headman of our village," Daggad went on, "goin' to fetch the three grown sons of a woman called Moonoom. These three were famous hunters, and it was their obligation to raid Canopy."

"They were free," Imeris said angrily. "They were under no such obligation!"

"The Headman never returned. The rest of us went without 'im. Without those three famous brothers. I wondered what became of them. I wondered what happenedta my wife, havin' lost me only weeks after we were wed. Slaves only get news from Understorey if someone else gets captured or they turn handy at trainin' birds."

Imeris's throat felt dry.

"What was your wife's name?"

"Nin."

"She married again." *Poor Daggad.* "She bore a daughter and called her Nirrin. Nirrin was my friend. She died." *Poor Nin. And poor Nirrin.*

At last, Imeris gave in to the urge to break away from him. She went to the window. Stared out at the lanterns. Kirrik was out there. The creature was out there. Students of Loftfol were out there.

Anahah was out there.

She wished she were the goddess of the winds, to search out with airy fingers all the ones she was so desperate to find. She wished she had killed Kirrik already, and everything was over with, and she could work out what it was she wished to do, and not simply what she had to do.

"I saw her wedding headdress," she said. "It had a sunburst carved in orange amber. Black and scarlet tail feathers, and the band was sky-blue silk."

When she turned her head, Daggad was sitting on the bed again, looking strangely loose, as if his legs had gone out from under him, his half-unbuckled sword forced high up above his head and tangled with his hair.

"I made it for Nin," he said. "Audblayin's bones. It is an age since I was unmanned by this depth of feelin'."

Imeris twined her fingers in the hanging fronds of mistletoe and sighed deeply.

"Feelings are not unmanly," she said. "How did you leave the king's service and become the property of the House of Epatut?"

"They trained us to become warrior-slaves. We learned swordsmanship. Other path- and platform-based fightin' styles unknown to the climbers and knife-wielders of Gannak. Some twenty years ago, there was a battle outside the gates of Audblayin's Garden. I think you were not born. It was a raid led by the sorceress that Ay spoke of. His goddess, Ehkis, was killed."

"I was born," Imeris said.

"Anyway, the merchant's house, the House of Epatut, was threatened by the fightin'. What hired guards it already 'ad turned out to be useless, somehow. Nobody told me exactly what 'appened, but the silk merchant wanted a stronger, more permanent presence outside 'is 'ome. Epatut bought me from 'is brother Otoyut, the king's Master of Sword."

Imeris's hands tightened into fists over the leaves and stems of the mistletoe, pulling slightly so that she could feel their connection to the host tree, the tallowwood, which was connected by its branch paths to other trees, and others.

"Everything is connected," she said. Then she laughed.

The raid in which Daggad had become a captive was the one her three fathers had narrowly avoided. The threat to Audblayinland, which had seen Daggad sold to the merchant, was the very same sorceress, Kirrik, who had killed both the rain goddess and Nirrin, the daughter of Daggad's wife.

"What makes you so sure," Daggad asked, "that the monster will return 'ere? To this room? What do you know that Oniwak does not?"

"Orin's creature is hunting *me*," Imeris answered, pulling so hard that some of the mistletoe broke away in her hands. "That is why I will not risk spreading my smell further among innocent people. I sheltered the traitor Anahah in this very room. The creature has my scent. It has visited all the places I have been, except for Odelland. There, I trust that Odel's Bodyguard, Aurilon, can turn it away. I pray that she can turn it away." Imeris let go of the mistletoe.

She turned to find Daggad on his feet again, bristling with fury.

"You coulda spoken of this before."

"I only just figured it out!"

"You coulda spoken of this before we went to Orinland! Before that poor Servant of Atwith fell!" Daggad drew his great sword over his shoulder, awkwardly, because the harness was half undone, and when his right and left hands went for the hilt and scabbard respectively, they found it at the wrong angle. "Tell me now 'ow to find the man Anahah. Let me slay 'im and 'ave this whole matter finished with."

Imeris's eyes narrowed. Her spines tingled.

"You heard Oniwak," she said. "The Hunt does not end with Anahah's death. It ends with the killing of the beast. It was Orin who killed the death god's Servant, not I."

"Do you not know what I—" He clamped his jaw shut, but Imeris goaded him.

"No, I do not know what you have been promised if you are the one to slay the beast," she said. "Tell me."

"Freedom." Daggad's face was white; his lips trembled. Fighting for his life against Orinland soldiers had not roused such emotion in him. "To see my wife again."

"Lies," Imeris snapped. "A fighting slave who slays a demon becomes even more valuable. You are an investment to them."

"You are a—I do not even know what you are. Friendta those who enslave the folk who were good enoughta raise you when you fell. I do not know the word for that, but it is repulsive."

Imeris felt the blood draining from her own face. She tried to speak, but no words came out. For a long moment, they stared at one another, breathing hard.

"I cannot give you back your broken spines, Daggad," she said at last. "I would not supply you with Anahah's whereabouts even if I knew them. I *can* give you the beast's head, if you will go into Ehkisland and find the items I have described."

Daggad swallowed. He shrugged his harness off the rest of the way and sheathed his sword. Then he slung it back over his shoulder again and began tightening the buckles.

"You 'ad better be right about the trap," he said.

"There is something else I may be right about, and that is the creature's intelligence. Do not let the others see you."

"Are you mad? How can I bring a couple of man-sized blades—"

"In a barrow. Or lowered in a net from an overhanging branch. In a fruit basket full of sex slaves. I do not—"

"What is so wrong with the others knowin' about the trap? With being prepared? We are all Hunters together—"

"You said it yourself," Imeris said flatly. "Each Hunter seeks glory for himself. I cannot risk this chance. The adze first, Daggad. So that I can start preparing the window and the doorway."

Daggad shook his head with something like awe.

"Very well, Imeris. Or should I call you Imerissiremi? The adze first."

He swaggered back out into the night.

TWENTY-FIVE

Drowsing by the door, Imeris dreamed of Horroh.

They faced one another in one of the training halls at Loftfol, darkness and the sounds of the monsoon all around, the floor beneath them polished by generations of students' bare feet. The river that ran through the school roared. Rain punched at flat leaves. It gurgled as it drained through bark crevices. One side of Horroh's grub-white, shaved head was lit. One doughy cheek. The iris of one eye, such a pale grey that it was almost white, around a pupil dilated by the dark.

Do not let them tell you that your skin decides what you are, Horroh said. He gripped her right palm in his, holding her forearm up so that her extended spines shone yellow in the light of the tallow candle. *This is what you are. An Understorian warrior. A student of Loftfol. My student. If you ever forget, let your spines remind you.*

Imeris blinked; found her spines smeared with blood. She looked up at Horroh, but his grip was loosening. His throat gaped open, striped red and white and black where the windpipe still held the memory of his last words.

The tallow candle flickered and went out.

Imeris's dream went with it.

She sat up on the floor in the Mistletoe Lodge, sweating and shaking. Daggad crouched beside her, an adze in his hand.

"No time for sleepin'," he whispered, grinning. "Make sure not to wake the others."

Imeris clutched the curved cooper's adze with both hands. It was heavy, made of floodgum and steel. The noise would be terrible. She would have to mask it somehow. If only she were the Godfinder and could carve the channels by the sides of the door and window with magic.

Imeris pulled off her boots and armour. On quiet feet, she crept past the other rooms into the dead innkeeper's kitchen, sighing with relief as she sized it up.

The kitchen window faced away from Southeats, where the watch was being kept.

Imeris found a clothesline. A cupboard full of wooden cutting boards and pots. Sealed gourds of magenta cherry jam. She tied the pots and boards to the end of the clothesline, smeared everything with jam, and dangled it out the window.

Shoving several wedges under the kitchen door so it was effectively locked from the inside, she then used her spines to climb out the kitchen window and into the closest empty guest room.

She'd been back in her own room only a few minutes when the first crash of boards and bowls against the tree sounded. Imeris hid the adze under the bed. She curled up on top of it, turning her back to the door, hiding her small satisfied smile.

The boards clacked and rattled again.

More. Louder.

Monkeys and gliders screamed, fighting over the jam-smeared boards. Every time an animal tried to make off with the treasure, the clothesline brought them up short and the utensils banged back into the side of the tree.

"What is that racket?" Oniwak grumbled from the hallway. Imeris heard her door creak open a hand-span. "Useless woman. Sound asleep."

Bare feet, shuffling carefully, came to a halt beside the partway-open door.

"Captain Oniwak," Ingaget said. "It's nocturnal animals, gliders and such, getting into the kitchen. The door's stuck. They'll go away when they've finished feeding."

When Imeris was sure the soldier and the old man were gone, she rolled over and fished around under the bed for her adze. She closed the door. Felt for the markings she'd made with her spines when she'd measured the frame. The first time she brought the adze down and a curl of pale, sinus-prickling tallowwood came away, she waited, holding her breath, to see if any of her fellow Hunters would come to investigate.

They didn't.

By the time Daggad returned with a barrow full of turpentine blocks and a note from a smith with a copy of the specifications for the blades together with a promise they'd be done on the morrow, Imeris had the first set of parallel grooves completely hollowed out.

"How did you get past Ibbin?" Imeris demanded.

"Gave 'im some bia. 'E wentta sleep."

"Gave him some bia?" She set the adze down and looked up at Daggad incredulously. "He cannot be older than . . . How many monsoons has he?"

"Would you rather I tied 'im to the other side of the tree?" Daggad slid the blocks under the bed. They squealed like rusty hinges. Imeris winced. "'E was tired anyway."

"Oniwak will be angry with him."

"There is no more room under the bed," Daggad observed, fists on hips.

"Too noisy," Imeris muttered. "Everything is too noisy. How can we get the others out of here tomorrow so we can build the gods-cursed trap?"

Daggad looked at her. He quirked an eyebrow.

"I 'ave an idea," he said.

IN THE morning, Oniwak hollered, "Up, woman!" and pounded on the door.

Imeris rubbed the grit from her grainy eyes and propped herself up on one elbow in bed. Daggad, however, was awake and ready. Before the Captain could barge in and notice the long channels chipped out of the wall to either side of the entry, the hulking man from Gannak went out to meet him.

Stark naked.

"Do not wake 'er," Daggad boomed.

Silence. Perhaps Oniwak was taken aback.

"You slaves behave like rutting animals," he said at last. "There is no time to waste. I have a message from Odelland. The creature has been seen there by Odel's emergent."

Daggad had sent that message himself at the crack of dawn. Imeris could foggily remember him sneaking back to the room with the lantern and enunciating Oniwak's name in a desperate whisper.

Imeris wondered if Daggad had his hands behind his back, hiding the charcoal smudges on his fingers.

"You go on ahead," he said. "We can follow after you."

"Don't bother! We four can travel to Odelland and back before nightfall. If we find and slay the creature, the better for this one who walks in the grace of Airak and the worse for you! You are both disgraces to the great name of Hunter. I should have your names removed from the monument tree!"

When Daggad came back into the room, Imeris expected to see a smirk on his face. Instead, he seemed lost in doubt, sitting absentmindedly on the bed where she lay. The great sword rested on the sheet alongside her, parallel to her body.

"Your plan worked," she whispered encouragingly.

"What if they find it?" Daggad stared out the window.

"They will not."

"But you said the creature might go to Odelland. What if they kill it?"

"Then I will help you to escape from the House of Epatut," Imeris promised. "Now I think you should put your clothes back on."

"Am I distractin' you?" There was the smirk. Imeris sighed.

"As soon as the others have gone, find the smith and redeem the receipt. After you get back you can—" Daggad stuck his tongue out at her, false childishness, and she was struck again by the odd familiarity of the sigil there. "Show me your slave-marking. Hold your tongue out like that."

She sat up, held his face between her hands and frowned at the interwoven wheel, cocoon, and loom burned into his tongue.

"Theen enuth?" he asked with his tongue between his teeth.

"This is not possible," Imeris murmured. "My sister Ylly had a silk blanket. A baby blanket. The edge was patterned like that."

Her stomach swooped. There was only one explanation. The baby blanket so jealously guarded by Ylly and later turned into a dress for her had not been Ylly's at all.

It was mine.

My blanket.

A silk blanket from the House of Epatut.

She felt like she was falling. There was no up. There was no down. She tried to push Daggad away. He was swinging her around and around; he must be. But she couldn't make him stop and eventually the spinning room slowed down and stopped.

"She dropped you off the edge of the silk market, eh?" Daggad said sympathetically.

Imeris hunched over the edge of the bed and retched violently.

It was the same spot where Ibbin had evacuated his gut the night before.

TWENTY-SIX

Imeris squatted on her heels in the gloom, guarding the greased pair of pins pushed into the wall.

It was an hour past sunset. Oniwak and the others had arrived back from Odelland empty-handed, to Daggad's great relief. Eeriez and his Audblayin-land contingent remained a day's travel away. Imeris imagined how their interrogation of Middle-Father would go, and hoped Youngest-Father was being as vigilant below the barrier as Middle-Father was above it. Had he gone to visit them while he was hiding from the Hunt? Had they discussed added defences against the sorceress, and secrecy to avoid Loftfol? Forbidden Middle-Mother her indulgent shopping trips to the villages, Oldest-Mother her healing jaunts, and Youngest-Mother her merry music-making in the ti-houses?

Over the window and over the door, the trap-blades in their wooden blocks waited, held high in their running grooves by strapleaf ropes; those ropes were connected to the pins whose handles rested within Imeris's reach. When the creature returned, when it stuck its monstrous head into either one of the room's entrances, Imeris would be waiting to pull the appropriate pin free. Top pin for the window. Bottom pin for the door.

Daggad had enlisted Ay, the reluctant Lakekeeper, in the scheme. *A pair of beheadin' machines, I suppose you could call them,* Daggad had explained, scratching his stubble. *One at each entrance.* The disgruntled Servant of the rain goddess now stood watch at Southeats with the instruction *not* to alert Oniwak upon the monster's arrival.

Only at some good indication of the beast's beheading was the Lakekeeper to summon a deluge and wash the body away.

Imeris should have felt calm. She'd completed the seven disciplines and the six flowing forms. Left her room, washed her face, eaten and drunk

her fill, made her toilet. All she could think about, though, was the way
Daggad had described her birth father and mother, the silk merchant Epatut and his wife, once called Igish, now subsumed by her husband's House
and called Wife-of-Epatut.

You should have told me immediately, Imeris had said.

I only just figured it out, Daggad protested in an echo of their earlier conversation. *You are tall and thin like 'e is, and you 'ave got the wife's little
round nose, and they did lose their firstborn, but I never imagined even someone like 'im would name 'is own daughter after a silkworm. I bet 'e gave tribute to the insect god instead of Odel, and that is why you fell.*

Someone like him? What does that mean?

I mean, Daggad had said, grinning, *someone who counts 'is coins like a
starvin' slave counts nuts. Someone who praises the beauty of rare dyes but never
the charms of 'is mate. And 'e does not hear 'er praises.*

What, then, Imeris demanded, *are his other children called?*

'E has got no fruit of his own loins, that one. Daggad shrugged. *Except
you, obviously, but 'e wanted a son. Adopted 'is nephew, Epi. Taught the lad
to love money and fine fabrics. I doubt the boy 'as ever held a weapon in 'is
life.*

That is why they needed you, she said, but she'd stopped imagining Daggad standing guard outside the house. Instead, she was seeing herself as she
might have been, a daughter of the House of Epatut, vain and pampered,
draped in colourful silks, helpless against the onslaught of enemies.

What enemies, she wondered as she waited to spring her trap in the Mistletoe Lodge, *would a silk merchant have?* One battle twenty years ago
hardly seemed a reason for ongoing paranoia. Canopy was a world of wealth
and leisure. So infrequently was it threatened, so rare was the intrusion of
any unpleasantness, that all the Hunters who had ever been summoned to
defend it could fit their names on a single gods-cursed tree.

She felt a terrible surge of gratitude and affection for her fathers below
the barrier. Oldest-Father, who had taught her about planes and pulleys,
scaffolds and springs. Middle-Father, who had put a knife in her hands and
shown her how to use it. Youngest-Father, who had given her wings.

The merchant Epatut was nothing. Imeris was determined to see him
separated from his precious fighting slave once the Hunt was over, whether
Daggad himself drew blood or not. And she would put her head together

with that of Ay the Lakekeeper, who knew of Kirrik and longed for something to be done about her. He would have Canopian resources to call upon that Imeris's own sister had denied her, but that would bring the enemy closer to her final doom; if the man could call a flood to a rogue creature, perhaps he could drown a sorceress in monsoon waters so deep that Kirrik's soul would never find the surface.

A snore wafted from under the bed.

Shifting gingerly away from the wooden pins, which were sunk arm-deep into the most solid section of wall yet so greasy they should come free in an instant, Imeris knelt by the bed, leaned down, and felt the scabbard of Daggad's great sword with her fingertips. She picked it up and prodded the sleeping lump under the bed with the pommel.

"Stay awake," she whispered.

A thud. The bed shuddered. It had sounded like skull against wood, like he'd tried to sit up.

"Ow," Daggad said softly, pitifully.

He crawled out from his hiding place.

"Get back in there," Imeris breathed. "You might scare it off."

"I 'ardly think one extra sword will frighten it."

"Not your stupid sword. Your smell. How is it supposed to know I am here when bia and onions ooze out of your every pore?"

"Somethin' is movin' out there," he murmured, and instead of returning to his hiding place, he went to the window. Imeris eyed the naked blade of the trap hovering barely a third of a pace over his head and bit her lip. It wasn't that she didn't have faith in her own calculations. It was not. Nor did she doubt the ropemaker. It simply was not necessary to take the risk of standing right under the trap.

"Monkeys," Imeris said, listening to the hoots and scuffles. "Gliders, too. Looking for more food."

Even as she said it, a small furry shape, black with two white stripes down its back, slipped in through the window and climbed up the ceiling. It hung from tiny claws, whiskered nose twitching.

"Shoo," Daggad said, waving his arms, moving back inside the room. Imeris sighed to see him out from under the gleaming steel. The glider didn't move.

"Daggad," she said, standing up suddenly, every muscle tense, the hair bristling on the back of her neck. Daggad picked up the mop, which he'd used to clean up again after Imeris had been sick, and poked at the animal with the handle.

It fell.

Twisted in midair.

When it reached the ground, it was human, lean green shoulders curved around the knees, fingers splayed on the floor to either side of the feet.

Anahah's eyes, when he raised them towards Imeris, were the darker green version. His greenish-gold hair was a little ragged, his previously hard-muscled abdomen looking fuller and flabbier.

"Audblayin's bones," Daggad said, too loudly. "The traitor."

"Hush," Imeris warned him, dragging Anahah by the arm over to the place by the pins where the lantern light from the window wouldn't shine on them directly. There, they crouched together. "Where have you been? What are you doing here?"

"Hello, Imeris," Anahah said. "I've been in Ulellinland. There's enough foliage covering Ulellin's emergent that I can stay comfortably camouflaged there. When I realised the pattern of the attacks, I came to check on you, though it seems there was no need. You've been chosen as a Hunter. You've made a pretty good trap. I thought the least I could do was lead Orin's beast into it." Daggad came and crouched beside them, big hands opening and closing like he'd like to choke Anahah to death, glaring unhelpfully from one companion to the unexpected other.

"So you think it will work?" Imeris asked.

"No." Anahah smiled apologetically.

"Why not?"

"I don't like to say. I could be wrong. In any case, it's not far behind me. We'll soon find out together."

"There is no 'together,'" Daggad said. "She and I are Hunters. You are a—Audblayin's bones, I do not know what you are. What in the goddesses' names are you?"

"I'm what they made me to be," Anahah replied coolly. "As is the creature. But when you've killed it and I'm free of her, I'll be what I please."

"You really think that when the beast is dead, Orin will give up searchin' for you?"

Anahah shrugged glumly and didn't answer.

The lamplight streaming through the window went out.

Darkness doused all three of them. It covered everything inside the room. Imeris shuddered, reminded of the room where Aurilon had enticed her, where they had fought in utter blackness.

"Do not move," she breathed, meaning Daggad, but she could sense from the movement of air and the slight sound of scabbard being scratched across tallowwood that he was already gone. The arms of the tree groaned. Mistletoe twigs swished and crackled at the window.

Hot breath, fouler than a mountain of onions, filled the guest room.

There was a sound. A snarl, a snort, a grunt. It sounded like the room itself was grunting. Like they were already inside the mouth of a wooden monster that had only to close its jaws to crush them.

No, Imeris thought, her hands on the pins. *The jaws are metal, and they are mine.*

But she could not tell if the thing had put its head inside the room; she needed light. Her hands left the pins and fumbled through the small pile of her things beside the bed. There was a taper there, and flint. Why hadn't she thought to keep a covered lantern with her?

Before she could find her fire-starting tools, there came the sound of Daggad's scabbard hitting the floor. Another, louder grumble. Daggad's blade clattered on the wood. Daggad himself howled.

Anahah's green-gold skin began to glow. He stood between Imeris and the creature, facing away from her, drawing himself to his full, diminutive height. Daggad seemed to have been thrown back against the wall to one side.

"Aaaagghh!" Daggad shrieked, holding both his hands up in front of his face. Something was wrong with them. They were fused together. Thick, black bristles sprouted from them.

It was the same coarse hair that unevenly coated the grotesque face of the monster.

The two long tusks almost touched the wall opposite the window. The snouted face was fractured like broken pottery, the way that Unar, the crossroads folk, and the crab-stick man had described. Each fleshy section of it bore a tiny pair of human eyes.

Orin's monster closed its stinking maw. It swallowed strings of drool. All of its eyes rested on Anahah. Little human noses and mouths began growing beneath each pair of eyes. Within seconds, the new mouths had opened.

"Help us, Anahah!" they implored as one.

"I can't help you," Anahah said, sounding heartbroken.

Imeris pulled out the upper pin.

TWENTY-SEVEN

THE FREED trap-blade slammed down. The entire tree shuddered.

For a horrible moment, Imeris feared she hadn't made the blade heavy enough. That it would rest on the monster's neck but not go all the way through.

Then she saw a glint of metal. The blade had embedded itself, as designed, in the window ledge. Now the light from outside was blocked by the trap-blade, not by the creature's bulk. The horrible head lay on the floor, gushing black blood in the golden-green light.

"Don't touch it," Anahah shouted, pushing Imeris back as the head rolled to one side, the tusks now one above the other instead of side by side. He skirted the enormous obstacle, pulling Daggad back as well. His golden glow spread into Daggad's transformed hands, reversing the magical change, allowing Daggad's palms and forearms to come apart.

The head stopped rolling, but the movement in the room didn't stop. Six semihuman faces in their semiseparate lumps of meat wriggled and screamed. A sudden rainstorm roared outside the window, beyond the blocking fallen blade. Oniwak's voice raised itself in the hallway. Imeris wondered how long it would take for the head to die.

Then six lumps of meat separated themselves from the inert ivory of the tusks. The upper tusk clattered down onto the lower one. Imeris shouted a warning to Daggad. Bulging in places and shrinking in others, the meat lumps flailed until they were upright, rough human shapes. Garbled speech issued from mouths choked by black tongues. The left or right sides of their bodies still covered in boar-bristles, they lurched, their other halves naked, skinless muscle and sinew. Imeris couldn't tell if they had been Canopians or Understorians.

Daggad's sword was lost. Imeris felt her spines tremble in their sheaths, but she feared closing with it in the face of its power to absorb and transform.

Clarity. The yellowrain longbow she had bought was in her hand. Without taking her eyes from the pieces of head that stumbled towards her on malformed feet, she stepped through the bow and strung it. She snatched a handful of arrows from the bed.

At such short range, her first pace-long arrow passed all the way through the chest of one of the pieces. It struck the piece behind, sticking into the neck.

"Hearts can regrow," Anahah shouted. "But not minds."

Imeris put her next arrow between the eyes of the closest miscreation. As the first arrow had, it passed through, but this time, the thing fell to the floor. It didn't move again.

Imeris shot smoothly, one arrow after another, with the elbow of her drawing arm hard up against the door. The second trap blade hovered overhead, gleaming in Anahah's glow just out of her field of vision. Daggad swore and dropped to the ground to avoid being hit by a pass-through.

The meat pieces were all down. Imeris found herself with one final drawn arrow, searching for a target, finding none, the fletching soft against her ear.

Behind her, the door flew open. It swung her elbow around. The nock of the arrow escaped her grip.

"What is going on?" Oniwak shouted in sudden darkness.

Imeris, knocked to her knees behind the door, clutched her longbow and tried not to replay in her mind what she'd seen before Anahah's glow had gone out.

Her last arrow had struck him. But where?

Hearts can regrow. But not minds.

Ibbin peered around Oniwak, holding a lantern. In the bright, blue-white light, Daggad and Imeris stared at one another in horror. Anahah was nowhere to be seen. He was invisible, somewhere.

Which means he is alive. He is alive!

"Is it dead?" Oniwak's bark was imperative. Insistent. "How have you done this? Why was I not told of this?"

"The creature's body," Imeris said hoarsely. "What has happened to the body? Did the Lakekeeper wash it away?"

Oniwak only stared imperiously down at her until Ingaget squeezed past him, holding his gourd flask with the potion of the winds out to her.

"The body," the old man said with an expression of mild concern, "is—"

But Imeris did not learn from him the fate of the monster's body, for the second pin came silently loose from the wall. The beheading machine cut Ingaget and his parchment stole into two halves, sealing Oniwak and Ibbin outside the room.

Imeris cried out involuntarily. She crawled to the still-trembling block and felt for Ingaget's body. What she felt and smelled made her want to retch. There was no way for him to be revived; not even Unar's skill could heal this.

She, Daggad, and Anahah were alone in the dark again.

"Anahah," she shouted, and Orin's ex-Bodyguard flickered to a lower grade of brightness like a half-crushed glowworm. Imeris looked quickly away from what remained of Ingaget, swallowing hard. Anahah lay on his back by the window. "Anahah, have I killed you, too?"

"I'm here," he whispered. There was no sign of the arrow. It must have passed through him. A wound in his chest slowly closed; the ability to change was even more useful than it seemed. "I'm not dying."

"Give me that potion-a winds," Daggad croaked, crawling through the congealing blood to the place where the gourd had fallen from Ingaget's papery hand. Imeris tried to pass it to him but found she couldn't move. Her knees still shivered with the shock of the second blade falling. Her eyes skittered away from what was in front of her.

"He did not know about the trap," she said as Daggad swigged from the gourd. "We did not warn him. I thought they would try to stop me. They do not see a Hunter when they see me."

"Get up," Daggad said, stoppering the gourd, shoving her shoulder. "Can you 'ear that? Somebody is fightin' the monster's body out there. We 'ave to help them."

"We cannot get out, Daggad," Imeris said flatly. "That was the entire purpose of the trap, to keep the head and body from joining back together."

Daggad staggered around the fallen mounds of flesh over to the window. There, he picked up the adze and started chopping at the side of the groove that held the turpentine block. Chips of tallowwood flew. Daggad's huge muscles bunched; his great arms swung. Water and blue-white lantern light started coming through the window at the side of the frame where he worked.

Imeris crawled over to Anahah. She touched his cheek. There was blood on her hand, and it made a brown streak on the glowing greenish-gold. His eyes had been closed; they opened at her touch, the irises palest green.

"Why did the creature ask you to help it?" she asked.

"They were my fellow Servants," Anahah said faintly. "Orin thought they should have predicted my so-called treachery. She punished them. She used them to form the beast."

Imeris shook her head and said nothing.

"I must leave Ehkisland, Imeris." Anahah tried to sit up, but he looked dizzy and sick. Imeris helped him. "What the creature knows, Orin knows. She knows I'm here, that her creature's between me and Ulellin's emergent, my safe haven. I shouldn't have come."

Imeris gripped his hands.

"Below the barrier," she said. "That is the way you must go back to Ulellin's emergent."

Anahah tried to pull back.

"My magic will not work below the barrier."

"Nor will the creature's."

"No," he admitted. "But I'll fall."

"I will show you what to do. I will take you to the tree. I know it."

Close to Loftfol. Close to the last place the sorceress Kirrik was seen, by my fathers and me.

Could it even be the same tree?

"Imeris," Daggad said, peering through the gap he'd made in the window frame. "Anahah. Come and see this."

Imeris didn't want to go.

"Any of that potion left?" Anahah asked.

Imeris brought it to him. Moments later, revived, he pressed the gourd on her and she accepted a swallow of nothing, a memory of Ingaget's gentle generosity. Somehow, she kept it down. Anahah eased himself to his feet and helped her up beside him. They squeezed beside Daggad to stare through the slit he'd made in the ruin of the arched window.

Raindrops caught in the lantern light like stars falling from the sky. Oniwak perched on a lateral branch at Southeats, sending crossbow bolts into the headless body of the creature as quickly as he could reload.

The headless, four-footed panther shape batted blindly at the men who stood before it on the branch road connecting Lodge and market. Water fell from nowhere, sheeting over the soggy monster's sides but not dislodging it from the path. Imeris saw Irrfahath at the forefront, swinging his bronze sword, and the Hunter from Ilanland with his double-bladed axe, chopping at the creature's neck.

Eeriez and his company had arrived back from Audblayinland.

"Eeriez poisoned one of the segments of it," Imeris guessed. A chunk of flesh at the monster's hindquarter spasmed uncontrollably. She couldn't see the Hunter from Eshland, did not expect to see him, considering his expertise at camouflage. As she watched, though, the shivering section of flesh shrivelled and fell away from the whole. The two pieces on either side of it closed seamlessly up together.

Yet the creature was made smaller.

"I suppose they will finish it without us, after all," Daggad said, sounding part relieved, part disappointed.

Then Orin's monster's padded forepaw connected with the swordsman. Imeris's breath caught, but Irrafahath was not swept into empty air. Instead, he stuck to the paw and was lifted, screaming, for the split instant it took for him to turn hairy and become absorbed.

A new, tiny, human-like head sprouted from the stump of the monster's neck.

"No," Daggad gasped.

"A terrible fate," Anahah said quietly.

Imeris watched, sickened, as two swift blows by the monster earned it two more pairs of eyes on its bubbling, expanding skull. Erth, the Hunter from Ilanland, and Ay, the Lakekeeper, were no more.

The rain stopped. Silence rang in Imeris's ears. The air above the creature emptied, and the last streams of water fell away from the hairy black hide. Ay was gone, his powers extinguished. He would drown neither the creature nor Kirrik.

"You can save them, Anahah," Imeris said, gripping his hand, pleading. "Just like you saved Daggad. You can bring them out again—"

"I can't, Imeris."

Omt, the soldier from Akkadland, was the final Hunter to be absorbed. His fine mace fell from his hand; it was the last part of him to remain recognisable. A mouth opened in the monster's new head, speckled with the teeth of four men. It made a sound like a lake draining.

Now that it could see, it lumbered all the way into Southeats. Finding Ibbin, lantern in hand, Oniwak, and Owun, the Hunter from Ukakland, out of reach, it scooped up a trio of howling shopkeepers who had been cowering behind their barrows.

"We took seven from it," Daggad said. "It took seven back. Will it come for you, now, traitor?"

"I think," Anahah said, "it's more likely that the Servants of Ehkis will come to drive it away. It ate their Lakekeeper. The rain goddess will have felt that."

"She is a child," Imeris said. She had let go of Anahah and was hugging herself. "The Lakekeeper said Ehkis was a child."

"Even a child goddess can deny water to the niche of Orinland if her anger is roused," Anahah said. "Nothing enrages a goddess like the use of another deity's power in her niche. You recall Ilan's anger. The creature can't stay."

As Anahah predicted, the monster didn't turn back towards Mistletoe Lodge. Instead, it pushed deeper through the market, headed all the way through and out the other side. Oniwak daringly climbed down from his perch to continue firing as it retreated.

A dozen crossbow bolts stuck in its backside. The monster ignored him, though Imeris's last glimpse of it hinted at the loss of another dead component, defecated over the edge like the dung of a skittish tapir.

"No use," she called out to him, knowing Oniwak couldn't hear her, suspecting he wouldn't heed her even if he could. "It will only take another innocent to replace whatever parts of itself it loses."

Anahah turned to look pointedly at the tusks on the floor.

"It can't replace those," he said. "This hasn't been a complete disaster."

"'As it not?" Daggad said angrily. "The Hunt is over! Barely 'alf of us are left alive!"

"What are they?" Imeris asked.

"They're Orin's own bones," Anahah said, "from a time when her shape was wilder and greater in size but much less mutable than it is now. They are valuable. Powerful. If we're going below the barrier, we should take them; they'll lose none of their potency there, and if nothing else, we can trade them."

"I cannot go below the barrier," Daggad said. "I am a slave of the 'Ouse of Epatut. Though with the beast following you, if I wanta kill it, I shall clearly need to stick closeta you."

"You are a slave of the House," Imeris said, "and I am a direct descendant of that House. Anahah, I am the owner of this slave, can you free him if I ask you to?"

Anahah's worn, frightened face brightened into a slow smile.

"Yes."

He turned to Daggad, put his thumb to the taller, bulkier man's lips, and pressed lightly. Daggad jerked back with a muffled cry. His eyes widened and he put out his tongue.

It was no longer marked. He put his fingers to it to feel the sudden smoothness, but there was another change left behind by Anahah's deceptively small movement.

A black thumb-imprint stained Daggad's lower lip.

"What is that?" Imeris asked.

"A reminder," Anahah said. "Let me tell you a story."

"No time for stories!" Daggad objected, but Anahah went on.

"When I was first made Orin's Bodyguard, she locked herself in seclusion for three days, telling me to go, to discover the limits of my new abilities. I transformed into a swamp harrier. I climbed high into the sky, feeling the sun blaze across my feathers, and when I spotted a red bit of flesh in the branches of the trees, I dived down on it so fast that my blood sang."

"Was it a trap?" Daggad guessed, and Anahah's smile widened.

"A flowerfowl farmer," he said. "My feet were caught by the snare. I thrashed around until he seized me by the neck. I was going to transform, to teach him a lesson, but then he whispered what a shame it was, that my chicks would starve to death in my absence, and that he would free me."

"Sentimental fool," Daggad said.

"I agree with you, Understorian. To protect himself and his interests, the farmer should've killed me, but he didn't. And I remembered to send a handful of wild cock-birds his way the next monsoon to increase the vigour of his flock. They will ask you, in Gannak, to lead them back to Canopy for revenge."

"You want me to remember this acta generosity. As if one kindness could earn forgiveness for all I 'ave lost."

"Canopy no longer has a hold on you," Anahah said, "just as the farmer no longer had a hold on me. He could only hope that I wouldn't return to kill again. I can only hope you'll leave the House that used you to its own devices."

Through the gap, Imeris watched Oniwak on the platform outside Southeats. Ibbin climbed down beside him, as did the Hunter from Ukakland.

At last, she was able to pick out the poised, utterly still shape of the poisoner, Eeriez of Eshland. His armour and tunic were not even dirty.

"You 'ad better 'ope," Daggad said, picking up the adze, "that this tool gets us out before newsa this night's farce reaches the House of Epatut."

Oniwak spun at the sound of chopping. Across the gap between trees, Imeris could feel his stare.

"Woman," he bellowed. "Can you hear me, whore—you and the slave you permitted to use you? You'd better escape from there while I'm finding my Hunters a healer! Because if I see either of you again, I'll kill you!"

He loosed a crossbow bolt in their direction, but his weapon was much less accurate than a longbow.

The missile spent itself aimlessly in the nothingness surrounding Southeats.

TWENTY-EIGHT

WHILE DAGGAD chopped at the window frame, Imeris dozed.

Not in the bed—that was taken up by half of Ingaget, whom she had set sliced side down and covered with the blanket. It was Canopian to roll corpses into the abyss; Understorian to seal them into tree hollows.

Imeris suspected that after Orin's creature had visited the lodge a second time, not only would nobody be in any hurry to return to it, but Southeats might also be abandoned. Ingaget and the slain, deformed remnants of Orin's Servants were as good as sealed in.

She slept in the sole unblooded corner.

Horroh came into her dream, again.

Whole.

Eyes burning with displeasure.

They stood in the training hall at Loftfol. The sound of falling water was the same as before. When he opened his mouth, Horroh spoke with Oldest-Father's voice.

You are the oldest child, Imeris. You have no choice but to look after your sister and brother when I am gone. They are dreamers. They do not like to work with their hands. You are the only chance they have to survive with the sorceress out there searching for all of us.

Imeris jerked awake.

Anahah knelt beside her, left hand on her shoulder, expression earnest. "It's time to go."

The boar tusks in his right hand no longer looked like tusks.

"You have changed them," she said groggily, blinking. "By magic." One ivory sword was longer than the other. Both were single-bladed and slightly curved. The longer sword had a hilt carved with birds. Leopards adorned the shorter sword. "But ivory does not cut, Anahah."

"These weapons will," he answered earnestly, "but only when brandished by human hands. They won't miss. Neither to parry nor to strike. And they can be used by adepts and nonadepts alike."

Daggad guffawed.

"If they are so great, why not take them yourself and slay the creature right now?"

"They won't work against the wild," Anahah said. "Only against mortal men and women. Domesticated beasts, perhaps. We'll barter the larger one for Understorian coin, weapons, ropes, food, whatever else we need. The shorter one is for you, Imeris."

Imeris took the white sword that had been a boar tusk.

"Why give me a sword that will fail against my enemy?"

"Don't you have other enemies?"

Imeris gazed into his glowing green eyes. *Kirrik is my enemy, but even a sword that never misses cannot parry her magic power. Loftfol is my enemy, but I do not wish them ill; I will avoid them if I can.*

"A weapon like this," she said, "would certainly surprise the Bodyguard of Odel. Yet I wonder if Aurilon is not too wild for the blade to become sharp against her crocodile skin."

Anahah smiled.

"It wouldn't do to seriously injure your future teacher, anyway," he said. "Daggad's made a hole big enough for us to get out. You said you'd show us the way."

When she poked her head out of the Mistletoe Lodge, Imeris saw two Servants of Ehkis on the platform outside Southeats. Sunrise was still several hours away.

"You had better turn invisible," she told Anahah, regathering the strong strapleaf ropes they had used for the trap and several other unused coils besides, taking a few moments while he transformed to expertly splice the ends together. She put the leather cap on her quiver to quiet the rustling of the fletches of her recovered arrows. "Daggad, follow as quietly as you can to the balcony below. The toilet will be the lowest part of the lodge, and it faces away from the food markets. We begin our descent there."

As the three of them slipped through the empty lodge, Imeris picked up one of Airak's lanterns, some tally-paper, and charcoal from the hapless innkeeper's study. She paused in the bathroom to set the lantern on the closed lid of the nearest toilet.

"Servants of Ehkis are headed here," Anahah reported, his disembodied voice issuing from just inside the arched window. "You have only moments before they enter the lodge."

Imeris scrawled out a message in her untidy handwriting. She opened the glass pane in the side of the lantern, thrust the message inside and cried out her brother's name.

The lantern flared. The message vanished. Imeris bit through her lip in an attempt to hold in a scream of pain.

Her right hand was badly burned. It hadn't happened to Oniwak when he'd done it. There had to be some trick to it, or some power bestowed on the soldiers of Airakland.

"Are you mad?" Daggad asked, swiping the lantern with the back of his hand so that it flew out the window. He seized her by the wrist of the injured hand. "That was a fire-startin' lantern. Not a cold one for light. Now you cannot climb without first salving this burn, or lose the dexterity of this 'and."

Imeris snapped her spines out angrily, barely missing him; he let go of her in a hurry.

"I can climb," she said through gritted teeth. "Onto the window ledge!"

"I 'ave no spines!"

"This is a tallowwood tree. My brother and my blood. Climb onto the window ledge, I said. I will show you what to do."

She sprang out the window ahead of him, ivory sword, quiver, adze, and longbow strapped across her back. She had to remember they were not wings. She had to remember the others could neither stick into tree bark nor, once they were below the barrier, fly. They were like children. She had to care for them.

You are the only chance they have to survive with the sorceress out there searching for all of us.

"Give me your great sword," she instructed, dangling by the spines of her right forearm, reaching up with her left hand for the sword. Daggad reluctantly unbuckled it. Holding it by the harness, he let it dangle into her palm.

Imeris thrust the sword, scabbard and all, horizontally through the bark of the tallowwood tree like a tailor putting a needle through cloth.

"Anahah must cling to you, Daggad, monkeyback style," she said. "All you need to do is hold one end of your great sword in each hand and do not let go." One-handed, Imeris secured one end of the single spliced rope to the harness of the great sword. The other end, she tied to one of the slanting support timbers of the protruding bathroom. "This coil is three hundred body lengths long. That is more than enough to get us below the barrier, yet not so long that you will come to Floor. Wait for me when you reach the end of it."

"What is down there?" Anahah's voice inquired. "Is it Loftfol?"

"It is the village of Het," Imeris answered, using her shin spines to swing her body to one side, making way for Daggad and his invisible rider. "There will be spies from Loftfol there, no doubt. We must keep ahead of them, while also keeping you below the barrier for no more than five or six hours at a time, lest you lose your arcane aura." She would have gained an aura herself in the course of the Hunt, and must not let it escape her.

"Sounds easy," Daggad said, laughing, taking hold of the great sword, one hand fractionally ahead of the other.

Vertical cords of grey tallowwood bark pulled away from the tree. The fresh bark was reddish-brown beneath. The gap that opened as the sword took Daggad's weight was only a hand's breadth, enough for the sword and its passengers to begin a slow slide downwards.

Imeris watched as their speed increased. She sucked her bleeding lip into her mouth, trying to feel confident. The strapleaf rope would hold. The splices were good. There would be no defects in the fibrous bark. The strip would be continuous to the base of the tree. And Daggad was strong.

He shrank away into darkness.

Doubt gnawed at her. She couldn't help but remember the moment her trap had ended the old man Ingaget. Images flashed before her eyes: her arms dangling, ungainly, upside down while her fathers battled the sorceress. Horroh had told her to trust her body, but it had betrayed her when she'd needed it most; she should have flown more, used her sword less, left her armour behind; if she'd been more Understorian, she would have known that. Her failure at Odel's emergent. The stupidity of her attempt to send a message to Leaper; if she'd been more Canopian, she would have known that.

Would the blond man with the birds be waiting in the village of Het?

Imeris shook her head. There was no choice but to go on. She could hear footsteps falling in the passages of the lodge, most likely those Servants of

Ehkis investigating the incursion of Orin's wild magic into their mistress's niche.

Ignoring the terrible pain and dangerous tightening in her right hand, not wanting to add her weight to the strapleaf rope that safeguarded her unspined companions, she began to climb carefully down after them.

TWENTY-NINE

IN THE dimness of Understorey, Anahah lost his invisibility as well as his ability to glow.

"Try to calm yourself, friend," Imeris heard his soft voice saying, over and over, as she neared the end of the rope where he and Daggad dangled.

"Is something wrong?" she called, her bottom lip scabbed and painful. Her arms and legs were covered in bark dust from the tallowwood tree. It was an hour or so since she'd last seen them on the other side of the barrier. She reached out to touch the rope with her left hand and found it jerking violently.

Daggad's body shook. His breathing stuttered, interrupted, as though his windpipe was being periodically squeezed by a huge fist, yet Anahah held him by the shoulders and not the throat.

Daggad still held the sword in both hands.

"Daggad," Imeris said urgently. "Where is the pain? I can take you back up, but it will not be quick. What is happening to you?"

As she spoke, she hung by her shin spines and freed the adze from her back. Less useful than an axe for splitting planks, she was nonetheless able to hack through the bark to the sapwood of the tree and bluntly batter until a piece resembling a plank splintered off into her raw and bloodied hands.

She dropped the adze before she could make a wedge to stick the plank in.

Careless. Hopeless. It seemed vital that he be able to sit or stand before the strength in his arms gave out and he fell down to Floor.

"Daggad," she said, trying to stay calm, "do you have a bore-knife? A skinning knife? Any kind of knife?"

Daggad bucked and trembled and strained for breath.

"Your arrowheads," Anahah suggested. "I have nothing but my bare hands, and he can't speak."

"Was he wounded on the way down? A branch? A sharp bit of bark?"

"I don't know."

Imeris hung backwards from her shin spines, arching her back, loosening the cap that held her arrows in their quiver. It was a fool move—*too impatient, but he is dying!*—the arrows fell out of their upside-down leather cocoon, and she was lucky to snatch a single shaft out of the air before they were all lost.

The point was less than a hand width long, its cutting edge quickly blunted against the bark. Imeris shouted with frustration, let it go when it stopped making headway, and finished the wedge with her aching forearm spines.

At last, she was able to stick the splintered plank deep enough into the tree that it would bear Daggad's weight. She and the ex-Bodyguard helped the huge Hunter into a sitting position, his legs dangling over the side of the plank. Anahah knelt beside him, but Imeris kept her weight on her spines.

She put her bloody palms to his cheeks.

"Daggad," she said. "Look at me. Speak to me. What is happening to you?"

"I cannot," Daggad managed between gasps. "Be here."

"Why not?" Imeris loosened the straps holding his shield and cloth-wrapped bundle to his back. Her hands found no punctures in his chest or in his throat.

"I am. The property. Of. The House of Epatut."

"No. Anahah lifted the sigil."

"There is. Other magic. Secret magic. They will. Not let. Me go!"

"There's no other magic," Anahah said gently. "I promise you. You are free."

It was almost too dark for staring into people's eyes, but Imeris took Daggad's face between her hands again and tried it.

"Look at me," she repeated. "You are not theirs. You are no one's but your own. Breathe in slowly. There is no magic to stop you. This is Understorey. Look at Anahah. Even a Servant of Orin has no power here."

Daggad exhaled a long, complete breath.

He breathed in, normally.

Out, and in.

"It cannot be this easy," he said, tears welling up. "It cannot be, or I could 'ave gone back to Nin twenty years ago."

"You are not weak," Imeris said. "It is not your fault you did not have what you needed."

She peeled her bloody hands from his face, drawing all eyes to them.

"We 'ad better find a spinewife or some other variety of 'ealer," Daggad said, "to get you what you need, woman."

"I think there's a bridge platform below us," Anahah said. "My powers have abandoned me, but I can still see."

THE SPINEWIFE of Het lived with three pet tree bears in a grey-barked poisonous milkwood tree.

Imeris stood on the near end of the bridge. Its planks rattled as Daggad and Anahah crossed behind her. They had waited some hours for the Headman of Het to set the bridges, and then waited again for the trickle of busily visiting villagers to dwindle, so there would be no witnesses to their crossings.

The spinewife's home had a pair of painted wooden signs hammered outside the arched opening. One was the emblem of the viper, letting villagers and visitors alike know who lived there. The other read DO NOT FEED THE BEARS.

"Seems safe," Daggad said over Imeris's shoulder.

"My youngest-father has been here," Imeris answered. "He told us stories about the bears."

"I don't like standing here in the open," Anahah said. "We don't have long before our auras fade. Life in Understorey might be fine for you, but it would not suit one who, above the barrier, has true wings to fly."

The high entry to the tree dripped a constant patter of toxic white sap droplets. Below the two signs, a pair of folded umbrellas rested in a fixed wooden tray. A corresponding tray sat on the inside of the open arch.

Imeris picked up an umbrella, opened it, and used it to keep the sap droplets off them for the few necessary strides. Then she folded it and set it in the second tray.

She rapped with her knuckles on the inner door, a hinged panel of spiny plum carved in the shape of heliconia flowers. The empty track of a small stream ran beneath the door. Imeris supposed it flowed only in the monsoon.

"Who is it?" a woman's voice sang out.

"A warrior. Bringing a candidate," Imeris called back.

"Eh?" Daggad spluttered behind her.

Water rushed through the hand-wide channel at the bottom of the door. Impossibly, it flowed upwards over the surface of the wood panel, filling the places between the flowers. As the door swung back into the dwelling, the water continued running upwards, twisting into a thin silver stream and funnelling itself into the open tap of a barrel on a head-high shelf.

A thin-faced old woman wearing silvery loincloth and breast bindings reached up and closed the tap. Then she closed her mouth, as though she had been singing, yet no sound had come out.

"Fairly old for a candidate," the spinewife said, eyeing Daggad, smiling a small, V-shaped smile at him before her eyes fixed on the leopard-carved hilt of the magical sword standing up over Imeris's shoulder. "Let me wrap that in chimera skin before you go any deeper, my dear. It will interfere with my clocks, not to mention the implantation of spines. Oh." Her gaze darted to Anahah's burden. "You have more than one."

"Please," Anahah said, offering her the bird-sword with a short bow. "I'd like to see those clocks. I knew a clockmaker, once."

"I knew a Canopian, once." The spinewife's pleasant tone stayed the same as she took the sword and wrapped it in precious, colour-changing cloth. "He'd been to visit a brothel in Het and stayed too long. He thought I could open the barrier for him and grew angry when I said that I could not. In the end, I had to kill him."

"Gentle healer," Imeris said quickly. "Revered spinewife. The sword you hold is made from the ivory of an Old God. It is yours, if you will help us. This man"—she patted his arm—"Daggad, a former slave and warrior of Gannak, has broken spines and needs them implanted anew. He will also need steel spines for climbing until his arms and legs have healed. That is if we are to avoid the fading of Canopian magic, the fate of the man that you described."

The spinewife's smile widened, and she tilted her head to one side.

Imeris took a deep breath. She showed her burned, scabbed palm. "I have injuries. If you would see to them, I would be grateful. We need salt if you have any to give. Arrows, if you can tell me where they may be sold. Lastly, I would ask for a route to Gannak via Ulellin's emergent. The bridges here are strange to me, and they say you have a copy of Eshland's master map. I would avoid—"

"Loftfol," the spinewife said keenly. "You would avoid Loftfol."

Imeris licked her lips.

"Yes."

"Items such as this"—she hefted the wrapped sword—"are in high demand at the Loftfol school. You would do better trading with them, unless you had some reason to avoid them. And you do have a reason, Imerissiremi, daughter of the man known here as Marram the Nightingale. Oh, yes. They search for you."

Imeris felt her spines quiver in their sheaths.

She was exhausted, her hand felt on fire, and likely she would be unable to fight a spinewife's magic. But she would try, rather than die here. She still carried the second, smaller, sword.

"I am afraid I do not know your name, revered spinewife," she said. "But I hope you can believe I am no traitor to Understorey. My father said that you found your bears as cubs in a trap and freed them. Perhaps you will allow the three of us to go free as well."

The spinewife stowed the sword in a drawer beneath a fine writing desk of purpleheart, completely unruffled.

"I am Sariras," she said. "You are safe from Loftfol here, Imerissiremi. Ten years ago, I heard your father play the thirteen-pipe flute. It was the sound of joy. A sound I will never forget."

IMERIS, HER hand bandaged, examined the clocks while Sariras prepared Daggad's new spines.

The bears snuffled at her boots and bundles, their black-furred shoulders at Imeris's hip-height. Their names were One-Eye, Stinky, and Nostrils, and their claws were filed so they wouldn't splinter Sariras's polished floor. When their bodies pressed against her, Imeris could feel their bones. It wasn't long since the monsoon had ended, and they'd come out of hibernation. They'd starved for five months.

The clocks dripped, downwards or upwards, according to the magic they'd been imbued with.

"These slivers of bone," Anahah said quietly, touching the inlay on a grey stone bowl, "must be from the Old God who became the rain goddess, Ehkis."

"You can sense that?"

"I can't sense anything." He turned gloomy. "An adept going below the barrier is like a hunter going deaf or having his hands tied. Still, these clocks could only keep time like this by Ehkis's power."

Some of the clocks were like ordinary water clocks, resin-sealed wooden bowls of water with measured leaks in the bottom and inscribed gradations down the sides: days, hours, even minutes. Water was plentiful in Ehkisland, and rich Canopian citizens would have slaves to fill their clocks for them. In Understorey, only a Headman or the master of a prosperous guild or family might own a clock, and these would be filled by the sons and daughters of the house or the lesser members of the guild.

Other clocks refilled themselves. Water droplets running out the bottom of the bowl leaped like living things up through carvings in the wood or channels in natural crystal to reach a secondary bowl set slightly above the first one. That bowl had a much wider hole in the bottom as well, yet no water escaped until the lower bowl was empty. Then, it all rushed through at once, resetting itself.

Made of rarer, more valuable materials, glazed clay or hammered copper, the members of this second type of clock had the tiny pieces of inlaid bone in common.

"The clockmaker you knew," Imeris said, touching the amulet that her sister found so offensive. "Did she use fragments of Old Gods, too?"

"Sometimes. Most of her clocks used the energy stored in metal springs, but the bodies and cogs were made of wood from Eshland, and in Eshland, the wood is the body of the god. By the time Esh comes into his full power, he hasn't got white bones like the rest of us. His skeleton is gap-axe wood."

Imeris didn't ask how he knew. As many attempts were made on the life of Esh as any other god.

They left the clocks to watch Sariras renew Daggad's broken spines. She strapped the hulking Hunter to a slab table and sang in a wild, startlingly loud voice that was dampened into silence almost as soon as it had begun.

Daggad lay still, sweating in his loincloth, staring at the milkwood ceiling with a fixed grimace. Under Sariras's hovering, empty palm, the seams in his forearms and shins peeled open, exposing bloodless bone.

Opening her mouth even wider, vibrating her throat as though singing at full volume and yet still silent, Sariras gently plucked the broken spines from the seams like a grandmother removing splinters. Imeris watched without expression as the spinewife brought out a steel knife and a board layered in reptiles that were stunned senseless but not dead. Sariras cut off snake's head after snake's head, ripped out fanged jaw after fanged jaw. The bloodless nature of the implantation was over.

Sariras dropped the knife onto the body-strewn board and sighed hoarsely when she was done.

"I am tired," she said. "I shall sit. Clean his skin, if you would, but do not disturb the spines."

Anahah filled a water bucket and found a cloth. They did as the old woman had said, Imeris trying to avoid wetting her bandages, using only the fingertips of her injured hand.

"I can see stars," Daggad said blearily.

"No you can't," Anahah said. "Close your eyes."

Daggad obeyed.

Imeris clumsily rubbed at the snakes' blood, clumped and clotting on Daggad's skin, on the table, and on the bindings holding him down. She darted a glance at Anahah.

"You flew higher than the forest," she said. "When you were a bird. What are the stars?"

"Airak's lanterns," Anahah said softly, without looking up from his task. "Carried above the clouds and abandoned there by the winged. Not even a Bodyguard of Orin dares fly that high."

"What are the winged?"

"Something between oversized human and flying snake, all made of fallen leaves." Anahah's cloth skirted the edge of a row of new spines. He frowned in concentration. "Kin to chimeras and titans, but where chimeras didn't have the brains to be a threat to their cousins, the winged did, and were banished for it."

"And what are titans?"

Anahah looked at her at last, his frown deepening.

"Weren't you a student at a famous school?"

"A fighting school." Imeris flicked her cloth back into the bucket and pressed her knuckles to her hips. "You know what kind of school."

"You know plenty about the titans." Anahah's hands went still. His eyes narrowed. "There were thirteen of them. The forest was raised when they died. Sometimes they looked like giant lizards, sometimes like men and women of a height with the great trees. You call them the Old Gods in Understorey. In Floor, they fossick for their bones."

THIRTY

IMERIS ACCEPTED the carefully tailored map with her head bowed in thanks.

Sariras had used different coloured inks to represent the great trees. Poinsettia pink for bloodwoods. Lichen grey for floodgums. Orchid bulb blue for quandong. Some of the trees were represented by dyes made from their own leaves or bark: strangler fig red, tallowwood green, and acacia brown.

Ulellin's emergent, windowleaf over floodgum, was shown as a blob of grey surrounded by a circle of pale citrine. It was the one. The tree where the Bird-Riders had led Imeris, where Kirrik's dovecote had been and Oldest-Father had died. Would Kirrik be more likely to build again in the same niche, or less likely? She could have asked Sariras for rumours, but the loss of Ay the Lakekeeper had cautioned her not to seek allies for the fight against the sorceress until the Hunt was done.

"Thank you," Imeris said. She hesitated with Anahah and Daggad in the grey milkwood archway, just short of the curtain of toxic sap-rain. Caught the spinewife's gaze and glanced upwards. "What will we find in your tree at the level of the city?"

"I do not know," Sariras said, raising her brows, passing Imeris an umbrella, "but a great deal of faeces comes down the south side, so you had best climb up the north."

Once on the other side of the dripping arch, Daggad grimaced as he set his steel spines into the tree. They were strapped onto his arms and legs over the top of the raw wounds of his new implants. Anahah, too, wore the beginner's attire, the metal more clumsy than living fangs and in need of sharpening every hundred body lengths or so. The sharpening would interrupt their upward advance, but they no longer had the option of Imeris going first and then throwing down a rope.

It was her imagination, yet she felt distinctly less welcome in Canopy already. Their auras were fading fast. Even an hour on the low roads would be enough to restore it, and then their route would take them back down to Understorey, where neither Orin's creature nor Oniwak could get revenge on them.

I can only trust Sariras's word, Imeris thought grimly, securing her own grip on the grey, oozing milkwood bark, *that she will not send Loftfol after us, seeing as she now knows every single tree we will be travelling on.*

At that moment, a feathery weight struck near her head. She ducked and shrugged, trying to dislodge the bird. It was grey speckled with black. *An owl? It must be confused.* There was daylight, somewhere above the trees. Maybe it was sick.

"Made a new friend?" Daggad drawled, looking down at her.

"It's a mimicbird," Anahah said. "They weave floating nests on the forest floor. It's rare to see one in Understorey."

Imeris jerked her head to one side, away from the bird, trying to see it clearly. It gripped her shoulder with long, splayed toes and blinked black, beady eyes. Then it stretched its long feathery throat towards Canopy and mimicked a young, male, human voice.

"Father's grave!" it cried.

It sounded like Leaper.

"Was that you or the bird?" Daggad asked.

"Father's grave!" the bird screeched. "Father's grave!"

It flew down towards Floor while Imeris remained frozen in astonishment.

"Never mind," she eventually called back up to Daggad, thinking, *Leaper got my message. The Godfinder has taught him her bird-taming tricks. He's agreed to meet me at Ulellin's emergent.*

Oldest-Father's grave.

THEY APPROACHED Ulellin's emergent at the level of the Temple.

It was a night and most of a day since they'd left Het. Much energy had been wasted passing back and forth through the barrier and avoiding as many eyes as possible. Imeris still wasn't sure whether she felt safer in Canopy or Understorey. Daggad's spines still weren't healed enough for him to use them.

Anahah avoided transformations when he was in Canopy, much as being invisible could have been useful to the party, because he said it would be like lighting a bonfire for Orin. As if the soldiers of Orinland with their feathered spears that pointed in his direction weren't bad enough.

"What do people ask Ulellin for, anyway?" Imeris wondered aloud, peering around the vine-wrapped trunk of a sweet-fruit pine at the emergent, only one tree away. Slaves and citizens burdened with tributes crossed two swaying bridges of windowleaves, high and low, to a polished, bronze-coloured structure shaped like two great wooden windowleaves, one above and parallel to the other, the sight of which made Imeris's skin crawl.

It looks just like Kirrik's dovecote, only larger, made of wood, and without the snakes.

Ulellin's Temple had come first, she supposed.

"Fortunes," Anahah said. "Prophecies." And Imeris remembered what the fiddler, Owun, had said to Ingaget about discovering his lost wife's fate.

Daggad, his mouth full of the sarsaparilla-flavoured leaves off the vine, gave Anahah a sceptical look, spat the leaves out, and waved a hand at some out-of-nichers in ragged shirts and skirts.

"I think those ones just want the vines they tend to produce more leaves. Ulellin is the goddess of leaves."

"Wind and leaves," Anahah said patiently. "Look at the man pushing the barrow on the high road." Imeris and Daggad turned their heads. The man wore silver-studded silk robes over split skirts and sandals whose silk ribbons wound all the way to his knees. His barrow was emblazoned with the orange hammer and tongs of what Imeris guessed was a coppersmith guild or wealthy House. It was stacked high with greenmango fruit. Anahah gave a low laugh. "Those won't be ordinary greenmangos. He's from Akkadland. They're metal-stone fruit, changed by the goddess to have copper stones inside instead of seeds. That's what it costs to know your future, citizens. Ulellin listens to the whispers of the wind. She interprets those whispers without error."

Daggad spat another ball of chewed leaf pulp as the man from Akkadland disappeared into the wooden Temple.

"What if she tells 'im 'e is goin' to get bit by a scorpion and die tonight? Think 'e will be allowedta have his metal-stone fruit back?"

"No," Anahah said.

"Follow me," Imeris said. "There is nobody on the lower crossing."

As they approached the Temple on the living, green bridge, single file with Imeris in front, she saw deeper into the Temple. Its lower entrance was crisscrossed with thousands upon thousands of orange-brown vines, each one perfectly straight, but forming the pattern of a spider's funnel, leading the eye to a lush topiary in the shape of an openmouthed woman's face.

Wind rushed in through the funnel. It caught the edges of the ragged family's clothes as they laid their tribute, a woven doll of windgrass and a fragrant fiveways fruit shaped like a man, inside the cavernous mouth of the leafy mask.

Imeris stepped off the side of the bridge before it reached the Temple. She caught herself on the juicy flesh of the windowleaf trunk with her spines, moved down out of the way, and waited for the others.

"Use your hands and feet," she told them. "There is a dead floodgum tree underneath. So many smaller trunks crossing the main trunk make easy holds, and you can save your metal spines." Sariras's gifts grew smaller with every sharpening.

"How far down is the . . . is your . . . is the grave?" Anahah asked.

Imeris tried not to recall the sight of the windowleaf trunks closing around Oldest-Father's body, covering his face, smothering him away from the light forever.

"It is quite a long way down," she said, "but Leaper does not know exactly how far. We will sleep for a few hours on this side of the barrier. Then we will descend as far as we must to find him."

THE TRIO stopped to break fast in a natural hollow in the crisscrossing windowleaf trunks.

It was shallow. They rested with floodgum bark at their backs and their heels dangling down, and it was there that Leaper found them, eating nut mix, fruit, and bean cake at the crack of dawn.

"A nest of owls!"

Imeris's chin jerked up at the sound of her brother's voice. Leaper's regrowing hair was backlit by one of Airak's lanterns that hung from a wooden pole strapped to his back. "One big and broad, one tall and thin, and one so small he's barely there—just like my three fathers used to be. Congratulations, Issi. You've got me back down here at last. I'm Leapael after all."

"Leaper," Imeris said, embracing him awkwardly around his climbing harness, coils of rope, axes, lantern, Skywatcher's black skirt, and brass bracers. "What is all this?"

"When we've finished talking and I've paid my respects to Oldest-Father," he said, "I'll need to rope a few trunk sections heavier than me, cut them free, and let the rope carry me back up to Ulellin's Temple. Why climb when you can fly?"

"You have lost your climbing fitness, you mean."

"Nothing of the sort! I'm being time-efficient. Besides, if I'd asked Airak to unlock my spines, he'd have known what I was up to. Introduce me to your fellow Hunters."

"This is Daggad, originally of Gannak," Imeris said. "He was chosen from the niche of Audblayinland." Dangling from his rope, Leaper put his right hand over his heart and made a foolish, twitchy bow that Imeris supposed he had learned in the royal court. "Are you in pain?" Imeris asked him, and he straightened his body satisfactorily. "This is Anahah."

Leaper peered keenly at the silent, unassuming-looking outcast. Here, the greenish-gold colour of Anahah's skin and eyes could be misconstrued as the combined effect of blue lantern and green foliage.

"However she chose you," Leaper murmured, "one who walks in the grace of Airak wonders if she'll choose your successor by some other method."

"Be polite," Imeris said sharply. "Orin has tried to kill all three of us. The other Hunters would like to kill Daggad and me. Oh, and Loftfol is bent on killing me."

"Fruit?" Daggad asked, offering Leaper an enormous handful. Leaper picked out a few magenta cherries.

"I need information," Imeris went on, "and everything learned by the Godfinder's birds seems to find its way to you."

"I didn't need Unar's birds," Leaper said, grinning, "to find out you killed several pieces of Orin's monster in Ehkisland."

"The only effect I had on it," Imeris answered with dismay, "was to force it to replace its dead pieces with the bodies of my companions."

"I wish I were a Hunter." Leaper sighed. "I'd finish that creature off in no time. Have you seen Ulellin's Temple up there? It's shaped like an eel trap. A perfect one-way tunnel to a room crisscrossed with vines. I'd replace every vine with copper wire. Once the beast was inside, I'd call lightning and laugh while it died. Every piece fried at once with no chance to replace any of them." He split the fruit with a thumbnail, evicted the seed, popped the sweet flesh into his mouth, and chewed thoughtfully. "Loftfol, though, I've no idea what to do about that."

THIRTY-ONE

IMERIS SHARED a glance with Daggad.

"You could kill the creature without having to be a Hunter," she pointed out, just as Daggad said, sounding shaken, "You could not call Airak's lightnin' to Ulellin's Temple!"

Leaper laughed and took some more magenta cherries from Daggad's hand.

"What about baiting the trap?" Imeris asked. "Whether you used me or used Anahah, the bait would die in the trap along with the creature."

Leaper threw seeds petulantly over his shoulder.

"Would not. I have better control over my power than that."

"Do you? Even in a different deity's niche?" Imeris's thoughts raced. This could be the end to an extremely undesirable situation, two Hunters on the run with the beast's intended prey; if Leaper really could kill the thing, life above the barrier would return to normal for her, leaving only Loftfol to worry about as she pursued the sorceress Kirrik. Daggad, grateful for his freedom, would no doubt help her in that enterprise, taking Oldest-Father's place, and if Anahah could transform into a chimera and chimeras could smell the soul of a sorceress, as the Godfinder had indicated, all could be set to rights, leaving Loftfol to be pacified by Kirrik's head and Imeris's explanations. *The curse would fall on me,* Anahah had said, *unless I used that form to save another's life,* but he would be saving a life: He would be saving Imeris and all of Kirrik's future victims.

"Whatever niche it is makes no difference to me," Leaper said carelessly.

"How can that be?" Imeris stilled his hand with her own. "This is no time for boasting, Leaper. Can you truly accomplish what you claim?"

"Will it help if I swear it on Oldest-Father's grave?" Leaper sneered abruptly in her face, so angry that he reverted to the Understorian syntax of their childhood. "Even the smallest and the weakest sibling has his own feelings and thoughts. You might have been his favourite, and Ylly might have turned out to be a goddess, but I have my uses, too!"

"Me? His favourite?" Imeris goggled at her brother. "Nothing I ever did was good enough for him. You called Middle-Father a slave, and he laughed. I called Oldest-Father a slave, and he never forgave me; he beat me half to death, took my weapons away, and did not call me by my real name ever again!"

"Not where you could hear him," Leaper retorted. He mimicked Oldest-Father's stiff carriage and said in a flat, harsh voice, "Issi is a Heightsman. Issi comes home. She steals away from Loftfol every chance she gets to visit her fathers. She shows the proper respect. She has the strength of a man. Never mind that Leapael is lazy and inept. Issi will defend the home when I am gone."

"I never—" Imeris tried to interrupt, stricken, but Leaper continued over the top of her, kicking at the tree in a fury.

"Issi this, Issi that! Too late for me to visit him now, isn't it? And where are you? Not defending the home, are you? You're here, hiding from Orin's beast, begging me to defend you! If only Oldest-Father could see us now!"

Imeris punched him in the mouth. Hanging from his rope, he escaped the full force of the blow. He tried to punch her back, but by then he was spinning, flailing; at some point they stopped trying to hit each other and just struggled to hold on to each other; it occurred to Imeris that he might fall, and then she would have killed her brother as well as her teacher, besides being responsible for Oldest-Father as well.

The sound of her own ugly crying was horrible in Imeris's ears. It didn't help that Leaper was bawling, too. Daggad pulled them both back into the hollow. He and Anahah said nothing while Imeris and Leaper cried and held each other. Leaper, like any young Skywatcher and regular at the king's court, had anointed himself with oils. He smelled like frangipani over sweat and char and sand.

"I pretended to be asleep," he gasped against her shoulder, "when he needed help checking the traps."

"I made fun of him," Imeris said hoarsely, "because he was afraid to fly."

"I despised him for having no magic ability."

"He would not let me visit Nirrin. I wished for him to die."

"I wished that Airak was my father instead. I told him so. To his face, Issi."

When she felt calm, and when Leaper's trembling subsided, Imeris pushed him out to arm's length.

"You are not the weakest," she said. "Nor the smallest, come to that."

He pulled a cord out of his shirt. It secured a chimera-leather pouch around his neck. Inside, there was a curved, flattened ivory shape like an animal's claw. It was the diameter of his palm.

"This is Tyran's Talon," he said, wiping his nose with the back of his other hand. "I overheard the Godfinder telling Aforis it was in the Earth-House of Hundar. That's a mud building below Airakland where Understorians from the village of Hundar meet and trade with the Floorians of Gui. Our Temple also trades with Gui. They're our source of black sands. For a price, I was able to convince one of the Gui traders to put the Talon into one of the bags of sand, which I intercepted."

"You have a long story about this thing and where it came from," Imeris said, staring at it, "but no mention of what it does."

Shame darkened Leaper's cheeks.

"It's a bone of the Old God who became Airak," he said in a rush.

Imeris understood at once.

"It makes you stronger than you should be in Airak's power."

"They'd take it from me if they knew. I'm only a Skywatcher, and—"

"And they do not like it when we have their bones," Imeris said softly, touching her amulet.

Leaper nodded.

"I wasn't boasting," he said. "I'll kill Orin's beast for you, if you want me to."

"Will the goddess not be in 'er Temple when you call lightnin' to it?" Daggad asked incredulously. "She and 'er Bodyguard and all others who serve 'er?"

"Ulellin lives in the leaves," Leaper said without taking his eyes from Imeris. "At the very branch tips, tossed by the wind. She and her Bodyguard and all others who serve her. They're wafer-thin, like leaves themselves, and the leaves move to catch their feet whenever they take a step. They come down every ten days or so to eat and drink and for the goddess to repeat in normal speech what the wind's told her. Lightning travels down through trees, not up. Springing a trap in the Temple wouldn't harm her."

"What about the king's fortune in wires? Where would they come from?"

"The copper in the metal-stone fruit, Daggad," Imeris said, touching his arm. "The tribute we saw the man wheeling along the bridge."

"You would need a coppersmith to shape them. It would take a week."

"I know the smith in Gannak," she said, surprising herself. "We were going to go there anyway. And Leaper said the goddess comes down only every ten days."

"You wouldn't really need to replace *every* vine with a wire," Leaper said. "The trap would still function with every second or third one replaced."

"Ulellin won't forgive you, Skywatcher," Anahah said softly, speaking to Leaper for the first time. "Her memory is long. You'd draw the mantle of future secrecy and fear from your sister's shoulders onto your own."

"A future like yours, you mean?" Leaper said scornfully. "Airak will protect me. I'm loyal to him."

"I don't question your loyalty," Anahah said. "I was a loyal Bodyguard for many years. It's their loyalty to us I no longer trust."

Leaper's chin lifted.

"My sister is Audblayin. She's Issi's sister, too. Slander her, and we'll see if your ability to survive lightning is any better than the creature's." Anahah's expression didn't change, but one hand fluttered reflexively to his abdomen.

"Stop it, Leaper," Imeris said.

"You fight like a young crocodile," Anahah said, "whose throat hasn't yet sealed against the water. You'd drag an adversary into the lake to drown him, not caring that you'd drown yourself as well."

Daggad, who had gobbled down a few bean cakes while he reconciled himself to the idea of desecrating the wind goddess's sanctuary, perked up interestedly.

"What do I fight like?" he asked.

"A tree bear," Anahah answered, still watching Leaper. "Very bold against enemies of your own size and calibre, but underestimating the efficacy of a spider's venom."

"And me?" Imeris prompted.

Anahah met her gaze in the blue light of Leaper's lantern. He hesitated.

"You should use whatever set bridges you can find at this level," he said. "We must all return to Canopy. Our auras are fading. I'll keep to this tree while you fetch your smith from Gannak. With new scent laid over old and plenty of greenery to camouflage myself in, I'll be safe until your return, but be careful. The beast will be close by."

"We will be careful," Imeris said, feeling a pang to part with him. Even without his powers, his presence and his knowledge were a comfort. "We have the map. The next time you see us, we will have the Silent Smith, Sorros, to help finish the beast once and for all."

"I'll leave the lantern here," Leaper said, "nailed to the tree. Send me a message when you need me again. This one burns cold, big sister. It's no good for starting cooking fires, but it'll be safe for you to put your hand into the light."

"Not one of yours, then?" Imeris laughed as he used the blunt end of his axe to fasten the lantern in the hollow.

"Not one of mine," he admitted. "I stole it from the Shining One myself."

THIRTY-TWO

"THAT CANNOT be all of it," Daggad said.

From their position in a rare Understorian-level lateral branch, the village of Gannak was visible all at once. Connected by the ropes and pale wooden boards of its bridges, all set by this hour of the morning, it comprised a dozen trees whose windows flickered with firelight. Their external platforms and some of the bridges were also lit, by scented bark torches for the midautumn festival day, Full-Belly, which would culminate by early evening in feasts and singing.

"Has it not grown since you left?" Imeris asked.

"It 'as shrunk. Or I 'ave grown."

"Or you have gotten used to Canopy." She shrugged a little. It seemed smaller to her, too. The sight and smell of the Full-Belly torches drew her back to a time when she raged against her fathers for forbidding her trips to Gannak. A child's careless tattling in the village could have been dangerous to her fathers then.

It was dangerous to them now. Loftfol had watchers in Gannak. She was glad to have approached it from the opposite direction to the tallowwood tree where her fathers had raised her.

"The forge is in the jackfruit tree," Imeris said, struck by the painful memory of how Nirrin and Vesev had died. "Nirrin's house—Nin's house—is in the ulmo tree." That other memory, of filching honey, made her smile. "The forge is closer, but Sorros might not be working on a festival day."

"What else would 'e be doin'?" Daggad asked grimly. "'Is children are dead, and you called 'im Sorros the Silent. Is 'e likely to be at the ti-house having a chat?"

"To the forge, then." Imeris didn't want to go to the forge. Not really.

Daggad went down ahead of her, roped to her harness, as he was trialling his new spines for the first time this morning and Imeris had talked him into using caution. He was a heavy man, and she wasn't sure that if he fell she'd be able to hold them both, but it made her feel slightly better.

They passed through a beaded curtain of dried, painted quandong seeds in the side of the jackfruit tree to find the forge fire dark and cold. Imeris's skin prickled at the haunting presence of Vesev and Nirrin. She felt sure their souls had been reborn by now, but the sensation of watching eyes remained present.

Forgive me, Oldest-Father. If I had known what Nirrin was that day, if I had killed her before she could escape . . .

Imeris lit a taper, dropped it into a ghost gourd, and hung the gourd at her waist. Daggad moved past her, deeper into the wide, circular space.

In the dim room, Imeris could now make out hammers and tongs hanging from pegs on the walls, cold-working tools and bell moulds on bench tops, bags of precious sand, lumps of beeswax, charcoal piles, sharpening stones, and immoveable-seeming anvils. Split skins of a very small number of half-rotted, mango-smelling fruit revealed seeds of iron, copper, silver, and gold.

"Not laminated." Daggad grunted, picking a half-polished sword blade up from a table. "It is the cast duplicate of a Canopian sword. Just like the weapon you carried when we met. I suppose I should be glad you 'ad solid steel and not tallowwood." He put down the blade and picked up a wooden sword, leather wrapped around the handle, razor-thin chips of metal set into the edge and point.

A black shape leaped out from under a table, swinging a hammer the size of Daggad's head.

"The smith! Do not harm him!" Imeris cried. Daggad's instinct must have been to slash his attacker with the wooden sword; he threw himself backwards instead, and the hammer crashed into the table over which Daggad had bent his head. "Sorros, stop, we are friends, I am Imeris-siremi!"

The silhouette turned to her, blanched, black-bearded face and short black hair revealed by the light of the gourd lantern, teeth bared.

"No traitor's spawn will steal from me," Sorros seethed. "I know who you are. They came 'ere, your fellow students. They warned us you would seek new weapons."

"I have weapons!" Her heart knocked hard against her ribs. She'd never seen Sorros like this before, and it was as frightening as if he were possessed by a sorceress himself. "I came seeking your wife and you."

"You will die before you raise a hand to 'er! It was no accident my son and daughter died when they were with you."

Imeris also hadn't heard Sorros speak so many words in the entirety of their acquaintance. She put another table between them when he raised the hammer and took two steps towards her.

"No," she said, holding her empty hands high. "It was no accident. The sorceress needed your daughter for the magic she would someday wield. Vesev died because he was in the way. That is not why I need Nin." As she spoke the words, she suspected it was useless. Sorros would never agree to help her. Loftfol had turned every weapons maker in Understorey against her, and Gannak had been against her fathers, especially Middle-Father, from the beginning. Sorros continued his advance, teeth gritted, hammer raised. What could she do? She couldn't kill him.

"Wait," Daggad said. "I know you. The boy who ate all the checkers pieces because 'e lost the game." Sorros lowered his hammer. Daggad smacked himself in the forehead with the hand not holding the wooden sword. "No. Why would she do that? Why would she marry House Gannak's youngest? Gods' bones! What an insult! The boy who ate the checkers!"

Sorros drew himself up indignantly.

"Who are you? 'Ow do you know me?"

Daggad put the wooden sword down, because he needed both hands to contain his laughter.

"The boy who ate the checkers," he hooted, pointing at Sorros. "The boy who shat splinters for a whole monsoon! It was too muchta hope that she would choose somebody sensible the second time around. Well met, Gannak Sorros, the Silent Smith, Lord of Checkers."

"Give me your name, dunderhead!"

"I am Daggad, sonna the spinewife Rididir. You and I shared a classroom, on the rare occasions you cameta school, before you went to your uncle's village to 'prentice to the smith. You were away when I set off on the raid, but we shared somethin' else besides the classroom. A wife, it turns out."

Sorros stared. He waited until Daggad stopped laughing. Imeris kept the table between them, still uncertain.

"Nin is at the ti-house," Sorros said at last. "Helpin' to prepare the feast." Imeris thought of the breakfast table of Audblayin, overflowing with greater amounts and varieties of dishes than Sorros had likely ever seen. *Feast* had a different meaning in Canopy. In Gannak, the name of the festival reflected the fact that only a once-yearly feast could result in a full belly. "I am regretful, Daggad, to tell you that your mother is dead. Our daughter, Nin's and mine, who would 'ave been the new spinewife, is dead also."

"May she be reborn a goddess," Daggad said lightly.

"Your companion could tell you more of Nirrin's death." Sorros frowned heavily at Imeris.

"My companion, as you call her, is enlisted by the Canopian Hunt to kill a demon set loose by the goddess of birds and beasts. I 'ave been named a Hunter also. If you cometa Canopy, if you help us, I promiseta make no claim to Nin, to your house or your belongin's."

"You 'ave no claim! They said you were dead!"

"I am not dead."

"'Er life is with me. She would not chooseta go with you." Sorros set his hammer down on the anvil with a clang. "And I do not believe you would force 'er."

Daggad sighed. He rubbed his chin. "No," he admitted. "I would not. Come along, Imeris. We must find ourselves another smith."

"Daggad," Imeris said, startled, "you must stay here. This is your home. Canopy cannot come after you here. Epatut and Otoyut cannot come after you. Forget the Hunt. Leave the creature to me."

"I 'ave no home," Daggad said. "I 'ave no wish to be a wedge between my once-wife and this man. Besides"—he ducked his head to hide his expression and waved in her direction—"a skinny girl like you could not carry the necessary equipment up to the Temple. Whether 'e makes wire by cuttin' thin strips from 'ammered sheets or by forcin' it through a confined channel in a die, drawplates, swage blocks, and 'ammers are 'eavy."

"I am curious," Sorros said, "about 'ow you intendta take me through the barrier to Canopy to make a wire snare for a demon."

"More than a simple wire snare is needed," Imeris said.

"The birth goddess owes my companion a favour," Daggad said.

"Wait a minute!" Imeris moved out from behind the table, towards Daggad. "No. It was my intention to bring the metal-stone fruit down for the smith to work on below the barrier where he would be safe from the creature."

"Many favours," Daggad told Sorros, ignoring her. "You could say Imeris and Audblayin were like sisters."

The smith tangled his fingers in his beard.

"Could these many favours extend," he asked, "to granting my Nin another child? It is late for us, I know. We 'ad not dared to 'ope. I might risk facing a demon, for a child's sake. Is the demon a dayhunter?"

"It is no dayhunter," Imeris growled.

"Leave a message for Nin," Daggad said. "Tell her you will be battling demons for ten or twenty days."

Sorros picked up a stick of charcoal and began riffling through a drawer for something to make marks on, but then he hesitated.

"Battling demons in Canopy when they care nothing for our demons down 'ere. Bah!" He shook his head and resumed rifling. "You 'ad better make it worth my while, once-'usband to my wife."

"Come with us to Audblayinland," Daggad said. "We will ask favours of the goddess together."

"Unless the asking meets with a favourable response," Imeris corrected him, still irritated, "there will be no passage to Audblayinland."

Sorros loaded himself and Daggad with the tools he thought he might need. He led them by quiet back bridges to the tree that was furthest from the centre of the village. It was a gobletfruit, uninhabited. The cool, smooth, richly coloured orange-brown bark was lightly pitted as though raindrops had made an impression on it.

The three of them had climbed only a dozen body lengths or so before Imeris, in the lead, noticed Daggad looking back towards the village, frozen against the tree trunk.

"What is it?" she called down to him, but when she saw where he looked, she caught her breath and covered her glowing gourd with one hand.

Outside the spiny plum which hosted the ti-house of Gannak, one of the torches had gone out. A tiny, distant figure stretched a taper to relight it.

"It is not 'er," Sorros said gruffly from below both of them. "Whoever it is, they are too far away to take notice of that weak excuse for a lantern. Carry on."

But Daggad didn't move.

"Daggad," Imeris said sharply. He looked up, and she lifted her hand from the ghost gourd at once; his expression was agony.

"I should 'ave done what your fathers did," he said, stricken.

"Commit murder and go into exile?" Imeris struck her spines, hard, into the bark of the tree. "You would have lost her anyway."

IMERIS FELT nothing as they passed through the barrier.

Daggad followed her easily. Yet when she looked back, Sorros pressed his hands against something invisible and unyielding. Light from Airak's lanterns and the full moon illuminated his awestruck face.

"Now what?" Imeris asked, inching along a lateral branch, making room for Daggad. Sorros could not reach them.

"Now," Daggad answered, shifting the pair of baskets laden with blacksmith's tools on his back, "you run aheadta the Garden. Get your sisterta come back 'ere and bargain with Sorros."

"It is the middle of the night," Imeris argued. "Even if the goddess Audblayin did come to the barrier to bargain with murderous outlawed Understorians in full view of her subjects, she would not come now."

"Somebody will come." Daggad plucked at the knots in the safety line holding him to Imeris. "You can do the bargainin'. Somebody with the power to open the barrier will listen to you."

"You forget." Imeris snatched her rope away from him. She coiled it efficiently in her all-but-healed hand. "I cannot enter the Garden."

"But you can try to get Sorros what 'e wants. Ulellin's Temple is waiting. Anahah is waiting."

She stuck her tongue out at him.

"Wait above the barrier," she said, "to refresh your aura, but do not lose sight of Sorros. We do not want him changing his mind just yet."

When she had climbed high enough to reach the low roads of Canopy, she stopped to empty her bladder, wash her hands, and splash some water on her face. It had been days or weeks since she had felt safe enough to have a proper, long rest; until the creature was slain, she had no choice but to carry on.

The Great Gates of the Garden were deserted. Lanterns lining the platform in front of the Gates threw the carvings into dramatic relief.

Battles. Audblayinland soldiers in two-by-two centipede formation, short swords raised and long spears levelled. They gripped branch roads beneath their studded sandals and faced Understorian warriors with wild eyes, thin lips, noses like blades, and spines out in all the usual places as well as some fanciful ones. Imeris had rarely looked at the finely detailed background carvings. She didn't care to see herself depicted as a beast.

Yet, this time, something caught her eye. One of those smaller, back-grounded scenes. A Gatekeeper of the Garden, lantern held high, summoned a maze of vines against a creature with a tusked head and what might have been spots or might have been twelve pairs of eyes. In another difficult-to-decipher, almost-hidden scene, the soaring Bodyguard of Aud-blayin met a winged animal made of leaves in the skies over the Garden.

Imeris touched the wood of the Gate, a subconscious gesture, as if she could brush away the bristling Servant in the foreground of the image and more clearly see the smaller shapes of Gardeners. They hurled seeds at a cohort of invaders who had hair and eyes half light and half dark. The seeds sprouted in the hair of the invaders, and roots tried to strangle them.

And lightning fell among the Gardeners.

These are not only battles of Canopy against Understorey. These are Airak's Servants attacking the Garden!

Then the gate cracked open, making her jump. Aoun stood there with his lantern, shadows under his deep-set eyes. When he recognised her, his attention drifted beyond the circle of light, as if he expected Orin's beast to be following behind her.

"It is not here," Imeris said softly, looking up at him. "I need to speak to my sister. I do not wish to wake my middle-father."

Aoun sighed.

"Unlike me," he said, "your father doesn't sleep. Remember?" Imeris grimaced. Lack of proper sleep must be impairing her more than she thought. "Go into his house, sister of my mistress. I'll rouse the goddess for you. Where are your companions?"

"I have not come to interview anyone on behalf of the Hunt. I wish to ask for the gift of a child, on behalf of an Understorian woman and man."

"That's not for you to ask," Aoun said, frowning. "She's a goddess of Canopy. Did Oos suggest that you come? She presumes much for a fallen Servant."

"I will ask Audblayin myself," Imeris said stubbornly.

She went to Middle-Father's house. The door was closed. She knocked on it in a pattern they had once used when hauling tree kangaroo carcasses in the dark. The door opened, and Middle-Father's hairy, hulking, tattooed form filled it.

"Middle-Father," Imeris said in the instant before they embraced.

"Is it dead?" Middle-Father murmured. "Have you killed it? They told me to go down below the barrier to avoid being named a Hunter. I am so sorry! I should have refused. I could have taken care of it."

"Magic will take care of it," Imeris said, letting him lead her inside, where the hearth fire that blazed, bringing beads of sweat in an instant to her skin, was an exact replica of home. "Leaper will take care of it. It will not be long now. Besides, being named a Hunter saved me from becoming a slave."

"I worry about you."

"Do not worry." Imeris detached from him, stepping past him, mesmerised by the flames.

"I am not talking about the beast. Leaper said Loftfol has turned against you."

"I killed Horroh the Haakim."

"Have you come for a tattoo?" Middle-Father indicated one of his oldest tattoos, of the head coming clean away from the Headman of Gannak's shoulders, but when his grin didn't bring a smile to her face, he sighed and squeezed her shoulder. "You respected him."

"He underestimated me." Imeris felt like the words were coming from somebody else. In the flames, she saw Horroh's face.

"I am sorry you needed to do it." Middle-Father went to the table, opened a great corked gourd of turnips pickled in brine, and gave her one to eat. "And proud of you at the same time." He ate one himself, relishing the salt. "Why have you come?"

"I need Ylly to—"

"You should call her Audblayin—" He gestured with his half-bitten turnip.

"I will call her whatever I—"

"Issi," Audblayin said from behind them. A gust of wind made the flames dance and the smoke sting Imeris's eyes. Stiffly, she turned towards the yellow-robed, jewel-draped woman in the doorway. "What exactly were you going to call me?"

"Little sister," Imeris said. "I need your help."

"Turnip?" Middle-Father offered. Audblayin made a repulsed face at him.

"I need to ask for a boon on behalf of an Understorian whose help I need," she explained. "Sorros the Silent Smith, you remember? Kirrik killed his children. He will help me if you will promise to give him and his wife another child."

"A random child from Canopy?" Audblayin asked carelessly. "You can buy them at any slave market."

"Of course not. A child of their own flesh."

Audblayin drew herself up then, in the manner indicating that Ylly had been pushed to the back of Audblayin's mind.

"You've forgotten how our world works, Issi. My people bring tribute to the Garden. Their love and devotion feeds my power. That is what allows me to grant their wishes. If I spend my resources below the barrier, where I am weak, on frivolous whimsies—"

"You would be spending it to help me defeat an enemy!"

"Orin's creature is not my enemy." Audblayin slammed her palm down on the table where the turnips sat.

"No?" Imeris said in a strangled voice. "It came here, tried to kill your Bodyguard, our own middle-father, did it not? I stood at the Gate of the Garden moments ago and saw a beast very like the one I am hunting facing down some long-dead Gatekeeper. My sister was not there in that moment, but you surely were, Holy One. You say you do not interfere with the affairs of other deities, but do you know what else I have noticed? Since the Hunt began, it has not rained."

"Ehkis must have other reasons for that. She does not care—"

"I think she does! You rarely communicate with one another, you do not see, hear, or touch one another, yet you fight like a human family and your memories are long. I cannot feel it, but somewhere here"—Imeris waved her hand around in the empty air—"your magics are all interwoven with one another's. Airak allowed his niche's king to make the call. Ehkis is aiding the Hunt. Ilan as well. You could if you wanted to."

"Have you finished interrupting me?" Audblayin leaned with both hands on the table. Green leaves curled out of the gourd; one of the pickled turnips was coming back to life, trying to grow close to her.

Imeris swallowed. "Yes."

THIRTY-THREE

"AND THEN," Imeris reported to Daggad, "she repeated what she'd said about the creature not being her enemy."

Daggad snorted.

"That one feels too safe. She relies too 'eavily on 'er Gates and wards."

The night had darkened, clouds screening the moon, yet whipbirds had begun calling, indicating the approach of dawn. The trio crouched in a bark crevice below the barrier, Imeris in the middle, with Daggad and Sorros on her left and right sides, the baskets full of tools roped to the lateral branch above them. Imeris and Daggad politely ignored the smell of Sorros's night-soil; he'd been unable to manoeuvre so that it fell completely clear of the tree.

"She said," Imeris went on quickly, "that Kirrik was her only enemy. She said that if Sorros was to catch the sorceress in some sort of magical metal snare that would stop her soul from fleeing, she would grant him a child in exchange for that tribute."

"A magical snare?" Sorros said angrily. "I 'ave never 'eard of such a thing."

"Who is this sorceress, again?" Daggad asked.

"She killed my oldest-father," Imeris said, at the same time as Sorros said, "She killed my children, Nirrin and Vesev."

Imeris and Sorros looked at one another.

"You admit, then," she said coolly, "that it was not I. The sorceress walks in Nirrin's body even now. I have seen it."

Sorros buried his face in his hands.

"I 'ave seen it myself," he said, voice muffled. "Since she was taken, she 'as been seen on several occasions by warriors and 'unters from the village. I wantedta believe that it was you. You are a killer. You were destined to be a killer. You are a child of killers!"

Imeris recoiled.

"What do you mean?"

He seemed to be weeping. She tried to gently take his elbow, to bring his arm down away from his face, but in an instant his spines were unsheathed, their blunt sides pressing into the flesh of her throat, and Sorros had only to pull his elbow down for the keen edges of them to catch, for her to die as swiftly as Horroh had.

"Your father killed my father," Sorros screamed into her face. "The 'unter Bernreb killed the 'Eadman of Gannak! Do you deny that?"

"No," Imeris said, suppressing the urge to swallow.

"'Ere, now, blacksmith," Daggad said mildly. "If you kill 'er, then I will 'ave to kill you. I would much rather we all killed the creature together, followed by the sorceress you Understorians keep mentioning. I 'ave hunted all sortsa things, but never an evil soul that could switch bodies. If that old clockmaker in Eshland could make a soul cage, I do not see why a famous smith could not find a way to forge a magical metal snare to keep a sorceress's soul inside 'er body."

"I am famous for my grief," Sorros said, staring wildly into Imeris's eyes. Traces of Nirrin and Vesev were in his prominent cheeks, olive-green eyes and whorl of black hair at his temple on the left side. "When my father died, I did not speak for seven years."

"Daggad, on the other hand, did exactly as your father the Headman asked," Imeris dared. "He has been a slave in Canopy far longer than seven years."

Sorros breathed heavily. Daggad's hand rested against Imeris's turned back; she felt a knife handle in it, but the Hunter made no move to reach past Imeris and plunge it into the smith. She tried to stay relaxed and still as Sorros looked from her face to Daggad's and back again.

Then Sorros opened the fist of his right hand and his spines went back into their seams.

"I am regretful," he panted. "You are right. If you are ta blame for your father's actions, I amta blame for the actions of my father." He looked to Daggad. "I am regretful you were taken as a slave."

"I am my own man now. I am sorry about your father."

"'E is reborn, I 'ope, in an 'appier place."

Imeris put her fingers to her throat. The skin bore the indents of Sorros's spines, but it was unbroken. She'd just been very close to being reborn, herself. Her sister would oversee the linking of her soul to a new body. But she had several tasks to complete first.

Her fingers travelled to the amulet around her neck.

"This is no metal snare," she said. "Yet this old bone keeps my soul inside my body, no matter how the sorceress's magic seeks to separate the two. Perhaps, around Nirrin's neck, it can keep Kirrik from escaping."

"I will 'elp you," Sorros wept, tears running into his beard. "I will 'elp you kill the creature and the sorceress, both. Only show me the way into Canopy. The goddess did grant us passage?"

"No," Imeris said.

"No?" Daggad repeated, dumbfounded.

Imeris adjusted the amulet on its woven cord.

"That is to say, she did not open us a way through the barrier. However, she told me that Oxor, goddess of the sun, has been recently killed by an assassin. Oxor's Bodyguard died in the Hunt"—she shared a glance with Daggad—"and her Servants were not able to protect her. There is a weakness in the barrier we can exploit."

As a result of Oxor's murder, Audblayin had said, *you may find her part of the barrier permeable at its most remote point.*

What point is that? Imeris had asked keenly.

Audblayin had turned to depart Middle-Father's dwelling. Over her shoulder, she said grudgingly, *The Falling Fig.*

"Last time I 'eard those words," Daggad murmured, "my wife stood by my side and the Headman thrust his fists towards the sky."

"Lead us to this weak place in the barrier," Sorros said, wiping his face with the back of his hand. "I will not falter again. I swear it by the souls of my two children and the soul of the third child that ista come. Did the goddess say whether I should bring Nin to the Garden, once I 'ave the sorceress's soul as my tribute?"

"No," Imeris said, beginning the climb back down to the level of the bridges in Understorey. "But by her bones, she will make good on her promise." *Even if I have to drag her down to Gannak by both ears.*

"Light a taper," Daggad whispered, "so that we can see the cursed map."

"I have no more tapers," Imeris whispered back.

The trees beneath the narrow end of the teardrop-shape of Oxorland were thinner-trunked. They put all their energy towards flowering year-round, monsoon season and dry. It meant the gaps between the trees were wider, the bridges scarcer and sometimes ill-set.

Imeris leaned back against deeply creviced suntree bark. The empty platform before them, which should have been receiver to the third-last bridge before the Falling Fig, hadn't been set at all, and Imeris struggled to see where on the map the spinewife had made for them they might backtrack and find another way.

"Sure would 'elp to 'ave your glowworm friend with us 'ere now."

"Maybe if you moved your fat head, I could catch a bit of sunlight."

"Maybe if you took over carryin' one of these tool baskets, I would cast a smaller shadow."

"Forget the map," Sorros murmured. "There is only one way back. We should cross to the rhododendron and try the isu tree."

Something swished on the other side of the suntree. The bark carried a faint tremor. If the tree had not been a mere dozen paces in diameter, Imeris might not have heard or felt the disturbance.

Imeris held up a hand for silence, the map forgotten.

Youngest-Father? she thought, but it couldn't be. She'd taken his wings and given them to Odel. He was trapped in the tallowwood tree.

Sorros pointed back along the bridge in the direction of the rhododendron. Two dark shapes moved there.

"Loftfol," Imeris shouted as loudly as she could, thrusting the map into Daggad's chest. "Show yourselves, cowards!" She seized Daggad by the ear, pulled his head down, and whispered, "Sorros must get through the barrier at the fig. I can get through anywhere. Make sure he gets there."

Daggad nodded. Twisted violently and threw Sorros down onto the bridge. The Hunter thrust his arms and legs between the wooden planking, urging the smith to do the same. Tool baskets rattled on their backs. Encumbered, they could not climb quickly. Imeris would have to give them more time.

Drawing the bone sword crafted for her by Anahah, she cut the ropes of the bridge. It was still connected at the rhododendron end. Daggad and Sorros fell away into darkness. Imeris could only hope that the students of Loftfol would ignore them and come after her.

She took a moment to string her bow, but the new arrivals did not wait

to be shot and killed; satisfaction surged in her as the two murky silhou-
ettes on the far trunk expanded into wing shapes and leaped into the gap
before she could nock one of the arrows from Het.

They would land on the suntree below her. She must stay ahead of them.
Reach the barrier first. Stashing the sword and bow across her back once
more, she lunged at the tree above eye level, spines ready.

The suntree betrayed her. Bark crumbled. Her right arm swung free.

A face appeared around the trunk, startled to find her so close. Imeris
swung her spines at it, and the student twisted away.

Kishsik. The one-handed boy that Imeris had maimed in training. She
remembered his hawk's stare on the day she had beaten him to Loftfol. He'd
had two hands then. She had still beaten him. All of them.

Six years ago.

A lifetime ago.

She could beat him again now.

Forcing her tired body to a burst of speed, Imeris surged up the side of
the tree. Spines struck deeply. Loudly. Bark fragments got in her eyes. She
closed them. She didn't need to see.

In her mind's eye, she saw herself in the Loftfol training hall, forearm
raised, Kishsik's encircling hand not around her wrist, where it was safe,
but around her seams. The action she'd taken, extruding the snake-fang
grafts, had been instinctive, as had the drawing back. Horroh had not reprimanded her. Simply taken the boy to the healing room. She had paid his
family thirteen yellow-bellied glider pelts, the set compensatory price for a
serious wounding.

It had not restored his hand, however.

She climbed the suntree with the same focus she'd brought to bear on the
river nut tree the day of the race, knowing that the merest slip meant death,
but climbing ferociously towards a future where she would kill Kirrik.

"I do not understand," Kishsik shouted up at her, a body length behind.
"Why betray us? Why whore for them when they failed you, when they let
you fall?"

Imeris was not fooled into wasting energy on a reply. She tried to close
her ability to hear him with the sheer force of her determination, but his
heartfelt words made their way past her defences, past the crash and crunch
of bark and spines, the pounding of her pulse and the buzz of cicadas in
Canopy. The words nestled against her chest.

She hadn't betrayed Loftfol.

Horroh had betrayed her.

He hadn't even listened to her! He had assumed she was guilty of reporting on him to Canopian masters.

I have no masters, she raged inwardly.

She climbed until the snorting of air through her sinuses sounded like the river running over the entrance to her fathers' house. She climbed until the red she saw behind her eyes became sunlight glaring through her lids.

Imeris opened her eyes and found herself in Canopy.

Kishsik and the other students of Loftfol, who could not pass through the barrier, were nowhere to be seen in the darkness below.

THIRTY-FOUR

FLOWERS COVERED the Irofland and Oxorland sides of the Falling Fig.

That was to say, since the flowers were internal, that the branches were covered in tiny, green, hard fruit that had not yet been entered and pollinated by wasps.

The Ehkisland portion of the tree glistened with a light lick of rain, giving the lie to Imeris's assertion that Ehkis was keeping the forest dry in order to favour the Hunt. Still, it had not been enough rain to reach Understorey.

Imeris wanted to journey through the grey folded boughs, bushy foliage, and fantastic formations of aerial roots to the Audblayinland side of the fig. She wanted to sleep in Middle-Father's comfortable bed for a week straight.

She wanted to stay there and never come out. Let him defend her from Orin's beast. Forget about being a Hunter. Forget Loftfol. Forget Kirrik.

But everywhere she went, she seemed to make more promises to people. To take on new and greater obligations. Had she really told Sorros she would make sure Audblayin gave him a child in exchange for his help?

Sorros and Daggad would be hungry and thirsty. Imeris went to look for them at the market called Jewel of All Seasons, which lay in the temple-like embrace of the Falling Fig's heart. She drank from the Stream of Fortune where it fell from a higher pool into one speckled with bright yellow fallen fig leaves. With a dripping mouth, she watched the surface of the broader pool, busy with ducks, spoonbills, and small children with baited twine trying to catch little red crayfish. When a pickpocket laid a hand on her sword, she whirled, ready to throw the thief headfirst into the water.

It was no pickpocket. Daggad and Sorros had scratched and tired faces, but they appeared unharmed. They still carried the baskets of tools. Sorros tried not to stare at the mayhem and noise around him, but the way he kept trying to avoid touching other people made him look suspicious.

"We should take a room at a lodge," Imeris said, sighing. "Get some food. Rest. When we are ready, we will take the low roads to Ulellinland."

"I may be recognised 'ere," Daggad said. "The House of Epatut trades at the Falling Fig in years of excess."

They would recognise a freed slave, a stolen belonging, Imeris thought, *but not their own blood.* Hooting sounds escaped her lips as she began walking towards the closest lodging.

"Why," Daggad asked, "are you laughing?"

"Perhaps I am going mad," Imeris replied, abruptly angry. "Too many plans, old and new, are jumbled up in my mind. I want too many things. Everything is complicated, and everything is hard. Kirrik. Orin's creature. Captain Oniwak and the other Hunters. Loftfol. A child for Sorros. Gannak and my fathers. The House of Epatut and me. Why do the goddesses and gods not solve all these wretched problems? Why is it left to a pair of Hunters that most Canopians take for slaves?"

"I am glad you no longer wish to tuck me into bed in Gannak," Daggad said lightly, bouncing a green fig on his palm. "I am glad that you finally see you are not alone. What a shame that this is a fig tree! I hate the taste of figs. Maybe that is something the goddesses and gods can fix while we are doing those other things."

Imeris couldn't suppress a smile at his forced cheer. She had thought the Hunt simply another obstacle in her path, but without it, she would not have Daggad on her side. Nor Sorros. Nor Anahah, wherever he was. Mere days, and she was beginning to forget the precise green of his eyes when he was angry or afraid; she felt a twinge in her chest at the thought that the creature might have caught up with him.

She had to make sure that he—that all three of them—survived. She would need them.

Once they had paid for a room, Sorros went to find a bathhouse, and Daggad was dispatched to bring back food from an eatery far away from any silk markets. In the cramped accommodation, Imeris stacked the furniture she found there, a low table and chocolate-preparing apparatus, on top of the bunks carved into the wall. She rolled up the carpet and evicted a snug brown tree-snake from the empty guest water jug.

Then she began the movements as best as she was able in the limited space.

Imeris sweated through the first six disciplines, allowing the plan to unfold in her mind as the sequences unfolded by rote in muscle and bone. A week. They needed a week for Sorros to make the wires. Perhaps as little as a day for Daggad to replace the Temple vines with copper, but what if the goddess sensed the tribute being taken away? What if there was no choice but for Sorros to work inside the Temple? Imeris would have to find some way to keep worshippers away.

She frowned. Ideas flashed into her mind and were discarded.

A chain saw would be suitable for cutting the main branch roads partway through and then letting them break under their own weight. Unless somebody examined the broken ends closely, it would seem natural, and how would anybody examine anything from the vantage point of another great tree? She could add the chain to Daggad's acquisition list. Perhaps trade some of Sariras's salt for it.

She would have to make sure Orin's creature was actually in Ulellin's emergent before she cut the roads. Anahah, too. There seemed no way to locate or signal to him, except to trust that he would find her before the creature did.

How to keep Daggad and Sorros safe from the creature while they worked? How to keep the goddess and her Bodyguard from coming down to investigate when she sensed her supply of tributes dwindling? Imeris shook her head. She began the final discipline.

Perhaps Leaper would have some better ideas. Once she reached Ulellin's emergent, Imeris would send him a message straightaway. Yet she did not know how long he could be away from Airak's Temple before he got into just as much trouble as she had at Loftfol for her extended absences.

Imeris's arms faltered. Trembled. The Discipline of Spines was interrupted in the moment before she would have half knelt and drawn her right arm in the motion that had ended the life of Horroh the Haakim.

There was trouble and then there was trouble, she supposed.

Leaper would never do to Airak what Imeris had done to Horroh.

Two DAYS later, Leaper met them at the spiny plum tree on the other side of the emergent.

In the bright noon blaze, Ulellin's Temple looked less like Kirrik's dovecote and more like the delicate weaving of a very large and gifted spider. Earlier in the morning, the goddess and her attendants had come down to refresh their spindly, wasted, wind-tossed bodies with what Imeris would have considered inadequate nourishment for a child.

Now they prepared to return to the heights.

Ulellin herself, from a distance, looked like a dark brown leaf pressed between the pages of a light green book. Two new, pale windowleaves, each as long as the goddess from neck to knees, adhered somehow to the front and back of her. She wore gauzy, pale green wrappings from her palms to her shoulders and from her knees to her ankles, leaving her feet and fingertips free. Her black hair streamed left and right in invisible breezes that Imeris could not feel.

The Servants and Bodyguard wore robes of the same light, thin, gauzy material, probably the dyed inner bark of a tree, over shirts and skirt-wraps made of leaves joined at the edges. These were made from smaller leaves, more like the red tunics of Audblayin's Gardeners, except that the smaller leaves also seemed magically adhered and not stitched together with thread.

When Ulellin and her adepts climbed, it was not as Canopians, nor Understorians, climbed. The invisible wind about Ulellin that Imeris could not feel picked them up and dashed them in a spiral pattern upwards, like butterflies in a whirlwind. When the wind died, Goddess, Bodyguard, and Servants caught at branches closest to them, clinging, waiting for the next gust, as though the wind were an animal breathing and could not carry them continuously.

"That's a useful trick," Leaper whispered to Imeris back from further around the spiny plum.

There were no worshippers to watch the Holy One go. The emergent and all of its visible branch paths, both origin roads and arrivals, were unusually still. Only monkeys picking at the spiny plum fruit and the rustle of leaves as the party departed disturbed the hush.

"Where is everyone?" Imeris wondered aloud.

Leaper cackled, and she turned in her crouch to face him. When he saw her face, his eyes widened.

"You haven't heard? Of course not; you've been in Gannak and missed the commotion. Orin's creature attacked a man on one of the high roads of Ulellin's emergent."

"It killed one of her worshippers? Why did you not say so in your reply to my message?"

Imeris's heart sank. If somebody had died, Ulellin surely would have done something to expel the creature from her niche. She would have activated some magical defence to prevent its return. The trap was useless, her promises to Sorros given for nothing.

"No," Leaper said. "It ate a cage of flowerfowl the worshipper was bringing for tribute. Must've gotten a taste for them at Unar's farm. Citizens have been scared off. They still send their slaves by the low roads if they've got them, but there's nobody on the high roads. One who walks in the grace of Airak is willing to wager that a bit of bird blood on the low roads will buy us the time we need."

"No sense in waitin'," Daggad said, shifting from foot to foot behind Leaper. The big baskets of tools forced him to bend his back as he leaned away from the tree. "We must take our chances. Go ahead with the plan. Or"—he guffawed—"run away to Floor."

"Anahah is here somewhere," Imeris murmured, putting her fingertips to her lips. "Orin's creature, too." She put one foot onto the branch road and hesitated, scanning the maze of huge, perforated windowleaf leaves and diamond-patterned branches crisscrossing the floodgum trunk.

"Well concluded, genius," Leaper said at her back. "Look, don't just stand there at the edge of the platform. If she's watching, she's watching. If she's not, the sooner we get started the better."

Imeris led them across the long, exposed road to the Temple. The back of her neck prickled. If the creature had taken some of Ulellin's tribute, word would have reached Oniwak. If he was steadfast, if he continued to prosecute the Hunt, he would be along soon to investigate. Which lodging would he choose this time? Imeris eyed the thatched cottage stuck to the side of a purple-leafed penda tree on the other side of the emergent to the spiny plum tree and overlooking the approach from the north.

Then she entered the Temple.

Inside the funnel of golden-brown vines, through the gap between carved, enormous imitation leaves, there was no movement and no sound louder than the increasing wheeze of the wind. The goddess and her retinue had taken little of the abundant food given as tribute. Imeris wrinkled her nose. Some of it was spoiling in the heat. Meanwhile, not even the most starving slave would dare steal a single crumb, lest Ulellin make some awful prophesy about their imminent demise.

Leaper found the barrow of metal-stone fruit inside the yawning mouth of the topiary woman. He stripped one fruit of its withering skin and rotting orange flesh, and held the fist-sized copper seed up to the sunlight filtering through the ceiling.

"Still here," he crowed.

Daggad dumped his baskets onto the floor of the Temple with an aggrieved sigh and began rubbing his shoulders where the leather straps had reddened his skin.

"Careful with those," Sorros admonished him.

"Where are you goin'?" Daggad asked Imeris.

"To keep watch," Imeris answered. "You had better stay. Sorros can use your strength."

"I shall get straight to work," Sorros said, crouching to sort through the spilled objects. "Leave me the boy as well as the brute."

"Do not command me as you would a slave," Daggad said.

"Don't call me boy," Leaper said. "I'm a Skywatcher of Airakland."

Imeris ignored them and slipped out of the Temple, not by the funnel-shaped entryway but by jumping and catching her spines on the ceiling, swivelling her body until her feet found the perforations and her knees were able to hook out through the holes.

She wriggled. Slithered out through gaps in the ceiling that would not have admitted Daggad. Windowleaves made a shady green roof over the wooden imitation-windowleaf roof. Imeris pushed them aside. Some predator, perhaps a snake or jaguar, had startled the monkeys. They abandoned the spiny plum, hooting.

There were two dozen or so substantial floodgum branches higher than the Temple. Up there, hidden by the lacework of windowleaf stems and foliage, the goddess and her servants surely would not tolerate the presence of Orin's creature. Where was it, then?

The faint sound of hammers floated up to her ears.

She moved a few body lengths upwards, deciding on a node where the windowleaves completely hid her yet she was able to monitor the south-bound paths through their perforations.

The smell of panther musk and banana leaves gave her warning.

Anahah called out softly to her while she sat cross-legged, unmoving.

"You still have the sword," he observed. "And you've brought the smith. I can smell the copper."

"Come here," Imeris replied. Moments later, he parted the leaves beside her. She made room for him, and he sat with one knee pressed against hers. His belly was noticeably more distended, after less than a week apart, and he had not been using his trick of invisibility. His hands were slim, green-skinned human hands.

Not the paws of a panther.

"You do not want Orin to know where you are," Imeris guessed. "You will not use her magic to transform."

"It's not that," Anahah said uneasily. He tilted his head, so that light through one of the leaves fell on his left eye; he did not trust her to watch the roads, or else he was watching for something other than what Imeris watched for. "You asked me, when we first met, how my rift with Orin began. You haven't asked again lately."

Imeris shrugged. "Lately I have not needed to know. You have been thoughtful. Helpful. You keep your promises. Does the Queen of Beasts need a reason to turn on those closest to her?"

"She had one," Anahah admitted. "A fairly good one. To turn on me, I mean. Not the others. They don't deserve to be part of the creature, to suffer that way. Death will free them."

"Tell me your long tale, then, Anahah. We have time. Three days."

"I'm afraid you won't have three days. My energy, my agility, which kept me ahead of the lumbering creature, is all used up. It's coming after me, and I'm too tired to move. I'm staying here. You have until sunset."

Imeris twitched the leaves aside, rising to her feet. She had to tell the others. They had to change the plan.

"Wait." Anahah sighed. "Wait and hear my story. Please."

Imeris knelt back down beside him.

"Your irises," she observed. "They just went dark. What is the matter, Anahah?"

He stared, grimacing, into some unpleasant past.

"Orin didn't give me permission to grow a womb," he said. "I grew one anyway."

THIRTY-FIVE

IMERIS BLINKED. She looked at his belly, then back at his face.

"What about permission to fornicate?" she asked, touching her mouth, remembering the kiss of slavery and the kiss of freedom he had given her.

"She didn't give permission for that, either." Anahah blinked, too, focusing on Imeris once again. "Adepts aren't allowed to touch one another. That's true of all Servants of goddesses and gods. It not only keeps them focused, but it keeps them from angling to capture deities' or Servants' souls for their unborn children." He lowered his lashes. "If our power was hereditary, we would be worse than royals. I never set out to entice anyone else to help me break that decree. Yet once I'd tried on the form of a chimera, I realised I could do it alone. Have a child. Love it. Raise it. Protect it, as I'd protected Orin for fifteen years, without a word of thanks. I was wrong, though. I failed to protect the boy hostage, Oul. I've made a mistake, but I can't go back. Fate must take its course."

Imeris reached towards his stomach, hesitated and caught his eye with her hand hovering over his skin. Only when he gave her a faint nod did she press her palm against the bulge in his abdomen.

Something rolled over underneath, and she drew her hand back, startled.

"It grows faster than a normal child," Anahah said. "Orin must have found out about it a month before she said anything to me. That's when the killing of my family and friends began. I heard about Oul from gossipy palace servants, and mourned, yet never suspected. When the goddess confronted me at last, she said she would feed it to the eagles. My child. My daughter."

"A daughter?" Imeris abruptly saw aspects of Youngest-Father in Anahah. Except that Anahah was not expecting another to watch his child while he retained the freedom to fly. "Are you sure?"

"I'm sure." Anahah's mouth twisted wryly. "I am both mother and father to this child. My daughter is a pulled-apart and reassembled version of me, the fruit of a self-pollinating tree. I fled Orinland to save her. I visited, in secret, the workshop of a clockmaker I'd heard malicious rumours about."

"In Eshland," Imeris said, nodding. It was all making sense.

"Yes. At first I thought I'd simply kill Orin and trap her soul forever." Anahah closed one fist as though he held the goddess's essence trapped there. "That way she'd be helpless to harm my child. To Floor with the needs of the forest and its people. I didn't tell the clockmaker what I wanted the soul trap for, though, and when I returned with payment, she revealed that a deity's soul could not be contained by a trap for very long. She said that Orin, of all deities, would be far too powerful! I realised my only chance would be to take that temporarily trapped spirit to some distant tree-branch, give birth there, open the trap, and ensure that Orin's soul entered my daughter's body."

"The sort of crazed grab for power that the decrees, the Bodyguards, and the Temple spells upon the adepts, are supposed to prevent," Imeris said with a snort of laughter.

Anahah opened his hand sadly, as though releasing some part of a sweet dream.

"It's no use," he said. "I didn't know that carrying a child would be so draining. In this state, I've no chance of getting close to Orin. Even if you Hunters kill the creature before my daughter is born, she'll never be safe."

"You could always let her fall," Imeris said lightly. "There are worse fates than being raised in Understorey. You can fly. We can, too."

"When I first saw you, I thought you were here on a raid." His face creased in sympathy. "You don't have a peaceful life, Imeris. You aren't safe."

"Nobody is safe," she said. "And I will have a peaceful life. When my duty is done. When the sorceress is gone. When Loftfol and I, and Gannak and my fathers, are reconciled."

Wind fluttered the foliage. In the dappled light, green on green, Anahah looked like a reflection in a pond. Like she could put her hand right through him if she reached for him again.

"You'd better go and tell your friends," he said, "that Orin's creature is coming." Imeris shifted her weight from her knees to the soles of her feet. "And listen, Imeris. I can't be the bait. I don't think I can transform any-more without harming the child. You must be the bait. Indeed, you have no choice, because the swords that I made for you from the tusks of the creature, whenever they appear above the barrier, will draw it more powerfully than even I ever could."

"You did not warn us of that fact before," Imeris said, frozen in her crouch.

"You were headed below the barrier."

"We had to come up periodically to keep our auras from fading," she cried. "We could have been ambushed or killed. What else have you not told us about them?"

Anahah lifted his chin. The shadow of a beard lay along his jaw, and his irises glittered the darker shade of green.

"When you fight the creature," he said. "When it touches you. Ordinarily, you would have mere moments before transforming. Before becoming part of it. Holding the sword will give you resistance. More time to do what you must do. But beware the sword's lure as you hold it. Orin's wildness is in it. You must think only kind thoughts towards your fellow humans when you carry it, or find yourself compelled to slaughter them. What I told you about the sword being unable to harm the creature is true, so you will need to kill it with some other weapon in your other hand."

Not, Imeris thought angrily, *such a great gift after all.*

"Are you not of the wild, Anahah?" she asked. "You gave me a sword that cannot harm the creature, but neither can it be turned against you. You always said you would not arm me against you. In case we fought against each other one day."

Anahah touched his abdomen.

"The eagle that kills the monkey's child," he said, "is as of the wild as the eagle nurturing the eaglet in the eyrie."

That was a thing Youngest-Father could easily have said.

"You have not been as open with me as I imagined," Imeris said.

"I am open." His tone entreated. "To you, I am. That's it. I've told you everything."

"Which animal, then," Imeris countered, "do I resemble in battle?"

"You fight like Imeris," he said softly. "I've never seen another, animal or human, who adapts as many techniques that should be contradictory into their fighting style as you. That hunter's trick with the mosquitoes, to locate a hidden sentry by his exhalation, could not be further from the fish-hips reversal made famous by the Fighting Slave of Scenting. You threw a short bolas by a wide, trunk-angled, underarm cast favoured by bee catchers in Irofland, but you switched knife hands like a net wrestler from Nessa."

Imeris was taken off guard. She responded to the last thing he had said.

"Have you been to Nessa?"

"No."

"Why will you not go to live in Understorey?"

The intensity of his gaze, the set of his jaw, the curl of his elbow around the child he carried; she half knew his answer before he spoke.

"Because you can't go there. Loftfol will hunt you forever, the same way that Orin will hunt me forever. Here, though, even if I was unable to transform, you could be a Bodyguard to my child the likes of which Canopy has never seen—"

"No!" Imeris wanted to slap him silly. She could not be a Bodyguard, not to Audblayin, not to Anahah's child, not to anyone else. She had to find Kirrik. She had to kill Kirrik. If the creature didn't kill her first. "When Canopy sees me, when it sees these"—she extruded the spines in both forearms—"it sees a slave, Anahah."

"You will change their minds! It will be as you hoped aloud just now. A great reconciliation, only it will be Canopian instead of Understorian. You will win their hearts and make peace between the two sides of the barrier." Anahah framed an oval with his hands, inviting her to imagine with him the section of the monument tree where her likeness would rise above the lake. "The victorious Hunter, a flesh-and-blood mortal without the merest magical crutch, who saved the city from the mad goddess's fury!"

For an instant, she saw it. Her noble profile. The bow in her hands and the outline of spines curving down from her shins. She glimpsed herself as Anahah saw her, and it was wonderful and terrible. Who would not love that person, the person that Anahah saw?

How could she not love Anahah, for seeing it?

No student of Loftfol had been able to see her as more than one thing at a time. She had been either weapon or breeder to them with no possible resolution of the two. Even her mothers and fathers had assumed she would have to make a choice, one path or the other. Mother or fighter. Understorian or Canopian.

Imeris convulsed silently with the realisation that the branch road leading to a future with a flowerfowl farm and few visitors now led, for her, to Anahah and a small green child.

"No," she said again.

Anahah reached for her face, but Imeris brought her extended spines between them. The instinct shocked her, but she thought that if he touched her, she would agree with whatever he said.

Now that she knew that she loved him, any physical interaction would be overwhelming; it would be painful in its intensity, and she would not allow it.

He took it for rejection. His expression turned crestfallen. What must he be thinking? How did he imagine that she was seeing him? Not a warrior emblazoned on a wooden wall, but something repulsive, weak, stunted, and unnatural? But she could not find the words to tell him that he was a wonder, an extraordinary counterbalance to Orin's far uglier creations.

"I have to kill the sorceress," she said. "I should have killed her already."

"If you had killed her that day, you would be battling me now."

"What do you mean?"

"Battling her in me, is what I mean," Anahah answered, his gaze steady, his self-possession recovered, and Imeris stared at him uncomprehendingly for a moment until his earlier words about the mosquitoes, throwing her weighted cords, and switching knife hands came back to haunt her. Those motions, drawn from the Disciplines of Balance, the Knife, and Administering Poison, were not ones she had used in her fight against Orin's creature.

Anahah had seen her fight the sentry. He had been on Ulellin's emergent the day that Oldest-Father had died.

What he meant was, if Imeris had succeeded in destroying Nirrin's body, Kirrik would simply have taken over Anahah's body, gaining his gift with beasts and birds in place of Nirrin's gifts.

"What were you doing there?" Imeris cried.

"Hiding from the monster in the foliage, of course. You know I've spent most of my time confined to this tree since Orin turned on me. Now you're acting surprised that the sorceress's activity, weaving a house out of leaves and snakes, drew my attention?"

"You could have—"

"What? What could I have done? I was below the barrier. I had no power. Not even my claws. I had a rope. I had my hiding place in the leaves. You didn't find me because I didn't smell like that sentry smelled or breathe the way he breathed."

She had no answer for him. Bit her lip. Tried to control the rush of anger.

Abruptly turning her back, she whisked away. Through the windowleaves. Found the hole that led into the Temple.

There, Daggad, Leaper, and Sorros had organised themselves into a production line, hammering the copper into thin sheets, cutting it into lengths, and drawing it through the dies.

Imeris breathed deeply and slowly. She waited until the flare of fury had died.

"We have a problem," she said.

Leaper looked up. He had mango juice and orange fibres stuck to his face. His hands were ruddy with rust from an iron shield he was using as an anvil. All of his fancy airs had fallen by the wayside. He looked like he'd never left Oldest-Father's workshop.

"The creature's coming now," he guessed cheerily. "The goddess Ulellin is coming as well. The goddess Orin is outside at the head of a horde of angry beasts. Aforis is coming to drag me back to Airakland. The barrier is down, Loftfol is attacking, and—"

"Will you stop?" Imeris folded her arms, scowling. "The first one that you said, and you do not need to sound so excited."

"'Ow long?" Sorros asked, halting with both hands wrapped around a piece of wire. It protruded from a die hung between two of the overhead vines that formed the funnel.

"We have until sunset, according to Anahah," Imeris said.

"So we've got six hours, maybe less, before the monster sticks its ugly head in here," Leaper said. He wiped his sticky, mango-spattered forehead with the back of his forearm. "That's not long enough. We'll have to abandon this design for the trap and think up some other plan."

"I wish Oldest-Father were here," Imeris said, thinking, *Oldest-Father would be here, if not for Anahah watching and doing nothing!*

Leaper laughed.

"But the old man is here." He tapped his temple with one rusty finger. Then he pointed it at Imeris. "Look at you. Look at me. We've brought him here. His strategies. His ways of thinking. You wouldn't catch Middle-Father building a trap, not if there were some direct way to wrestle the monster. And Youngest-Father would give it a smug little smile right before flying past its face and away."

"There is nowhere to fly to."

"I'm not actually suggesting flight."

"Maybe wrestling," Daggad said, one eyebrow raised, fists on hips.

"What do you mean?" Imeris asked.

Daggad shrugged. He gestured around at the setup for wire making.

"Suppose Anahah spoke truth and we cannot finish enough wire ta replace all the vines of the Temple. Maybe we do not need to. One good wire, wrapped many times around the creature's body to encompass all the different parts of it, might carry the lightnin' in a satisfactory way." He glanced at Leaper.

"Sure," Leaper said. "But who's going to volunteer to wrestle the monster and tie it into a neat package with a bow on top? Even if the volunteer doesn't get bitten in half or shredded to pieces, didn't you say, Daggad, that you started to turn into the thing as soon as you touched it?"

"Should I keep makin' the wire?" Sorros asked simply as the three others looked helplessly at one another.

"If you would, Sorros, please," Imeris said. She squared her shoulders. Tossed her head. *Middle-Father is my father, too. Why should I not bring him with me to the battle?* "I have studied weighted ropes and wire strangulation under Yolmoloy the Scentingim." *Anahah said holding the sword would give me the ability to resist.* "I have an idea of how the wire may be secured to the beast's body."

But I wish I still had Youngest-Father's chimera wings.

Just in case.

Anahah.

You were the Bodyguard of Orin. You could have done something.

THIRTY-SIX

An hour before sunset, men's arguing voices on the northern high roads prompted Imeris to climb around the circumference of the emergent.

As stealthily as she could, trying not to make the windowleaves rustle or shake, she selected windowleaf trunks with plenty of rootlets that would bear her weight without pulling away from the floodgum host.

On a smooth, grey branch road arriving from the penda tree, a dozen rangy soldiers stood. Their leather armour was stained Ulellin's green and blue, and they contended with a stockier, black-clad soldier with feathers in his hair and a crossbow over his shoulder who suspiciously resembled Captain Oniwak.

Behind Oniwak stood a little boy, head cocked attentively. At the boy's side hovered a man of middle height in mulberry silks carrying a fiddle. *Ibbin and Owun.* Imeris systematically searched the other paths and platforms. After several long minutes of scrutiny, in which Oniwak's voice grew louder and began to carry enough for her to decipher his words, she finally located Eeriez against the penda tree trunk, armour and tunic smeared convincingly in ash and perfectly still, as always.

"It's lovely that you're defending the Temple," Oniwak argued, "but understand, king's men are no deterrent to the creature. I'm a king's officer. The thing did not hesitate to attack me. I just told you that my company has lost both a Servant of Atwith and the gods-protected Bodyguard of Oxor!"

"Our charge is to keep this road safe for worshippers of Ulellin," the leader of the Ulellinland soldiers answered. "You are not here to pay tribute to the Speaker of Truth."

"How observant are the keen-eyed knives of the wind," Oniwak sneered. "Our charge is to hunt the beast and kill it no matter where it goes!"

Besides Orinland, Imeris thought.

She climbed down into the Temple, avoiding the node where Anahah lay curled and quiet; she'd brought him food from the Temple only to find him sleeping. Which worried her, since Bodyguards didn't need sleep, and why hadn't she realised something was sapping his strength when he'd slept in her room at the Mistletoe Lodge?

"Come to tell us of another problem, have you?" Leaper whispered. He, Sorros, and Daggad were taking a break from their labour in the mouth of the face-shaped topiary.

Imeris looked at the wire coiled on the floor. She was a good judge of rope lengths from their bundled size. What they had in copper looked to be forty paces or twenty body lengths, no more, which would barely be enough to wrap Orin's monster three times around. She'd have no spare lengths for binding the legs. That would leave at least four sections of the monster free to re-form.

"Soldiers," she said. "Ulellinland soldiers. They are arguing with Oniwak on one of the north roads, but when they get here, they will want to put a pair of guards on every path leading to the Temple. Once they put someone on the south road, that person will only have to turn around to see straight through the funnel and discover exactly what we are doing."

"We are worshipping!" Leaper said, raising a gourd of magenta cherry wine.

"Put that down and help me get the wire closer to the entrance."

She'd barely arranged it the way she wanted before scraping sounds and shouts came close by. Motioning for Leaper to get out of sight, she strung her bow and moved her quiver to her hip, keeping one eye on the entrance the whole time.

Something moved in the open air, but it wasn't Ulellinland soldiers, or even Captain Oniwak.

Orin's creature, grunting and snuffling, stuck its face into the funnel. Imeris had not yet expected it. At the very least, Oniwak should have seen it and raised a cry. She lost her grip on the arrow as she took a few paces back. Leaper and Daggad shouted a warning to Sorros. Imeris smelled spilled wine and heard blades sliding free as the whole building shuddered.

The grotesque new head, empty of tusks, too tight in some places, like a poorly felted blanket, and too loose in others, like the abdominal skin of a gutted carcass, filled the opening. All of its tiny human eyes were as wide as they would go, gathering the paltry available light. Daggad, Sorros, and Leaper had not lit any candles to replace the fading sun, and Leaper had removed those of Airak's lanterns that might flicker to life as the day dwindled.

Imeris found another arrow. Nocked it and went to full draw. Loosed. Allowed the motion of her fingers falling away from the string to turn into a reach for her next arrow.

She didn't aim for the eyes. She did not want to kill the component pieces until they were all snugly trussed together. Instead, she sank her shafts up to the feathers into nonvital joints and folds.

They would be her anchor points.

Seven of them, and the creature snarled and clawed at the shafts. Several snapped off close to the skin. The protruding splinters were still long enough for her to use.

Imeris tossed the bow aside. She heaved a coil of copper over her shoulder, taking to hand the stiff, bladed end of the metal sheet where Sorros had run out of time to draw the wire; he had unhinged the die to set free the unfinished section.

The creature reached for her with the one foreleg it had managed to stuff into the funnel-shaped Temple entrance. Sorros, moving past Imeris, bravely swung one of his hammers at the scrabbling, clawed cat toes, making the animal roar. *Oniwak must have heard that.* He and the other Hunters must be on their way. Imeris focused hard.

Under the tongue and between the jawbones. That was where her huge copper darning needle and thread must pass, if she was to keep the monster from withdrawing from the Temple before her work was done. Yet who was to say that its skeleton was built in the usual way? She hesitated, holding the copper blade in her right hand, the hilt of the sheathed boar-tusk sword in her left.

Sorros swung his hammer. The creature roared again. Imeris charged forwards, head down, a human arrow with a head of copper. The wind of its breath brought back her failure at Mistletoe Lodge; it mingled with the magic wind of Ulellin that had once helped cook Oldest-Father's fish.

She speared the copper blade through the floor of the monster's mouth. It felt like pushing her arms into wet padded armour; like upholstering a

chair. Imeris dropped the coil of copper rope into a pool of frothing saliva.
Jerked backwards before the mouth could snap shut. Dropped to the floor
and rolled under its chin. There, she pulled the copper blade free.

She needed both hands to pull the bloodied wire through. As soon as she
let go of the sword hilt, she felt a wrinkling heaviness in her skin, like she'd
fallen into water wearing quilted clothes. Pausing to pick up the sword
again, she stuck the crossguard between her teeth, letting the blunt edge of
the blade lie along her breastbone, and immediately felt lighter.

More time to do what you must do.

In the corner of her eye, Sorros rolled and moaned on the floor, sprout-
ing fur from hands that had dropped the hammer. She could spare no
thought for him. Imeris used her spines to climb. She sank them in the
creature's fur and face, climbing through sagging gore so unlike the solid
purchase of a tree, until she swung one arm and her spines connected with
a satisfying thunk to the Temple's wooden, perforated roof.

She went up through one hole, carrying the copper blade, and down
through another. She stabbed the monster through the snout a second time
and secured the blade to the loose end of the copper wire.

It thrashed and squealed. Imeris had stitched its head to the entryway.

She could not stop, terrified that it would come apart and re-form. Seizing
the loose end of the metal rope, she went up through the ceiling again,
coming down on the platform outside the Temple where the monster's body
hunched, its four feet scrabbling at the door frame for purchase, straining
backwards.

Oniwak and the three other Hunters clustered there. Crossbow bolts and
poison darts stuck out from the creature's rump. Ibbin darted in, stabbed,
and darted out again. Owun played his fiddle, and a cloud of hornets, seeming hypnotised by the tune, swarmed in and out, buzzing and stinging.

"Back!" Imeris tried to bellow with the sword between her teeth. "Get
back, for your lives!"

Oniwak looked up at her with something akin to hatred. Nevertheless,
he obeyed. They all did. Imeris climbed over the fetid skin, dragging the
wire, until the creature's body was wrapped three times in copper.

Then there was no more wire. She bent the nubby end around another
piece of itself and dropped back down onto the platform. She lost the sword
as she landed on her back and her bones jarred. Chunks of loose hair, leaf

litter, and waist-high splinters carved up by the beast's claws obscured the place where the sword had landed. She knew it hadn't fallen to Floor; she'd heard it clatter on the wood.

Her skin started to feel thick again. All her many harness straps, ropes, and fittings were too tight. Her body deformed. Her arms grew longer and her legs shorter.

Oniwak lifted his crossbow. The bolt pointed at her heart.

I would rather be dead, she had time to think, *than be part of the monster. But who will kill Kirrik?*

Her searching hands closed over the hilt of the sword and for the second time, the prickling transformation reversed, spreading from palms to shoulders and from there up and down her spine. She shook herself off. Rolled free of the debris. Sucked in a sweet breath; yet another chance at life.

Oniwak's crossbow bolt thudded into the place where she had lain, but she had as little time for him as she had for Sorros.

Holding the bone blade in her left hand, she stabbed with a bore-knife at the ends of the creature's limbs not contained by the rope. Searched out the pairs of human eyes and drove the knife between them. Did not flinch when she recognised the mournful eyes of Irrafahath, the Bodyguard of Oxor, despite the wasp-stung swellings, or the tear-scarred tracks beneath the lower lids of Ay, once Lakekeeper of Ehkisland, who might have helped her defeat Kirrik.

Legless, tailless, the creature squirmed, a hairy worm wound with gleaming copper ribbon. Imeris staggered back from the beast. She looked up and saw Leaper standing on top of the upper leaf of the Temple, the curving relic of the Old Gods, Tyran's Talon, in his upraised hands.

"Now, Leaper!" she cried.

Spears of lightning struck between the widespread boughs of the emergent. The crack was deafening. Imeris fell backwards as the whole tree convulsed. Her hair stood on end. She resheathed her spines. Threw a forearm up to shield her eyes as a second bolt struck, and then a third.

She smelled charred flesh. Heard sizzling. A final scream sounded before the silence.

When she lowered her arm, she saw a burned black mountain of meat. Long, jagged cracks in it oozed juices that bubbled and stank. No part of it was recognisable as once human.

No part of it moved.

Imeris blinked, shook her head, and blinked again at the sight of the goddess Ulellin standing on top of the Temple beside Leaper. Ulellin struck Leaper across the face with the back of her slim hand. Wrenched the relic out of his grasp. Leaper dropped to his knees, his expression horrified.

Imeris's heart was in her throat. They had done it. They had killed Orin's monster, and the Hunt was complete. She should have been weeping with joy, but her brother had been touched by a deity.

That meant he would have to die.

PART III

The Wings &
the Sword

THIRTY-SEVEN

THE GODDESS of wind and leaves had the face of a starved child.

Up close, her large eyes looked sunken. Her brown cheeks were thin. Her black hair, thick and straight, blew to one side in a strong gust nobody else could feel, exposing the nape of a reedy neck.

She stood before the mountain of cooked monster flesh, considering it for a moment. Then, with a flick of her wrist, a gust of wind that everyone could feel blasted the abomination off the branch road.

Imeris watched it fall in silence. She should have felt relief. Orin's creature was dead. All distractions were past. She was not a Hunter anymore. It was time to hunt Kirrik, the true quarry, at last.

Yet the goddess must pronounce a terrible judgement on Leaper, the boy who had been so determined to go one way only, up into the sun, and stay there. He had always been a talker, chattering away even while the children were on the toilet, so that Ylly and Imeris had impersonated him by making fart sounds between words, and Youngest-Mother had listened, bemused, for hours while he described the battles of ants and tarantulas.

He had nothing to say now.

Ulellin turned away from the char mark where the creature had died, towards the platform where five of the six surviving Hunters stood: Imeris still gripping the bone sword with the leopard-carved hilt that Anahah had made for her, Oniwak holding his crossbow limply at his side, Eeriez with poison knives, Ibbin with his dagger, and Owun with his fiddle, the cloud of stinging insects dispersed.

Daggad came out of the Temple. Imeris was reassured to see him walking unaided and with normal skin and symmetry; she'd imagined him becoming contaminated by Sorros, the pair of them fusing into the creature's final, much-diminished incarnation. She beckoned, and he circled the seething goddess, joining Imeris and the others.

"The smith?" she asked him out of the corner of her mouth.

"Tied a rope to 'im and threw 'im out the window," Daggad said under his breath. "Figured if 'e fell below the barrier, 'e might escape the—"

"Silence," the goddess Ulellin said with all the fierceness and sibilance of the wind.

The six Hunters knelt before her, instinctively, in unison. Imeris peeked up through her eyelashes. On top of the Temple, Leaper remained kneeling. He had not moved, had hardly breathed, since Ulellin had taken the relic. Imeris was so afraid for him.

She could do nothing.

"Holy One," Oniwak said with his head bowed. "The Hunt is complete. One who walks in the grace of Airak begs your forgiveness for trespassing in your Temple. Permit us to return to the court of my master, the king of Airakland, he who called this Hunt, to have him formally dissolve it."

"Your master?" Ulellin asked derisively, striding closer to him. "A mortal who believes his will is more important than the inviolable laws of goddesses and gods?"

"The king of Airakland sought to defend his people, Holy One," Oniwak said carefully without rising.

"And the Skywatcher of Airak who has dared to call lightning in my domain, was he acting under the Hunt's compulsion, under the orders of your master, the king of Airakland?"

"No." Oniwak raised his eyes to Leaper. "One who walks in the grace of Airak has never seen that adept before. He's no part of the Hunt."

"He is part of it," Imeris and Daggad objected at the same time. They looked at one another.

"We employed him," Imeris said.

"We brought 'im into the compact," Daggad said, pressing his knuckles harder into the wooden platform.

"If you did, you should've known better," Oniwak said, volume rising. "Hunters don't employ mercenaries. We aren't merchants, to buy protection. We're warriors chosen by Ilan's compass for the skills—"

"The creature is dead," Daggad observed cuttingly. "Killed by lightnin', not by your skills."

"The Hunt was never meant to oppose rogue goddesses," Imeris said, turning her head to the other side where she could glare at Oniwak. "Mortal hunters might have a chance against ordinary demons—"

"SILENCE," Ulellin said again.

Imeris looked hopelessly up at Leaper. She found him looking equally hopelessly back down at her. He had been so proud of his idea. Of his ability to help her. To save her.

Now he was going to die for her. And Oldest-Father had charged her with his protection. But what could she do? Try to kill the goddess? The same wind that had carried the remains of the creature away would knock her a thousand body lengths down to Floor before she was permitted to disobey Ulellin.

"Will you sentence one who walks in the grace of Airak—no, one who serves him, for make no mistake, I am his Skywatcher, Oniwak!—to death, Holy One?" Leaper called, his voice enviably steady.

Ulellin turned her back on the Hunters. Fists on hips, she lifted her chin haughtily in Leaper's direction.

"Kill Leaper the Skywatcher? No! There's no need." Imeris's heart raced at this pronouncement. Ulellin elaborated with increasing malice. "The wind spoke to me of your path. I doom you, by my power, to wander far from home until your mate, your true love, your heart's desire, grows to love another more than you. Only then will you be permitted to return." She looked at the relic in her hand, gripping it tighter as though the sight of it stirred her to unimaginable rage. "A much more fitting punishment than mere falling."

She thrust the relic at Oniwak's face.

"Holy One—" Oniwak began hesitantly.

"Take this to Airakland at once," she spat. "Place it into the hands of the Lord of Lightning and no other. Don't stop to rest until you've crossed my border, lest I change my mind about sparing you."

"Yes, Holy One. Thank you, Holy One."

Imeris, frozen in dismay by the horror of the wind goddess's prophecy, was slow to stand. Daggad tugged her elbow to get her to rise.

"Come on, woman," he said gruffly. "We dare not go back inta the Temple. But remember that Sorros 'as 'is spines. No doubt 'e will untangle 'imself and make 'is way 'ome to Gannak. We must go with Oniwak. This way, to Ilanland."

She stood but didn't take a step until Leaper climbed down from the roof of the Temple and stood beside her. They embraced.

"That was close," Leaper said, a tremor in his voice that hadn't been there when he'd so boldly demanded that the goddess address his fate.

"What do you mean?" Imeris cried. "Did you not hear what she said?"

"One who walks in the grace of Airak heard her perfectly." Leaper shrugged. He grinned. "So I won't leave the forest. Who cares? So what?" He hunched a little, as if realising the goddess might still be within earshot, but there was no sign of her. Daggad waved his hand to indicate she'd floated back up into the foliage. Leaper stood straighter and threw out his chest. "I did it. I killed Orin's creature. It worked. Get me a lantern as we go. I'll send a message to Ilanland. A crowd of grateful citizens will meet us at the border. They'll carry us on their shoulders to the monument tree."

Imeris, Leaper, and Daggad lagged behind the other Hunters. Every few minutes, Oniwak looked suspiciously over his shoulder at them.

"Woman, I don't like having you at my back," he said at last.

"You shot at me," Imeris reminded him.

"You were transforming into the creature."

"Also, the last time we spoke, you said you would kill me if you saw me again."

"He's run out of bolts," Ibbin piped up helpfully. "Walk with us."

"It makes it less obvious," Eeriez said drily, "how many we have lost."

Imeris shared a glance with Daggad. He nodded. They dragged themselves tiredly across the intervening space. Leaper looked longingly at Tyran's Talon, secured by rope to Oniwak's weapons belt.

As they started off again along a branch road, a light rain began to fall.

THE BLACK-ETCHED white walls of the monument tree ran with rainwater.

"'Ow," Daggad grumbled, standing where the curving wooden wall sheltered the great entryway lanterns, squeezing out his long tail of straight black hair, "are we supposed to celebrate properly in the wet?"

Imeris tried to make out the place, across the lake, where the legend of her Hunt was written, but she couldn't see it through the screen of the downpour.

"Ehkis is crying," she said. "Her Lakekeeper is dead."

"She'll have a new one by now," Leaper said, sighing. "Let's just hope Airak hasn't declared me fallen and chosen a new Skywatcher to fill my place."

His prediction about the crowd came true. People who had followed them, cheering and pressing food and drinks upon them, now ran ahead down the paths that encircled the lake. They returned with fisher-women and child divers at their head, urging the Hunters to take shelter around cooking fires. The fires were sheltered from the rain by upturned boats set onto forked posts that formed the fisherfolks' cramped little houses.

Imeris refused their wine. Refusal didn't help her to stay awake. Within minutes of sitting down at someone's fireside, she fell asleep, Leaper on one side of her, Daggad and his great sword and shield on the other, the black mark of his freedom on his drowsy lower lip.

When she woke, it was night. Fresh leaves smouldering on the fire kept the mosquitoes away. She felt safe and comfortable enough to stay motion-less for a long time, enjoying the ability to do nothing, then realised that the forked posts were used for smoking fish in times of abundance and the lingering smell reminded her of Oldest-Father and home.

After that, it occurred to her that someone else by the fireside was awake. Two someones. A fat, curious-eyed, scarf-wrapped young woman in the fancy orange robes of a silk merchant, and an angry, frowning, brown-shirt-and-trouser-clad out-of-nicher with her hair in two untidy braids.

"Godfinder," Imeris said, startled, sitting forwards suddenly and caus-ing the sleeping mountain that was Daggad to shift and moan.

"Congratulations," Unar said. "You survived."

"Did you doubt it?"

"The odds were against you."

"Did you come to see for yourself whether I needed healing? Again?"

"I'd like to pretend that's why." Unar waved vaguely in a northeasterly direction. "I was busy finding the new incarnation of Oxor. Again. These careless deities don't live long, for all their Bodyguards and barricades."

It was Imeris's turn to frown.

"Irrafahath did his duty," she said. "More than most of them, including—"

"Including Bernreb?"

"I was going to say Aurilon." Imeris picked up a twig to fidget with.

"Will you go back to Aurilon," Unar asked, "once you've seen the king of Airakland? Do you think finishing the Hunt will have surprised Odel's Bodyguard? She'd expect nothing less from you."

I will go to Aurilon after I have seen the king, Imeris thought, *but not to become her student.*

What she said was, "Godfinder, this is a fortuitous meeting. You are well informed. I must have word from Gannak. I must know if Sorros the smith is safe."

"As to that," the other woman said, who had been silent so far, "I drew up the coil of rope that Daggad left behind." She pulled a green coil out from under layers of shining orange fabric. Her hands looked strangely familiar. Imeris stared into the pleasant features and bright eyes, abruptly recognising Anahah.

"I thought you could not take the shape of another person," she said, taking the coil of rope. "I thought you were afraid to do harm by altering yourself at this late stage."

Anahah looked mildly offended.

"This is my shape." His voice was the same, after all. "This is my shape while I'm bearing a child in this body, in any case. You went to so much trouble to slay the beast, should I be ungrateful and walk about in Bodyguard's clothing in broad daylight with my green skin showing?"

"You let my father die. I have nothing to say to you."

"Don't say anything, then. But listen when I say this is the rope that Daggad dangled Sorros from, out of Ulellin's emergent into Understorey. The knots were secure. The smith couldn't have freed himself from it without human wit and human dexterity. He hasn't gone back to Gannak as the last remnant of a demon, but as his own man."

Imeris fastened it to her harness.

"I made him a promise," she said.

"What promise?" Unar asked.

"We have to catch Kirrik. Trap her soul forever. So that my sister will give Sorros and his wife another child."

"It can't be done," Unar said flatly. Anahah and Imeris both gazed at her, taken aback by her vehemence.

"You make pronouncements like a king or god," Anahah said, seeming amused.

"How can you be sure?" Imeris wanted to know. "The last time Oniwak spoke of a soul cage, you said nothing."

"Kirrik turned my little sister against me." Unar's lip curled. "She killed Eilif, the Servant of Audblayin who was my teacher. She has killed the goddess Ehkis twice in my lifetime, and it's because of her that I . . . that I . . . I have magical gifts more powerful than you can imagine, Imeris. Yes, I've healed your broken bones, grown dwellings, trained birds to speak, but I also cut down Airak's emergent. Don't you think, if there was a way of trapping dangerous souls like Kirrik's, I would have found it?"

"Powerful you may be, Godfinder," Imeris said, "but you trained your birds to speak because you were not taught to read. There may be information in ancient writings or the memories of goddesses or gods—"

"Oh, do deities share their knowledge with you?" Unar's eyes snapped back into focus on Imeris's face. "Has your sister, Audblayin, explained why your amulet offends her? Did you speak the name of that relic"—she flung a finger in Oniwak's direction—"in front of Ulellin? You did not. And you must not." Unar took a deep breath. It rattled as she let it out slowly, calming herself. "She would kill you for knowing it. Any of them would. I should never have told Aforis where it was."

"I will never fear Audblayin," Imeris said stubbornly, but this time the shared glance was between Unar and Anahah, and Imeris felt herself excluded from what they knew about the ruthlessness of immortals. "I will speak with her. I will try."

Anahah tried to hide his smile, but Unar caught it.

"Encouraging her, Anahah?" she admonished him. "Haven't you got enough problems of your own? Wanted a child so badly you thought you'd go ahead alone, and now look at you. Where are you going to go? Who do you know with young children? Anyone?"

Anahah's smile vanished.

"No," he admitted.

"You could shelter him at your farm, Godfinder," Imeris said smartly, "if you are so concerned about the unborn child."

"No," Unar squawked.

"You must be concerned. You served Audblayin, whose domain is new life."

"I live by myself. I like it that way."

"Leaper lived with you," Imeris reminded her.

"Not for long, and I've never taken care of a newborn."

"What?" Imeris said with mock outrage. "What about me? You were there, too. My three fathers, my three mothers, and you."

"I was sleeping."

"I thought," Anahah confessed, "that if I didn't know what to do, I could transform into some animal with strong mothering instincts. It would be like transforming into territorial animals when I fight."

"What, and leave whole broods of newborn creatures motherless?" Imeris said.

"That would lead Orin straight to you," Unar said, "and besides, animals are no fit mothers for babes. They raise human children only in conveniently long-ago legends." She swallowed hard then, and looked at Imeris. "What I mean is—"

"Come to the Gate of the Garden with me, Anahah." Imeris did not know why those words had left her lips. She was angry with Anahah. Helping him again would only get her into more trouble. "My sister will not turn you away."

"Will she not?" Unar said with exasperation. "Her own Servants turned her away when she was little more than a year old! How do you think she came to be raised in Understorey with you? Besides, he's no innocent. He can't enter the Garden any more than you or I can."

"I was having a good dream," Leaper groaned, yawning and turning over. He rubbed his eyes. "You three are noisy."

"I'm not staying," Unar said, rising to her feet.

"Nor am I," Anahah said, doing the same.

Imeris realised the rain had stopped.

"You heard about the curse?" she asked Unar. "You heard about the curse that Ulellin placed on Leaper?"

"What curse?" the Godfinder asked sharply.

"No curse," Leaper lied. "Don't be ridiculous, Issi. Just the chattering of a goddess with no power in my niche. If I ever talk about leaving the forest, you've got permission to slap me till I come to my senses."

THIRTY-EIGHT

THE KING'S palace in Airakland rested in the pale arms of a living flood-gum.

It was near sunset, two days since they had left the monument tree. Imeris followed Daggad, who walked with a bowed head on account of his great height, through bone-white corridors that opened to arching walkways of wood glazed with black glass. Darkening overcast skies lay above them. The lantern-lit roads of Canopy lay below. Occasional lightning strikes visited Airak's emergent, barely ten thousand paces to the west of the palace, but as the palace manservants and maids paid no attention to the flashes or resounding whip-cracks, Imeris did her best to also ignore them.

Oniwak led the party, looking resplendent in a more ornate dress uniform that his soldiers had provided. Ibbin had been taken in hand by the maids and scrubbed until he shone, but Eeriez and Imeris had both resisted the temptation of heated, fragrant baths, choosing eucalyptus-oil scrapings instead, nodding at one another outside the bath hall door in silent acknowledgement of each other's commitment to a camouflaged scent. Daggad, of the widest shoulders and most apparent musculature, had spent several hours in the palace kitchen being wooed by the cooks and Airak knew who else. He had returned, bathed and looking very pleased with himself.

Leaper, however, bringing up the rear behind Imeris, looked guilty and hunched his shoulders. He'd tried to vanish on arrival in Airakland, but Oniwak had insisted he remain with the party to explain Ulellin's animosity to the king.

Never mind, Imeris had told him drily. *If anyone can turn a tale from a disaster into a hero's epic, it is you, Leaper. The king will probably reward you with a fortune in glass.*

Yet it was not the king of Airakland who left Leaper sweating where they waited in a mirrored hall outside the king's reception chamber. A group of courtiers clustered there, merchants and royal relatives, famed beauties and decorated solders.

Aforis, too.

When Leaper laid eyes on his superior Skywatcher, he pivoted on the ball of his foot as though he would march straight back down the hall of mirrors and make a tidy escape, but the guards at the door had come in behind him and were using a stick with a hook on the end to pull down a rope and give it a single, emphatic swing.

Leaper turned back to Aforis just as the deafening note from the bell made the mirrors tremble. Leaper's nervous face, reflected a hundred times or more in the opposing walls of silver-backed glass, might have shivered as a result of the bell or in anticipation of his reprimand, Imeris couldn't be sure.

The hundred reflections of Aforis looked stern. His arms, bulging to rival Daggad's, were crossed over his black robes and bearskin, his black hair in short braids, one white eye a reminder of his previous status. Adepts who did not obey could be cast aside, that eye seemed to say.

"It wasn't without reservations that I agreed to help shelter and tutor you, Leapael," he said.

Leaper winced.

"But, Aforis—"

"I was a firsthand witness to the wickedness of your soul. Still, I felt sorry for you. In logic, mathematics, and philosophy you were so far behind the others of your age. The Godfinder convinced me that I could guide you towards better choices." His voice grew quieter, not louder, forcing Imeris and Leaper to lean in to hear what he was saying over the babble from the other occupants of the hall. "My mother was a teacher. My father was a teacher. Teaching was in my blood, Unar insisted. Why else had the Temple kept me on, though I'd become afraid to use my power, barely able to summon lightning even under the direct watch of my deity? I could redeem myself through you, she said, and I wasn't completely fooled. I knew you were part of her redemption, too."

"Just let me explain," Leaper pleaded.

"You will explain to the Lord of Lightning. Come."

"Aforis," Imeris said quickly. "Skywatcher. Warmed One. Captain Oniwak wishes that Leaper first appear before the king."

"Airak does not serve the king," Aforis said in his quietest, most velvet voice yet, and somehow the Hunters, soldiers, and courtiers, wide-eyed and askance, all heard him and edged back from him, Oniwak included. "The king serves Airak. So do I. So do you, Leapael, though you oft forget it." He put his right hand to the back of Leaper's neck as though he would drag him off by the scruff, but Leaper cringed beneath it so there was no actual contact. Aforis extended his left hand imperatively towards Oniwak. "Give me the bone of the Old Gods."

Oniwak, who had been told by Ulellin not to give the bone to anyone besides the Lord of Lightning himself, handed over Tyran's Talon like an obedient child.

The soldiers who had rung the bell moved out of the way so that Aforis and Leaper could leave.

Imeris looked after him anxiously for only a moment before the doors at the other end of the hall opened. The returning victors of the Hunt were ushered into the reception chamber.

It was perhaps a hundred paces long and wide, a straight, square space hollowed from the floodgum tree. There were no windows. Airak's lanterns, these ones smelted from silver, hung from silver chains.

Standing on a dais that glittered with glazing in many shades of green, giving the impression of a jewelled meadow beneath their bare, silver-ankletted feet, the king and queen of Airakland gazed over the sparsely occupied chamber with filled chalices raised to their lips as though they had been interrupted at dinner by the sound of the bell. Shorter and plumper than their guards, they wore long, grey stormbird feathers in their hair. Cylindrical sheaths of swirling, cloud-coloured silk encased them from shoulders to knees. Silver streamers and strings of miniature blue-lit lanterns hung from the grey cloth. From a distance, they looked like small cities in themselves.

"Welcome, Hunters," the king called, raising his chalice in tribute to them. The group of courtiers from the hall of mirrors, spilling into the chamber at the Hunters' backs, cheered, applauded, and stamped their feet on the grey-carpeted wood floor. Imeris tried to feel welcome. She tried not to feel overwhelmed by the lustre of the room, or dimmed by the dazzle of the king and queen. She tried not to resent them for setting old men, children, and slaves against a goddess, and for showing no sorrow at the absence of over half the group.

She tried not to calculate how many slaves they must keep, for the palace to be maintained in this state of splendour.

Oniwak went to the foot of the dais, bowed deeply, and left the compass which had chosen Imeris in the palace of the king of Odelland near the foot of the king of Airakland.

"We feel only gratitude for this great honour, My King. Orin's beast is no more. Order is restored. Our people are safe."

He said it a bit pompously, Imeris thought, for a man who had very little to do with the actual killing of the creature. *I am not safe,* Imeris thought. Now that the Hunt was over, she was safe from the creature, and Oniwak, at least, but Loftfol and Kirrik still loomed in her mind.

Then she heard Daggad's quiet chortle beside her, becoming aware of his heavy, solid presence, and remembered that he was with her now. That she had bought for Anahah a measure of safety, in exchange for the sword that had saved her from transforming, and that she stood in the audience chamber of the king of Airakland, being cheered by Canopian nobility. She could use her new fame, and their goodwill, to forge the peace she had longed for, once Sorros had built her a trap for Kirrik's soul and she had filled it.

I will fill it. The Hunt has not injured me. It has made me stronger. I have more allies. I am more determined than ever. Her spines quivered in their sheaths.

"What," the king asked Oniwak, "are the names of the Hunters who have returned? I would reward them."

"Their names are Oniwak of Airakland," Oniwak said, taking two steps back before standing straight and stiff with his shoulders thrown back. "Owun of Ukakland. Eeriez of Eshland. Ibbin of Irofland. Daggad of Audblayinland. Imeris of Odelland."

At the sound of Imeris's name, one of the women amongst the courtiers gave an exaggerated gasp. Imeris turned and saw a wide, big-bosomed woman clasping at her heart. She met the woman's astonished protuberant eyes with cool curiosity an instant before it occurred to her who this must be.

Wife-of-Epatut. My birth mother. Here to reclaim Daggad, her stolen slave.

Imeris took a step back. Her gaze felt nailed to the woman's goggle-eyed face and stubby-fingered hands. She searched for traces of herself, but she was not accustomed to seeing herself and owned no expensive handheld looking glasses of her own. Did her eyes bulge that way? Were they the same colour? Aside from height, they seemed to be the opposite in everything; Imeris was small-breasted and long-fingered.

She had to have guessed wrong. The woman must be mourning another whose name she'd expected to come after Imeris's.

Then Imeris's gaze shifted to the two men flanking the woman. One was older, white-haired, with sharp cheekbones and long-fingered hands.

My birth father, Epatut.

The other man was dimple-cheeked, stubble-chinned, and chubby. He was a year or two younger than Imeris and had Wife-of-Epatut's bright, slightly bulging eyes.

The adopted heir to the House. Imeris couldn't remember what Daggad had said his name was. He was weighed down with more colourful cloth than the king and queen. When he raised a goblet almost identical to theirs and opened his heart-shaped mouth, Imeris thought he might propose a toast to her, to claim her immediately back into the House.

"To Daggad, a slave of the House of Epatut!" he said in a high-pitched voice instead.

"An ex-slave of the House," Imeris contradicted him loudly, angrily, and at once. "Freed by the ex-daughter of the House!"

Gasps, tutting, and commentary erupted from the court.

"My daughter," Wife-of-Epatut moaned. "My daughter! You can't be a birth mother's ex-daughter!"

"And if you can," Epatut said acerbically, "then you have no right to give away the House's property. Your Highness, I entreat you to surrender the slave of the House back into the custody of the House."

The king passed his goblet to a recently arrived man Imeris supposed was his vizier and clapped his hands once.

The sound echoed through the suddenly silent room.

"If surviving the Hunt," the king said sternly, "cannot earn a slave his freedom, then what can? One who walks in the grace of Airak hasn't called the Hunters here to shackle them, but rather to reward them. Daggad, Hunter of Audblayinland, you have helped make my niche safe, not only for my citizens and slaves but for my person and my family, and I thank you most sincerely. Where are the thanks of the House of Epatut?"

Epatut, his wife, and his heir immediately went to their knees before the king of Airakland.

"I beg your pardon, Highness," Epatut said tightly. "We are very, very thankful."

Daggad bowed courteously from the waist.

"Your Highness is kind," he boomed.

The king took his drink back from the vizier. He ordered food and fine glass knives to be brought for Ibbin, Oniwak, Daggad, Owun, and Imeris. Imeris swept the room constantly with her gaze, telling herself she was staying alert to threats but actually wanting to sneak glimpses of Wife-of-Epatut, who still knelt behind her husband and whose downcast features looked pensive.

When the time came for Imeris to receive her knives, she accepted them gratefully from a slave whose green eyes locked with hers.

It could have been envy in those green eyes, or it could have been scorn. It could have been an accusation: *While even one of us is still a slave, you do not deserve honours.*

Imeris would have answered, *I am fighting as hard as I can, but I am not a god!*

After the royals had retired to wherever they had been enjoying their feast, Imeris approached the representatives of the House of Epatut, the crowd parting ahead of her, all interested eyes fixed on the weapons. Perhaps they wondered if she was going to use the black glass blades to carve out Epatut's heart; how sensational it would have been if she had.

Instead, she offered them to him.

"You lost a slave," she said. "Twenty monsoons ago, you lost me. I have my reward, a sword made from a tusk of the monster. Take these to equip your future guards, or indeed your heir. You will not see me again."

Those last words startled her even as they passed her lips. She hadn't known, until she said them, whether she would want to know them, to understand them, or to part with them. The slave's stare must have decided for her. Reminded her, that for all its airs, Canopy was uncivilised. That being godless and battling demons was better than keeping magically imprisoned people inside impenetrable wards. Imeris still carried the slave-making coin of the king of Odelland in her belt pouch.

Anything was better than that.

Epatut took the knives. He peered into her face as though his true daughter was inside her somewhere, at the end of a long tunnel, and if only he squinted enough, she would come into focus.

"I spent all my wealth trying to find you," he said at last.

"I was raised by a chimera." She matched his blunt coldness.

"You're wild." He nodded to himself. "You'd rather live among savages."

"I have not seen true savagery," Imeris said, "except in Canopy." It was a lie. She thought of Loftfol. She thought of Sorros wanting to kill her for Bernreb's crime. Wherever there was humankind, there was savagery.

"I'm called Epi," the fat, cloth-heaped boy said, eyes shining. "I'm your cousin by blood, Imeris."

Imeris looked at him through slitted eyes.

"Do not mention blood to me, Epi," she said. "It might arouse my savagery."

She turned on her heel and left them, looking for Daggad, but he was surrounded by women again. Instead, she found a gloomy, isolated alcove with a view of Airak's Temple.

There she was free to stare at the lightning strikes and set her mind adrift. It was not a true time of triumph but a lull before the storm. Kirrik was out there, and this time there would be no blinding spears of Airak's power to aid in the enemy's destruction.

THIRTY-NINE

Two days later, Imeris and Daggad stood within sight of Odel's emergent.

Imeris found the sweet-fruit pine boughs and fish-shaped building, gleaming in the rain and bathed with the orange cloud-light of late afternoon oddly comforting, though she had ended all her days there in defeat. This day would be different.

"I 'ad not seen Odel's Temple before," Daggad said. "I did not ever imagine to 'ave a use for it. Childless, as far as I knew, and my master and mistress 'ad given up on producing a true-born heir."

"The first time I saw it," Imeris said, "I was a nine-year-old child on an adventure. It seemed much bigger and more wondrous."

"You saw Canopy durin' your Understorian childhood?"

"My fathers arranged for tribute to be paid in my name at the Temple." Imeris sighed. "Even though I lived below the barrier, Odel was able to save me when I should have fallen a second time. That is how I know my sister is lying when she says she cannot grant Sorros a child below the barrier. She does not want to. She does not want to think about them, about the life she had there, because that would set her at war with her immortal self, the self who does not care about Understorians and slaves."

"She freed the Garden slaves," Daggad pointed out.

"Odel freed his slaves as well," Imeris replied, "and he has no wards to keep me out. Even murderers love their children. Some days I like him better. He and Aurilon have done much for me, with no bond of blood."

The Temple itself was crowded with people bringing tributes for babies born during the monsoon, when mothers were more confined and could not come on long journeys between niches. Priceless items from tiny pearls to great chunks of pink rock salt were laid beside humbler items like leaf plates of seed porridge and tail feathers of colourful birds. Odel knew when a family or individual was making a real sacrifice and when not, and extended his protection accordingly.

Imeris stood and watched the supplicants in silence as dusk drew nearer and Airak's lanterns blazed to life across the high roads of the city. Daggad chatted amicably with anyone who would talk to him, and though by his speech and dress he seemed a slave, even noblewomen could not resist the chance to brag about their babes. Imeris thought on what Epatut had said about spending his fortune to recover her. If only he had thought to spend it before she fell and not after, but perhaps he had hoped, at that stage, to have plenty of sons.

She thought on Oldest-Father, who had woven a great net to catch gold-fruit stones from Akkadland when Imeris was only a few years old. Risking the wrath of the Headman of Dul for poaching, Youngest-Father had flown out with the net and flown back with three seed-shaped ingots. Two had been sent up the side of the tree to Youngest-Mother's old friend, the Gate-keeper of the Garden, who had agreed to send them on as tribute to Odel.

The third metal seed had been intended to decorate a wedding headdress, but instead had been put to the exact same purpose as the others when Leaper was born.

Three golden fruit. Three children to protect. Three fathers with nowhere near the resources of a man like Epatut, yet they had guarded their children far better than the Canopian merchant had.

At last, the main open space of the Temple was empty but for Imeris and Daggad. Aurilon emerged with slow caution. Odel was not far behind her.

Daggad bowed. Imeris did not.

"I have a remnant of Orin's creature," she said without preamble. "An artefact of the Old Gods."

"I feel it," Odel said wryly. "It itches my mind. I wish you'd take it away."

Imeris didn't try to hide her disappointment.

"I thought you would want it," she said, extricating the bone sword from a tangle of harness and other tools and weapons. Holding it recalled the battle against the creature and the way her skin had started to transform; in that manner, it itched her mind, too. "I thought you would take it. I wanted to trade it for the chimera skin I left behind, if you felt the items were of equal value."

"They're not of equal value," Odel said, disappointing Imeris even further. He smiled. "The pelt was a welcome tribute in nobody's name. It's been a long time since anyone made an unspecified gift so generous. The greatest source of my personal suffering is the foreknowledge that children will fall and that I'll be unable, in most cases, to save them. I was helpless to save even Aurilon when she fell as a child, though I knew she would one day be the most worthy of Bodyguards. I had to let her go. Nobody had brought me any gifts that day and begged me to save somebody they could not name."

"So Youngest-Father's wings did some good, then?" Imeris folded her arms across her chest. "They saved someone?"

"They saved many."

"But you are saying I cannot have them back."

Odel's smile deepened.

"I'm not saying that. Aurilon will fetch the wings for you. Don't bring the sword any closer to my floating dish. Their magics will interfere with one another."

"But you said they were not of equal value, Holy One."

"They aren't. The sword is much more valuable. Chimeras can breed and replenish their numbers. Bones of the Old Gods can be consumed, but they can't ever be replaced. What else would you ask for to trade?"

Imeris brightened.

"Books," she said at once. "Scrolls. Do you have anything that deals with metalworking and magic in combination? Could you have copies made for me?"

He raised an eyebrow, but simply said, "I could."

Aurilon, when she returned, brought both the frame-strapped chimera skin that Youngest-Father had lent Imeris and the shimmering skin of the chimera that Aurilon had killed herself.

"Let me wrap the sword in this skin," she said, and Imeris handed her the ornate weapon that Anahah had crafted from the tusk of the monster.

"I was warned," Imeris said, "that this sword would make me wild. That I might, in using it, turn on my friends. I was warned that it could not be used against the wild, only against people and perhaps domesticated animals."

"It is not to be used," Aurilon said, "but to be proffered as payment in turn, at some future hour when Orin rages against Odel and requires pacification."

"Oh," Imeris said. She couldn't imagine how Odel might offend Orin, but she supposed Aurilon knew best. The Bodyguard rolled the sword neatly in the colour-changing cloth, so that it became not only shielded but nearly invisible. Meanwhile, Imeris checked the struts and pins of the wings, pulling them around her, attaching them to her harness, shrugging her shoulders until they felt right.

The two women looked up from their tasks at the same time, eyes meeting. They stood a pace apart.

"Will you go back to Understorey," Aurilon asked, "despite the enmity of the Loftfol school?"

"Will you teach me," Imeris replied just as quietly, "so that I might survive Loftfol and destroy the sorceress who murdered my friends and my father?"

Aurilon sighed.

"I should have told you this years ago. I am not the teacher you need. Nor are the instructors of Loftfol." She put one hand to Imeris's shoulder. "All you need to know is this. In battle, every technique is best suited to a certain size and shape of form and also best used against a certain size and shape of form. You will never be as tall or wide as those low-dwelling warriors, but you know that already; already you have adapted many fighting styles taught to you by men. My biggest mistake was to allow the Crocodile-Riders to remove my breasts so that I could use their men's techniques. I would rather have spent my lifetime learning to fight in my own true style. You are your own teacher. You are the only teacher you need."

"No," Imeris said, feeling like she was falling, as if a branch she had reached for was not really there, had never been there. Aurilon's words were too similar to Anahah's. She could not accept them. There had to be some final lesson. "You sound just like him. He would not tell me what my weaknesses were."

Aurilon compressed her lips. Her fingers squeezed.

"Do you mean that I sound like the instructor that you killed? Your weakness when you fought me was impatience. Your weakness when you fought the sorceress was your care for your fathers. Fight her alone. Fight when time is not a factor. Fight without a care for anybody else."

"You fight with Odel as your care," Imeris said.

"Odel cannot be killed," Aurilon replied, lifting the skin of the chimera who had killed Odel in her other hand. "Not truly. Nor can any soul."

"Then why take the chimera's curse upon yourself, Bodyguard?"

Aurilon smiled.

"Because I have a gift," she said, letting her fingers lift lightly from Imeris's shoulder. "And gifts are meant to be used."

OUTSIDE THE Gate of the Garden, Imeris waited in the moonlight for the goddess Audblayin.

"Come inside," Middle-Father called around a mouthful of tapir in pomegranate sauce. "You cannot sit there all night."

In the doorway of his dwelling, he and Daggad made a matched pair, each as brawny and cheerful as the other. After a brief scuffle over which of them should've done what he was told by the Headman of Gannak and which one should have killed the Headman twenty-five years ago, they shared bia and swapped gossip while Imeris practiced the seven disciplines and the six flowing forms on the platform outside Audblayin's Temple.

Aoun must have seen her, or sensed her, but he made no appearance; apparently Imeris had disturbed the goddess's sleep too often of late.

"Maybe I should go down to Gannak ahead of you," Daggad suggested, waving his gourd full of bia. "I can take the scrolls to Sorros. Make sure 'e is well. 'Elp 'im to read them. We could 'ave a strategy all worked out before the goddess 'as even spoken to you."

"You could be killed by Loftfol," Imeris called back without taking her eyes from the Gate, "before you reached Gannak. You could lose the scrolls."

"You could visit my wife," Middle-Father told Daggad, "and she could berate you for a few days for not forcing me to return to her."

"What possible reason could I 'ave to want to do that?"

"She would feed you while she was berating you. Also, Loftfol holds certain superstitious misconceptions about the emergents of goddesses and gods, including that they cannot be bored into. It is one reason Esse chose this tree in which to hide our home."

"The more people you tell," Imeris said, "the less hidden it is."

"I like this man," Middle-Father declared. "His jokes are good for a weakling from Gannak."

"Your jokes are good," Daggad replied generously, "for a criminal from nowhere."

I have to pacify Loftfol, Imeris thought, *but I have already given the sword to Odel. How else can I make amends?*

While Bernreb told stories of all the fools and madmen he'd dispatched outside the Garden Gate and Daggad boasted of all the soldiers who had wet themselves when they realised the slave they'd spoken down to easily outmatched them, Imeris wandered back to the closed Gate and put her hand to a representation of Audblayin.

She is not doing all she can to help me.

Imeris sat with her back to the Gate. In her mind's eye, she saw the first time Middle-Father had asked Audblayin, Ylly as she had been then, to break the neck of a bird caught in a snare. *Hit the neck bones hard between the heel of your hand and the edge of the plank,* Middle-Father suggested. *Or hold it by the head and whirl it sharply through the air. The neck will break.*

Ylly, frozen in hesitation, had helplessly held the woodcreeper between both hands as if it were her own child.

Let me do it, Imeris had said. *The longer you hold it without killing it, the more frightened it is.*

Ylly had fumbled as she'd passed the bird to Imeris. It had escaped in panicked flight, leaving a few red-barred feathers behind.

She had no warrior self then. But she does now.

Crickets droned and moths flew towards the moon outside the Gate of the Garden. Imeris let her limbs go, slumping sleepily against the carved wood. Ylly had only ever once been physically punished by Oldest-Father. That was when she had broken the rope jig that led down to the pool. Little did she know that Imeris had actually broken it, but loosely twined it back into place to give the appearance that it was still sound, not thinking that the next person to use it might be killed.

Later, with Ylly's weeping stirring her to unbearable levels of guilt, Imeris had cried too. She had confessed. Oldest-Father had beaten her twice as hard as usual. To remind her that he loved her, he said. To remind her that he could not keep her safe if she did not remember and obey.

Imeris nodded drowsily. She napped. When she woke, the Gate at her back had left impressions in her flesh; it was dawn and birdsong washed over her.

She stretched, blinking away dreams of woodcreepers and Oldest-Father with a whipping stick in his hand. Middle-Father watched her from the open front door of his house, arms folded, sleepless and alert.

Daggad must be inside. Sleeping in the bed she'd politely refused, Imeris assumed.

She listened to the birds again. Their chorus was a soothing wave when tuned to background noise but an ongoing war when listened to call by call, some crying for mates, others to summon their family groups to a source of food.

Humans were savage, Imeris had decided, but birds were no better. So much of the song humans considered beautiful was actually territorial. Bird kingdoms carved by strength from the Great Trees, defended by blood when necessary, and starving hatchlings fell as often as starving children from the broad boughs.

Imeris leaped to her feet, finding fresh spiderwebs with her face. Middle-Father laughed as she clawed them away.

"Come inside," he told her. "Eat and drink. Make water where the bugs will not find your bare backside so quickly. What are you so angry about?"

"*She,*" Imeris said, stalking stiffly into the dwelling, "is not doing all she can to help me."

"And are you," Middle-Father answered gently, "doing all you can to help her?"

FORTY

Imeris left Daggad snoring in Middle-Father's bed.

"You," she said when the Gate cracked open and her barefooted, diamond-draped, loose-haired sister appeared, "are not doing all you can to help me."

The white-robed Gatekeeper, Aoun, stood silently behind Audblayin, one step back from the gap. Imeris saw in the corner of her eye that Middle-Father had moved to a position where he could better survey the scene. He held a barbed, white-apple-wood javelin in a spear-thrower in his right hand.

He smiled at her when he saw her looking.

Vines growing up the walls of the Garden twitched towards Audblayin's lithe body, wanting to be closer. Flowers opened out of season, turning to green-flecked purple fruits almost immediately.

"Perhaps you should make it clearer to me," the goddess replied reasonably, "exactly what you're trying to do."

She had always been the gentler one. The prettier one. With Middle-Mother's smile and Middle-Mother's laugh; Middle-Mother's favourite, her daughter by blood, and perhaps that was why Oldest-Father had not thrashed her as much. He had always been a little bit afraid of Middle-Mother.

"Stop the sorceress," Imeris said flatly. "It is what I have been raised to do. What I have always tried to do. Meanwhile, you flit about pretending it is not important. You pretend Understorey is not important."

"You pretend Canopy isn't important."

"Of course it is important. Half my family is here."

"I should never have opened the barrier for you," Audblayin said, and Imeris took a step back. *I called you my little sister, but your soul is by far the older. Now you dare condescend to me, to yearn to take my choices out of my hands!* "It's my fault you feel torn between two worlds. I should have made you stay below, a clean break, as clean as when you fell as a baby, but I missed you, and you wanted so badly to beat Aurilon."

"Yes," Imeris replied, stung. "If you had only left me alone down there with Oldest-Father, I would be a Leader of Loftfol by now. My mission would be to hunt you. Kill you."

"You'd never have agreed to that. No matter what."

"So what am I supposed to do? You will not open the barrier for me again? Is that the help you will give me, to help me get over losing you? Loftfol will find us, eventually, if Kirrik does not." Middle-Father, who pretended to be scanning the surroundings, gave himself away by shifting uncomfortably.

"Make peace with Loftfol," Audblayin said, and Imeris was taken aback by hearing her thoughts spoken aloud.

"How?" she demanded, as if she had not been turning it over in her mind ever since the pursuit by Kishsik.

"You'll think of something."

"You are confusing me with Leaper. Our brother is the one who speaks fancy words and makes the murderous see reason. I am the hunter he taught me to be." Imeris pointed at Middle-Father without taking her eyes from Audblayin. "I trap things. I cut their throats and skin them. Right now there is a soul I need to trap, and you know more about it than me. You are immortal, and you are not telling me what you know."

"I cannot."

"Help me with what you can help me with, then," she demanded. "Grant a child to Sorros the Silent Smith and his wife, Nin. Give me three golden metal-stone fruits to take to the Temple of Odel. One for Sorros's child. One for Ibbin, who helped me on the Hunt." She would have liked to bestow the deity's protection on every surviving member of the Hunt, even Oniwak, but Ibbin was the only one who was still a child. "And one for Anahah's child."

Before Imeris could dwell on Anahah, Audblayin surprised her with a long, angry, incredulous laugh that made her seem more like Middle-Mother than ever.

"You want me to give you gold from my Garden so you can pay tribute to a rival god? You're mad."

"You are the mad one. You think I do not care for Canopy? I saved Canopy from a monster. My name is on the monument tree. It will be there after I am dead and born again. The king of Airakland presented me with gifts of gratitude, so why not you?"

It was Audblayin's turn to take a long, deep breath.

"I'll give you gold," she said at last. "I'll give you another amulet of my old bone. A piece of myself from when I was a monster. Don't dare say I haven't helped you. You know how I feel about such fragments of the past. Place the amulet around Nin's neck, and she'll conceive. Bring it back to me a month later, when she's sure she's carrying. I'll open the barrier for you one last time."

"I will bring it back when she is sure," Imeris said solemnly, gratefully. She heard Daggad yawning and scratching himself in the doorway of Middle-Father's dwelling.

One last time.

"Promise," Audblayin said, "not to give my amulet to Odel, whom you love more than you love me."

"That is ridiculous." Imeris's skin prickled. Could the goddess have overheard her remarks to Daggad, somehow?

"Gods and goddesses are jealous creatures."

"Only when it comes to worshippers. I am your sister." *But you are not the sister I could torment, whose little ears I could pull. Middle-Father was wrong to suggest I am not helping you. I am helping take care of our mothers so that you do not have to.*

"You worship Odel's Bodyguard," Audblayin said.

"Is that why you are set on keeping me from seeing Aurilon again? Fighting her again?" *She said she was not the teacher I needed. She will never teach me. Leaper was right all along.*

"I'm saving her for you." Audblayin smiled wanly. "We don't worship what we've defeated."

"Do you know what would be better than locking me out of Canopy forever? Dissolving the barrier. Merging Canopy and Understorey into one."

Why is it my task to make peace? Why not yours, when you have so much power?

"That's not possible." The smile vanished.

Imeris turned to find Daggad knuckling his back, all his straps creaking and buckles jingling, great sword on his hip, hip-length hair falling around his funny-angled face.

"Are we going back to Odelland?" he asked, tonguing the black mark on his lip. "I sure am getting tired of that walk."

"Not today," Imeris answered.

Daggad fell on her. His unexpected weight crushed her down onto the platform. The great sword hilt drove up into her solar plexus, and she gasped for breath beneath him, wondering, *What is this? Is he trying to kill Audblayin? Was I a fool to trust him all along?*

Then she realised Audblayin was beside her, smothered under the white robes of the Gatekeeper.

A single arrow stuck into the Gate.

Writhing under her fellow Hunter, Imeris spotted a thin green strapleaf rope. It led from the attachment point of Middle-Father's door lintel to a swaying weight a hundred paces away, off the edge of one of the smaller tallowwood paths.

Middle-Father hauled on the rope. His face looked furious. After a while, the other end came visible on the path. It was a dead body, struck through the rib cage by the barbed, white-apple javelin. Imeris hadn't realised the throwing spear had a rope swaged to the end with a metal ferrule, which brought the plainly dressed, presumed slave up like a fish on a line.

If the dead man had held a bow, it was gone. Fallen. The arrows, likewise.

"Let me up, Aoun," Audblayin gasped. "Bernreb says the danger is over."

Imeris hadn't heard Middle-Father make a sound, but the Gatekeeper obeyed the instruction. Daggad rolled away, too, and together the sisters sat upright, Imeris sucking at the air, recovering from a stunned diaphragm. Eventually, she was able to stand.

Middle-Father brought the would-be assassin along the path, gripping one arm and one leg, the man's bulk across his shoulders. He dumped the corpse at their feet with a sigh. Imeris pictured him back in their family home; that sigh was the exact sound Imeris had heard thousands of times as he'd dumped a dead beast on their table and sighed in the face of the long task of skinning and butchering.

Imeris recognised the sad, lifeless face.

It was the blond, brown-eyed slave from Mistletoe Lodge who had sent the bird to Loftfol.

"He was not trying to shoot you, Holy One," Imeris concluded imme-diately. "He was here to kill me. He was an agent of Loftfol. Perhaps he was a student there before becoming a slave. If I had not been here with you, if Middle-Father had not been watching over us, I might have died. Are you sure you want to banish me down below the barrier?"

"Are you sure you won't stay and be my Bodyguard?" The Gatekeeper seemed startled, but Audblayin's focus was on Imeris's face.

"I am sure." Imeris grimaced. She thought of Anahah and his little green child, and her fingers rose reflexively to her lips.

"Then I'm going into the Garden," Audblayin said. "I'll return with the items you've asked for, Issi."

"Thank you, Holy One," Imeris said. When Audblayin and Aoun were gone, she stood by while Middle-Father wriggled his javelin free. At length, she told Daggad, "I want to go to the silk market on the way down to Gannak."

"Bribes for your three mothers?" Daggad guessed. "To keep them from 'aranguing you about the danger you keep leapin' into? Or to distract them from the question of grandchildren?"

"No," Imeris said, scowling. She was beginning to understand Oniwak better every day she spent with Daggad. "I want to see the place she dropped me. You know where it is."

"I know where it is, but I do not—"

A clean break.

"I want to see the place where I fell."

THE SILK market nestled between the boughs of three great mulberry trees.

Imeris breathed in the bitter steam of brown silkworm pupae being boiled in cauldrons alongside the intersecting lanes of the market. Daggad already snacked on a leaf-cup of spiced, fried worms. He held it up to her, grin-ning, like the king of Airakland proposing a toast with a glass goblet.

"Imeris," he said with great satisfaction, "would you like to taste your-self?"

Imeris pushed his hand down out of her face. Great sheets of shining silk hung down from the branches like red and gold rivers; others were tightly rolled and protected from the sun and rain by awnings of leaves or leather. Scarves and skirts fluttered on lines beside vendors of dried roots and pots of liquid dye.

"Show me where my family trades," she said curtly.

"Look for the banner I once bore on my tongue," Daggad replied drily. "Most of the silk they sell is from Ukakland and Ulellinland. One is a better niche for the insects, the other for mulberry leaves. 'Ere is the best for sellin'. 'Ere, silk prices are 'ighest."

Imeris spotted the sigil almost before he'd finished speaking. The wheel, cocoon, and loom was pressed into a bearskin resting on tent poles of purpleheart. Wife-of-Epatut scolded a pair of slave girls, her back to Imeris and Daggad but her broad silhouette and silk-woven hair unmistakeable.

"That is where she dropped me?" Imeris asked doubtfully. Nothing in the market had triggered any memories. What if the chimera had eaten more than one fallen child? What if the cloth she'd had with her was some other baby's wrappings?

No. Her physical resemblance to Epatut could not be wished away.

"Go and ask 'er," Daggad suggested, crunching down on a fried silkworm at the same time; it made a popping sound and flecked his lips and Imeris's cheek with juice. "As I am a free man, I will stay right 'ere."

"You might as well take the books and scrolls Odel gave us down to Sorros, then," Imeris said, watching Wife-of-Epatut. She absently wiped her juice-flecked cheek with the back of her hand. "Make sure he is well. Begin searching through the writings for the information we need. I will follow you to Gannak."

But before he could leave, Wife-of-Epatut turned. She locked eyes with Imeris across the press of customers. Turning, she lifted a bundle out from under the display bench of the stall and began squeezing through the crowd towards them.

Imeris straightened her shoulders. She braced herself. This was it; her birth mother was coming to recognise her. To present her with some kind of heirloom.

"Daggad," Wife-of-Epatut said with a nod, "Hunter of Audblayinland. In the past few days, these gifts have been presented to me in your name by strangers, citizens of Aublayinland. They're tokens of gratitude for your part in the slaying of the monster. I pass them on to you."

Daggad tipped the last few silkworms hastily into his mouth, freeing both hands to accept the bundle. It was silk-wrapped. Inside were wooden boxes, perfumed gourds, stoppered glass bottles, and other, smaller silk bundles tied with embroidered ribbons.

He slanted a glance at his former owner.

"You did not know I would come 'ere," he said. "You would 'ave kept these."

"You did not leave me," Wife-of-Epatut answered, "any forwarding address."

Imeris touched an exquisitely carved bowl of scented satinwood packed with pink salt. If she had gifts like these, she would not need gold from her sister to pay tribute to Odel. Was Daggad receiving them because he was Canopian? Because he was a man?

"Where are mine?" she asked.

"You're the Hunter of Odelland," Wife-of-Epatut said levelly. "I imagine your gifts are being left at Odel's emergent."

"I knew it," Daggad said. "I knew we would 'ave to go back there."

"Not yet," Imeris said sharply. Tribute could not be paid on behalf of children not conceived. First, she had to deliver the fertility amulet to Nin.

"I am not sure," Daggad said with a slight swagger, "I can carry all the books and scrolls as well as my new gifts. I might hafta make two trips—"

"Will you come to my house, Imeris?" Wife-of-Epatut interrupted. "It was your house. It is the house where you were born."

"You will excuse me," Daggad told Imeris, ignoring Wife-of-Epatut, "if I do not return to the scene of so many wasted years. I will go to the smith's 'ome, like you said."

"Why invite me to your house?" Imeris blurted at Wife-of-Epatut. "What for?" Wife-of-Epatut gazed at her for what seemed like a long time.

"For the sake of what might have been."

FORTY-ONE

WIFE-OF-EPATUT'S HOUSE, the extravagant crown of a gobletfruit tree, was crammed full of—Imeris did not know how else to describe them—a great many *things*.

It was a market with no customers. A village's worth of goods for just one family. There were rooms full of merchandise, bales of silk, piles of clothing, wooden worm-breeding assemblages, and components of giant weaving apparatus. But there were also things kept that others might have cast away, such as a stack of old, gilt-framed paintings of Ukak, Ulellin, and their prior incarnations, previously in pride of place over the dining table where Audblayin's portrait now hung. There were stands of hung children's clothes in a place with no children and preserved dead birds in lifelike positions that had no use besides decoration.

"Greetings, sister," Imeris murmured to the portrait as she passed.

"This way," Wife-of-Epatut said skittishly, leading her on through the wide, winding halls. There was so much silk on the walls, and so few windows, that Imeris began to feel as though she'd entered the enormous cocoon of her namesake.

Then they halted in an open doorway. This room, at least, had a skylight of translucent bone.

"My bedchamber," the older woman said. "You were born here, Imeris."

Imeris stared at the round, magenta-silk-draped, eucalyptus-smelling room that might have been familiar and beloved. At the knots and splinters in the ceiling that might have witnessed the secret hopes and fears of her childhood.

With her reflexes and quiet understanding of the wild, might she have rebelled against her merchant parents and grown to serve as a soldier of Audblayinland? Or, without enemies and threats to shape her, would she have enjoyed the company of silent silkworms and whispering looms as she hoped one day to enjoy the company of flowerfowl and sacks of feed?

"I thank you," she said, "and my birth father Epatut for the gift of my life."

"I kept your cradle," Wife-of-Epatut said. "In the nursery. I'll show you."

The nursery was draped in orange and yellow, a perpetual sunrise. The cradle was fine work, woven of black wattle and set in a rocking frame of sweet-fruit pine. Imeris tried to imagine herself matched to a man like Epatut, absent all the day but useful for his wealth and connections. She looked again at her birth mother, who had been called Igish before marriage, who had tried her best but made an error of judgement when it came to the gods, and seen her whole life shaped by that mistake.

"What does the name Igish mean?" she asked.

"It's a little bee-eating bird," Wife-of-Epatut replied. "Rainbow-coloured. You don't have them . . . down below?"

"We have dayhunters," Imeris said grimly, touching the thin, worn furs in the cradle. The animal hides provided by her three fathers were the bedding of royal babes in Canopy. "We have the spotted swarm. We have chimeras."

Wife-of-Epatut touched the wings folded along Imeris's back.

"It's almost as soft as silk," she said slowly. "I couldn't have given a skin like this to you. I wouldn't have known where to find the warrior teachers you needed. Since seeing you in Airakland, Epi is a boy possessed. He never cared about weapons or training before. Now he's discovered that soldiering skills are passed down through soldiering families, and my husband will never allow him to leave this family and be adopted by soldiers."

"Do you wish me to stay and train him?" Imeris asked guardedly, ready to refuse.

"I wish you would stay and marry him."

Imeris shook her head. She lifted her hand from the cradle, thinking again with a pang of Anahah. He had made mistakes too, but he understood her, and she thought she understood him. She had decided that she loved him, yet she did not yearn for him as the songs and sagas said that lovers yearned. Did she really love him? It seemed thrilling enough that she should brush against the secret thought of him, sometimes. If he was nearby, she'd only get angry at him again for letting Oldest-Father die, and besides, she would never see him again.

"I am banished by my sister, Audblayin, back to Understorey," she said.

Maybe she would see him again, though. Audblayin said Imeris's home was Understorey and was intent on sealing her away below the barrier, but what if attempts to make peace with Loftfol failed? Marrying Epi, returning to the House of Epatut, would be one way of defying the interfering deity. Marking her tongue with the slave-making token she still carried would be another.

"For what crime?" Wife-of-Epatut wanted to know.

"Every time she opens the barrier for me, Audblayinland is endangered." *And she is angry that I do not behave slavishly towards her. She blames me for not knowing who I am.*

"I see."

"Aside from Daggad and me, there are four Hunters who survived." Despite how it had gone, Imeris was pleased to think of them returning to their own niches, gathering their gifts. "Oniwak, Eeriez, Owun, and Ibbin. If you wish me to write letters, to ask them to tutor your heir, ask now. I am headed back to Understorey. I will be permitted one final visit to Canopy next moon. If there is anything else you want from me, ask now."

Wife-of-Epatut smiled.

"Don't write letters," she said. "But go back to Understorey knowing I'm proud of you. I'll go to Atwith knowing I brought something of value into the world. And although I love Epi with all my heart, more than I've ever loved anything—aside from you, when I had you, before you fell—he is no warrior. He never will be. Safe journey, Imeris."

"Thank you, Birth Mother," Imeris said, briefly bowing her head.

Then her thoughts skittered ahead of her, to Gannak, wondering what secrets of the gods Daggad and Sorros had unlocked.

HOPING FOR unlocked secrets, Imeris found the forge unlocked, instead.

The air was bitter with the smell of spilled bia. It was the early hours before morning, and slow-roiling mist separated the great trees, hiding all but the brightest lanterns of the village nearby.

Imeris hesitated on the threshold as usual, hating the assault of memories that accompanied her presence in the forge.

"Sorros!" Imeris called, her voice echoing through the gloomy rooms, and heard Daggad's sleepy chuckle from the toilet chamber. She found him sitting on the hole, drunk and bare-arsed.

"Musta fallen asleep," he mumbled when she prodded him in the forehead.

"Where is Sorros?"

"In 'is 'ouse. With 'is wife. Could not watch them together. She was mine."

"What about the writings, Daggad? Has he looked at them? Did you look at them together?"

"Not yet."

Imeris dragged him off the toilet and back to his blankets before leaving the forge by the front door. She climbed high enough in the jackfruit tree to give her an easy glide to the ulmo where Sorros and Nin lived.

The house where she had visited Nirrin.

Night air whistled over her eyes and ears. She slapped hard against the wrinkled ulmo bark in the dark, efficiently setting her spines, folding her wings, dropping down to the platform outside the smith's door.

The woman who opened the door was small and stout with a wrinkled neck and silver-blond hair braided in rings around her crown. She rubbed sleep out of her eyes and hid a yawn.

"I do not know you. Do you need moonflower? Wait." She wrinkled her nose. Imeris knew she smelled of bark, sap, and eucalyptus oil. "How did you get 'ere?"

Imeris had only ever seen Nirrin and Vesev's mother from a distance before. Now she saw Nirrin's sky-blue eyes in Nin. Wondered at the deceptive, bland exterior, which hid a history with Daggad that ended in disaster, the loss of her two children, and life with a man who was famous for saying nothing.

"Many things have conspired to bring me here," Imeris said. "My mother who dropped me. My fathers' refusal to obey orders. The prejudice of the Loftfol school. The goddess Orin. The king of Airakland. Your husband, Sorros. Your son, Vesev, and your daughter, Nirrin. The sorceress Kirrik."

"Imerissiremi," Nin said, standing immediately back from the doorway so that Imeris could enter. Inside, the brightest light was the orange glow from three oil lanterns hung over a tallowwood table. The books and scrolls Daggad had brought were spread out. Sorros's black-haired head was bent over them. "Will you take ti?"

Imeris shed her wings at the door.

"I can make the ti," she said. The memory of her visit came back to her startlingly strongly. "I remember where you keep the honey."

Nin tilted her head inquisitively, but when Imeris didn't say anything else, she nodded and went to the table. She propped her straight arms against its edge and looked down at the rough notes her husband made with charcoal on pieces of wood.

"I fear," Nin said, "that what you ask of us will cost a fortune in metal."

"It is possible, then?" Imeris hesitated at the hanging tapestry which covered the opening to the kitchen. Excitement and hope expanded her chest. Anger as well. Odel had helped her where her own sister had refused. "You can do it? You can make a trap for Kirrik's soul?"

"Yes," Sorros said, looking up at her with purpose and determination she'd never seen on his bearded face before.

"I will make ti," Imeris said again, and found herself seeming to step back in time, confronted with the cluttered but well-organised gourds and herb boxes, and the wooden shutters over the little square windows with their insectivorous-plant-smothered sills, which had so amazed her as a child, when her own family's cooking area was little more than the open hearth and a series of spits.

She was a head taller now than she had been.

Nirrin's ghost lingered.

We only have honey on feast days, she had said, and Imeris had quizzed her about feast days, which her fathers had hardly mentioned. Meat and fish were so abundant in the dwelling of the three hunters, she supposed every day was a feast compared to the way things were in Gannak.

Imeris made the tea, trying not to remember the ti-house, Breeze, where Oldest-Father had cooked his last fish.

FORTY-TWO

THE NEXT day, after the bridges were set, she went to the ti-house at Gannak.

It was where Nin sold moonflowers every morning. If agents of Loftfol were watching for Imeris, the ti-house was bound to draw their attention.

Imeris instructed Sorros and Nin to stay locked in their house. She could only assume Daggad was still snoring at the forge. If her plan went wrong and she ended up dead, she didn't want them involved.

She didn't go by the bridges. Instead, while the mist still lingered, she glided down from a high point on the ulmo tree where Nin and Sorros lived to the spiny plum where the ti-house of Gannak was bored through the mottled grey-and-brown bark. It was a much older tree than other spiny plums she had seen. Opportunistic white and orange fungi decorated the old slashes left behind by the spines of prior climbers.

Imeris set two simple noose snares at the small, paired rear doors that seemed the most likely unobtrusive exit.

Then she waited for a gap in human traffic, glided down onto the bridge, and entered by the main door, folding her colour-shifting chimera wings behind her.

The ti-house had no name. Most villages only had one. This one looked like it had been carved long before Loftfol, with moss and glowworms covering the domed ceiling of the reception area. There, a dozen villagers had shucked their nets, tools, harnesses, and raincloaks, and a smiling order taker with charcoal finger marks on her apron stood behind a counter where bowls of dried ti displayed the various types of available leaf.

Imeris shed none of her belongings. She asked the order taker for a bowl of duck broth, paid in shell coins, and walked into the C-shaped common room where a few blond, bearded men looked up from their game of sticks and a small boy selling wine from a gourd started hopefully towards her, probably tricked by her short hair and the low light into thinking she was a man. Women in Gannak were not supposed to get drunk, Nirrin had told her once. It reduced their fertility.

Imeris sat with her back to the wall in the centre of the C so she could see almost everyone. Nobody else sat there. It was too close to the fire. She wanted them to be able to see her face clearly. The stick players, seeming to ignore her, drew their colours one at a time from the jumbled tower of sticks on their table. The stage beyond them was empty of players, though a flute rested on a stool in promise of some future performance.

Half an hour later, one of the stick players finished off his wine and shuffled away to the distant end of the C, shifting the belt of his trousers as though his bladder was uncomfortably full.

Imeris waited, her ears pricked. Probably she wouldn't be able to hear him urinating from the common, but she might hear the rear doors opening. She heard the flap of a batted tapestry. The rap of a wooden spoon across knuckles and the squeals of children in the kitchen.

The stick player returned. Beckoned the boy over for some more wine. A thin man came in, holding a bowl of ti, sipping it too quickly and grimacing when he burned his mouth, but apparently in a hurry to finish it and get up on stage. He had to be the flute player.

When he saw Imeris, he set his ti-bowl down abruptly. He went to the distant end of the ti-house. There was a creak. It might have been a door.

At the sound of his strangled yelp, Imeris followed after him, dodging tables and stools as quickly as she could manage.

She didn't want him to completely hang.

His face, when she found him kneeling and choking in the rear doorway, was purple.

"Stop struggling," she told him coldly, removing the noose. "Who are you?"

"Greerg," he managed, clear grey eyes bulging in the light from the brazier that burned beside the back door.

"Take me with you," she said, "to the house where you were going to inform on me, or I will cut your throat. I am sure you have heard that I am a killer."

They went back through the ti-house, Greerg nervous and twitching,

Imeris calm and arm in arm with him, smiling softly as though they were father and doting daughter. Outside the main door, they crossed a dozen bridges, circumventing the market tree and the trade-houses, towards the Headman's house. Sorros had lived in it, before he gave up his claim to being Headman. It was difficult to give advice and sit in judgement when you did not speak. One of his cousins became the respected elder of Gannak.

Their destination lay one level above a signposted school in a wide and twisted bloodwood tree. Children's chanted genealogies and insect-repelling smoke wafted from a lower window. The Headman's house was positioned in a bend of the great trunk so that his toilet sat well away from the school-house. There had been fire or a lightning strike in the past, so that the bark was burned black. Epicormic shoots sprouted vigorously from cracks where hardened sap the colour of heart's blood glittered, jewel bright.

A ring of ballista platforms hosted bridges stretching off in five different directions. Two thin young men who could have been the flute player's brothers stood watch over the ballistae. They looked nervous at Imeris's approach, lowering the crossbows in their hands. She smiled bitterly at them, thinking of a time when she would have given anything to have more friends her own age, when a Headman's sons would have seemed like kings.

Inside the house, she found the Headman himself, a broad, silver-braided man. He wore slightly too-small silver-tooled red leather armour that he'd probably owned since his own stint at Loftfol, and she interrupted him feeding kept birds, which she suspected would fly to Loftfol at once if she was to open the cage door.

After an exchange of blows that demonstrated how lazy his practice of the Gannakim's curved knife techniques had become in old age, Imeris tied him to his flute-playing relation, the pair of them back-to-back in the writing room, and completed feeding the birds.

It was gloomy in the room. She lit a pair of oil lanterns and half a dozen tallow candles. There were plenty to spare. No matter how long she had to wait.

"You will write to Loftfol," she told the Headman. He hadn't screamed for help when he might have, and now he was gagged with a long, thick braid of his own severed silver hair. "Tell them to send someone with the authority to negotiate with me. If they proceed in good faith, many slaves may be saved. No attack, or I'll make both of you slaves of Odelland before anyone can kill me, and if the climb does not kill you, you will live out your days scrubbing the shit holes of Canopy."

LOFTFOL SENT the one-handed student, Kishsik.

I do not understand, his last words had been to her. *Why betray us? Why whore for them when they failed you, when they let you fall?*

She answered him now, in the birdcage room of the Headman's house, a night and a day since she had captured them, her two prisoners beside her and the magic bone coin from Odelland bouncing on her palm.

"I have not slept in two days," she told Kishsik. "I cannot ever sleep a truly restful sleep because the sorceress Kirrik is out there. She killed my father. She killed the son of one of the villagers. She took the body of my best friend for her own. I went to Canopy to learn the skills to fight her, the same reason I went to Loftfol. Horroh the Haakim tried to kill me before I could explain, else I would never have raised a hand to him."

Kishsik stood thin and strong as a cidergum sapling in gliding harness and bark skirt, head cocked to one side so that his long, reddish-brown fringe fell away from one baleful hazel eye where reflected candle flames leaped. He reached for no weapons, but like her, Kishsik had trained hardest with his own spines. The missing hand affected his climbing and woodcraft but not the swing of a forearm full of snake's teeth.

"Horroh the Haakim defended you to the other teachers like you were his own blood," he said, making Imeris's heart lurch. "He begged to be the one to confront you when news came of your sighting in Canopy. *She will speak the truth to me,* he swore. We could only guess that the truth you spoke was one he could not bear to hear from one who had restored his faith in the future of Loftfol."

"I told him the truth!" Imeris rubbed her forehead with a knuckle, distressed by the revelation, struggling to remember exactly how it had happened. "I told him some of the truth. But only after he caught me in a lie. I did not want to endanger my fathers. Why must the ones I love war with one another, and why must I always be forced to choose?" She bared her teeth. "I am sick to death of choosing."

"Sleep does not come easily to me, either," Kishsik said softly. "My father was murdered when I was a child. We all have our reasons for wanting revenge on Canopy."

"Each time you try for revenge, all you do is make more slaves," Imeris said. "What if there was a better way to help our people, both those below and those already taken?"

He did not take objection of her use of *our people* to include herself and him.

"You would reinstate the practice of buying back slaves?" he guessed calmly instead. "We have nothing with which to pay. Only the scraps that fall from their table."

"Loftfol could generate wealth. Teach Canopian youngsters to kill demons. Those skills are a rarity up there. Both the meat and skins *and* the luxury of boasting. They would like nothing better than to risk their lives demon-hunting in Understorey, so long as their lessons and the hunt itself were kept to brief enough time periods that they could keep their auras and return home." Imeris slipped the bone coin into her pouch and held up both empty hands, pleading for him to picture it. "Our villages would be safer. Canopian students would give Loftfol their metal coins and take all the foolish risks on themselves. Take their money and rid us of dayhunters and needleteeth."

"They could not be trusted."

"Even city-dwellers know Loftfol by its fearsome reputation. Use it!"

"I would rather use it to slay their goddesses and gods."

"That is Kirrik's alleged aim, but she has killed as many Understorians that I love—" Imeris tried to keep her voice from breaking; she was so tired. Why couldn't he just agree? Why was he going to force her to kill him? "—as she has killed goddesses and gods."

Kishsik stood, still and proud, for a quiet moment. The two prisoners watched him, wide-eyed, over their gags.

"I have heard of the sorceress," he said at last.

"At the very least, give me leave to hunt her freely. You can kill me after she is done."

"That is," he qualified, "I have heard of a rogue spinewife from Dul who once went by that name. That Kirrik once killed Audblayin, Odel, Airak, Ilan, and Ehkis in a single day."

"Audblayin died of old age," Imeris corrected him, outraged. "Odel was killed by a chimera. Airak was unharmed. What she did manage was to steal the body of Ehkis for about five minutes before getting her throat cut by a Bodyguard, and for that she needed to have her minions kidnap Ilan.

She cannot steal bodies across the barrier without a goddess or god to make an opening for her."

"You know a lot about it."

"I know a lot about Loftfol, and I tell you I have never betrayed it!" Her voice did crack with emotion now, and there was nothing she could do about it. "I brought an ex-slave with me to Gannak. His name is Daggad. You could have freed him years ago under an exchange like this. You could have bought back his life, for him to live as he wished, before it was half over. Please, Kishsik. Take this plan to them. Convince them. I can even give you the name of your first pupil. He is Epi, a silk merchant's son from Audblayinland."

FORTY-THREE

IMERIS PUT her hand up to feel for the barrier.

It was open. Her sister had made a hole for her as promised.

One last time.

Her month in Gannak had flown by. She looked at her upraised hand. It trembled.

Curse you, Ylly. You have no right to make me choose.

Sap from the tallowwood was fragrant on her spines. She rose into the dawn birdsong cloud, distracted by her calculations. Sorros had told her he needed one hundredweight of steel and fifty of silver to finish the trap for Kirrik's soul. That, and a piece of bone from the Old Gods.

Imeris had considered giving him the amulet that protected her from Kirrik. She had considered letting him use the bone coin that turned humans into marked Odelland slaves. Or sending a message to Leaper to say that she needed him to steal back Tyran's Talon.

No, Sorros had said, consulting his compilation of notes from the writings given to them by Odel. *That coin is a piece of the Old God who became Odel. We need a piece of the god who became Atwith or the goddess who became Audblayin. No other artefact will do.*

She had considered going back on her promise to her sister to return the fertility pendant which had, to Nin's delight, and some degree of nausea, functioned exactly as promised.

No, she had said slowly to Sorros, holding the pendant up to the firelight in the forge. *I swore to take it back to her, and I will. But there is another piece of the old birth goddess that I think I know how to reach.*

She was thinking of the protective amulet worn by Oldest-Father when Ulellin's emergent had swallowed him whole.

As she climbed, Oldest-Father's heaviest, most durable adze hung from one side of her harness, his best bore-knife on the other. The three gold seeds given to her by Audblayin stretched the seams of her belt pouch. Once she had filled the empty sack she'd brought for the steel and silver, she would be much too heavy for gliding. The chimera wings remained at home on the top shelf in the fishing room.

When she reached the platform outside the Garden of Audblayin, Canopians lined up outside the Gate looked on with fear mixed with curiosity as an Understorian warrior, spines and all, appeared to pound on the Bodyguard's door.

She whirled, startled, as Middle-Father spoke her name from behind her.

"Imerissiremi." He enfolded her in a hug. "Your sister has not yet woken. I will call her."

"First of all," Imeris answered, searching about her person for the rolled parchment she'd brought from the Headman of Gannak, "this is for you."

She swapped it for a nut cake and a water gourd, gulping gratefully while he read the document. The proclamation was slightly crushed from its journey but still quite legible. Middle-Father's eyebrows rose higher and higher. His beard trembled, and his mouth opened widely in an incredulous laugh.

"All my offers to slay demons for them," he said, "and it is my dangerously daft daughter who brings me a pardon at last."

"Sorros helped," Imeris said quickly. "It was his father that you killed, after all, and his cousin who is Headman of Gannak. Now all of you, my mothers and fathers, will be able to visit openly. Trade. Play music in the ti-house. Buy your own bloody blades."

"This is wonderful, Issi." He hesitated. "But the sorceress. If she knew where your mothers lived—"

"We are halfway to defeating her." Imeris washed her face with the last of the water and handed the empty gourd back to Middle-Father. "Sorros is building a woman-sized cage of magic-infused metal for her body and soul."

She would have told him more, but the Gate cracked open. Suppliants who had come to present tribute or ask Audblayin's Servants for care fell to their knees before the resplendent birth goddess. Middle-Father reached into the open door of his dwelling, exchanging the Gannak Headman's proclamation for the bloodstained wooden javelin.

Imeris fell to her knees among the suppliants for the sake of appearances, holding up the fertility charm. Audblayin walked by the other slaves and citizens to claim it.

"Thank you, Holy One," Imeris intoned. "Wife-of-Sorros is with child, and grateful for your gift."

"Holy One indeed," Audblayin muttered. Loudly, she responded with, "Wife-of-Sorros has my blessing." Then, quietly again, she added, "Imeris, come and see me again at dusk. We'll talk."

"I go to Odelland," Imeris whispered back. "To pay the tribute that you gave me and to fetch the gifts I hope I have been given. It might take a few days." *Or weeks. I need that pendant from Ulellinland.*

"However long it takes. Come to see me before you go." *Forever.*

"I promise."

Middle-Father could not drop his guard while the goddess was out in the open, but he spoke to Imeris out of the side of his mouth while he scanned the surrounding branches for attackers.

"News reached us of your deal with Loftfol."

Imeris stood straighter before she could help herself.

"Loftfol has its first three Canopian students," she said, "paid for with the lives of three freed slaves."

"I am proud of you, Issi. Take extra care on your journey to Odelland. You will be sad to hear that one of your fellow Hunters, the one called Oniwak of Airakland, was killed by agents of the goddess Orin."

Imeris's heart sank.

"I have negotiated away the threat of one group with a grudge against me, and now I must avoid another?"

"You killed her beast."

"I had no choice! I was called to the Hunt by the power of a different goddess, by the order of a king. This is not justice. Ilan should—"

"Ilan has power in her own niche, Issi. Only her own niche, if she does not wish to make enemies of her own kind." Middle-Father's gaze left Audblayin for just long enough to assess the weapons that his other daughter carried on her person. He grunted his approval. "Just watch your back."

"I always do," Imeris answered. "This may be Audblayinland, but it is still a part of Canopy. I may be brown, but my spines are white. I will see you again soon, Middle-Father."

TWO HOURS later, she was watching her back when she saw somebody familiar bounding up to her from the direction of the silk market.

Oh, no, she thought despairingly as Epi, heir to the House of Epatut, approached her along an almost-straight mulberry path. Once she'd arranged for him to become a student of Loftfol, she thought she'd seen the end of him and her birth family. Her debt to them felt like it was sufficiently discharged, that no more visits, no more awkward conversations, would be required.

He wore silks as ornately embroidered as the ones he'd worn in the king's court, but the puppy fat in his face was gone and the sashes at his waist were definitely wound tighter than before.

Imeris stopped to wait for him. A white-skinned slave girl in a plain brown silk wrap followed a step behind him, carrying a small wooden chest. If he had gifts for her, she would take them. She would buy metal with them.

"My Lady Hunter," Epi said, eyes bright, stopping at arm's length and bowing his head. Imeris spotted a jewelled knife handle half buried in his sash. Pale ridges of callus lined the outer edges of his hands and splotched his knuckles where his skin had been sleekly soft before.

"Call me Imeris," she said. "Or sister."

He jerked a little in surprise, bulging eyes widening, and her suspicions were confirmed; Epi, like his mother, wanted them married.

"C-c-cousin," he spluttered. *Oh, yes. Cousins can marry. Brother and sister cannot.* "Are you thirsty?"

Before Imeris could say she was not, the slave girl opened the chest and Imeris's attention was drawn by the wave of cold that floated out of it. It held glittering, white, feathery-looking stuff in which two wine gourds nestled.

The white stuff was not duck down.

"Is that . . . ice?" She silently calculated the season. Three months of spring. Five months of monsoon. One month of autumn. Three of winter. It was winter.

"Snow," Epi answered, grin wide and white teeth perfect. "Oxor is weak, for the first time I can remember. She died recently, so we've had less sun. Have you ever seen snow before?"

"No." Imeris stared. The slave's hands trembled. She must have been instructed to keep the lid of the thick-walled chest closed at all times to keep the snow from melting. Her blue eyes darted nervously at Epi. "I have seen slaves before, though. What is your name?"

Epi moved between them before the girl could answer, lifting both gourds out of the snow and pressing one into Imeris's hands, looking embarrassed.

"The girl's mother was freed," he said quickly, "as first payment for my tuition. One who walks in the grace of Audblayin will free this slave next, once his hired servant has been trained. I beg you, cousin, drink while it's still chilly. You've never tried anything like it."

Imeris frowned. Perhaps he was nervous because he wanted to impress her.

Or perhaps he was nervous because Loftfol had not forgiven her, after all, but slipped him a poison to use on her. He was not her real family. She could not trust him.

Yet the gourd was so deliciously *cold*.

"I do not want wine," she said, pressing the gourd back on him, to his great consternation. "But I will take the snow."

She took the chest from the white-skinned girl. Scooped out half a handful of the stuff, which felt grainy and sharp like broken glass or honey tree sawdust. Wondered at the sensation of her fingertips growing numb.

Snow.

She put it in her mouth, and it turned to cool nothing against her tongue.

"Epi," she said between her third and fourth scoop, "this stuff is amazing."

His face glowed with pleasure, and he swigged both gourds of wine and said nothing as she ate it all.

When there was no more snow, Imeris gave the wet box back to the slave.

"Thank you," she said. "That was very refreshing. Now I must go to Odelland."

"Stay," Epi implored her. "Marry me. Be my wife."

"Forty days at Loftfol," Imeris said, shaking her head, adjusting her harness, "and a box full of snow, and you imagine to win my favour?" *And Wife-of-Epi is a foolish-sounding name.*

"Yes! My teacher Kishsik says I'm at least as gifted as you were when you began."

"Does he say so?" Imeris asked dangerously.

"It's because I'm a man." Epi nodded to himself stupidly, and Imeris realised the two gourds of wine had affected him.

"It is because you are paying him," Imeris murmured, turning away, but Epi bumped up against her, blustering.

"Shall we race, then, cousin?"

"No," Imeris said.

"You're afraid of being beaten!" He put his hand to the hilt of the jew-elled dagger as though it had a hope of availing him against her. His chest could not be puffed any higher. "They put your name with the other Hunt-ers on the monument tree, but you're not so great! If you don't race me, I'll tell everyone you were afraid to face me!"

Imeris smiled thinly. It was not fair, to punish him for his pride, but her own pride demanded it. He called her Hunter, but that was not what he saw when he looked at her.

"Very well," she said. "A race. To the Falling Fig on the border of Aud-blayinland and Ehkisland. It is seven thousand paces away. To win the title of Heightsman and become accepted at Loftfol, I won a climbing race, but you have no spines. A climbing race would not be fair. We will run a footrace." She had to go in that direction, anyway, though she hadn't intended to run.

She felt the drag of her heavy weapons, tools and three golden seeds. Her muscles were fatigued from the climb, but most of that was in her shoul-ders and back, and she had no glider to tangle her heels or bang against her legs as she ran.

Epi laughed triumphantly, as though the race were already over.

"I have a lesson, later on," he informed her. "If we waited, they could witness."

"No." He would be pleased, later on, that there were no witnesses. "Let Loftfol wait."

"If I win the race, will you marry me?"

"Yes." She said it easily. He would not win.

"When do we start?"

"We start now, of course."

Epi stared at her a little longer. Then he gave a single, decisive nod. Strip-ping off his ridiculous heeled boots and the outer layers of his fancy garb, he gave them to the girl, instructing her to take them back to his stall at the silk market.

"Who will say when?" he asked, swinging his bared arms back and forth as though limbering up. How his arms would help him in a footrace, Imeris couldn't be sure.

"Count to three," Imeris told him, cinching her harness tighter behind her, drawing the adze and the bore-knife into the small of her back. She took note of the position of the sun; it was behind thin cloud cover and still low in the east. The Falling Fig lay due south. It would not do to lose her way.

"One," Epi all but shouted, abruptly quivering with excitement. His gaze turned from her to the mulberry branch ahead. The high road narrowed as it curved gently towards the next crossroads, a meeting of mulberry and floodgum. There, a couple of merchant women with barrows, their heads together in deep conversation, provided the first obstacle. "Two. Three!"

Imeris leaped into the lead.

FORTY-FOUR

IMERIS TOOK the low roads.

For a while, as she warmed to the task, when she turned her head she could see Epi labouring along the high roads, mouth open in a ragged O, armpits damp, the silk streaky with sweat, his eyes bulging more than usual.

Then she forgot him, lengthening her stride, enjoying the wind of her passage as it broke over her brow. The dappled sunlight of Canopy made patterns on the road that were unique, never to be repeated again. As the day grew hotter, less suitable for trussing a squealing tapir calf and taking it to market, most people retreated to the shade if they were able, so that sometimes Imeris was the only witness to the shadow-play.

Any snow that had fallen overnight without being saved in a box would have melted ten times over. The air smelled of human waste that had not quite made it over branch edges, lemon ironwood and sweet-fruit pine oils, the powder down of parrot flocks, banked fires of floodgum bark, and winter flowers with a whiff of flying fox.

She was perhaps a quarter of the way to the Falling Fig when the sound of heavy shapes slapping the leaves of the passionflower-vine-covered gap-axe she was in made her slow down in order to search out its origin. One of the leaf-concealed, rapidly moving shapes gave a long, wild wail. Imeris glimpsed golden fur.

Gibbons, she thought. Their meat tasted tolerable when well spiced but otherwise worked better as bait. *Nothing to worry about.*

Still, she wanted them to pass before she sped up again. She could not keep an eye on the troupe and run safely at the same time without slipping. Something about the answering wails of the other gibbons recalled the wildness of the bone sword Anahah had made for her, made an image of Orin's many-eyed monster flash though her mind.

Then she remembered where she'd last seen a gibbon: the cave-like entrance of the palace in Orinland.

From a branchlet that split off from the high road, an ape swiftly arced, one-handed. It was the size of a just-walking human child. Its fine yellow body fur turned white in a ring around its black, bare face. White canines gleamed in a black hole-mouth as it swung towards her, screaming.

Imeris sidestepped the fast-flung, hairy body, feeling the wind of its passage. The gibbon's long arms caught in a hanging vine beside her and its trailing legs, feet as dexterous as hands, grabbed the harness across her back. Imeris felt it with the finality of dropping to the end of a rope. It jerked her towards the edge with surprising strength. When she braced herself and spun, swinging angrily at it with her spines, the gibbon did not abandon her.

Instead, holding on by its feet, it swung the opposite way and wrapped itself around her eyes, a smothering blanket that smelled of rancid oil.

A second gibbon slammed into one shoulder, unbalancing her again towards the edge. Then a third. She couldn't turn her forearms around enough to cut the first animal; the angle needed was one as if to cut her own face. Blunt teeth chewed her ear in a lightning strike of pain. Blood ran down her neck.

Imeris reached her adze. Freed it with difficulty. Wedged the blade of it between the first gibbon and her forehead, prising it loose. Once it was away from her, she was able to insert her other forearm into the gap and cut through the animal's hide. It took a piece of her ear along with it when it fell. The other two gibbons, swinging about with their feet open, seeking a hold, she didn't strike at directly. Instead, she slashed with her spines at the vines they were using as ropes.

They fell, but not far. Almost faster than her eye could follow, they swung back to the high road and aimed themselves at her from different directions.

Now that she was prepared for it, Imeris had no trouble slicing them along their breastbones as they came. Her spines stayed magically sharp, unlike the skinning knives she'd used on monkeys under Middle-Father's eye. Their naked lungs deflated as their chests opened. Imeris blinked more ape blood out of her eyes.

She stood, red-smeared and panting, on the gap-axe road, trying to look in all directions for more gibbons.

Covered in gore, she must have presented a curious sight to Epi. She heard him coming, puffing and wheezing like forge bellows. She saw his face, a hundred paces back along the high road. Goggling at her. No sign of recognition.

He was so absorbed in the spectacle of her that he made a misstep. The branch road kinked. Epi kept running straight ahead.

He seemed to hang in the air. Imeris's heart seized; for a moment she thought he was young enough that the protection of Odel would still hold. He opened his hands and waved desperately about. Passionflower leaves came loose from their vines in his grip but failed to slow or check his plunge.

Imeris started running towards him, spreading her arms as if to fly and catch him, but her glider wasn't there.

He plummeted into darkness. Imeris fell to her knees.

Her chimera wings. The angles were all wrong. She couldn't have caught him anyway.

I still would have tried.

FORTY-FIVE

CAKED IN dried ape-blood, Imeris entered Odel's Temple.

She half expected Aurilon to descend on her, but once again, there were only worshippers in the wide main chamber.

Her gore-covered right forearm spines needed to be cleaned before they could be retracted. Flesh seemed to stick where sap never did. Canopians, citizens and slaves alike, performed a slow but sure evacuation, edging away from her in a strained silence, all but tossing their tributes in retreat and warning the others they met along the paths in whispers.

"Aurilon," Imeris said loudly, hoarsely, but nobody came. She placed the three golden seeds one by one on the floating dish and added, "Ibbin, a Hunter of Irofland. He is still a child. That is for him, if Orin has not murdered him yet. The second seed is for the not-born child of Sorros the Silent Smith and his wife, Nin, the moonflower seller of Gannak. The third is for the child of Anahah, who was once Bodyguard to Orin. I do not know if that baby is born or not." She smiled, and the movement stung her bloody, chewed ear.

Imeris went to the sweet-fruit pine plug in the floor, sunk her left forearm spines into it and tried to pull it open, but it resisted.

"Protector of Children," she shouted. "Holy One!"

There was no response. When she peered through the fish-mouth door, she saw the whisperers, heads together, still blocking the roads to the Temple. She wondered if someone had gone to the palace to alert the king's soldiers.

She needed to ask for her gifts before she returned to Wife-of-Epatut in disgrace.

Imeris began washing her bloody arms in the clear, perfumed water on top of the central platform where the bronze tribute-dish floated. If anything got a reaction, desecrating the water would.

Moments later, the trapdoor in the floor flew open.

Odel's amber eyes were red-rimmed from crying. Imeris was shocked by his dirt-streaked face. Scabs covered his head where he'd apparently inexpertly shorn off his own hair. The strong, ink-stained hands were uncovered. He wore a loose, pink, rumpled robe and a long wrap skirt slit up the side, but nothing on his feet.

"How dare you pollute my—" he snarled before encompassing her own wretched appearance. His mouth flattened. His nostrils flared. He swallowed. "Orin attacked you."

"I have not seen gibbons attack of their own accord before," Imeris said, staring at him, wanting to ask why he looked so dishevelled, but knowing there could only be one answer, and that the answer was one she did not want to hear.

"Imeris, Aurilon is dead."

"No," Imeris whispered.

"I've summoned the king's vizier, who was once my Servant, back to be my new Bodyguard. You bring tribute for Anahah's child, oblivious to the harm he has done the balance by becoming pregnant, an essentially female act, but if Orin can't contain the damage by killing him, I'll counteract it in the opposite direction by making my new Bodyguard a man. I've given him three days to bid his family farewell. Three days, I hoped to have to mourn my most faithful Servant in private. Yet somehow here I am, talking to you."

Imeris hardly registered what he said about Anahah.

"No," she repeated. "Aurilon cannot be dead."

"Many gifts intended for you, as Hunter of Odelland, were brought here." Odel was now calm. His voice held no further trace of bitterness. "Aurilon opened them all to be certain they were safe. This one looked like a knife but it was a mirage. Orin's doing. A rival god's spell that reached out and borrowed power from the blade you brought to trade for the skin." Imeris hung her head, but Odel hadn't finished speaking. "The spell compelled her to take up the blade, and to use it. Aurilon couldn't let go of the bone sword's hilt once she seized it. She leaped to her death rather than start laying about her and slaughtering innocents in my Temple."

No. Imeris couldn't say it anymore; she could only think it. *My miscalculation again.*

"Orin's magic in the seat of my power." Odel sighed. "If I had power to harm her, I would, but I can't withhold my power from her niche and let children die. I'm not the Mistress of the Wild, to be fickle with my people's lives. But nor can I forgive her. Oxor is weak this season and so even gods can't find it in their hearts to love and forgive."

Imeris wiped tears from her cheeks and made a sound suspiciously like a sniffle.

"Please forgive me, Holy One."

"I don't blame you," Odel said. "I blame Orin, and I blame the chimera's curse. The chimera Aurilon killed, the one that killed me, was of the wild before it died. Orin may be to blame for sending the box, but Aurilon shouldn't have succumbed to the spell in the seat of my domain. Would not have, if not for the curse on her. I suppose I was lucky to keep her as long as I did. Could anyone but Aurilon have survived twenty years with a chimera's curse hanging over them?"

"No," Imeris said, trying to smile.

"I'm sorry you weren't able to beat her, Imeris. She would have liked to die that way, too old, her reflexes too slow, with young blood come to take her place. But I never believed that you would have stayed. Would you?"

"No."

"I didn't think so. Canopy is not your home."

IT WAS nightfall when Imeris pounded on the door of the House of Epatut.

On either side of the entry, the armed guards watched her but made no move to restrain her. Epi's pale child-slave unbarred and opened the door, her timid face turned blue by the blaze of Airak's lanterns.

"Can I help you, citizen?" the girl asked.

"I am no citizen," Imeris said harshly. "I need to see the master and mistress of the House."

"Master Epatut is away in Ukakland. Master Epi hasn't returned home."

"Let me in. I must speak with Igish."

"I'm here, Imeris," Wife-of-Epatut said, bringing an upraised oil lantern to the door. "Come inside. It's late."

When her eyes locked with Imeris's, she sucked in a sharp, hissing breath. She knew.

"No," she whispered, sounding exactly as Imeris had sounded at the sight of Odel.

"Your son, Epi, challenged me to a footrace, and I accepted," Imeris said, sparing herself no part of the blame in the telling. "I told him I would marry him if he won the race. At the quarter mark, I was winning. Instruments of Orin fell upon me; I fought them off. Epi was distracted by the fight."

"No."

"He lost concentration. He stepped wrong, straight off the edge. He fell."

Igish did not cry or scream. Her protuberant eyes glazed with grief. In silence, moving stiffly as if every joint suddenly ached, she turned away and walked into the House. Imeris moved to follow, glancing hopelessly, questioningly at the girl for a moment, who shrugged in response to the unasked question: *Am I still welcome in the House?*

But Igish had told her to come inside, so in she went, around a sharp corner, and through a vestibule containing a smoke-curtain, past the gallery of stuffed birds, and into the great feast hall where the portrait of Audblayin hung by the head of the table.

Imeris wasn't able to follow Igish any further then, for the mistress of the House went to her bedroom and barred the door.

Imeris stood before it, biting her lip. Then she went back to the feast hall.

"Please," she asked the girl, "may I have something to eat and drink?"

The trembling, pasty slave freely shed tears that Igish had not.

"Is Master Epi really dead?"

"He fell. I saw it."

"But you fell. Once."

"True. I was lucky." Imeris sat on one of the heavy, throne-like dining chairs. She traced the seams along both her forearms with her fingers. Glanced across at the girl, who should have had spines as her birthright. Epi could not free this younger slave now, as payment for his training. She would stay here forever, the mark of the House of Epatut on her tongue until she died.

"He had . . . there is . . . Master Epi had another chest of snow," the girl offered mournfully.

Imeris laughed, low and sad.

"What is your name?"

"Haftfah. I was named after my—"

"After your mother," Imeris said. *Whom you will not see again, so long as the barrier between Canopy and Understorey survives.*

Haftfah nodded.

"Leave the snow, Haftfah. I will have water and fish, if there is any."

"There is, citiz—Hunter Imeris."

After she'd eaten, drunk, and relieved herself, Imeris curled up to sleep on a pile of tapestries beside the cot that Igish had told her had once been hers.

She dreamed of Aurilon, naked and long-clawed, the bark in her hair replaced by a crown of lotus flowers. Aurilon's back remained marked like a Crocodile-Rider's, but it was a chimera she rode through the empty tunnels of Odel's Temple. Tallow candles flickered in niches that had not been there in life. The chimera's eyes glowed.

Imeris sensed it was the curse-chimera. The one that had been waiting to take Aurilon's soul along with it into the ether. A man stood silently beside them, cheeks streaked with red, wearing only a skirt of bones. It was Aoun, the Gatekeeper of the Garden.

Watch your back, Imeris, Aurilon advised. *Spend your life wisely.*

Aoun waved his hand, and the candles went out, plunging the dream into darkness.

FORTY-SIX

IMERIS STAYED seven days and nights in the House of Epatut.

Igish didn't say a word the entire time. When Haftfah, who was bright as brass, brought a filled inkwell and freshly trimmed quill, Wife-of-Epatut wrote a message on parchment. Her hand shook so much that the writing was barely legible. A paid runner took it to Ukakland to inform Epatut that his heir had fallen.

Epatut returned four days later in a rage at Imeris, with no gesture of kindness or consolation to spare for his wife. He cursed the day Imeris had been born. He lamented that the chimera had saved her. He cursed his own blood that flowed through her veins.

Imeris returned a blank stare to him. Though he ordered her out of his House, she didn't leave. Though he ordered the slaves not to feed her, she helped herself whenever she was hungry. Epatut didn't dare try to force her out himself, or risk the lives of his door guards by instructing them to remove her. She realised it wasn't blind submission to authority that had made her obey Oldest-Father but true love and respect, neither of which she held for Epatut.

She had hoped to be some kind of comfort to Igish, but as the sun set on the seventh day, she accepted she could delay her travel to Ulellinland no longer. She had to retrieve Oldest-Father's amulet and help Daggad and Sorros to complete the soul trap.

"I wish fate had been kinder to you," she told Igish, trussing her tools tightly in anticipation of departure. "I wish there were something I could do."

Igish, lying motionless on her mattress, gazed through Imeris and made no response.

ULELLIN'S EMERGENT gleamed in the moonlight.

Smooth, dark windowleaves shivered in the breeze.

Imeris watched the northern approach to the charred, semirebuilt Temple of Ulellin for a time. She wasn't tired. She'd slept the day away at the lodge, stuck to the side of the purple-leafed penda where she'd once suspected Oniwak of lurking.

He couldn't lurk anywhere any longer. Orin had done him in. The vengeful goddess would likewise do for Imeris if she had the chance, but at least Ibbin was protected by Odel.

Late-leaving worshippers trailed out of the place where Ulellin had spoken Leaper's curse. Imeris wasn't sure she was safe from Ulellin. The goddess of wind and leaves had let them all go in the aftermath of the slaying of Orin's creature but on further reflection might have changed her mind.

Curse Orin and Ulellin and their senseless, selfish ways. I do not need them. I will go to Understorey as Audblayin bids me, and curse Audblayin, too.

She ran lightly down the penda path to the windowleaf-wrapped floodgum, secured a pulley to the tree, and threaded one end of her longest rope through it. She secured that end of the rope to her harness and let the other end fall loosely out of its coils to dangle below. Using one metal hook against the dangling section of rope to smooth her journey and a crimp-like tool in the other to slow her when needed, she dropped as speedily and recklessly below the barrier into Understorey as she had dropped down into Floor by her fathers' sides, a seeming eternity ago.

On the wrong side of the tree for finding Oldest-Father's grave, she nonetheless knew the level she wanted at once.

There was something about the air. Perhaps the constant breezes set blowing by the wind goddess made her able to judge the depth by the stillness. In any other tree, she would have had to pull out her tools and begin making herself some walking planks.

In this one, all she had to do was climb around, crab-like, with the juicy windowleaf stems offering easy hand- and footholds. Her sense that she was in the right place was confirmed when she saw the blue glow of the lantern Leaper had stolen, still fixed to the alcove with his axe.

Below it, an empty hole gaped where Oldest-Father's body had been imprisoned by Kirrik.

Imeris could hardly believe what she was seeing. She climbed back up to the lantern, pulled the axe free, and juggled the lantern into place where the wide wound in windowleaf trunks had been gored by some keen Understorian blade.

The lantern showed bloodstains and some half-rotted harness that Imeris recognised.

This is where he was.

Holding the lantern stupidly out from the trunk, she looked down, as if she might be able to see all the way to Floor and discover whether Oldest-Father's bones were there or if his remains had been stolen along with the protective amulet that she needed.

The amulet that was no longer there.

Imeris knew she shouldn't do it, but she did anyway; she climbed into the hole. She imagined the thick trunks crowding in, squeezing the life out of her. Curled around the cold, bright lantern, she wept yet again for Oldest-Father. Then she wept for herself.

How am I to finish the soul trap without the amulet?

Imeris left the lantern in the hole. She wiped her tears away. Borrowing one of Leaper's better ideas, she caught the loose end of the rope and tied it to a thick section of windowleaf trunk. The adze she'd intended to use on Oldest-Father's grave gleamed in the light of the lantern.

She cut the section of windowleaf trunk free. It was only slightly heavier than she was, so she rose at a slow, even pace which gave her plenty of time to think.

I shall have to beg Audblayin for the fertility amulet back. I need good lies to tell to her. Or else I need to use my own protective amulet.

She couldn't think of any convincing-sounding lies.

IMERIS STOPPED several afternoons later at the House of Epatut, intent on bidding her grieving birth mother farewell forever.

The day had been one constant shower. Faded grey winter bark was beginning to peel from the tree. Small streams seeped into the cracks, turning the skin-soft, new pink bark wound-red. The wet, clustered husks of last season's gobletfruit glinted like chandeliers against the clouds, one droplet hanging from the pointed tip of each brown ridge.

When Igish opened her front door, her bright countenance was not that of a grieving mother.

"Mighty Hunter-child," she exclaimed, clapping her hands delightedly together. "Imeris, Slayer of Monsters! Come inside at once. Apologies, but your worthy father has unfortunately absented himself. I shall make us some tea."

Imeris stared at her.

"Where is Haftfah?" she asked. Igish, who had already begun leading Imeris into the House, hesitated halfway through the smoke-curtain.

"Who?"

"The slave girl."

"Oh." One hand waved carelessly through the smoke. "I freed her. She has gone to join her mother in Dul."

Imeris looked to her left at one of the door guards. She looked to her right, at the other guard.

"Has grief driven Wife-of-Epatut mad?" she whispered to them, but they returned her scrutiny with blank expressions and minute shrugs. "How long has she been alone? When was Haftfah freed? When did Epatut leave?"

Of course, they did not accept her as a daughter of the House and made no reply.

Imeris gave them a final glare before going inside. Water dripping from her hair and clothes hissed in the brazier as she stepped through the smoke-curtain. The usual smouldering green gobletfruit leaves had been placed on top of what looked like a charred log, and the scent of it was sharp and as repellent to Imeris as she supposed it was to insects.

Strangely, Igish neither led her to the changing closet and offered a dry robe, nor indicated that Imeris should stay back from the expensive carpets laid on the floor beyond the hall. Instead, she took a turn into the sitting room she reserved for wealthy patrons and called, "Come and sit in here, daughter dear!"

Imeris went, dripping all the way.

"I did not know the girl's mother was from Dul," Imeris said in the doorway of the sitting room. "I did not know you knew the names of the villages of Understorey."

"Strange that umbrellas are not more popular here," Igish said, ignoring Imeris's remark, sprawling belly down, feet up, on the silk-upholstered couch that was normally reserved for Epatut. "Short of good leather, I imagine. Too many people in Canopy, not enough room left for the animals."

"You will find plenty of animals in Orinland," Imeris answered tightly, and did not sit down. It wasn't bad enough that she had failed Oldest-Father, killed Horroh, watched her fellow Hunters be absorbed by a monster, and later helped slay them. Fate had decided that bringing a curse down on

Leaper, goading Orin into an attack that had killed Aurilon instead, and then being responsible for her cousin's fall, were not enough for her to bear.

Now she must stare into the face of a birth mother so changed by trauma that she was unrecognisable.

"Have you lived here long?" Igish asked brightly.

"I do not live here, Birth Mother. I have come to say good-bye before my sister Audblayin seals me away below the barrier forever."

"Why would she do that? Have you done something wrong? You are famous. You are adored. You are one of us."

"I am not one of you." *I can never be. Hunter or not.* "And I am sad to see you are not yourself. Good-bye, Birth Mother."

Igish bounded to her feet, her bulging eyes frenzied.

"But the ti! We must have ti! Am I to truly lose you below the barrier a second time and you will not stay for ti?"

"I do not want any, thank you. I am not thirsty."

"Why are you in such a hurry?" Igish advanced towards her. "Are you going to the Garden?"

"Yes." Imeris backed away slowly, but her host kept pace.

"How can you go inside the Gate when you are a Hunter, when you have killed? The wards there are stronger than they have been for hundreds of years. Does that amulet you wear help you to get inside?"

"No," Imeris said, frowning. "I will not go inside. My sister will come out to see me."

Igish's mouth snapped shut and her head jerked up. She stopped where she was at the edge of the carpet, her eyes narrowed to contemplative slits. For a moment, Imeris dared hope she was coming to her senses.

"Igish?" she asked softly.

Wife-of-Epatut stood like a statue, silent.

"Birth Mother," Imeris went on, "I am so sorry about your Epi. I wish I had not raced him. I wish I could undo what happened. I wish that Odel had the power to protect everyone in Canopy from falling."

"Odel," Igish repeated in a weird, flat tone. "Audblayin. Ehkis. Oxor. Airak. Ulellin. Ukak. Atwith. Ilan. Esh. Orin. Irof. Akkad. Each of them with one-thirteenth of Canopy's power and wasting it against one another. What if they would use it only for the common good? What if they would meet, make peace, and work together? They could protect everyone from Canopy to Floor."

Imeris licked her lips. It was her turn to stay silent. Igish had never spoken like this before. Imeris had accepted that Wife-of-Epatut's indifference to the plight of anyone not a citizen was a blindness instilled by her upbringing and had forgiven her for it.

To suggest that all the goddesses and gods meet and resolve their differences? Impossible.

"You would be one of us then," Igish went on, "because there would be no us and them. We would all be one. One forest."

"They will not," Imeris said haltingly. "They cannot—"

"They can. They are lazy. They are selfish. Audblayin is your sister. Convince her."

"To dissolve the barrier? I have tried!"

"She wishes to protect the people of Canopy from demons? You are a Hunter. Tell her you will protect the House of Epatut." Igish mimed a knife thrust. "Tell her that all the warriors of Understorey, and all the students of Loftfol, will stop being enemies of the goddesses and gods and protect the people instead."

Imeris imagined it for one joyful moment.

"I cannot convince her," she said, but as she said it she remembered convincing Audblayin to lend her the fertility amulet. She was the one who had convinced Loftfol to make peace. Perhaps she was more like Leaper than she knew. Perhaps, at the very least, she could convince the deities of Canopy to gather and speak to one another. She could stop any further disasters like the wasteful, accidental death of Aurilon.

"I will dress you for your audience," Igish said, tugging Imeris by the hand in the direction of her bedroom.

WRAPPED IN enough silk to dress four women, Imeris presented herself at the Gate.

It stood open. The Gatekeeper, Aoun, was there, robed in white as usual, watching over the departure of supplicants in the moments before the Gate closed at dusk. The people passed through the invisible wards with dreamy smiles or frustrated frowns on their faces, which told who had been successful in their requests and who was returning home with bad news.

Imeris did not mention the dream in which Aoun had appeared blood-streaked in a skirt of bones. Wife-of-Epatut, silent and with downcast eyes, stood a pace behind and beside her. Imeris could not understand the sudden shyness. Her birth mother had been to the Garden many times before, when she'd still hoped to have another child of her own body.

"Gatekeeper," Imeris said, "I wonder if you might fetch my sister. I wish to say good-bye. My middle-father does not seem to be here, or I would ask him to call her."

"Hunter," Aoun said with a bow of his head, "Wife-of-Epatut. The Bodyguard of Audblayin lies wounded in the king's palace. There was an attack on this, his dwelling, by the goddess Orin."

Imeris felt cold. Her heart shook her whole body with each beat.

"Tell me he is alive," she gasped.

Aoun smiled apologetically.

"He will be fine. He was wounded by a pair of panthers, though he killed them in the end. Your sister had him taken to Eshland for his broken bones to be healed. She would have come out of the Garden to heal him, but he insisted she stay behind the Gate. Bernreb will rest in the palace until he's fully recovered. He can't come into the Garden, and my wards can't protect him while he's outside of it."

"Will you call Audblayin, or not? She told me to come and see her, but I cannot go into the Garden, and you are saying she would not come out. Not even to heal her own Bodyguard."

"On Bernreb's insistence."

"They have to do something," Imeris blurted. "The goddesses and gods. They have to stop fighting each other. They have to work together." She expected Igish to step forwards and add her voice, her agreement, but she stayed behind Imeris, half bent.

"The last time they were unified in purpose," Aoun said regretfully, "was when they raised this great forest from the Bright Plain and put the barrier in place. That was a time of crisis."

"This is a time of crisis! Aurilon is dead! The surviving Hunters are being picked off one by one! My father—" Her voice fractured, and she stopped to swallow and lower her pitch. "My middle-father is injured. Our deities should form a council. Like the teachers of Loftfol. Like a guild council." She turned to look at Wife-of-Epatut, who had told her about the silk merchant's guild and their council, where each had an equal voice, but the silk-decorated head remained bowed. "They could gather at the Falling Fig. Settle disputes. Speak freely. Make peace."

Audblayin stepped out from behind the shadow of the Gate.

"One small success with a gang of bloodthirsty boys," she said, shaking her head, "and you think you've got the answers to all our problems."

"You," Imeris said angrily, accusingly, "are supposed to be a goddess, but you allowed Middle-Father to be harmed."

"He guards me," Ylly shot back. "I don't guard him."

"You need to speak to Orin. All of you. Face-to-face!"

"It's not just Orin. Thanks to our little brother, Ulellin's been cursing Airak and his Servants every time she comes down from her tree. She used the wind to blow all the bees of Ukakland away from the flowering trees of Irofland as retribution for the use of bespelled insects by the Hunter from Ukakland within her niche. She blew a few children out of their cradles to spite Odel, whom she blames for your actions. We're not friends, Imeris. We can't be. Power-giving tributes paid to one deity are tributes that can't be paid to another. The only reason we don't normally strike directly at one another is that it would be a waste of our bodies and weaken the barrier."

"You could make friends," Imeris beseeched her. She turned a third time to Wife-of-Epatut for support. The movement opened up a direct line of sight between Igish and Audblayin.

"Kirrik," the goddess said with astonishment.

Wife-of-Epatut's lips drew ferociously back from her teeth.

FORTY-SEVEN

Imeris's spines tried to spring from their sheaths.

But Kirrik, in Wife-of-Epatut's body, had wrapped her arms and legs in so many layers of silk she was rendered temporarily helpless.

"I hoped you would all gather together," Kirrik told Audblayin over Imeris's shoulder, "so that I could kill you all at once. A council of Canopian deities! But this brainless Hunter was never going to succeed at that task. I should have known. I shall settle for just you, Audblayin."

In a nonmagical body, how can she attack a goddess? Imeris wondered, tearing off ribbons and sashes, struggling to find her weapons. *Did somebody kill Nirrin? If they did, how could Kirrik's soul cross the barrier? Wife-of-Epatut is—was—not gifted. She was neither spinewife nor Servant.*

Imeris's eyes rose to Aoun, then, who stood with no amulet to protect his naked soul. No weapon to hand but his magic, which would be extinguished as soon as Kirrik struck him from the body that housed him. Audblayin, too, was vulnerable; Imeris had heard somewhere that Kirrik had once stolen the body of the goddess of rain. Instead of turning to slash at Kirrik, Imeris launched herself at her sister and the Gatekeeper, arms outstretched.

"Into the Garden," she screamed at them, sweeping them up, feeling first her fingers and then her arms and face rebounding from nothing she could see; but they were safe; they were behind the wards.

Now she could turn. Put the Gate at her back. Fling down the last of her silk wrappings and hold Oldest-Father's bore-knife out between her body and Kirrik's.

I do not have my chimera skin.

"How did you get through the barrier?" Imeris snarled, striking hard from the strength of her extended back leg, but Kirrik danced back, teeth bared.

"Go ahead and kill me, Hunter. Kill the one who speaks of One Forest, who speaks what is in your heart!"

"You do not speak what is in my heart," Imeris shouted, thrusting again with the bore-knife in her right hand. "Killing my sister is not in my heart!" Kirrik dodged the knife, but Imeris brought out her spines, stepping through and swinging from the elbow, a tight movement to bring her fist close to her hip, and then, dropping to one knee, the swifter, deadlier, cutting-edge reversal.

It caught Wife-of-Epatut—Kirrik—in the back of her extended right knee. Silk parted. Blood spurted. The joint tore, and Kirrik went down on her side, knuckles white against the wooden platform, still snarling.

"That is not your sister," Kirrik insisted, undaunted by Imeris's knee on her chest. "Your sister lived for only one breath before that thief stole her body. Audblayin is a parasite in human clothing, a power-hungry soul that drank the blood of a Titan to become what it is today. Kill me, protect it, and it will not reward you. It will never abolish the barrier. None of them will. One day you—"

Imeris pressed the blunt curve of her bore-knife to Kirrik's throat. It was not the threat of death that silenced the sorceress but the physical restriction of air.

I will cut my birth mother's throat, but Kirrik will not die.

"What is the use of killing you like this?" she muttered, trying not to see Wife-of-Epatut in the choking, darkening face. "You will only murder somebody else."

The smell of panther musk and crushed banana leaves reached her nostrils before the small green hand appeared over her shoulder. She did not flinch or move to strike when she felt Anahah's body against her from behind.

She let his hand close over her knife hand and draw it back. When he tried to take the knife from her, she allowed that, too.

Kirrik sucked in a deep, desperate breath.

Anahah dug at Imeris's belt pouch. He put something in her hand. The slave-making coin. Imeris wanted to turn her head, to meet his eyes, to laugh, but she couldn't let her attention drift away from Kirrik. Using her adze-handle in her left hand, she prised open Kirrik's jaw. Took the bone coin between her right thumb and forefinger.

"You told my oldest-father that your son was a slave," she said. "You said you refused to pay his ransom. Maybe now you will meet him in the Palace of Odelland."

But Kirrik had also told Oldest-Father that switching bodies was a way to escape slavery. As the bone coin touched her squirming tongue, Kirrik's whole body relaxed.

"Anahah," Imeris said, sitting abruptly back on her haunches, "she is leaving! I did not know she could leave before the host body died!"

Where will she go? To the closest unprotected body.

Imeris jolted to her full height, careless of Wife-of-Epatut's long, still form at her feet. She reached for her bore-knife but Anahah had taken it. Raising the adze instead, she put out her spines, quivering in horrified expectation.

Anahah stood there in his short, brown skirt, his green hair shifting in the wind, one corner of his mouth upturned. His pot-belly was gone. He looked lean and tired. Between his hands, a tiny cage made of bone held a single smouldering fragment of something colour-shifting and difficult to see.

"What is that?" Imeris asked, daring to hope that it was still Anahah and not the sorceress that she spoke to. "What is that inside the cage?"

"It's burning chimera skin," was the reply, and she could not tell if it was really him; did not trust herself to tell. Kirrik, or Anahah, raised the cage to pursed lips and blew sharply.

Black smoke billowed from the bars of the fist-sized cage, far more than should be possible for anything less than a bonfire. Imeris coughed and waved her hands. In moments, the smoke was dispersed, but what was left behind was a hovering, multilimbed apparition of sooty haze. A branch shifted in the wind, and the last sunbeams touched the shifting shape, turning it brown. Audblayin and Aoun stared at it from behind the wards of the Garden but made no move to approach.

Anahah stepped forwards, passing the little bone cage through the haze. Some part of the shape shrank, solidified and stayed within the contained space.

What remained was the smoky shape and glowing eyes of a chimera. Imeris only just had time to recognise it. The next gust of wind blew it away. All that remained was the silently railing, shrunken human smoke-shape, confined by the tiny white bars between Anahah's hands.

"I know just what to do with this," he said, smiling, giving it a shake near his ear like a child with a new rattle.

FORTY-EIGHT

WHILE IGISH's still-breathing but soulless body slept, Imeris practiced the seven disciplines and the six flowing forms in the House of Epatut.

Once the silk carpets were drawn back, the sanded sapwood floor of the gobletfruit tree provided as smooth and uninterrupted a surface as Imeris could have wished. She let all her guilt and all her fears float away as her body went through the motions.

When she was finished, she drank a gourd of water, put the carpets back, and went to the main bedroom to check on Igish.

The woman's empty husk had not so much as rolled over in its sleep.

Imeris trickled a little water into the dry, open mouth. Wife-of-Epatut could still swallow. It was three days since Imeris had carried her injured, unresponsive body back to the bed where she'd given birth.

Three days since Anahah had trapped Kirrik's soul and taken it away.

Imeris should have felt free. Her debt to Nirrin, Vesev, and Oldest-Father was paid. *Your spirit can be reborn now, Oldest-Father. You do not need to watch over me any longer.* No urgent matters demanded her attention. No monster rampaged. Nobody needed her protection.

Still, she could not seem to bring herself to leave the House of Epatut.

A parchment lay on the chair beside the bed. Imeris picked it up and sat down. She didn't need to look at it. She'd read it so many times she knew it by heart, had curled and uncurled it so often that it would never again lie flat.

Most Formal and Humble Greetings to the House of Epatut, it read. *We, the pale warriors down below, were most surprised two days past to be the recipients of a well-fed young man fallen from your wondrous realm. He is alive and unhurt. We are unable to pass through the formidable magical barrier erected by your fearsome gods to deliver him. Please burn the log en-closed in this basket. The fragrant smoke will guide him home.*

Anahah, who had been the one to find the note, had soberly explained to Imeris how Kirrik's sorcery had worked. By adding a dark spell to the crushed bone from Oldest-Father's amulet, she was able to form the log from sawdust into a conduit for her soul. Imeris could hardly bear to imagine Wife-of-Epatut crouched before the sharp-smelling flames, breathing the smoke, imagining desperately that she was welcoming Epi home, when in fact she was welcoming her own end.

Is there a chance that Epi really is alive? Imeris had asked, but Anahah had given her such a look that she regretted asking.

"All you ever wanted was loving family around you," she said to the in-ert form on the bed. "Youngest-Father would have been the right kind of husband for you."

Impulsively, she rose to find a fire upon which to burn the treacherous parchment. The insect-repelling brazier wasn't lit, but coals in the kitchen hearth could be coaxed to life. Imeris set the parchment over them. It smoked copiously and stung her throat, but it was a good, familiar sting, unlike the sharp smell that she now knew was the stench of burnt Old God's powdered bone.

This burning parchment smelled much the same as the one she'd received from Epatut's brother, Otoyut, and burned within a day of the sorceress's defeat. Nobody had seen or heard from Epatut since the last time Imeris had seen him. She was inclined to agree with Anahah when he said that Kirrik had probably simply pushed the merchant out the window of his own House.

Still, there was no reason for Otoyut to so hastily claim what he described as his rightful inheritance. Especially while Wife-of-Epatut, technically, still lived.

On her way back to the bedroom, Imeris put her hand to her throat, touching smooth skin where the leather thong holding her bone amulet had rested for so long. The amulet was back in Audblayin's hands. Imeris didn't need it anymore.

Your soul trap, Imeris had said to Anahah outside the Garden, correctly identifying the bone cage. *You were going to use it on Orin to keep yourself and your baby safe.*

I'm still not sure, Anahah had replied, shaking the little cage again and peering at Kirrik's black, agitated soul, *that I did the right thing.* The source of the bone for the trap, Anahah had not deigned to reveal. He'd also refused to tell Imeris where he was going to put the trapped sorceress for safekeeping. *If you don't know, you can't tell anyone. Not even by accident.*

He had, however, told her where he'd been staying with his newborn for the past week or so.

With the Godfinder? Imeris had repeated, incredulous. *After the fuss she made? About living alone and liking it that way?*

She likes the baby. Anahah flashed a grin. *You'll like her, too. Come to Airakland when you can.*

Imeris did not know if she could go to Airakland. Last night, a runner had brought a message from the Garden. The goddess Audblayin would call on her before noon. Perhaps it was just to see if she could offer any more healing on Wife-of-Epatut than her Servants had already managed, though it seemed obvious to Imeris, who was no expert on magical healing, that without a soul, Wife-of-Epatut would never walk or speak again.

Perhaps Imeris's goddess-allotted time in Canopy was up, though, and Audblayin was coming to send her down to Understorey for good.

That is not your sister, Kirrik had said. *It will never abolish the barrier. None of them will.*

Imeris felt shamed by her inclination to half believe the former and completely agree with the latter. She was too worn down to resist anymore. Too tired to try and bridge two worlds. Let the whims of deities blow her where they would. She would be Understorian by default, by the simple process of elimination.

Igish wet herself on schedule. Imeris changed the wrappings and cleaned her birth mother's female parts, thinking, *I came from here. This was my doorway to life. I had no soul when I came through this door and then I took my first breath.*

She sat back down in the bedside chair.

The clang of somebody's foot catching on the brazier in the entrance hall brought her head up sharply. A male voice cursed. Was it Epatut? Who else would come in without knocking and without resistance from the door guards? Then she remembered Epatut was presumed dead. Her eyes focused blearily on Audblayin's face, gold-lit by the long-wicked oil lanterns.

The portrait. She had fallen asleep in the dining room.

No, she was still in the bedroom.

Richly dressed Canopians surrounded her. The smell of incense filled the room.

Imeris blinked.

Audblayin stood there in the flesh, her hair caught in a net of live monkey-ladder vine. She was gloved and gowned in pale green with white trim to match the slowly opening white flower clusters of the vine. A man stood beside her in a metal-thread-embroidered black silk wrap that covered him from chest to knees. He wore a headdress consisting of a blue-glowing silver tree, sharply forked like frozen lightning, emerging from a length of black silk wound around his head. Silver rings hung from his ears, and his haughty, full-lipped face was night-black on the left side and bone-white on the right. He could only be Leaper's master, Airak, the lightning god. When Imeris looked at his curly-haired legs, she saw his right shin was black-skinned and his left shin was white.

"Good evening, Hunter Imeris," Odel said politely, drawing Imeris's eyes back up again. Odel's long, luxuriant body wrap, boots and high-collared jacket were the colour of sunrise. His new Bodyguard, the bearded king's vizier, in yellow jacket and red split skirt, stood beside a towering fighter in Ilan's purple who leaned on a silver scythe.

Ilan herself wore the same painted silks resembling armour that Imeris had seen before. *Four of them in one room.*

Two goddesses. Two gods.

The man who had cursed in the hallway and stumbled over the brazier, marked by ashy smears on one bare, pale knee, was Daggad. He hesitated in the unenviable position of wanting to push through the crowd without touching any goddesses or gods. He wore a short wrap skirt and a harness to hold his ridiculously long sword.

He carried the limp form of a dark-haired Understorian woman with a leg brace, whom Imeris had last seen sending lethal magic in her direction.

Nirrin.

In a heartbeat, Imeris recognised the slack-mouthed stillness, identical to Igish's, which characterised the soulless. Daggad negotiated the crowd and finally managed to get Nirrin down onto the bed beside Igish. He blew out his breath, pinched the black mark on his lip, and knuckled his back.

"I am dreaming," Imeris said, gazing from one deity to another, adding a belated, "Holy Ones."

"Move away from the bedside," Ilan said briskly. "It is time for justice."

"It is time to raise the fallen," Odel said, the corner of his mouth quirking, "and to bestow on them the safety of a second childhood."

"It is time to fuse body and soul with the first spark," Airak said, glowering.

Imeris vacated the chair and dragged it back. Audblayin took her place, putting one hand on Igish's wrist and the other on Nirrin's. White flowers bloomed beside her earlobe. A green tendril curled around her cheekbone.

"It is time for new life," she said simply.

The goddesses and gods closed their eyes.

Lantern flames did not flicker. There were no wondrous, thundering sounds, lightning strikes, or levitation. The deities opened their eyes again. For a moment, Imeris thought they had failed.

Nothing had happened.

Then Nirrin yawned and sat up, blinking. The spines of her leg brace caught in the sheets as she drew her legs in. Her jaw dropped at the sight of the deities around the bed. She shook her head. Tried to swallow. Tears brimmed in her eyes.

"Where am I? My mouth is dry." Imeris gave her some water. Nirrin clutched her arm. "Issi, where am I?"

"In Canopy."

"She killed me. I felt it. She killed me."

"Your soul hadn't been reborn," Ilan said, frowning. "I don't know why not. It waited. Together, we were able to retrieve it. The same goes for the merchant woman." Igish's slack-lipped blankness had turned to deep, ordinary slumber, complete with impressive snores.

"It is strange," Audblayin said softly. "Most are reborn almost at once."

"Ulellin speaks to the wind," Odel said, "and sees the future most clearly, but I have prescient dreams. Maybe Atwith does, too. Maybe that's how he knew not to let these two souls pass through him."

"We should have invited him to the party," Airak said stonily.

"No," Audblayin answered. "It's one thing for the four of us to meet. But birth and death can never be in the same room. Our world would end."

"Why did you decide to meet?" Imeris asked loudly from her place at a safe distance, shoulder blades against the wall. She caught her sister's gaze and held it. "Why have you done all this? Why bother to restore my birth mother and my friend? I thought you were rivals. I thought you did not spend your magic on unworthy Understorians!"

The Bodyguards bristled. Daggad smirked.

"I thought about what you said, Imeris," Audblayin answered tranquilly. "About the squabbles of immortals playing havoc with ordinary people's lives. About me turning my back on the blameless people born below. About my refusal to open the barrier for you anymore. Instead of cursing me for it, you saved my life."

Airak stepped up beside her.

"Audblayin has a resident pest in you," he said, "but in Airakland I have two. They are the Godfinder, Unar, and her ward, my Skywatcher Leapael. After their interference in the Hunt, I had two choices: either listen to them or kill them."

"Orin would have loved you to kill them," Audblayin murmured.

"In the past I've killed blasphemers as a general rule," Airak said as though he hadn't heard her. "It hasn't secured my domain. This time I chose to listen."

"I told you when we met upon the border," Ilan said, one finger upraised, "that mortals had little hope of placating Orin. I warned it would be better for the matter to be resolved by diplomacy among deities. Perhaps we can't take Audblayin with us into Atwithland, but we can go to Orin. We can go to Ulellin. We must strengthen the bonds between us. We created this forest together."

This is my Great Deed, Imeris thought. *My Great Deed was never going to be the slaying of a creature, or even destroying Kirrik.*

It was to bring these four deities here, together in the same niche.

All eyes went to Odel. He shrugged disingenuously and glanced at the former king's vizier.

"I have a new Bodyguard," he said. "I wanted to take him for a test outing. He's fatter than he was before he went to serve the king."

Igish's snore rose to greater heights. Attention shifted to the bed. Only Imeris kept her eye on Odel.

When he saw her looking, he winked at her.

Imeris put the slave-making coin on a bedpost, where he could take it without touching her hand.

FORTY-NINE

IMERIS DUCKED inside the entry to the satinwood burl that was the Godfinder's home.

The caramel smell made her nostrils flare. She vacillated on the doorstep. Daggad almost ran into her from behind. Unar's thief-catching vine was not yet repaired, but that didn't mean she hadn't applied some other form of magical security that might erupt out of the walls and attack strangers.

Behind them, in the open canopy, the sun crept over the horizon. Thin cries of black cockatoos cracking open the last of the satinwood nuts replaced the summer swooping of insect-eating birds after bugs attracted to the pink-tinged, creamy flowers.

Leaper popped up in front of her, grinning. His shin and forearm spines had been unchained.

"Come in, dimwit. You haven't got the wrong farm."

Imeris followed him to the main room where Unar, Anahah, and Aforis sat on cushions, drinking ti in the blue light of the lamp.

"Godfinder," Imeris announced. "You remember Daggad, my fellow Hunter."

"I remember," Unar said, pouring another ti, rising to her feet and extending the cup to Daggad. "I thought you had gone to Gannak with Nirrin, Daggad."

"I went," Daggad admitted, taking the ti. "We both spent some three weeks there. Imeris stayed in the House of Epatut with 'er birth mother while we were gone. Then we both came back. Nirrin finds Gannak overwhelmin', she says. Full of too many uncomfortable memories."

"The girl says so," Unar asked shrewdly, "or you do? Does she remember the things that the sorceress made her body do?"

"No." Daggad sipped the ti, avoiding Unar's gaze. "But she remembers dyin'. She will not go into 'er father's forge. I 'ave left her with the Servants in the Garden of Audblayin. Bernreb is teachin' 'er the use of weapons. The Gatekeeper is teachin' 'er to use her spinewife skills in the service of the goddess. It is obvious they plan for 'er to replace Audblayin's Bodyguard, if she shows an aptitude for it."

Unar's laugh was a little too abrupt.

"If she shows an aptitude," she repeated bitterly.

"This is good ti," Daggad said quickly.

"But women can't be the Bodyguards of women," Leaper said, looking outraged.

"After your deities all got together for their little chat," Daggad drawled, "they discovered a whole lotta rules they decided they did not need anymore."

"My sister has asked me to guard her before," Imeris said, accepting her own cup from Unar. The look Unar gave her was dagger-sharp.

"The balance," Aforis said, "will be preserved. Odel's new Bodyguard is a man."

"Leaper," Imeris said, changing the subject, settling on a cushion and trying to avoid looking at Anahah; he sat cross-legged and quiet on a cushion across from her, dressed plainly in a man's shirt and short skirt, in need of a shave, but with neither infant nor panther parts in evidence. "Have you been in danger from Orin or Ulellin lately?"

"No," Leaper answered cheerfully. "I told you Airak would look after me. He went to meet with Orin and Ulellin at the Falling Fig and came back in a good mood. So it must've gone well." His expression sobered, and he lowered his voice. "I've been having dreams about calling lightning to kill the creature, though. Bad dreams, Issi."

"I have had some bad dreams myself," Imeris said with sympathy.

"I felt the lightning go through Orin's Servants, and they didn't do anything wrong. They were only doing what Orin made them do. At the time I was a bit giddy that Ulellin hadn't killed me on the spot, but now it's haunting me. Maybe the gods can make peace with each other, but they can't make me forget what I did."

Imeris shook off the memory of her glider snagging. Her body swinging upside down through the air.

"We remember," she said, "so we do not make the same mistakes again."

"You're right," Leaper said, raising his cup. "I've vowed never to do violence to thinking creatures again."

"Not even if Airak commands it?" Anahah asked, laughing his quiet, stuttering laugh.

"He won't," Leaper said, scowling. "He's not like Orin."

"Nobody is like Orin," Anahah agreed.

"I thought the Queen of Airakland looked a little like Ilan," Imeris said, remembering.

"The Queen of Airakland," Leaper said, licking his lips, "looks like perfection as described by a poet, like loveliness made flesh. I wish she was in my dreams instead."

"Imeris," Anahah said suddenly, "I've got something to show you." He stood up. Imeris stood up too, so quickly that she sloshed ti all over herself.

"Show me," she said, setting the ti on one of the blue chests. She followed Anahah to the mouth of a gloomy tunnel she could have sworn had not been there before. When she glanced back, she saw Leaper still wistfully pondering the Queen of Airakland, Daggad lost in his own thoughts, Aforis opening the door of the stove to add more charcoal, and Unar watching her go with a knowing expression, ti half raised to her lips.

The tunnel was long and dark. They strolled along inside the satinwood branch, beyond the burl that formed the farm. At the end, a new room, smelling even more strongly of caramel, had been formed with wide, clear-glass ceiling panes and chest-high, gauze-screened openings opposite to let the breeze blow through.

The room held little more than table and cot. The cot held a sleeping babe, wrapped in a silk blanket stamped with the sigil of the House of Epatut. For all her protests, Unar, who must have made the room, had decorated the walls with story carvings, slyly including the tale of the giant silkworm, and provided a stuffed toy shaped like a flowerfowl.

Imeris couldn't look away from the tiny, perfect face. A single clenched fist escaped the blanket, smaller than a spiny plum. The child was black-skinned, but in direct sunlight, even blacker leopard-rosettes were faintly visible.

"She is beautiful," Imeris said at last. "Does she have that pattern all over her, Anahah?"

She looked up and caught a guilty expression sliding across his face.

"Childbirth was extremely painful."

"So I have heard. Did you not expect that?"

"It went for hours and hours."

Imeris laughed. She felt like she had not laughed for a lifetime.

"I have heard that, too."

Anahah gripped the cot railing with one small, green hand, hanging his head.

"At the last moment, I turned us into a pair of panthers. The pain went away. She came out easily. It was over. She and I were only nonhuman for a minute. Two at most. We were still connected by the cord. I thought I could still change her all the way back, but I couldn't."

Imeris smiled. Her hand covered his, but it was too much. Feelings flooded her, and she took her hand away as if his cool skin had burned her. She put her fingers to her lips.

"What have you named her?" she asked, self-conscious.

"I haven't named her yet."

"Igish?" Imeris blurted despite herself. "Can her name be Igish? It means—"

"I know what it means. Yes." He lifted his head. Imeris was relieved to see an answering smile. "She can be Igish. You've left Igish the Older for good, haven't you? Audblayin hasn't changed her mind about opening the barrier for you."

"No." Imeris shook her head. "She has not changed her mind. It is true that I will not see my birth mother again. When I go below the barrier, it will be for good."

"If I go with you," Anahah said gravely, "I won't be able to change anymore. I'll need to sleep as much as an ordinary person. I won't be able to protect Igish from demons. But at least she'll be safe from Orin."

Imeris's heart twisted like a wrung cleaning rag.

"Orin has made peace—"

"Orin has made peace with the other goddesses and gods. Not with me."

"I will protect you both," Imeris said, and when Anahah took her hand this time, she didn't pull away. "I will protect you both from humans and demons and gods." Anahah's irises turned a darker shade of green. Would they still do that, below the barrier? "We will go to Understorey together. Today, if you wish. I will live anywhere in Understorey with you that is not the home my oldest-father made in Audblayin's emergent."

She still loved her sister. But she could not forgive her. Did not want to live beneath her.

"Why stop at Understorey?" Anahah said. "Let's take Igish with us to Floor. I've been there before, at the edge of the forest where the bamboo and long grasses grow. It's not all darkness, trespasses, and death."

Imeris's head spun at the possibilities.

"If we go," she said, "you have to stop sneaking around. You have to stop following me without me knowing. When you are close to me, you have to call out and let me know."

"Are you still angry I didn't save him?" Anahah squeezed her hand tighter. "I was sneaking around because Orin wanted to kill me. I was sneaking around because Kirrik would have killed me. If I hadn't been sneaking around the Garden, I couldn't have captured Kirrik's soul."

"Kirrik is finished. When we leave Canopy behind, we leave Orin behind, and all that has happened."

"You're right. In that case, I agree."

"Would I have to marry you?" she asked, feeling a pang for Epi, who had been so certain she was destined to be with him.

"You don't even have to love me," Anahah answered sadly, and she realised too late she could have framed the question with greater sensitivity. He shifted so the cot was no longer between them and captured her other hand, holding them both tightly, looking intensely up into her eyes. "Love the child, though."

"I will."

"I can't have more children. When I leave Canopy I'll have all human, all male parts again."

"I see."

"You might find a use for those. Later."

"I think I might," Imeris said in a strangled voice. "Later."

Anahah let go of her hands.

"What is it?" he asked gently. "Do you need more time to make sure?"

"No," Imeris said. "I am sure about Igish, and I am sure about you. It is Daggad I am not sure about. He followed me here. I do not think he knows where to go. We should take him with us. He was miserable in Gannak, and he is almost as good a Hunter as I am. He can help protect Igish, too."

"Let's ask him," Anahah said without hesitation.

Imeris paused to touch Igish's tiny nose with the tip of her little finger.

"Enjoy the sunlight, little panther, little rainbow-coloured bird," she whispered. "You will not pass between two realms, like me. You will belong to one."

Outside the window, a cluster of nuts chewed free by a cockatoo spun through the air, destined to fall though Canopy and Understorey on its way, inevitably, to Floor.